DATE DUE		
JAN 05 1999		
MAR 0 9 2001		

THE EYE OF THE TIGER

By Wilbur Smith

The Eye of the Tiger

WILBUR SMITH

DOUBLEDAY & COMPANY, INC., GARDEN CITY, NEW YORK
1976

ISBN: 0-385-11264-5
LIBRARY OF CONGRESS CATALOG CARD NUMBER 75-14841
COPYRIGHT © 1975 BY WILBUR SMITH
PRINTED IN THE UNITED STATES OF AMERICA
FIRST EDITION IN THE UNITED STATES OF AMERICA

For my wife, Danielle, with love

'TIGER! TIGER! burning bright
In the forests of the night . . .
In what distant deeps or skies
Burnt the fire of thine eyes?'

William Blake

THE EYE OF THE TIGER

It was one of those seasons when the fish came late. I worked my boat and crew hard, running far northwards each day, coming back into Grand Harbour long after dark each night, but it was November the 6th when we picked up the first of the big ones riding down on the wine purple swells of the Mozambique current.

By this time I was desperate for a fish. My charter was a party of one, an advertising wheel from New York named Chuck McGeorge, one of my regulars who made the annual six-thousand mile pilgrimage to St Mary's Island for the big marlin. He was a short wiry little man, bald as an ostrich egg and grey at the temples, with a wizened brown monkey face but the good hard legs that are necessary to take on the big fish.

When at last we saw the fish, he was riding high in the water, showing the full length of his fin, longer than a man's arm and with the scimitar curve that distinguishes it from shark or porpoise. Angelo spotted him at the instant that I did, and he hung out on the foredeck stay and yelled with excitement, his gipsy curls dangling on his dark cheeks and his teeth flashing in the brilliant tropical sunlight.

The fish crested and wallowed, the water opening about him so that he looked like a forest log, black and heavy and massive, his tail fin echoing the graceful curve of the dorsal, before he slid down into the next trough and the water closed over his broad glistening back.

I turned and glared down into the cockpit. Chubby was already helping Chuck into the big fighting chair, clinching the heavy harness and gloving him up, but he looked up and caught my eye.

Chubby scowled heavily and spat over the side, in complete contrast to the excitement that gripped the rest of us. Chubby is a huge man, as tall as I am but a lot heavier in the shoulder and gut. He is also one of the most staunch and consistent pessimists in the business.

'Shy fish!' grunted Chubby, and spat again. I grinned at him.

'Don't mind him, Chuck,' I called, 'old Harry is going to set you into that fish.'

'I've got a thousand bucks that says you don't,' Chuck shouted back, his face screwed up against the dazzle of the sun-flecked sea, but his eyes twinkling with excitement.

'You're on!' I accepted a bet I couldn't afford and turned my attention to the fish.

Chubby was right, of course. After me, he is the best billfish man in the entire world. The fish was big and shy and scary. ,

Five times I had the baits to him, working him with all the skill and cunning I could muster. Each time he turned away and sounded as I brought *Wave Dancer* in on a converging course to cross his beak.

'Chubby, there is a fresh dolphin bait in the icebox: haul in the teasers, and we'll run him with a single bait,' I shouted despairingly.

I put the dolphin to him. I had rigged the bait myself and it swam with a fine natural action in the water. I recognized the instant in which the marlin accepted the bait. He seemed to hunch his great shoulders and I caught the flash of his belly, like a mirror below the surface, as he turned.

'Follow!' screamed Angelo. 'He follows!'

I set Chuck into the fish at a little after ten o'clock in the morning, and I fought him close. Superfluous line in the water would place additional strain on the man at the rod. My job required infinitely more skill than gritting the teeth and hanging on to the heavy fibreglass rod. I kept *Wave Dancer* running hard on the fish through the first frenzied charges and frantic flashing leaps until Chuck could settle down in the fighting chair and lean on the marlin, using those fine fighting legs of his.

A few minutes after noon, Chuck had the fish beaten. He was on the surface, in the first of the wide circles which Chuck would narrow with each turn until we had him at the gaff.

'Hey, Harry!' Angelo called suddenly, breaking my concentration. 'We got a visitor, man!'

'What is it, Angelo?'

'Big Johnny coming up current.' He pointed. 'Fish is bleeding, he's smelt it.'

I looked and saw the shark coming. The blunt fin moving up

2

steadily, drawn by the struggle and smell of blood. He was a big hammerhead, and I called to Angelo.

'Bridge, Angelo,' and I gave him the wheel.

'Harry, you let that bastard chew my fish and you can kiss your thousand bucks goodbye,' Chuck grunted sweatily at me from the fighting chair, and I dived into the main cabin.

Dropping to my knees I knocked open the toggles that held down the engine hatch and I slid it open.

Lying on my belly, I reached up under the decking and grasped the stock of the FN carbine hanging in its special concealed slings of inner tubing.

As I came out on to the deck I checked the loading of the rifle, and pushed the selector on to automatic fire.

'Angelo, lay me alongside that old Johnny.'

Hanging over the rail in *Wave Dancer*'s bows, I looked down on to the shark as Angelo ran over him. He was a hammerhead all right, a big one, twelve feet from tip to tail, coppery bronze through the clear water.

I aimed carefully between the monstrous eyestalks which flattened and deformed the shark's head, and I fired a short burst.

The FN roared, the empty brass cases spewed from the weapon and the water erupted in quick stabbing splashes.

The shark shuddered convulsively as the bullets smashed into his head, shattering the gristly bone and bursting his tiny brain. He rolled over and began to sink.

'Thanks, Harry,' Chuck gasped, sweating and red-faced in the chair.

'All part of the service,' I grinned at him, and went to take the wheel from Angelo.

At ten minutes to one, Chuck brought the marlin up to the gaff, punishing him until the great fish came over on his side, the sickle tail beating feebly, and the long beak opening and shutting spasmodically. The glazed single eye was as big as a ripe apple, and the long body pulsed and shone with a thousand flowing shades of silver and gold and royal purple.

'Cleanly now, Chubby,' I shouted, as I got a gloved hand on the steel trace and drew the fish gently towards where Chubby waited with the stainless-steel hook at the gaff held ready.

Chubby withered me with a glance that told me clearly that he had been pulling the steel into billfish when I was still a gutter kid in a London slum.

'Wait for the roll,' I cautioned him again, just to plague him a little, and Chubby's lip curled at the unsolicited advice.

The swell rolled the fish up to us, opening the wide chest that glowed silver between the spread wings of the pectoral fins.

'Now!' I said, and Chubby sank the steel in deep. In a burst of bright crimson heart blood, the fish went into its death frenzy, beating the surface to flashing white and drenching us all under fifty gallons of thrown sea water.

I hung the fish on Admiralty Wharf from the derrick of the crane. Benjamin, the harbour-master, signed a certificate for a total weight of eight hundred and seventeen pounds. Although the vivid fluorescent colours had faded in death to flat sooty black, yet it was impressive for its sheer bulk—fourteen feet six inches from the point of its bill to the tip of its flaring swallow tail.

'Mister Harry done hung a Moses on Admiralty,' the word was carried through the streets by running bare-footed urchins, and the islanders joyously snatched at the excuse to cease work and crowd the wharf in fiesta array.

The word travelled as far as old Government House on the bluff, and the presidential Land-Rover came buzzing down the twisting road with the gay little flag fluttering on the bonnet. It butted its way through the crowd and deposited the great man on the wharf. Before independence Godfrey Biddle had been St Mary's only solicitor, island-born and London-trained.

'Mister Harry, what a magnificent specimen,' he cried delightedly. A fish like this would give impetus to St Mary's budding tourist trade, and he came to clasp my hand. As State Presidents go in this part of the world, he was top of the class.

'Thank you, Mr President, sir.' Even with the black homburg on his head, he reached to my armpit. He was a symphony in black, black wool suit, and patent leather shoes, skin the colour of polished anthracite and only a fringe of startlingly white fluffy hair curling around his ears.

'You really are to be congratulated.' President Biddle was dancing with excitement, and I knew I'd be eating at Government House on guest nights again this season. It had taken a year or two—but the President had finally accepted me as though I was island-born. I was

4

one of his children, with all the special privilege that this position carried with it.

Fred Coker arrived in his hearse, but armed with his photographic equipment, and while he set up his tripod and disappeared under the black cloth to focus the ancient camera, we posed for him beside the colossal carcass. Chuck in the middle holding the rod, with the rest of us grouped around him, arms folded like a football team. Angelo and I were grinning and Chubby was scowling horrifically into the lens. The picture would look good in my new advertising brochure—loyal crew and intrepid skipper, hair curling out from under his cap and from the vee of his shirt, all muscle and smiles—it would really pack them in next season.

I arranged for the fish to go into the cold room down at the pine-apple export sheds. I would consign it out to Rowland Wards of London for mounting on the next refrigerated shipment. Then I left Angelo and Chubby to scrub down *Dancer's* decks, refuel her across the harbour at the Shell basin and take her out to moorings.

As Chuck and I climbed into the cab of my battered old Ford pick-up, Chubby sidled across like a racecourse tipster, speaking out of the corner of his mouth.

'Harry, about my billfish bonus—' I knew exactly what he was going to ask, we went through this every time.

'Mrs Chubby doesn't have to know about it, right?' I finished for him.

'That's right,' he agreed lugubriously, and pushed his filthy deep-sea cap to the back of his head.

   ＊ ＊ ＊

I put Chuck on the plane at nine the next morning and I sang the whole way down from the plateau, honking the horn of my battered old Ford pick-up at the island girls working in the pineapple fields. They straightened up with big flashing smiles under the brims of the wide straw hats and waved.

At Coker's Travel Agency I changed Chuck's American Express traveller's cheques, haggling the rate of exchange with Fred Coker. He was in full fig, tailcoat and black tie. He had a funeral at noon. The camera and tripod laid up for the present, photographer became undertaker.

Coker's Funeral Parlour was in the back of the Travel Agency

5

opening into the alley, and Fred used the hearse to pick up tourists at the airport, first discreetly changing his advertising board on the vehicle and putting the seats in over the rail for the coffins.

I booked all my charters through him, and he clouted his ten per cent off my traveller's cheques. He had the insurance agency as well, and he deducted the annual premium for *Dancer* before carefully counting out the balance. I recounted just as carefully, for although Fred looks like a schoolmaster, tall and thin and prim, with just enough island blood to give him a healthy all-over tan, he knows every trick in the book and a few which have not been written down yet.

He waited patiently while I checked, taking no offence, and when I stuffed the roll into my back pocket, his gold pince-nez sparkled and he told me like a loving father, 'Don't forget you have a charter party coming in tomorrow, Mister Harry.'

'That's all right, Mr Coker—don't you worry, my crew will be just fine.'

'They are down at the Lord Nelson already,' he told me delicately. Fred keeps his finger firmly on the island's pulse.

'Mr Coker, I'm running a charter boat, not a temperance society. Don't worry,' I repeated, and stood up. 'Nobody ever died of a hang-over.'

I crossed Drake Street to Edward's Store and a hero's welcome. Ma Eddy herself came out from behind the counter and folded me into her warm pneumatic bosom.

'Mister Harry,' she cooed and bussed me, 'I went down to the wharf to see the fish you hung yesterday.' Then she turned still holding me and shouted at one of her counter girls, 'Shirley, you get Mister Harry a nice cold beer now, hear?'

I hauled out my roll. The pretty little island girls chittered like sparrows when they saw it, and Ma Eddy rolled her eyes and hugged me closer.

'What do I owe you, Missus Eddy?' From June to November is a long off-season, when the fish do not run, and Ma Eddy carries me through that lean time.

I propped myself against the counter with a can of beer in my hand, picking the goods I needed from the shelves and watching their legs as the girls in their mini-skirts clambered up the ladders to fetch them down—old Harry feeling pretty good and cocky with that hard lump of green stuff in his back pocket.

6

Then I went down to the Shell Company basin and the manager met me at the door of his office between the big silver fuel storage tanks.

'God, Harry, I've been waiting for you all morning. Head Office has been screaming at me about your bill.'

'Your waiting is over, brother,' I told him. But *Wave Dancer*, like most beautiful women, is an expensive mistress, and when I climbed back into the pick-up, the lump in my pocket was severely depleted.

They were waiting for me in the beer garden of the Lord Nelson. The island is very proud of its associations with the Royal Navy, despite the fact that it is no longer a British possession but revels in an independence of six years' standing; yet for two hundred years previously it had been a station of the British fleet. Old prints by long-dead artists decorated the public bar, depicting the great ships beating up the channel or lying in Grand Harbour alongside Admiralty Wharf—men-of-war and merchantmen of John Company victualled and refitted here before the long run south to the Cape of Good Hope and the Atlantic.

St Mary's has never forgotten her place in history, nor the admirals and mighty ships that made their landfall here. The Lord Nelson is a parody of its former grandeur, but I enjoy its decayed and seedy elegance and its associations with the past more than the tower of glass and concrete that Hilton has erected on the headland above the harbour.

Chubby and his wife sat side by side on the bench against the far wall, both of them in their Sunday clothes. This was the easiest way to tell them apart, the fact that Chubby wore the three-piece suit which he had bought for his wedding—the buttons straining and gaping, and the deep-sea cap stained with salt crystals and fish blood on his head—while his wife wore a full-length black dress of heavy wool, faded greenish with age, and black button-up boots beneath. Otherwise their dark mahogany faces were almost identical, though Chubby was freshly shaven and she did have a light moustache.

'Hello, Missus Chubby, how are you?' I asked.

'Thank you, Mister Harry.'

'Will you take a little something, then?'

'Perhaps just a little orange gin, Mister Harry, with a small bitter to chase it down.'

While she sipped the sweet liquor, I counted Chubby's wages into her hand, and her lips moved as she counted silently in chorus. Chubby watched anxiously, and I wondered once again how he had managed all these years to fool her on the billfish bonus.

Missus Chubby drained the beer and the froth emphasized her moustache.

'I'll be off then, Mister Harry.' She rose majestically, and sailed from the courtyard. I waited until she turned into Frobisher Street before I slipped Chubby the little sheath of notes under the table and we went into the private bar together.

Angelo had a girl on each side of him and one on his lap. His black silk shirt was open to the belt buckle, exposing gleaming chest muscles. His denim pants fitted skin-tight, leaving no doubt as to his gender, and his boots were hand-tooled and polished westerns. He had greased his hair and sleeked it back in the style of the young Presley. He flashed his grin like a stage lamp across the room and when I paid him he tucked a banknote into the front of each girl's blouse.

'Hey, Eleanor, you go sit on Harry's lap, but careful now. Harry's a virgin—you treat him right, hear?' He roared with delighted laughter and turned to Chubby.

'Hey, Chubby, you quit giggling like that all the time, man! That's stupid—all that giggling and grinning.' Chubby's frown deepened, his whole face crumpling into folds and wrinkles like that of a bulldog. 'Hey, mister barman, you give old Chubby a drink now. Perhaps that will stop him cutting up stupid, giggling like that.'

At four that afternoon Angelo had driven his girls off, and he sat with his glass on the table top before him. Beside it lay his bait knife honed to a razor edge and glinting evilly in the overhead lights. He muttered darkly to himself, deep in alcoholic melancholy. Every few minutes he would test the edge of the knife with his thumb and scowl around the room. Nobody took any notice of him.

Chubby sat on the other side of me, grinning like a great brown toad—exposing a set of huge startlingly white teeth with pink plastic gums.

'Harry,' he told me expansively, one thick muscled arm around my neck. 'You are a good boy, Harry. You know what, Harry, I'm going to tell you now what I never told you before.' He nodded wisely as he gathered himself for the declaration he made every pay day. 'Harry, I love you, man. I love you better than my own brother.'

I lifted the stained cap and lightly caressed the bald brown dome

8

of his head. 'And you are my favourite eggshell blond,' I told him.

He held me at arm's length for a moment, studying my face, then burst into a lion's roar of laughter. It was completely infectious and we were both still laughing when Fred Coker walked in and sat down at the table. He adjusted his pince-nez and said primly, 'Mister Harry, I have just received a special delivery from London. Your charter cancelled.' I stopped laughing.

'What the hell!' I said. Two weeks without a charter in the middle of high season and only a lousy two-hundred-dollar reservation fee.

'Mr Coker, you have got to get me a party.' I had three hundred dollars left in my pocket from Chuck's charter.

'You got to get me a party,' I repeated, and Angelo picked up his knife and with a crash drove the point deeply into the table top. Nobody took any notice of him, and he scowled angrily around the room.

'I'll try,' said Fred Coker, 'but it's a bit late now.'

'Cable the parties we had to turn down.'

'Who will pay for the cables?' Fred asked delicately.

'The hell with it, I'll pay.' And he nodded and went out. I heard the hearse start up outside.

'Don't worry, Harry,' said Chubby. 'I still love you, man.'

Suddenly beside me Angelo went to sleep. He fell forward and his forehead hit the table top with a resounding crack. I rolled his head so that he would not drown in the puddle of spilled liquor, returned the knife to its sheath, and took charge of his bank roll to protect him from the girls who were hovering close.

Chubby ordered another round and began to sing a rambling, mumbling shanty in island patois, while I sat and worried.

Once again I was stretched out neatly on the financial rack, God how I hate money—or rather the lack of it. Those two weeks would make all the difference as to whether or not *Dancer* and I could survive the off-season, and still keep our good resolutions. I knew we couldn't. I knew we would have to go on the night run again.

The hell with it, if we had to do it, we might as well do it now. I would pass the word that Harry was ready to do a deal. Having made the decision, I felt again that pleasurable tightening of the nerves, the gut thing that goes with danger. The two weeks of cancelled time might not be wasted after all.

I joined Chubby in song, not entirely certain that we were singing

9

the same number, for I seemed to reach the end of each chorus a long time before Chubby.

It was probably this musical feast that called up the law. On St Mary's this takes the form of an Inspector and four troopers, which is more than adequate for the island. Apart from a great deal of 'carnal knowledge under the age of consent' and a little wife-beating, there is no crime worthy of the name.

Inspector Peter Daly was a young man with a blond moustache, a high English colour on smooth cheeks and pale blue eyes set close together like those of a sewer rat. He wore the uniform of the British colonial police, the cap with the silver badge and shiny patent leather peak, the khaki drill starched and ironed until it crackled softly as he walked, the polished leather belt and Sam Browne cross-straps. He carried a malacca cane swagger stick which was also covered with polished leather. Except for the green and yellow St Mary's shoulder flashes, he looked like the Empire's pride, but like the Empire the men who wore the uniform had also crumbled.

'Mr Fletcher,' he said, standing over our table and slapping the swagger stick lightly against his palm. 'I hope we are not going to have any trouble tonight.'

'Sir,' I prompted him. Inspector Daly and I were never friends—I don't like bullies, or persons who in positions of trust supplement a perfectly adequate salary with bribes and kick-backs. He had taken a lot of my hard-won gold from me in the past, which was his most unforgivable sin.

His mouth hardened under the blond moustache and his colour came up quickly. 'Sir,' he repeated reluctantly.

Now it is true that once or twice in the remote past Chubby and I had given way to an excess of boyish high spirits when we had just hung a Moses fish—however, this did not give Inspector Daly any excuse for talking like that. He was after all a mere expatriate out on the island for a three-year contract—which I knew from the President himself would not be renewed.

'Inspector, am I correct in my belief that this is a public place—and that neither my friends nor I are committing a trespass?'

'That is so.'

'Am I also correct in thinking that singing of tuneful and decent songs in a public place does not constitute a criminal act?'

'Well, that is true, but—'

'Inspector, piss off,' I told him pleasantly. He hesitated, looking at

Chubby and me. Between the two of us we make up a lot of muscle, and he could see the unholy battle gleam in our eyes. You could see he wished he had his troopers with him.

'I'll be keeping an eye on you,' he said and, clutching at his dignity like a beggar's rags, he left us.

'Chubby, you sing like an angel,' I said and he beamed at me.

'Harry, I'm going to buy you a drink.' And Fred Coker arrived in time to be included in the round. He drank lager and lime juice which turned my stomach a little, but his tidings were an effective antidote.

'Mister Harry, I got you a party.'

'Mister Coker, I love you.'

'I love you too,' said Chubby, but deep down I felt a twinge of disappointment. I had been looking forward to another night run.

'When are they arriving?' I asked.

'They are here already—they were waiting for me at my office when I got back.'

'No kidding.'

'They knew that your first party had cancelled, and they asked for you by name. They must have come in on the same plane as the special delivery.'

My thinking was a little muzzy right then or I might have pondered a moment how neatly one party had withdrawn and another had stepped in.

'They are staying up at the Hilton.'

'Do they want me to pick them up?'

'No, they'll meet you at Admiralty Wharf ten o'clock tomorrow morning.'

❋   ❋   ❋

I was grateful that the party had asked for such a late starting time. That morning *Dancer* was crewed by zombies. Angelo groaned and turned a light chocolate colour every time he bent over to coil a rope or rig the rods and Chubby sweated neat alcohol and his expression was truly terrifying. He had not spoken a word all morning.

I wasn't feeling all that cheerful myself. *Dancer* was snugged up alongside the wharf and I leaned on the rail of the flying bridge with my darkest pair of Polaroids over my eyes and although my scalp itched I was afraid to take off my cap in case the top of my skull came with it.

The island's single taxi, a '62 Citroën, came down Drake Street and stopped at the top end of the wharf to deposit my party. There were two of them, and I had expected three, Coker had definitely said a party of three.

They started down the long stone-paved wharf, walking side by side, and I straightened up slowly as I watched them. I felt my physical distress fade into the realms of the inconsequential, to be replaced by that gut thing again, the slow coiling and clenching within, and the little tickling feeling along the back of my arms and in the nape of the neck.

One was tall and walked with that loose easy gait of a professional athlete. He was bare-headed and his hair was pale gingery and combed carefully across a prematurely balding pate so the pink scalp showed through. However, he was lean around the belly and hips, and he was aware. It was the only word to describe the charged sense of readiness that emanated from him.

It takes one to recognize one. This was a man trained to live with and by violence. He was muscle, a *soldier,* in the jargon. It mattered not for which side of the law he exercised his skills—law enforcement or its frustration—he was very bad news. I had hoped never to see this kind of barracuda cruising St Mary's placid waters. It gave me a sick little slide in the guts to know that it had found me out again. Quickly I glanced at the other man, it wasn't so obvious in him, the edge was blunted a little, the outline blurred by time and flesh, but it was there also—more bad news.

'Nice going, Harry,' I told myself bitterly. 'All this, and a hangover thrown in.'

Clearly now I recognized that the older man was the leader. He walked half a pace ahead, the younger taller man paying him that respect. He was a few years my senior also, probably late thirties. There was the beginnings of a paunch over the crocodile skin belt, and pouches of flesh along the line of his jawbone, but his hair had been styled in Bond Street and he wore his Sulka silk shirt and Gucci loafers like badges of rank. As he came on down the wharf he dabbed at his chin and upper lip with a white handkerchief and I guessed the diamond on his little finger at two carats. It was set in a plain gold ring and the wristwatch was gold also, probably by Lanvin or Piaget.

12

'Fletcher?' he asked, stopping below me on the jetty. His eyes were black and beady, like those of a ferret. A predator's eyes, bright without warmth. I saw he was older than I had guessed, for his hair was certainly tinted to conceal the grey. The skin of his cheeks was unnaturally tight and I could see the scars of plastic surgery in the hair line. He'd had a facelift, a vain man then, and I stored the knowledge.

He was an old soldier, risen from the ranks to a position of command. He was the brain, and the man that followed him was the muscle. Somebody had sent out their first team and, with a clairvoyant flash, I realized why my original party had cancelled.

A phone call followed by a visit from this pair would put the average citizen off marlin-fishing for life. They had probably done themselves a serious injury in their rush to cancel.

'Mr Materson? Come aboard—' One thing was certain, they had not come for the fishing, and I decided on a low and humble profile until I had figured out the percentages, so I threw in a belated '—sir.'

The muscle man jumped down to the deck, landing soft-footed like a cat and I saw the way that the folded coat over his arm swung heavily, there was something weighty in the pocket. He confronted my crew, thrusting out his jaw and running his eyes over them swiftly.

Angelo flashed a watered-down version of the celebrated smile and touched the brim of his cap. 'Welcome, sir.' And Chubby's scowl lightened momentarily and he muttered something that sounded like a curse, but was probably a warm greeting. The man ignored them and turned to hand Materson down to the deck where he waited while his bodyguard checked out *Dancer's* main saloon. Then he went in and I followed him.

Our accommodation is luxurious, at a hundred and twenty-five thousand pounds it should be. The air-conditioning had taken the bite out of the morning heat and Materson sighed with relief and dabbed again with his handkerchief as he sank into one of the padded seats.

'This is Mike Guthrie.' He indicated the muscle who was moving about the cabin checking at the ports, opening doors and generally over-playing his hand, coming on very tough and hard.

'My pleasure, Mr Guthrie.' I grinned with all my boyish charm, and he waved airily without glancing at me.

'A drink, gentlemen?' I asked, as I opened the liquor cabinet. They

13

took a Coke each, but I needed something medicinal for the shock and the hangover. The first swallow of cold beer from the can revitalized me.

'Well, gentlemen, I think I shall be able to offer you some sport. Only yesterday I hung a very good fish, and all the signs are for a big run—'

Mike Guthrie stepped in front of me and stared into my face. His eyes were flecked with brown and pale green, like a hand-loomed tweed.

'Don't I know you?' he asked.

'I don't think I've ever had the pleasure.'

'You are a London boy, aren't you?' He had picked up the accent.

'I left Blighty a long time ago, mate,' I grinned, letting it come out broad. He did not smile, and dropped into the seat opposite me, placing his hands on the table top between us, spreading his fingers palm downwards. He continued to stare at me. A very tough baby, very hard.

'I'm afraid that it is too late for today,' I babbled on cheerfully. 'If we are going to fish the Mozambique, we have to clear harbour by six o'clock. However, we can make an early start tomorrow—'

Materson interrupted my chatter. 'Check that list out, Fletcher, and let us know what you are short.' He passed me a folded sheet of foolscap, and I glanced down the handwritten column. It was all scuba diving gear and salvage equipment.

'You gentlemen aren't interested in big game fishing then?' Old Harry showing surprise and amazement at such an unlikely eventuality.

'We have come out to do a little exploring—that's all.'

I shrugged. 'You're paying, we do what you want to do.'

'Have you got all that stuff?'

'Most of it.' In the off-season I run a cut-rate package deal for scuba buffs which helps pay expenses. I had a full range of diving sets and there was an air compressor built into *Dancer*'s engine room for recharging. 'I don't have the air bags or all that rope—'

'Can you get them?'

'Sure.' Ma Eddy had a pretty good selection of ships' stores, and Angelo's old man was a sail-maker. He could run up the air bags in a couple of hours.

'Right then, get it.'

I nodded. 'When do you want to start?'

'Tomorrow morning. There will be one other person with us.'

'Did Mr Coker tell you it's five hundred dollars a day—and I'll have to charge you for this extra equipment?'

Materson inclined his head and made as if to rise.

'Would it be okay to see a little of that out front?' I asked softly, and they froze. I grinned ingratiatingly.

'It's been a long lean winter, Mr Materson, and I've got to buy this stuff and fill my fuel tanks.'

Materson took out his wallet and counted out three hundred pounds in fivers. As he was doing so he said in his soft purry voice, 'We won't need your crew, Fletcher. The three of us will help you handle the boat.'

I was taken aback. I had not expected that. 'They'll have to draw full wages, if you lay them off. I can't reduce my rate.'

Mike Guthrie was still sitting opposite me, and now he leaned forward. 'You heard the man, Fletcher, just get your niggers off the boat,' he said softly.

Carefully I folded the bundle of five pound notes and buttoned them into my breast pocket, then I looked at him. He was very quick, I could see him tense up ready for me and for the first time he showed expression in those cold speckled eyes. It was anticipation. He knew he had reached me, and he thought I was going to try him. He wanted that, he wanted to take me apart. He left his hands on the table, palms downwards, fingers spread. I thought how I might take the little finger of each hand and snap them at the middle joint like a pair of cheese sticks. I knew I could do it before he had a chance to move, and the knowledge gave me a great deal of pleasure, for I was very angry. I haven't many friends, but I value the few I have.

'Did you hear me speak, boy?' Guthrie hissed at me, and I dredged up the boyish grin again and let it hang at a ridiculous angle on my face.

'Yes, sir, Mr Guthrie,' I said. 'You're paying the money, whatever you say.'

I nearly choked on the words. He leaned back in his seat, and I saw that he was disappointed. He was muscle, and he enjoyed his work. I think I knew then that I was going to kill him, and I took enough comfort from the thought to enable me to hold the grin.

Materson was watching us with those bright little eyes. His interest was detached and clinical, like a scientist studying a pair of labo-

15

ratory specimens. He saw that the confrontation had been resolved for the present, and his voice was soft and purry again.

'Very well, Fletcher.' He moved towards the deck. 'Get that equipment together and be ready for us at eight tomorrow morning.'

I let them go, and I sat and finished the beer. It may have been just my hangover, but I was beginning to have a very ugly feeling about this whole charter and I realized that after all it might be best to leave Chubby and Angelo ashore. I went out to tell them.

'We've got a pair of freaks, I'm sorry but they have got some big secret and they are dealing you out.' I put the aqualung bottles on the compressor to top up, and we left *Dancer* at the wharf while I went up to Ma Eddy's and Angelo and Chubby took my drawing of the air bags across to his father's workshop.

The bags were ready by four o'clock and I picked them up in the Ford and stowed them in the sail locker under the cockpit seats. Then I spent an hour stripping and reassembling the demand valves of the scubas and checking out all the other diving equipment.

At sundown I ran *Dancer* out to her moorings on my own, and was about to leave her and row ashore in the dinghy when I had a good thought. I went back into the cabin and knocked back the toggles on the engine-room hatch.

I took the FN carbine from its hiding-place, pumped a cartridge into the breech, set her for automatic fire and clicked on the safety catch before hanging her in the slings again.

*   *   *

Before it was dark, I took my old cast net and waded out across the lagoon towards the main reef. I saw the swirl and run beneath the surface of the water which the setting sun had burnished to the colour of copper and flame, and I sent the net spinning high with a swing of shoulders and arms. It ballooned like a parachute, and fell in a wide circle over the shoal of striped mullet. When I pulled the drag line and closed the net over them, there were five of the big silvery fish as long as my forearm kicking and thumping in the coarse wet folds.

I grilled two of them and ate them on the veranda of my shack. They tasted better than trout from a mountain stream, and afterwards I poured a second whisky and sat on into the dark.

Usually this is the time of day when the island enfolds me in a

16

great sense of peace, and I seem to understand what the whole business of living is all about. However, that night was not like that. I was angry that these people had come out to the island and brought with them their special brand of poison to contaminate us. Five years ago I had run from that, believing I had found a place that was safe. Yet beneath the anger, when I was honest with myself, I recognized also an excitement, a pleasurable excitement. That gut thing again, knowing that I was at risk once more. I was not sure yet what the stakes were, but I knew they were high and that I was sitting in the game with the big boys once again.

I was on the left-hand path again. The path I had chosen at seventeen, when I had deliberately decided against the university scholarship which I had been awarded and instead I bunked from St Stephen's orphanage in north London and lied about my age to join a whaling factory ship bound for the Antarctic. Down there on the edge of the great ice I lost my last vestige of appetite for the academic life. When the money I had made in the south ran out I enlisted in a special service battalion where I learned how violence and sudden death could be practised as an art. I practised that art in Malaya and Vietnam, then later in the Congo and Biafra—until suddenly one day in a remote jungle village while the thatched huts burned sending columns of tarry black smoke into an empty brazen sky and the flies came to the dead in humming blue clouds, I was sickened to the depths of my soul. I wanted out.

In the South Atlantic I had come to love the sea, and now I wanted a place beside it, with a boat and peace in the long quiet evenings.

First I needed money to buy those things—a great deal of money—so much that the only way I could earn it was in the practice of my art.

One last time, I thought, and I planned it with utmost care. I needed an assistant and I chose a man I had known in the Congo. Between us we lifted the complete collection of gold coins from the British Museum of Numismatology in Belgrave Square. Three thousand rare gold coins that fitted easily into a medium-sized briefcase, coins of the Roman Caesars and the Emperors of Byzantium, coins of the early states of America and of the English Kings—florins and leopards of Edward III, nobles of the Henrys and angels of Edward IV, treble sovereigns and unites, crowns of the rose from the reign of Henry VIII and five-pound pieces of George III and Vic-

17

toria—three thousand coins, worth, even on a forced sale, not less than two million dollars.

Then I made my first mistake as a professional criminal. I trusted another criminal. When I caught up with my assistant in an Arab hotel in Beirut I reasoned with him in fairly strong terms, and when finally I put the question to him of just what he had done with the briefcase of coins, he snatched a .38 Beretta from under his mattress. In the ensuing scuffle he had his neck broken. It had been a mistake. I didn't mean to kill the man—but even more I didn't mean him to kill me. I hung a 'DON'T DISTURB' sign on his door and I caught the next plane out. Ten days later the police found the briefcase with the coins in the left-luggage department at Paddington Station. It made the front page of all the national newspapers.

I tried again at an exhibition of cut diamonds in Amsterdam, but I had done faulty research on the electronic alarm system and I tripped a beam that I had overlooked.

The plain clothes security guards who had been hired by the organizers of the exhibition rushed headlong into the uniformed police coming in through the main entrance and a spectacular shoot-out ensued, while a completely unarmed Harry Fletcher slunk away into the night to the sound of loud cries and gunfire.

I was halfway to Schipol airport by the time a cease-fire was called between the opposing forces of the law—but not before a sergeant of the Dutch police received a critical chest wound.

I sat anxiously chewing my nails and drinking innumerable beers in my room in the Holiday Inn near Zürich Airport, as I followed the gallant sergeant's fight for life on the TV set. I would have hated like all hell to have another fatality on my conscience, and I made a solemn vow that if the policeman died I would forget for ever about my place in the sun.

However, the Dutch sergeant rallied strongly and I felt an immense proprietary pride in him when he was finally declared out of danger. And when he was promoted to assistant inspector and awarded a bonus of five thousand crowns I persuaded myself that I was his fairy godfather and that the man owed me eternal gratitude.

Still, I had been shaken by two failures and I took a job as an instructor at an Outward Bound School for six months while I considered my future. At the end of six months, I decided for one more try.

This time I laid the ground-work with meticulous care. I emigrated to South Africa, where I was able with my qualifications to obtain a post as an operator with the security firm responsible for bullion shipments from the South African Reserve Bank in Pretoria to overseas destinations. For a year I worked with the transportation of hundreds of millions of dollars' worth of gold bars, and I studied the system in every minute detail. The weak spot, when I found it, was at Rome—but again I needed help.

This time I went to the professionals, but I set my price at a level that made it easier for them to pay me out than put me down and I covered myself a hundred times against treachery.

It went as smoothly as I had planned it, and this time there were no victims. Nobody came out with a bullet or a cracked skull. We merely switched part of a cargo and substituted leaded cases. Then we moved two and a half tons of gold bars across the Swiss border in a furniture removals van.

In Basle, sitting in a banker's private rooms furnished with priceless antiques, above the wide swift waters of the Rhine on which the stately white swans rode in majesty, they paid me out. Manny Resnick signed the transfer into my numbered account of one hundred and fifty thousand pounds sterling and he laughed a fat hungry little laugh.

'You'll be back, Harry—you've tasted blood now and you'll be back. Have a nice holiday, then come to me again when you've thought up another deal like this one.'

He was wrong, I never went back. I rode up to Zürich in a hire car and flew to Paris Orly. In the men's room there, I shaved off the beard and picked up the briefcase from the pay locker that contained the passport in the name of Harold Delville Fletcher. Then I flew out Pan Am for Sydney, Australia.

Wave Dancer cost me one hundred and twenty-five thousand pounds sterling and I took her under a deck load of fuel drums across to St Mary's, two thousand miles, a voyage on which we learned to love each other.

On St Mary's I purchased twenty-five acres of peace, and built the shack with my own hands—four rooms, a thatched roof and a wide veranda, set amongst the palms above the white beach. Except for the occasions when a night run had been forced upon me, I had walked the right-hand path since then.

It was late when I had done my reminiscences and the tide was pushing high up the beach in the moonlight before I went into the shack, but then I slept like an innocent.

* * *

They were on time the following morning. Charly Materson ran a tight outfit. The taxi deposited them at the head of the wharf while I had *Dancer* singled up at stem and stern and both engines burbling sweetly.

I watched them come, concentrating on the third member of the group. He was not what I had expected. He was tall and lean with a wide friendly face and dark soft hair. Unlike the others, his face and arms were darkly suntanned, and his teeth were large and very white. He wore denim shorts and a white sweatshirt and he had a swimmer's wide rangy shoulders and powerful arms. I knew instantly who was to use the diving equipment.

He carried a big green canvas kit bag over one shoulder. He carried it easily, though I could see that it was weighty, and he chatted gaily with his two companions who answered him in monosyllables. They flanked him like a pair of guards.

He looked up at me as they came level and I saw that he was young and eager. There was an excitement, an anticipation, about him, that reminded me sharply of myself ten years previously.

'Hi,' he grinned at me, an easy friendly grin and I realized that he was an extremely good-looking youngster.

'Greetings,' I replied, liking him from the first and intrigued as to how he had found a place with the wolf pack. Under my direction they took in the mooring lines and, from this brief exercise, I learned that the youngster was the only one of them familiar with small boats.

As we cleared the harbour, he and Materson came up on to the flying bridge. Materson had coloured slightly and his breathing was raggedy from the mild exertion. He introduced the newcomer.

'This is Jimmy,' he told me, when he had caught his breath. We shook hands and I put his age at not much over twenty. Close up I had no cause to revise my first impressions. He had a level and innocent gaze from sea-grey eyes, and his grip was firm and dry.

'She's a darling boat, skipper,' he told me, which was rather like telling a mother that her baby is beautiful.

'She's not a bad old girl.'

'What is she, forty-four, forty-five feet?'

'Forty-five,' I said, liking him a little more.

20

'Jimmy will give you your directions,' Materson told me. 'You will follow his orders.'

'Fine,' I said, and Jimmy coloured a little under his tan.

'Not orders, Mr Fletcher, I'll just tell you where we want to go.'

'Fine, Jim, I'll take you there.'

'Once we are clear of the island, will you turn due west.'

'Just how far in that direction do you intend going?' I asked.

'We want to cruise along the coast of the African mainland,' Materson cut in.

'Lovely,' I said, 'that's great. Did anybody tell you that they don't hang out the welcome mat for strangers there?'

'We will stay well offshore.'

I thought a moment, hesitating before turning back to Admiralty Wharf and packing the whole bunch ashore.

'Where do you want to go—north or south of the river-mouth?'

'North,' said Jimmy, and that altered the proposition for the good. South of the river they patrolled with helicopters and were very touchy about their territorial waters. I would not go in there during daylight.

In the north there was little coastal activity. There was a single crash boat at Zinballa, but when its engines were in running order, which was a few days a week, then its crew were mostly blown out of their minds with the virulent palm liquor brewed locally along the coast. When crew and engines were functioning simultaneously, they could raise fifteen knots, and *Dancer* could turn on twenty-two any time I asked her.

The final trick in my favour was that I could run *Dancer* through the maze of off-shore reefs and islands on a dark night in a roaring monsoon, while it was my experience that the crash boat commander avoided this sort of extravagance. Even on a bright sunny day and in a flat calm, he preferred the quiet and peace of Zinballa Bay. I had heard that he suffered acutely from sea sickness, and held his present appointment only because it was far away from the capital, where as a minister of the government the commander had been involved in a little unpleasantness regarding the disappearance of large amounts of foreign aid.

From my point of view he was the ideal man for the job.

'All right,' I agreed, turning to Materson. 'But I'm afraid what you're asking is going to cost you another two-fifty dollars a day— danger money.'

'I was afraid it might,' he said softly.

I brought the *Dancer* around, close to the light on Oyster Point. It was a bright morning with a high clear sky into which the stationary clouds that marked the position of each group of islands towered in great soft columns of blinding white.

The solemn progress of the trade winds across the ocean was interrupted by the bulwark of the African continent on which they broke. We were getting the backlash here in the inshore channel, and random squalls and gusts of it spread darkly across the pale green waters and flecked the surface chop with white. *Dancer* loved it, it gave her an excuse to flounce and swish her bottom.

'You looking for anything special—or just looking?' I asked casually, and Jimmy turned to tell me all about it. He was itchy with excitement, and the grey eyes sparkled as he opened his mouth.

'Just looking,' Materson interrupted with a ring in his voice and a sharp warning in his expression, and Jimmy's mouth closed.

'I know these waters. I know every island, every reef. I might be able to save you a lot of time—and a bit of money.'

'That's very kind of you,' Materson thanked me with heavy irony. 'However, I believe we can manage.'

'You are paying,' I shrugged, and Materson glanced at Jimmy, inclined his head in a command to follow and led him down into the cockpit. They stood together beside the stern rail and Materson spoke to him quietly but earnestly for two minutes. I saw Jimmy flush darkly, his expression changing from dismay to boyish sulks and I guessed that he was having his ear chewed to ribbons on the subject of secrecy and security.

When he came back on to the flying bridge he was seething with anger, and for the first time I noticed the strong hard line of his jaw. He wasn't just a pretty boy, I decided.

Evidently on Materson's orders, Guthrie, the muscle, came out of the cabin and swung the big padded fighting chair to face the bridge. He lounged in it, even in his relaxation charged with the promise of violence like a resting leopard, and he watched us, one leg draped over the arm rest and the linen jacket with the heavy weight in its pocket folded in his lap.

A happy ship, I chuckled, and ran *Dancer* out through the islands, threading a fine course through the clear green waters where the reefs lurked darkly below the surface like malevolent monsters and the islands were fringed with coral sand as dazzling white as a snowdrift, and crowned with dark thick vegetation over which the palm stems curved gracefully, their tops shaking in the feeble remnants of the trade.

It was a long day as we cruised at random and I tried to get some hint of the object of the expedition. However, still smarting from Materson's reprimand, Jimmy was tight mouthed and grim. He asked for changes of course at intervals, after I had pointed out our position on the large scale admiralty chart which he produced from his bag.

Although there were no extraneous markings on his chart, when I examined it surreptitiously I was able to figure that we were interested in an area fifteen to thirty miles north of the multiple mouths of the Rovuma River, and up to sixteen miles offshore. An area containing perhaps three hundred islands varying in size from a few acres to many square miles—a very big haystack in which to find his needle.

I was content enough to perch up on *Dancer's* bridge and run quietly along the seaways, enjoying the feel of my darling under me and watching the activity of the sea animals, and birds.

In the fighting chair Mike Guthrie's scalp started to show through the thin cover of hair like strips of scarlet neon lighting.

'Cook, you bastard,' I thought happily, and neglected to warn him about the tropical sun until we were running home in the dusk. The next day he was in agony with white goo smeared over his bloated and incarnadined features and a wide cloth hat covering his head, but his face flashed like the port light of an ocean-goer.

By noon on the second day I was bored. Jimmy was poor company for although he had recovered a little of his good humour he was so conscious of security that he even thought for thirty seconds before accepting an offer of coffee.

It was more for something to do than because I wanted fish for my dinner that when I saw a squadron of small kingfish charging a big shoal of sardine ahead of us, I gave the wheel to Jimmy.

'Just keep her on that heading,' I told him and dropped down into the cockpit. Guthrie watched me warily from his swollen crimson face as I glanced into the cabin and saw that Materson had my bar open and was mixing himself a gin and tonic. At seven hundred and fifty a day I didn't grudge it to him. He hadn't emerged from the cabin in two days.

I went back to the small tackle locker and selected a pair of

23

feather jigs and tossed them out. As we crossed the track of the shoal I hit a kingfish and brought him out kicking, flashing golden in the sun.

Then I recoiled the lines and stowed them, wiped the blade of my heavy bait-knife across the oil stone to brighten up the edge and split the kingfish's belly from anal vent to gills and pulled out a handful of bloody gut to throw it into the wake.

Immediately a pair of gulls that had been weaving and hovering over us screeched with greed and plunged for the scraps. Their excitement summoned others and within minutes there was a shrieking, flapping host of them astern of us.

Their din was not so loud that it covered the metallic snicker close behind me, the unmistakable sound of the slide on an automatic pistol being drawn back and released to load and cock. I moved entirely from instinct. Without thought, the big bait-knife spun in my right hand as I changed smoothly to a throwing grip and I turned and dropped to the deck in a single movement, breaking fall with heels and left arm as the knife went back over my right shoulder and I began the throw at the instant that I lined up the target.

Mike Guthrie had a big automatic in his right hand. An old-fashioned naval .45, a killer's weapon, one which would blow a hole in a man's chest through which you could drive a London cab.

Two things saved Guthrie from being pinned to the back of the fighting chair by the long heavy blade of the bait-knife. Firstly, the fact that the .45 was not pointed at me and, secondly, the expression of comical amazement on the man's scarlet face.

I prevented myself from throwing the knife, breaking the instinctive action by a major effort of will, and we stared at each other. He knew then how close he had come, and the grin he forced to his swollen sunburned lips was shaky and unconvincing. I stood up and pegged the knife into the bait chopping board.

'Do yourself a favour,' I told him quietly. 'Don't play with that thing behind my back.'

He laughed then, blustering and tough again. He swivelled the seat and aimed out over the stern. He fired twice, the shots crashing out loudly above the run of *Dancer*'s engines and the brief smell of cordite was whipped away on the wind.

Two of the milling gulls exploded into grotesque bursts of blood and feathers blown to shreds by the heavy bullets, and the rest of the flock scattered with shrieks of panic. The manner in which the birds were torn up told me that Guthrie had loaded with explosive bullets, a more savage weapon than a sawn-off shotgun.

He swivelled the chair back to face me and blew into the muzzle of the pistol like John Wayne. It was fancy shooting with that heavy calibre weapon.

'Tough cooky,' I applauded him, and turned to the bridge ladder, but Materson was standing in the doorway of the cabin with the gin in his hand and as I stepped past him he spoke quietly.

'Now I know who you are,' he said, in that soft purry voice. 'It's been worrying us, we thought we knew you.'

I stared at him, and he called past me to Guthrie.

'You know who he is now, don't you?' and Guthrie shook his head. I don't think he could trust his voice. 'He had a beard then, think about it—a mug-shot photograph.'

'Jesus,' said Guthrie. 'Harry Bruce!' I felt a little shock at hearing the name spoken out loud again after all these years. I had hoped it was forgotten for ever.

'Rome,' said Materson. 'The gold heist.'

'He set it up.' Guthrie snapped his fingers. 'I was sure I knew him. It was the beard that fooled me.'

'I think you gentlemen have the wrong address,' I said with a desperate attempt at a cool tone, but was thinking quickly, trying to weigh this fresh knowledge. They had seen a mug-shot—where? When? Were they law men or from the other side of the fence? I needed time to think—and I clambered up to the bridge.

'Sorry,' muttered Jimmy, as I took the wheel from him. 'I should have told you he had a gun.'

'Yeah,' I said. 'It might have helped.' My mind was racing, and the first turning it took was along the left-hand path. They would have to go. They had blown my elaborate cover, they had sniffed me out and there was only one sure way. I looked back into the cockpit but both Materson and Guthrie had gone below.

An accident, take them both out at one stroke, aboard a small boat there were plenty of ways a greenhorn could get hurt in the worst possible way. They had to go.

Then I looked at Jimmy, and he grinned at me.

'You move fast,' he said. 'Mike nearly wet himself, he thought he was going to get that knife through his gizzard.'

The kid also? I asked myself—if I took out the other two, he would

25

have to go as well. Then suddenly I felt the same physical nausea that I had first known long ago in the Biafran village.

'You okay, skipper?' Jimmy asked quickly, it had shown on my face.

'I'm okay, Jim,' I said. 'Why don't you go fetch us a can of beer.'

While he was below I reached my decision. I would do a deal. I was certain that they didn't want their business shouted in the streets. I'd trade secrecy for secrecy. Probably they were coming to the same conclusion in the cabin below.

I locked the wheel and crossed quietly to the corner of the bridge, making sure my footsteps were not picked up in the cabin below.

The ventilator there funnels fresh air into the inlet above the saloon table. I had found that the ventilator made a reasonably effective voice tube, that sound was carried through it to the bridge.

However, the effectiveness of this listening device depends on a number of factors, chief of these being the direction and strength of the wind and the precise position of the speaker in the cabin below.

The wind was on our beam, gusting into the opening of the ventilator and blotting out patches of the conversation in the cabin. However, Jimmy must have been standing directly below the vent for his voice came through strongly when the wind roar did not smother it.

'Why don't you ask him now?' and the reply was confused, then the wind gusted and when it cleared, Jimmy was speaking again. 'If you do it tonight, where will you—' and the wind roared, '—to get the dawn light then we will have to—' The entire discussion seemed to be on times and places, and as I wondered briefly what they hoped to gain by leaving harbour at dawn, he said it again. 'If the dawn light is where—' I strained for the next words but the wind killed them for ten seconds, then 'I don't see why we can't—' Jimmy was protesting and suddenly Mike Guthrie's voice came through sharp and hard. He must have gone to stand close beside Jimmy, probably in a threatening attitude.

'Listen, Jimmy boy, you let us handle that side of it. Your job is to find the bloody thing, and you aren't doing so good this far.'

They must have moved again for their voices became indistinct and I heard the sliding door into the cockpit opening and I turned quickly to the wheel and freed the retaining handle just as Jimmy's head appeared over the edge of the deck as he came up the ladder.

He handed me the beer and he seemed to be more relaxed now.

The reserve was gone from his manner. He smiled at me, friendly and trusting.

'Mr Materson says that's enough for today. We are to head for home.'

I swung *Dancer* across the current and we came in from the west, past the mouth of Turtle Bay and I could see my shack standing amongst the palms. I felt a sudden chilling premonition of loss. The fates had called for a new deck of cards, and the game was bigger, the stakes were too rich for my blood but there was no way I could pull out now.

However, I suppressed the chill of despair, and turned to Jimmy. I would take advantage of his new attitude of trust and try for what information I could glean.

We chatted lightly on the run down the channel into Grand Harbour. They had obviously told him that I was off the leper list. Strangely the fact that I had a criminal past made me more acceptable to the wolf pack. They could reckon the angles now. They had found a lever, so now they could handle me—though I was pretty sure they had not explained the whole proposition to young James.

It was obviously a relief for him to act naturally with me. He was a friendly and open person, completely lacking in guile. An example of this was the way that his surname had been guarded like a military secret from me, and yet around his neck he wore a silver chain and a Medic-alert tag that warned that J. A. NORTH, the wearer, was allergic to penicillin.

Now he forgot all his former reserve, and gently I drew small snippets of information from him that I might have use for in the future. In my experience it's what you don't know that can really hurt you.

I chose the subject that I guessed would open him up completely.

'See that reef across the channel, there where she's breaking now? That's Devil Fish Reef and there is twenty fathoms sheer under the sea side of her. It's a hangout of some real big old bull grouper. I shot one there last year that weighed in at over two hundred kilos.'

'Two hundred—' he exclaimed. 'My God, that's almost four hundred and fifty pounds.'

'Right, you could put your head and shoulders in his mouth.'

The last of his reserves disappeared. He had been reading history and philosophy at Cambridge but spent too much time in the sea, and had to drop out. Now he ran a small diving equipment supply

27

company and underwater salvage outfit, that gave him a living and allowed him to dive most days of the week. He did private work and had contracted to the Government and the Navy on some jobs.

More than once he mentioned the name 'Sherry' and I probed carefully.

'Girl friend or wife?' and he grinned.

'Sister, big sister, but she's a doll—she does the books and minds the shop, all that stuff,' in a tone that left no doubt as to what James thought about book-keeping and counter-jumping. 'She's a red-hot conchologist and she makes two thousand a year out of her sea-shells.' But he didn't explain how he had got into the dubious company he was now keeping, nor what he was doing halfway around the world from his sports shop. I left them on Admiralty Wharf, and took *Dancer* over to the Shell basin for refuelling before dark.

※　　※　　※

That evening I grilled the kingfish over the coals, roasted a couple of big sweet yams in their jackets and was washing it down with a cold beer sitting on the veranda of the shack and listening to the surf when I saw the headlights coming down through the palm trees.

The taxi parked beside my pick-up, and the driver stayed at the wheel while his passengers came up the steps on to the stoop. They had left James at the Hilton, and there were just the two of them now—Materson and Guthrie.

'Drink?' I indicated the bottles and ice on the side table. Guthrie poured gin for both of them and Materson sat opposite me and watched me finish the last of the fish.

'I made a few phone calls,' he said when I pushed my plate away. 'And they tell me that Harry Bruce disappeared in June five years ago and hasn't been heard of since. I asked around and found out that Harry Fletcher sailed into Grand Harbour here three months later—inward bound from Sydney, Australia.'

'Is that the truth?' I picked a little fish bone out of my tooth, and lit a long black island cheroot.

'One other thing, someone who knew him well tells me Harry Bruce had a knife scar across his left arm,' he purred, and I involuntarily glanced at the thin line of scar tissue that laced the muscle of my forearm. It had shrunk and flattened with the years, but was still very white against the dark sun-browned skin.

'Now that's a hell of a coincidence,' I said, and drew on the cheroot. It was strong and aromatic, tasting of sea and sun and spices. I wasn't worried now—they were going to make a deal.

'Yeah, isn't it,' Materson agreed, and he looked around him elaborately. 'You got a nice set-up here, Fletcher. Cosy, isn't it, really nice and cosy.'

'It beats hell out of working for a living,' I admitted.

'—Or out of breaking rocks, or sewing mail bags.'

'I should imagine it does.'

'The kid is going to ask you some questions tomorrow. Be nice to him, Fletcher. When we go you can forget you ever saw us, and we'll forget to tell anybody about that funny coincidence.'

'Mr Materson, sir, I've got a terrible memory,' I assured him.

After the conversation I had overheard in *Dancer's* cabin, I expected them to ask for an early start time the following morning, for the dawn light seemed important to their plans. However, neither of them mentioned it, and when they had gone I knew I wouldn't sleep so I walked out along the sand around the curve of the bay to Mutton Point to watch the moon come up through the palm trees. I sat there until after midnight.

✵　　✵　　✵

The dinghy was gone from the jetty but Hambone, the ferry man, rowed me out to *Dancer's* moorings before sun-up the following morning and as we came alongside I saw the familiar shape shambling around the cockpit, and the dinghy tied alongside.

'Hey, Chubby.' I jumped aboard. 'Your Missus kick you out of bed, then?'

Dancer's deck was gleaming white even in the bad light, and all the metal work was brightly burnished. He must have been at it for a couple of hours; Chubby loves *Dancer* almost as much as I do.

'She looked like a public shit-house, Harry,' he grumbled. 'That's a sloppy bunch you got aboard,' and he spat noisily over the side. 'No respect for a boat, that's what.'

He had coffee ready for me, as strong and as pungent as only he can make it, and we drank it sitting in the saloon. Chubby frowned heavily into his mug and blew on the steaming black liquid. He wanted to tell me something.

'How's Angelo?'

29

'Pleasuring the Rawano widows,' he growled. The island does not provide sufficient employment for all its able-bodied young men—so most of them ship out on three-year labour contracts to the American satellite tracking station and Air Force base on Rawano Island. They leave their young wives behind, the Rawano widows, and the island girls are justly celebrated for the high temperature of their blood and their friendly dispositions.

'That Angelo going to shag his brain loose, he's been at it night and day since Monday.'

I detected more than a trace of envy in his growl. Missus Chubby kept him on a pretty tight lead—he sipped noisily at the coffee.

'How's your party, Harry?'

'Their money is good.'

'You not fishing, Harry.' He looked at me. 'I watch you from Coolie Peak, man, you don't go near the channel—you are working inshore.'

'That's right, Chubby.' He returned his attention to his coffee.

'Hey, Harry. You watch them. You be good and careful, hear. They bad men, those two. I don't know the young one—but the others they are bad.'

'I'll be careful, Chubby.'

'You know the new girl at the hotel, Marion? The one over for the season?' I nodded, she was a pretty slim little wisp of a girl with lovely long legs, about nineteen with glossy black hair, freckled skin, bold eyes and an impish smile. 'Well, last night she went with the blond one, the one with the red face.' I knew that Marion sometimes combined business with pleasure and provided for selected hotel guests services beyond the call of duty. On the island this sort of activity drew no social stigma.

'Yes,' I encouraged Chubby.

'He hurt her, Harry. Hurt her bad.' Chubby took another mouthful of coffee. 'Then he paid her so much money she couldn't go to the police.'

I liked Mike Guthrie a little less now. Only an animal would take advantage of a girl like Marion. I knew her well. She had an innocence, a child-like acceptance of life that made her promiscuity strangely appealing. I remembered how I had thought I might have to kill Guthrie one day—and tried not to let the thought perish.

'They are bad men, Harry. I thought it best you know that.'

'Thanks, Chubby.'

'And don't you let them dirty up *Dancer* like that,' he added accusingly. 'The saloon and deck—they were like a pigsty, man.'

He helped me run *Dancer* across to Admiralty Wharf and then he set off homewards, grumbling and muttering blackly. He passed Jimmy coming in the opposite direction and shot him a single malevolent glance that should have shrivelled him in his tracks.

Jimmy was on his own, fresh-faced and jaunty.

'Hi, skipper,' he called, as he jumped down on to *Dancer*'s deck, and I went into the saloon with him and poured coffee for us.

'Mr Materson says you have some questions for me, is that right?'

'Look, Mr Fletcher, I want you to know that I didn't mean offence by not talking to you before. It wasn't me—but the others.'

'Sure,' I said. 'That's fine, Jimmy.'

'It would have been the sensible thing to ask your help long ago, instead of blundering around the way we have been. Anyway, now the others have suddenly decided it's okay.'

He had just told me much more than he imagined, and I adjusted my opinion of Master James. It was clear that he possessed information, and he had not shared it with the others. It was his insurance, and he had probably insisted on seeing me alone to keep his insurance policy intact.

'Skipper, we are looking for an island, a specific island. I can't tell you why, I'm sorry.'

'Forget it, Jimmy. That's all right.' What will there be for you, James North, I wondered suddenly. What will the wolf pack have for you once you have led them to this special island of yours? Will it be something a lot less pleasant than penicillin allergy?

I looked at that handsome young face, and felt an unaccustomed flood of affection for him—perhaps it was his youth and innocence, the sense of excitement with which he viewed this tired and wicked old world. I envied and liked him for that, and I did not relish seeing him pulled down and rolled in the dirt.

'Jim, how well do you know your friends?' I asked him quietly, and he was taken by surprise, then almost immediately he was wary.

'Well enough,' he replied carefully. 'Why?'

'You have known them less than a month,' I said as though I knew, and saw the confirmation in his expression. 'And I have known men like that all my life.'

'I don't see what this has to do with it, Mr Fletcher.' He was

31

stiffening up now, I was treating him like a child and he didn't like that.

'Listen, Jim. Forget this business, whatever it is. Drop it, and go back to your shop and your salvage company.'

'That's crazy,' he said. 'You don't understand.'

'I understand, Jim. I really do. I travelled the same road, and I know it well.'

'I can look after myself. Don't worry about me.' He had flushed up under his tan, and the grey eyes snapped with defiance. We stared at each other for a few moments, and I knew I was wasting time and emotion. If anyone had spoken like this to me at the same age I would have thought him senile.

'All right, Jim,' I said. 'I'll drop it, but you know the score. Just play it cool and loose, that's all.'

'Okay, Mr Fletcher.' He relaxed slowly, and then grinned a charming and engaging grin. 'Thanks anyway.'

'Let's hear about this island,' I suggested and he glanced about the cabin.

'Let's go up on the bridge,' he suggested, and out in the open air he took a stub of pencil and a scrap pad from the map bin above the chart table.

'I reckon it lies off the African shore about six to ten miles, and ten to thirty miles north of the mouth of the Rovuma River—'

'That covers a hell of a lot of ground, Jim—as you may have noticed during the last few days. What else do you know about it?'

He hesitated a little longer, before grudgingly doling out a few more coins from his hoard. He took the pencil and drew a horizontal line across the pad.

'Sea level—' he said, and then above the line he raised an irregular profile that started low, and then climbed steeply into three distinct peaks before ending abruptly, '—and that's the silhouette that it shows from the sea. The three hills are volcanic basalt, sheer rock with little vegetation.'

'The Old Men—' I recognized it immediately; '—but you are a long way out in your other calculations, it's more like twenty miles offshore—'

'But within sight of the mainland?' he asked quickly. 'It has to be within sight.'

'Sure, you could see a long way from the tops of the hills,' I

32

pointed out as he tore the sheet from the pad and carefully ripped it to shreds, and dropped them into the harbour.

'How far north of the river?' He turned back to face me.

'Offhand I'd say sixty or seventy miles,' and he looked thoughtful.

'Yes, it could be that far north. It could fit, it depends on how long it would take—' He did not finish, he was taking my advice about playing it cool. 'Can you take us there, skip?'

I nodded. 'But it's a long run and best come prepared to sleep on the boat overnight.'

'I'll fetch the others,' he said, eager and excited once more. But on the wharf he looked back at the bridge.

'About the island, what it looks like and all that, don't discuss it with the others, okay?'

'Okay, Jim,' I smiled back at him. 'Off you go.' I went down to have a look at the admiralty chart. The Old Men were the highest point on a ridge of basalt, a long hard reef that ran parallel to the mainland for two hundred miles. It disappeared below the water, but reappeared at intervals, forming a regular feature amongst the haphazard sprinkling of coral and sand islands and shoals.

It was marked as uninhabited and waterless, and the soundings showed a number of deep channels through the reefs around it. Although it was far north of my regular grounds, I had visited the area the previous year as host to a marine biology expedition from UCLA who were studying the breeding habits of the green turtles that abounded there.

We had camped for three days on another island across the tide channel from the Old Men, where there was an all-weather anchorage in an enclosed lagoon, and brackish but just drinkable water in a fisherman's well amongst the palms. Looking across from the anchorage, the Old Men showed exactly the outline that Jimmy had sketched for me, that was how I had recognized it so readily.

Half an hour later, the whole party arrived; strapped on the roof of the taxi was a bulky piece of equipment covered with a green canvas dust sheet. They hired a couple of lounging islanders to carry this, and the overnight bags they had with them, down the wharf to where I was waiting.

They stowed the canvas package on the foredeck without unwrapping it and I asked no questions. Guthrie's face was starting to fall off in layers of sun-scorched skin, leaving wet red flesh exposed. He had smeared white cream over it. I thought of him slapping little Marion around his suite at the Hilton, and I smiled at him.

'You look so good, have you ever thought of running for Miss Universe?' and he glowered at me from beneath the brim of his hat as he took his seat in the fighting chair. During the run northwards he drank beer straight from the can and used the empties as targets, firing the big pistol at them as they tumbled and bobbed in *Dancer's* wake.

A little before noon, I gave Jimmy the wheel and went down to use the heads below deck. I found that Materson had the bar open and the gin bottle out.

'How much longer?' he asked, sweaty and flushed despite the air-conditioning.

'Another hour or so,' I told him, and thought that Materson was going to find himself with a drinking problem the way he handled spirits at midday. However, the gin had mellowed him a little and—always the opportunist—I loosened another three hundred pounds from his wallet as an advance against my fees before going up to take *Dancer* in on the last leg through the northern tide channel that led to the Old Men.

The triple peaks came up through the heat haze, ghostly grey and ominous, seeming to hang disembodied above the channel.

Jimmy was examining the peaks through his binoculars, and then he lowered them and turned delightedly to me.

'That looks like it, skipper,' and he clambered down into the cockpit. The three of them went up on to the foredeck, passed the canvas-wrapped deck cargo, and stood shoulder to shoulder at the rail staring through the sea fret at the island as I crept cautiously up the channel.

We had a rising tide pushing us up the channel, and I agreed to use it to approach the eastern tip of the Old Men, and make a landing on the beach below the nearest peak. This coast has a tidal fall of seventeen feet at full springs, and it is unwise to go into shallow water on the ebb. It is easy to find yourself stranded high and dry as the water falls away beneath your keel.

Jimmy borrowed my hand-bearing compass and packed it with his chart, a Thermos of iced water and a bottle of salt tablets from the medicine chest into his haversack. While I crept cautiously in towards the beach, Jimmy and Materson stripped off their footwear and trousers.

When *Dancer* bumped her keel softly on the hard white sand of the beach I shouted to them.

'Okay—over you go,' and with Jimmy leading, they went down the ladder I had rigged from *Dancer's* side. The water came to their armpits, and James held the haversack above his head as they waded towards the beach.

'Two hours!' I called after them. 'If you're longer than that you can sleep ashore. I'm not coming in to pick you up on the ebb.'

Jimmy waved and grinned. I put *Dancer* into reverse and backed off cautiously, while the two of them reached the beach and hopped around awkwardly as they donned their trousers and shoes and then set off into the palm groves and disappeared from view.

After circling for ten minutes and peering down through the water that was clear as a trout stream, I picked up the dark shadow across the bottom that I was seeking and dropped a light head anchor.

While Guthrie watched with interest I put on a face-plate and gloves and went over the side with a small oyster net and a heavy tyre lever. There was forty feet of water under us, and I was pleased to find my wind was still sufficient to allow me to go down and prise loose a netful of the big double-shelled sun clams in one dive. I shucked them on the foredeck, and then, mindful of Chubby's admonitions, I threw the empty shells overboard and swabbed the deck carefully before taking a pailful of the sweet flesh down to the galley. They went into a casserole pot with wine and garlic, salt and ground pepper and just a bite of chilli. I set the gas-plate to simmer and put the lid on the pot.

When I went back on deck, Guthrie was still in the fighting chair.

'What's wrong, big shot, are you bored?' I asked solicitously. 'No little girls to kick around?' His eyes narrowed thoughtfully. I could see him checking out my source of information.

'You've got a big mouth, Bruce. Somebody is going to close it for you one day.' We exchanged a few more pleasantries, none of them much above this level, but it served to pass the time until the two distant figures appeared on the beach and waved and halloed. I pulled up the hook, and went in to pick them up.

Immediately they were aboard, they called Guthrie to them and assembled on the foredeck for one of their group sessions. They were all excited, Jimmy the most so, and he gesticulated and pointed out into the channel, talking quietly but vehemently. For once they seemed all to be in agreement, but by the time they had finished talking there was an hour of sunlight left and I refused to agree to Materson's demands that I should continue our explorations that evening. I had no wish to creep around in the darkness on an ebb tide.

Firmly I took *Dancer* across to the safe anchorage in the lagoon across the channel, and by the time the sun went down below a blazing horizon I had *Dancer* riding peacefully on two heavy anchors, and I was sitting upon the bridge enjoying the last of day and the first scotch of the evening. In the saloon below me there was the interminable murmur of discussion and speculation. I ignored it, not even bothering to use the ventilator, until the first mosquitoes found their way across the lagoon and began whining around my ears. I went below and the conversation dried up at my entry.

I thickened the juice and served my clam casserole with baked yams and pineapple salad and they ate in dedicated silence.

'My God, that is even better than my sister's cooking,' Jimmy gasped finally. I grinned at him. I am rather vain about my culinary skills and young James was clearly a gourmet.

I woke after midnight and went up on deck to check *Dancer's* moorings. She was all secure and I paused to enjoy the moonlight.

A great stillness lay upon the night, disturbed only by the soft chuckle of the tide against *Dancer's* side—and far off the boom of the surf on the outer reef. It was coming in big and tall from the open ocean, and breaking in thunder and white upon the coral of Gunfire Reef. The name was well chosen, and the deep belly-shaking thump of it sounded exactly like the regular salute of a minute gun.

The moonlight washed the channel with shimmering silver and highlighted the bald domes of the peaks of the Old Men so they shone like ivory. Below them the night mists rising from the lagoon writhed and twisted like tormented souls.

Suddenly I caught the whisper of movement behind me and I whirled to face it. Guthrie had followed me as silently as a hunting leopard. He wore only a pair of jockey shorts and his body was white and muscled and lean in the moonlight. He carried the big black .45, dangling at arm's length by his right thigh. We stared at each other for a moment before I relaxed.

'You know, luv, you've just got to give up now. You really aren't my type at all,' I told him, but there was adrenalin in my blood and my voice rasped.

36

'When that time comes, Fletcher, I'll be using this,' he said, and lifted the automatic, 'all the way up, boy,' and he grinned.

*　　*　　*

We ate breakfast before sun-up and I took my mug of coffee to the bridge to drink as we ran up the channel towards the open sea. Materson was below, and Guthrie lolled in the fighting chair. Jimmy stood beside me and explained his requirements for this day.

He was tense with excitement, seeming to quiver with it like a young gundog with the first scent of the bird in his nostrils.

'I want to get some shots off the peaks of the Old Men,' he explained. 'I want to use your hand-bearing compass, and I'll call you in.'

'Give me your bearings, Jim, and I'll plot it and put you on the spot,' I suggested.

'Let's do it my way, skipper,' he replied awkwardly, and I could not prevent a flare of irritation in my reply.

'All right, then, eagle scout.' He flushed and went to the port rail to sight the peaks through the lens of the compass. It was ten minutes or so before he spoke again.

'Can we turn about two points to port now, skipper?'

'Sure we can,' I grinned at him, 'but, of course, that would pile us on to the end of Gunfire Reef—and we'd tear her belly out.'

It took another two hours of groping about through the maze of reefs before I had worked *Dancer* out through the channel into the open sea and circled back to approach Gunfire Reef from the east.

It was like the child's game of hunt the thimble; Jimmy called 'hotter' and 'colder' without supplying me with the two references that would enable me to place *Dancer* on the precise spot he was seeking.

Out here the swells marched in majestic procession towards the land, growing taller and more powerful as they felt the shelving bottom. *Dancer* rolled and swung to them as we edged in towards the outer reef.

Where the swells met the barrier of coral their dignity turned to sudden fury, and they boiled up and burst in leviathan spouts of spray, pouring wildly over the coral with the explosive shock of impact. Then they sucked back, exposing the evil black fangs, white

37

water cascading and creaming from the barrier, while the next swell moved up, humping its great slick back for the next assault.

Jimmy was directing me steadily southwards in a gradual converging course with the reef, and I could tell we were very close to his marks. Through the compass he squinted eagerly, first at one and then the other peak of the Old Men.

'Steady as you go, skipper,' he called. 'Just ease her down on that heading.'

I looked ahead, tearing my eyes away from the menacing coral for a few seconds, and I watched the next swell charge in and break—except at a narrow point five hundred yards ahead. Here the swell kept its shape and ran on uninterrupted towards the land. On each side, the swell broke on coral, but just at that one point it was open.

Suddenly I remembered Chubby's boast.

'I was just nineteen when I pulled my first jewfish out of the hole at Gunfire Break. Weren't no other would fish with me—don't say as I blame them. Wouldn't go into the Break again—got a little more brains now.'

Gunfire Break, suddenly I knew that was where we were heading. I tried to remember exactly what Chubby had told me about it.

'If you come in from the sea about two hours before high water, steer for the centre of the gap until you come up level with a big old head of brain coral on your starboard side, you'll know it when you see it, pass it close as you can and then come round hard to starboard and you'll be sitting in a big hole tucked in neatly behind the main reef. Closer you are on the back of the reef the better, man—' I remembered it clearly then, Chubby in his talkative phase in the public bar of the Lord Nelson, boastful as one of the very few men who had been through the Gunfire Break. 'No anchor going to hold you there, you got to lean on the oars to hold station in the gap—the hole at Gunfire Break is deep, man, deep, but the jewfish in there are big, man, big. One day I took four fish, and the smallest was three hundred pounds. Could have took more—but time was up. You can't stay in Gunfire Break more than an hour after high water—she sucks out through the Break like they pulled the chain on the whole damned sea. You come out the same way you went in, only you pray just a little harder on the way out—'cos you got a ton of fish on board, and ten feet less water under your keel. There is another way out through a channel in the back of the reef. But I don't even like to talk about that one. Only tried it once.'

Now we were bearing down directly on the Break, Jimmy was going to run us right into the eye of it.

'Okay, Jim,' I called. 'That's as far as we go.' I opened the throttle and sheered off, making a good offing before turning back to face Jimmy's wrath.

'We were almost there, damn you,' he blustered. 'We could have gone in a little closer.'

'You having trouble up there, boy?' Guthrie shouted up from the cockpit.

'No, it's all right,' Jimmy called back, and then turned furiously to me. 'You are under contract, Mr Fletcher—'

'I want to show you something, James—' and I took him to the chart table. The Break was marked on the admiralty chart by a single laconic sounding of thirty fathoms, there was no name or sailing instruction for it. Quickly I pencilled in the bearings of the two extreme peaks of the Old Men from the Break, and then used the protractor to measure the angle they subtended.

'That right?' I asked him, and he stared at my figures.

'It's right, isn't it?' I insisted and then reluctantly he nodded.

'Yes, that's the spot,' he agreed, and I went on to tell him about Gunfire Break in every detail.

'But we have to get in there,' he said at the end of my speech, as though he had not heard a word of it.

'No way,' I told him. 'The only place I'm interested in now is Grand Harbour, St Mary's Island,' and I laid *Dancer* on that course. As far as I was concerned the charter was over.

Jimmy disappeared down the ladder, and returned within minutes with reinforcements—Materson and Guthrie, both of them looking angry and outraged.

'Say the word, and I'll tear the bastard's arm off and beat him to death with the wet end,' Mike Guthrie said with relish.

'The kid says you pulling out?' Materson wanted to know. 'Now that's not right—is it?'

I explained once more about the hazards of Gunfire Break and they sobered immediately.

'Take me close as you can—I'll swim in the rest of the way,' Jimmy asked me, but I replied directly to Materson.

'You'd lose him, for certain sure. Do you want to risk that?'

He didn't answer, but I could see that Jimmy was much too valuable for them to take the chance.

'Let me try,' Jimmy insisted, but Materson shook his head irritably.

'If we can't get into the Break, at least let me take a run along the reef with the sledge,' Jimmy went on, and I knew then what we were carrying under the canvas wrapping on the foredeck.

'Just a couple of passes along the front edge of the reef, past the entrance to the Break.' He was pleading now, and Materson looked questioningly at me. You don't often have opportunities like this offered you on a silver tray. I knew I could run *Dancer* within spitting distance of the coral without risk, but I frowned worriedly.

'I'd be taking a hell of a chance—but if we could agree on a bit of old danger money—'

I had Materson over the arm of the chair and I caned him for an extra day's hire—five hundred dollars, payable in advance.

While we did the business, Guthrie helped Jimmy unwrap the sledge and carry it back to the cockpit.

I tucked the sheath of banknotes away and went back to rig the tow lines. The sledge was a beautifully constructed toboggan of stainless steel and plastic. In place of snow runners, it had stubby fin controls, rudder and hydrofoils, operated by a short joystick below the perspex pilot's shield.

There was a ring bolt in the nose to take the tow line by which I would drag the sledge in *Dancer*'s wake. Jimmy would lie on his belly behind the transparent shield, breathing compressed air from the twin tanks that were built into the chassis of the sledge. On the dashboard were depth and pressure gauges, directional compass and time elapse clock. With the joystick Jimmy could control the depth of the sledge's dive, and yaw left or right across *Dancer*'s stern.

'Lovely piece of work,' I remarked, and he flushed with pleasure.

'Thanks, skipper, built it myself.' He was pulling on the wet suit of thick black neoprene rubber and while his head was in the clinging hood I stooped and examined the maker's plate that was riveted to the sledge's chassis, memorizing the legend.

'Built by North's Underwater World.
5, Pavilion Arcade.
BRIGHTON. SUSSEX.'

I straightened up as his face appeared in the opening of the hood.
'Five knots is a good tow speed, skipper. If you keep a hundred

40

yards off the reef, I'll be able to deflect outwards and follow the contour of the coral.'

'Fine, Jim.'

'If I put up a yellow marker, ignore it, it's only a find, and we will go back to it later—but if I send up a red, it's trouble, try and get me off the reef and haul me in.'

I nodded. 'You have three hours,' I warned him. 'Then she will begin the ebb up through the break and we'll have to haul off.'

'That should be long enough,' he agreed.

Guthrie and I lifted the sledge over the side, and it wallowed low in the water. Jimmy clambered down to it and settled himself behind the screen, testing the controls, adjusting his face-plate and cramming the mouthpiece of the breathing device into his mouth. He breathed noisily and then gave me the thumbs up.

I climbed quickly to the bridge and opened the throttles. *Dancer* picked up speed and Guthrie paid out the thick nylon rope over the stern as the sledge fell away behind us. One hundred and fifty yards of rope went over, before the sledge jerked up and began to tow.

Jimmy waved, and I pushed *Dancer* up to a steady five knots. I circled wide, then edged in towards the reef, taking the big swells on *Dancer's* beam so she rolled appallingly.

Again Jimmy waved, and I saw him push the control column of the sledge forwards. There was a turmoil of white water along her control fins and then suddenly she put her nose down and ducked below the surface. The angle of the nylon rope altered rapidly as the sledge went down, and then swung away towards the reef.

The strain on the rope made it quiver like an arrow as it strikes, and the water squirted from the fibres.

Slowly we ran parallel to the reef, closing the Break. I watched the coral respectfully, taking no chances, and I imagined Jimmy far below the surface flying silently along the bottom, cutting in to skim the tall wall of underwater coral. It must have been an exhilarating sensation, and I envied him, deciding to hitch a ride on the sledge when I got the opportunity.

We came opposite the Break, passed it and just then I heard Guthrie shout. I glanced quickly over the stern and saw the big yellow balloon bobbing in our wake.

'He found something,' Guthrie shouted.

Jimmy had dropped a light leaded line, and a sparklet bulb had

41

automatically inflated the yellow balloon with carbon dioxide gas to mark the spot.

I kept going steadily along the reef, and a quarter of a mile farther the angle of the tow line flattened and the sledge popped to the surface in a welter of water.

I swung away from the reef to a safe distance, and then went down to help Guthrie recover the sledge.

Jimmy clambered into the cockpit, and when he pulled off his face-plate his lips were trembling and his grey eyes blazed. He took Materson's arm and dragged him into the cabin, splashing sea water all over Chubby's beloved deck.

Guthrie and I coiled the rope, then lifted the sledge into the cockpit. I went back to the bridge, and took *Dancer* on a slow return to the entrance of Gunfire Break.

Materson and Jimmy came up on to the bridge before we reached it. Materson was affected by Jimmy's excitement.

'The kid wants to try for a pick up.' I knew better than to ask what it was.

'What size?' I asked instead, and glanced at my wristwatch. We had an hour and a half before the rip tide began to run out through the break.

'Not very big—' Jimmy assured me. 'Fifty pounds maximum.'

'You sure, James? Not bigger?' I didn't trust his enthusiasm not to minimize the effort involved.

'I swear it.'

'You want to put an air bag on it?'

'Yes, I'll lift it with an air bag and then tow it away from the reef.'

I reversed *Dancer* in gingerly towards the yellow balloon that played lightly in the angry coral jaws of the Break.

'That's as close as I'll go,' I shouted down into the cockpit, and Jimmy acknowledged with a wave.

He waddled duck-footed to the stern and adjusted his equipment. He had taken two air bags as well as the canvas cover from the sledge, and was roped up to the coil of nylon rope.

I saw him take a bearing on the yellow marker with the compass on his wrist, then once again he glanced up at me on the bridge before he flipped backwards over the stern and disappeared.

His regular breathing burst in a white rash below the stern, then began to move off towards the reef. Guthrie paid out the bodyline after him.

I kept *Dancer* on station by using bursts of forward and reverse, holding her a hundred yards from the southern tip of the Break. Slowly Jimmy's bubbles approached the yellow marker, and then broke steadily beside it. He was working below it, and I imagined him fixing the empty air bags to the object with the nylon slings. It would be hard work with the suck and drag of the current worrying the bulky bags. Once he had fitted the slings he could begin to fill the bags with compressed air from his scuba bottles.

If Jimmy's estimate of size was correct it would need very little inflation to pull the mysterious object off the bottom, and once it dangled free we could tow it into a safer area before bringing it aboard.

For forty minutes I held *Dancer* steady, then quite suddenly two swollen green shiny mounds broke the surface astern. The air bags were up—Jimmy had lifted his prize.

Immediately his hooded head surfaced beside the filled bags, and he held his right arm straight up. The signal to begin the tow.

'Ready?' I shouted at Guthrie in the cockpit.

'Ready!' He had secured the line, and I crept away from the reef, slowly and carefully to avoid up-ending the bags and spilling out the air that gave them lift.

Five hundred yards off the reef, I kicked *Dancer* into neutral and went to help haul in the swimmer and his fat green air bags.

'Stay where you are,' Materson snarled at me as I approached the ladder and I shrugged and went back to the wheel.

The hell with them all, I thought, and lit a cheroot—but I couldn't prevent the tickle of excitement as they worked the bags alongside, and then walked them forward to the bows.

They helped Jimmy aboard, and he shrugged off the heavy compressed air bottles, dropping them to the deck while he pushed his face-plate on to his forehead.

His voice, ragged and high-pitched, carried clearly to me as I leaned on the bridge rail.

'Jackpot!' he cried. 'It's the—'

'Watch it!' Materson cautioned him, and James cut himself off and they all looked at me, lifting their faces to the bridge.

'Don't mind me, boys,' I grinned and waved the cheroot cheerily. They turned away and huddled. Jimmy whispered, and Guthrie said, 'Jesus Christ!' loudly and slapped Materson's back, and then they were all exclaiming and laughing as they crowded to the rail

43

and began to lift the air bags and their burden aboard. They were clumsy with it, *Dancer* was rolling heavily, and I leaned forward with curiosity eating a hole in my belly.

My disappointment and chagrin were intense when I realized that Jimmy had taken the precaution of wrapping his prize in the canvas sledge cover. It came aboard as a sodden, untidy bundle of canvas, swathed in coils of nylon rope.

It was heavy, I could see by the manner in which they handled it— but it was not bulky, the size of a small suitcase.

They laid it on the deck and stood around it happily. Materson smiled up at me.

'Okay, Fletcher. Come take a look.'

It was beautifully done, he played like a concert pianist on my curiosity. Suddenly I wanted very badly to know what they had pulled from the sea. I clamped the cheroot in my teeth as I swarmed down the ladder, and hurried towards the group in the bows. I was halfway across the foredeck, right out in the open, and Materson was still smiling as he said softly, 'Now!'

Only then did I know it was a set-up, and my mind began to move so fast that it all seemed to go by in extreme slow motion.

I saw the evil black bulk of the .45 in Guthrie's fist, and it came up slowly to aim into my belly. Mike Guthrie was in the marksman's crouch, right arm fully extended, and he was grinning as he screwed up those speckled eyes and sighted along the thick-jacketed barrel.

I saw Jimmy North's handsome young face contort with horror, saw him reach out to grip the pistol arm but Materson, still grinning, shoved him roughly aside and he staggered away with *Dancer's* next roll.

I was thinking quite clearly and rapidly, it was not a procession of thought but a set of simultaneous images. I thought how neatly they had dropped the boom on me, a really professional hit.

I thought how presumptuous I had been in trying to make a deal with the wolf pack. For them it was easier to hit than to negotiate.

I thought that they would take out Jimmy now that he had watched this. That must have been their intention from the start. I was sorry for that. I had come to like the kid.

I thought about the heavy soft explosive lead slug that the .45 threw, about how it would tear up the target, hitting with the shock of two thousand foot pounds.

Guthrie's forefinger curled on the trigger and I began to throw

44

myself at the rail beside me with the cheroot still in my mouth, but I knew it was too late.

The pistol in Guthrie's hand kicked up head high, and I saw the muzzle flash palely in the sunlight. The cannon roar of the blast and the heavy lead bullet hit me together. The din deafened me and snapped my head back and the cheroot flipped up high in the air leaving a trail of sparks. Then the impact of the bullet doubled me over, driving the air from my lungs, and lifted me off my feet, hurling me backwards until the deck rail caught me in the small of the back.

There was no pain, just that huge numbing shock. It was in the chest, I was sure of that, and I knew that it must have blown me open. It was a mortal wound, I was sure of that also and I expected my mind to go now. I expected to fade, going out into blackness.

Instead the rail caught me in the back and I somersaulted, going over the side head-first and the quick cold embrace of the sea covered me. It steadied me, and I opened my eyes to the silver clouds of bubbles and the soft green of sunlight through the surface.

My lungs were empty, the air driven out by the impact of the bullet, and my instinct told me to claw to the surface for air, but surprisingly my mind was still clear and I knew that Mike Guthrie would blow the top off my skull the moment I surfaced. I rolled and dived, kicking clumsily, and went down under *Dancer*'s hull.

On empty lungs it was a long journey, *Dancer*'s smooth white belly passed slowly above me, and I drove on desperately, amazed that there was strength in my legs still.

Suddenly darkness engulfed me, a soft dark red cloud, and I nearly panicked, thinking my vision had gone—until suddenly I realized it was my own blood. Huge billowing clouds of my own blood staining the water. Tiny zebra-striped fish darted wildly through the cloud, gulping greedily at it.

I struck out, but my left arm would not respond. It trailed limply at my side, and blood blew like smoke about me.

There was strength in my right arm and I forged on under *Dancer*, passed under her keel and rose thankfully towards her far waterline.

As I came up I saw the nylon tow rope trailing over her stern, a bight of it hanging down below the surface and I snatched at it thankfully.

I broke the surface under *Dancer*'s stern, and I sucked painfully for air, my lungs felt bruised and numb, the air tasted like old copper in my mouth but I gulped it down.

My mind was still clear. I was under the stern, the wolf pack was in the bows, the carbine was under the engine hatch in the main cabin.

I reached up as high as I could and took a twist of the nylon rope around my right wrist, lifted my knees and got my toes on to the rubbing strake along *Dancer*'s waterline.

I knew I had enough strength for one attempt, no more. It would have to be good. I heard their voices from up in the bows, raised angrily, shouting at each other, but I ignored them and gathered all my reserve.

I heaved upwards, with both legs and the one good arm. My vision starred with the effort, and my chest was a numbed mass, but I came clear of the water and fell half across the stern rail, hanging there like an empty sack on a barbed-wire fence.

For seconds I lay there, while my vision cleared and I felt the slick warm outpouring of blood along my flank and belly. The flow of blood galvanized me. I realized how little time I had before the loss of it sent me plunging into blackness. I kicked wildly and tumbled headlong on to the cockpit floor, striking my head on the edge of the fighting chair, and grunting with the new pain of it.

I lay on my side and glanced down at my body. What I saw terrified me, I was streaming great gouts of thick blood, it was forming a puddle under me.

I clawed at the deck, dragging myself towards the cabin, and reached the combing beside the entrance. With another wild effort I pulled myself upright, hanging on one arm, supported by legs already weak and rubbery.

I glanced quickly around the angle of the cabin, down along the foredeck to where the three men were still grouped in the bows.

Jimmy North was struggling to strap his compressed air bottles on to his back again, his face was a mask of horror and outrage and his voice was strident as he screamed at Materson.

'You filthy bloody murderers. I'm going down to find him. I'm going to get his body—and, so help me Christ, I'll see you both hanged—'

Even in my own distress I felt a sudden flare of admiration for the kid's courage. I don't think it ever occurred to him that he was also on the list.

'It was murder, cold-blooded murder,' he shouted, and turned to the rail, settling the face-plate over his eyes and nose.

Materson looked across at Guthrie, the kid's back was turned to them, and Materson nodded.

I tried to shout a warning, but it croaked hollowly in my throat, and Guthrie stepped up behind Jimmy. This time he made no mistake. He touched the muzzle of the big .45 to the base of Jimmy's skull, and the shot was muffled by the neoprene rubber hood of the diving-suit.

Jimmy's skull collapsed, shattered by the passage of the heavy bullet. It came out through the glass plate of the diving mask in a cloud of glass fragments. The force of it clubbed him over the side, and his body splashed alongside. Then there was silence in which the memory of gunfire seemed to echo with the sound of wind and water.

'He'll sink,' said Materson calmly. 'He had on a weight belt—but we had better try and find Fletcher. We don't want him washed up with that bullet hole in his chest.'

'He ducked—the bastard ducked—I didn't hit him squarely—' Guthrie protested, and I heard no more. My legs collapsed and I sprawled on the deck of the cockpit. I was sick with shock and horror and the quick flooding flow of my blood.

I have seen violent death in many guises, but Jimmy's had moved me as never before. Suddenly there was only one thing I wanted to do before my own violent death overwhelmed me.

I began to crawl towards the engine-room hatch. The white deck seemed to stretch before me like the Sahara desert, and I was beginning to feel the leaden hand of a great weariness upon my shoulder.

I heard their footsteps on the deck above me, and the murmur of their voices. They were coming back to the cockpit.

'Ten seconds, please God,' I whispered. 'That's all I need,' but I knew it was futile. They would be into the cabin long before I reached the hatch—but I dragged myself desperately towards it.

Then suddenly their footsteps paused, but the voices continued. They had stopped to talk out on the deck, and I felt a lift of relief for I had reached the engine hatch.

Now I struggled with the toggles. They seemed to have jammed immovably, and I realized how weak I was, but I felt the revitalizing stir of anger through the weariness.

I wriggled around and kicked at the toggles and they flew back. I fought my weakness aside and got on to my knees. As I leaned over the hatch a fresh splattering of bright blood fell on the white deck.

'Eat your liver, Chubby,' I thought irrelevantly, and prised up the hatch. It came up achingly slowly, heavy as all the earth, and now I felt the first lances of pain in my chest as bruised tissue tore.

The hatch fell back with a heavy thump, and instantly the voices on deck were silent, and I could imagine them listening.

I fell on my belly and groped desperately under the decking and my right hand closed on the stock of the carbine.

'Come on!' There was a loud exclamation, and I recognized Materson's voice, and immediately the pounding of running footsteps along the deck towards the cockpit.

I tugged wearily at the carbine, but it seemed to be caught in the slings and resisted my efforts.

'Christ! There's blood all over the deck,' Materson shouted.

'It's Fletcher,' Guthrie yelled. 'He came in over the stern.'

Just then the carbine came free and I almost dropped it down into the engine-room, but managed to hold it long enough to roll clear.

I sat up with the carbine in my lap, and pushed the safety catch across with my thumb, sweat and salt water streamed into my eyes blurring my vision as I peered up at the entrance to the cabin.

Materson ran into the cabin three paces before he saw me, then he stopped and gaped at me. His face was red with effort and agitation and he lifted his hands, spreading them in a protective gesture before him as I brought up the carbine. The diamond on his little finger winked merrily at me.

I lifted the carbine one-handed from my lap, and its immense weight appalled me. When the muzzle was pointed at Materson's knees I pressed the trigger.

With a continuous shattering roar the carbine spewed out a solid blast of bullets, and the recoil flung the barrel upwards, riding the stream of fire from Materson's crotch up across his belly and chest. It flung him backwards against the cabin bulkhead, and split him like the knife-stroke that guts a fish while he danced a grotesque and jerky little death jig.

I knew that I should not empty the carbine, there was still Mike Guthrie to deal with, but somehow I seemed unable to release my grip on the trigger and the bullets tore through Materson's body, smashing and splintering the woodwork of the bulkhead.

Then suddenly I lifted my finger. The torrent of bullets ceased and Materson fell heavily forward.

The cabin stank with burned cordite and the sweet heavy smell of blood.

Guthrie ducked into the companionway of the cabin, crouching with right arm outflung and he snapped off a single shot at me as I sat in the centre of the cabin.

He had all the time he needed for a clean shot at me, but he hurried it, panicky and off-balance. The blast slapped against my ear drums, and the heavy bullet disrupted the air against my cheek as it flew wide. The recoil kicked the pistol high, and as it dropped for his next shot I fell sideways and pulled up the carbine.

There must have been a single round left in the breech, but it was a lucky one. I did not aim it, but merely jerked at the trigger as the barrel came up.

It hit Guthrie in the crook of his right elbow, shattering the joint and the pistol flew backwards over his shoulder, skidded across the deck and thudded into the stern scuppers.

Guthrie spun aside, the arm twisting grotesquely and hanging from the broken joint and at the same instant the firing pin of the carbine fell on an empty chamber.

We stared at each other, both of us badly hit, but the old antagonism was still there between us. It gave me strength to come up on my knees and start towards him, the empty carbine falling from my hand.

Guthrie grunted and turned away, gripping the shattered arm with his good hand. He staggered towards the .45 lying in the scuppers.

I saw there was no way I could stop him. He was not mortally hit, and I knew he could shoot probably as well with his good left hand. Still I made my last try and dragged myself over Materson's body and out into the cockpit, reaching it just as Guthrie stooped to pick the pistol out of the scuppers.

Then *Dancer* came to my aid, and she reared like a wild horse as a freak swell hit her. She threw Guthrie off balance, and the pistol went skidding away across the deck. He turned to chase it, his feet slipped in the blood which I had splashed across the cockpit and he went down.

He fell heavily, pinning his shattered arm under him. He cried

49

out, and rolled on to his knees and began crawling swiftly after the glistening black pistol.

Against the outer bulkhead of the cockpit the long flying gaffs stood in their rack like a set of billiard cues. Ten feet long, with the great stainless steel hooks uppermost.

Chubby had filed the points as cruelly as stilettos. They were designed to be buried deep into a game fish's body, and the shock of the blow would detach the head from the stock. The fish could then be dragged on board with the length of heavy nylon rope that was spliced on to the hook.

Guthrie had almost reached the pistol as I knocked open the clamp on the rack and lifted down one of the gaffs.

Guthrie scooped up the pistol left-handed, juggling it to get a grip on it, concentrating his whole attention on the weapon and while he was busy I came up on my knees again and lifted the gaff with one hand, throwing it up high and reaching out over Guthrie's bowed back. As the hook flashed down over him I hit the steel in hard, driving it full length through his ribs, burying the gleaming steel to the curve. The shock of it pulled him down on to the deck and once again the pistol dropped from his hand and the roll of the boat pushed it away from him.

Now he was screaming, a high-pitched wail of agony with the steel deep in him. I tugged harder, single-handed, trying to work it into heart or lung and the hook broke from the stock. Guthrie rolled across the deck towards the pistol. He groped frantically for it, and I dropped the gaff stock and groped just as frantically for the rope to restrain him.

I have seen two women wrestlers fighting in a bath of black mud, in a nightclub in the St Pauli district of Hamburg—and now Guthrie and I performed the same act, only in place of mud we fought in a bath of our own blood. We slithered and rolled about the deck, thrown about mercilessly by *Dancer*'s action in the swell.

Guthrie was weakening at last, clawing with his good hand at the great hook buried in his body, and with the next roll of the sea I was able to throw a coil of the rope around his neck and get a firm purchase against the base of the fighting chair with one foot. Then I pulled with all the remains of my strength and resolve.

Suddenly, with a single explosive expulsion of breath, his tongue fell out of his mouth and he relaxed, his limbs stretched out limply and his head lolled loosely back and forth with *Dancer*'s roll.

50

I was tired beyond caring now. My hand opened of its own accord and the rope fell from it. I lay back and closed my eyes. Darkness fell over me like a shroud.

*   *   *

When I regained consciousness my face felt as though it had been scalded with acid, my lips were swollen and my thirst raged like a forest fire. I had lain face up under a tropical sun for six hours, and it had burned me mercilessly.

Slowly I rolled on to my side, and cried out weakly at the immensity of pain that was my chest. I lay still for a while to let it subside and then I began to explore the wound.

The bullet had angled in through the bicep of my left arm, missing bone, and come out through the tricep, tearing a big exit hole. Immediately it had ploughed into the side of my chest.

Sobbing with the effort I traced and probed the wound with my finger. It had glanced over a rib, I could feel the exposed bone was cracked and rough ended where the slug had struck and been deflected and left slivers of lead and bone chips in the churned flesh. It had gone through the thick muscle of my back—and torn out below the shoulder blade, leaving a hole the size of a *demi tasse* coffee cup.

I fell back on to the deck, panting and fighting back waves of giddy nausea. My exploration had induced fresh bleeding, but I knew at least that the bullet had not entered the chest cavity. I still had some sort of a chance.

While I rested I looked blearily about me. My hair and clothing were stiff with dried blood, blood was coated over the cockpit, dried black and shiny or congealed.

Guthrie lay on his back with the gaff hook still in him and the rope around his neck. The gases in his belly had already blown, giving him a pregnant swollen look.

I got up on to my knees and began to crawl. Materson's body half-blocked the entrance to the cabin, shredded by gunfire as though he had been mauled by a savage predator.

I crawled over him, and found I was whimpering aloud as I saw the icebox behind the bar.

I drank three cans of Coca Cola, gasping and choking in my eagerness, spilling the icy liquid down my chest, and moaning and

51

snuffling through each mouthful. Then I lay and rested again. I closed my eyes and just wanted to sleep for ever.

'Where the hell are we?' The question hit me with a shock of awareness. *Dancer* was adrift on a treacherous coast, strewn with reefs and shoals.

I dragged myself to my feet and reached the blood-caked cockpit. Beneath us flowed the deep purple blue of the Mozambique, and a clear horizon circled us, above which the massive cloud ranges climbed to a tall blue sky. The ebb and the wind had pushed us far out to the east, we had plenty of sea room.

My legs collapsed under me, and I may have slept for a while. When I woke my head felt clearer, but the wound had stiffened horribly. Each movement was agony. On my hand and knees I reached the shower room where the medicine chest was kept. I ripped away my shirt and poured undiluted acriflavine solution into the cavernous wounds. Then I plugged them roughly with surgical dressing and strapped the whole as best I could, but the effort was too much.

The dizziness overwhelmed me again and I crashed down on to the linoleum floor unconscious.

I awoke light-headed, and feeble as a new-born infant.

It was a major effort to fashion a sling for the wounded arm, and the journey to the bridge was an endless procession of dizziness and pain and nausea.

Dancer's engines started with the first kick, sweet as ever she was.

'Take me home, me darling,' I whispered, and set the automatic pilot. I gave her an approximate heading. *Dancer* settled on course, and the darkness caught me again. I went down sprawling on the deck, welcoming oblivion as it washed over me.

It may have been the altered action of *Dancer*'s passage that roused me. She no longer swooped and rolled with the big swell of the Mozambique, but ambled quietly along over a sheltered sea. Dusk was falling swiftly.

Stiffly I dragged myself up to the wheel. I was only just in time, for dead ahead lay the loom of land in the fading light. I slammed *Dancer*'s throttle closed, and kicked her into neutral. She came up and rocked gently in a low sea. I recognized the shape of the land—it was Big Gull Island.

We had missed the channel of Grand Harbour, my heading had been a little southerly and we had run into the southernmost straggle of tiny atolls that made up the St Mary's group.

Hanging on to the wheel for support I craned forward. The canvas-wrapped bundle still lay on the foredeck—and suddenly I knew that I must get rid of it. My reasons were not clear then. Dimly I realized that it was a high card in the game into which I had been drawn. I knew I dare not ferry it back into Grand Harbour in broad daylight. Three men had been killed for it already—and I'd had half my chest shot away. There was some strong medicine wrapped up in that sheet of canvas.

It took me fifteen minutes to reach the foredeck, and I blacked out twice on the way. When I crawled to the bundle of canvas I was sobbing aloud with each movement.

For another half-hour I tried feebly to unwrap the stiff canvas and untie the thick nylon knots. With only one hand and my fingers so numb and weak that they could not close properly it was a hopeless task, and the blackness kept filling my head. I was afraid I would go out with the bundle still aboard.

Lying on my side I used the last rays of the setting sun to take a bearing off the point of the island, lining up a clump of palms and the point of the high ground—marking the spot with care.

Then I opened the swinging section of the foredeck railing through which we usually pulled big fish aboard, and I wriggled around the canvas bundle—got both feet on to it and shoved it over the side. It fell with a heavy splash and droplets splattered in my face.

My exertions had re-opened the wounds and fresh blood was soaking my clumsy dressing. I started back across the deck but I did not make it. I went out for the last time as I reached the break of the cockpit.

The morning sun and a raucous barnyard squawking woke me, but when I opened my eyes the sun seemed shaded, darkened as though in eclipse. My vision was fading, and when I tried to move there was no strength for it. I lay crushed beneath the weight of weakness and pain. *Dancer* was canted at an absurd angle, probably stranded high and dry on the beach.

I stared up into the rigging above me. There were three black-backed gulls as big as turkeys sitting in a row on the cross stay. They twisted their heads sideways to look down at me, and their beaks were clear yellow and powerful. The upper part of the beak ended in a curved point that was a bright cherry red. They watched me with glistening black eyes, and fluffed out their feathers impatiently.

53

I tried to shout at them, to drive them away but my lips would not move. I was completely helpless, and I knew that soon they would begin on my eyes. They always went for the eyes.

One of the gulls above me grew bold and spreading his wings, planed down to the deck near me. He folded his wings and waddled a few steps closer, and we stared at each other. Again I tried to scream, but no sound came and the gull waddled forward again, then stretched out his neck, opened that wicked beak and let out a hoarse screech of menace. I felt the whole of my dreadfully abused body cringing away from the bird.

Suddenly the tone of the screeching gulls altered, and the air was filled with their wing beats. The bird that I was watching screeched again, but this time in disappointment and it launched itself into flight, the draught from its wings striking my face as it rose.

There was a long silence then, as I lay on the heavily listing deck, fighting off the waves of darkness that tried to overwhelm me. Then suddenly there was a scrabbling sound alongside.

I rolled my head again to face it, and at that moment a dark chocolate face rose above deck level and stared at me from a range of two feet.

'Lordy!' said a familiar voice. 'Is that you, Mister Harry?'

I learned later that Henry Wallace, one of St Mary's turtle hunters, had been camped out on the atolls and had risen from his bed of straw to find *Wave Dancer* stranded by the ebb on the sand bar of the lagoon with a cloud of gulls squabbling over her. He had waded out across the bar, and climbed the side to peer into the slaughterhouse that was *Dancer's* cockpit.

I wanted to tell him how thankful I was to see him, I wanted to promise him free beer for the rest of his life—but instead I started to weep, just a slow welling up of tears from deep down. I didn't even have the strength to sob.

❊　❊　❊

'Little scratch like that,' marvelled MacNab. 'What's all the fussing about?' and he probed determinedly.

I gasped as he did something else to my back; if I had had the strength I would have got up off the hospital bed and pushed that probe up the most convenient opening of his body. Instead I moaned weakly.

'Come on, Doc. Didn't they teach you about morphine and that stuff back in the time when you should have failed your degree?'

MacNab came around to look in my face. He was plump and scarlet-faced, fiftyish and greying in hair and moustache. His breath should have anaesthetized me.

'Harry, my boy, that stuff costs money—what are you, anyway, National Health or a private patient?'

'I just changed my status—I'm private.'

'Quite right, too,' MacNab agreed. 'Man of your standing in the community,' and he nodded to the sister. 'Very well then, my dear, give Mister Harry a grain of morphine before we proceed,' and while he waited for her to prepare the shot he went on to cheer me up. 'We put six pints of whole blood into you last night, you were just about dry. Soaked it up like a sponge.'

Well, you wouldn't expect one of the giants of the medical profession to be practising on St Mary's. I could almost believe the island rumour that he was in partnership with Fred Coker's mortician parlour.

'How long you going to keep me in here anyway, Doc?'

'Not more than a month.'

'A month!' I struggled to sit up and two nurses pounced on me to restrain me, which required no great effort. I could still hardly raise my head. 'I can't afford a month. My God, it's right in the middle of the season. I've got a new party coming next week—'

The sister hurried across with the syringe.

'—You trying to break me? I can't afford to miss a single party—'

The sister hit me with the needle.

'Harry old boy, you can forget about this season. You won't be fishing again,' and he began picking bits of bone and flakes of lead out of me while he hummed cheerily to himself. The morphine dulled the pain—but not my despair. If *Dancer* and I missed half a season we just couldn't keep going. Once again they had me stretched out on the financial rack. God, how I hated money.

MacNab strapped me up in clean white bandages, and spread a little more sunshine.

'You going to lose some function in your left arm there, Harry boy. Probably always be a little stiff and weak, and you going to have some pretty scars to show the girls.' He finished winding the bandage and turned to the sister. 'Change the dressings every six hours, swab out with Eusol and give him his usual dose of Aureo Mycytin every four hours. Three Mogadon tonight and I'll see him on my rounds tomorrow.' He turned back to grin at me with bad teeth under the untidy grey moustache. 'The entire police force is waiting outside this very room. I'll have to let them in now.' He started towards the door, then paused to chuckle again. 'You did a hell of a job on those two guys, spread them over the scenery with a spade. Nice shooting, Harry boy.'

Inspector Daly was dressed in impeccable khaki drill, starched and pristine, and his leather belts and straps glowed with a high polish.

'Good afternoon, Mr Fletcher. I have come to take a statement from you. I hope you feel strong enough.'

'I feel wonderful, Inspector. Nothing like a bullet through the chest to set you up.'

Daly turned to the constable who followed him and motioned him to take the chair beside the bed, and as he sat and prepared his shorthand pad the constable told me softly, 'Sorry you got hurt, Mister Harry.'

'Thanks, Wally, but you should have seen the other guys.'

Wally was one of Chubby's nephews, and his mother did my laundry. He was a big, strong, darkly good-looking youngster.

'I saw them,' he grinned. 'Wow!'

'If you are ready, Mr Fletcher,' Daly cut in primly, annoyed by the exchange. 'We can get on.'

'Shoot,' I said, and I had my story well prepared. Like all good stories, it was the exact and literal truth, with omissions. I made no mention of the prize that James North had lifted, and which I had dumped again off Big Gull Island—nor did I tell Daly in which area we had conducted our search. He wanted to know, of course. He kept coming back to that.

'What were they searching for?'

'I have no idea. They were very careful not to let me know.'

'Where did all this happen?' he persisted.

'In the area beyond Herring Bone Reef, south of Rastafa Point.' This was fifty miles from the Break at Gunfire Reef.

'Could you recognize the exact point where they dived?'

'I don't think so, not within a few miles. I was merely following instructions.'

Daly chewed his silky moustache in frustration.

56

'All right, you say they attacked you without warning,' and I nodded. 'Why did they do that—why would they try to kill you?'

'We never really discussed it. I didn't have a chance to ask them.' I was beginning to feel very tired and feeble again, I didn't want to go on talking in case I made a mistake. 'When Guthrie started shooting at me with that cannon of his I didn't think he wanted to chat.'

'This isn't a joke, Fletcher,' he told me stiffly, and I rang the bell beside me. The sister must have been waiting just outside the door.

'Sister, I'm feeling pretty bad.'

'You'll have to go now, Inspector.' She turned on the two policemen like a mother hen, and drove them from the ward. Then she came back to rearrange my pillows.

She was a pretty little thing with huge dark eyes, and her tiny waist was belted in firmly to accentuate her big nicely shaped bosom on which she wore her badges and medals. Lustrous chestnut curls peeped from under the saucy little uniform cap.

'What is your name, then?' I whispered hoarsely.

'May.'

'Sister May, how come I haven't seen you around before?' I asked, as she leaned across me to tuck in my sheet.

'Guess you just weren't looking, Mister Harry.'

'Well, I'm looking now.' The front of her crisp white uniform blouse was only a few inches from my nose. She stood up quickly.

'They say here you're a devil man,' she said. 'I know now they didn't tell me lies.' But she was smiling. 'Now you go to sleep. You've got to get strong again.'

'Yeah, we'll talk again then,' I said, and she laughed out loud.

The next three days I had a lot of time to think for I was allowed no visitors until the official inquest had been conducted. Daly had a constable on guard outside my room, and I was left in no doubt that I stood accused of murder most vile.

My room was cool and airy with a good view down across the lawns to the tall dark-leafed banyan trees, and beyond them the massive stone walls of the fort with the cannons upon the battlements. The food was good, plenty of fish and fruit, and Sister May and I were becoming good, if not intimate, friends. She even smuggled in a bottle of Chivas Regal which we kept in the bedpan. From her I heard how the whole island was agog with the cargo that *Wave Dancer* had brought into Grand Harbour. She told me they

57

buried Materson and Guthrie on the second day in the old cemetery. A corpse doesn't keep so well in those latitudes.

In those three days I decided that the bundle I had dropped off Big Gull Island would stay there. I guessed that from now on there would be a lot of eyes watching me, and I was at a complete disadvantage. I didn't know who the watchers were and I didn't know why. I would keep down off the skyline until I worked out where the next bullet was likely to come from. I didn't like the game. They could deal me out and I would stick to the action I could call and handle.

I thought a lot about Jimmy North also, and every time I felt myself grieving unnecessarily I tried to tell myself that he was a stranger, that he had meant nothing to me, but it didn't work. This is a weakness of mine which I must always guard against. I become too readily emotionally bound up with other people. I try to walk alone, avoiding involvement, and after years of practice I have achieved some success. It is seldom these days that anyone can penetrate my armour the way Jimmy North did.

By the third day I was feeling much stronger. I could lift myself into a sitting position without assistance and with only a moderate degree of pain.

They held the official inquest in my hospital room. It was a closed session, attended only by the heads of the legislative, judicial and executive branches of St Mary's government.

The President himself, dressed as always in black with a crisp white shirt and a halo of snowy wool around his bald pate, chaired the meeting. Judge Harkness, tall and thin and sunburned to dark brown, assisted him—while Inspector Daly represented the executive.

The President's first concern was for my comfort and well-being. I was one of his boys.

'You be sure you don't tire yourself now, Mister Harry. Anything you want you just ask, hear? We have only come here to hear your version, but I want to tell you now not to worry. There is nothing going to happen to you.'

Inspector Daly looked pained, seeing his prisoner declared innocent before his trial began.

So I told my story again, with the President making helpful or admiring comments whenever I paused for breath, and when I finished he shook his head with wonder.

58

'All I can say, Mister Harry, is there are not many men would have had the strength and courage to do what you did against those gangsters, is that right, gentlemen?'

Judge Harkness agreed heartily, but Inspector Daly said nothing.

'And they were gangsters too,' he went on. 'We sent their fingerprints to London and we heard today that those men came here under false names, and that both of them have got police records at Scotland Yard. Gangsters, both of them.' The President looked at Judge Harkness. 'Any questions, Judge?'

'I don't think so, Mr President.'

'Good.' The President nodded happily. 'What about you, Inspector?' And Daly produced a typewritten list. The President made no effort to hide his irritation.

'Mister Fletcher is still a very sick man, Inspector. I hope your questions are really important.'

Inspector Daly hesitated and the President went on brusquely, 'Good, well then we are all agreed. The verdict is death by misadventure. Mister Fletcher acted in self-defence, and is hereby discharged from any guilt. No criminal charges will be brought against him.' He turned to the shorthand recorder in the corner. 'Have you got that? Type it out and send a copy to my office for signature.' He stood up and came to my bedside. 'Now you get better soon, Mister Harry. I expect you for dinner at Government House soon as you are well enough. My secretary will send you a formal invitation. I want to hear the whole story again.'

Next time I appear before a judicial body, as I surely shall, I hope for the same consideration. Having been officially declared innocent I was allowed visitors.

Chubby and Mrs Chubby came together dressed in their standard number one rig. Mrs Chubby had baked one of her splendid banana cakes, knowing my weakness for them.

Chubby was torn by relief at seeing me still alive and outrage at what I had done to *Wave Dancer*. He scowled at me fiercely as he started giving me a large slice of his mind.

'Ain't never going to get that deck clean again. It soaked right in, man. That damned old carbine of yours really chewed up the cabin bulkhead. Me and Angelo been working three days at it now, and it still needs a few more days.'

'Sorry, Chubby, next time I shoot somebody I'm going to make

59

them stand by the rail first.' I knew that when Chubby had finished repairing the woodwork the damage would not be detectable.

'When you coming out anyway? Plenty of big fish working out there on the stream, Harry.'

'I be out pretty soon, Chubby. One week tops.'

Chubby sniffed. 'Did hear that Fred Coker wired all your parties for rest of the season—told them you were hurt bad and switched their bookings to Mister Coleman.'

I lost my temper then. 'You tell Fred Coker to get his black arse up here soonest,' I shouted.

Dick Coleman had a deal with the Hilton Hotel. They had financed the purchase of two big game fishing boats, which Coleman crewed with a pair of imported skippers. Neither of his boats caught much fish, they didn't have the feel of it. He had a lot of difficulty getting charters, and I guessed Fred Coker had been handsomely compensated to switch my bookings to him. Coker arrived the following morning.

'Mister Harry, Doctor MacNab told me you wouldn't be able to fish again this season. I couldn't let my parties down, they fly six thousand miles to find you in a hospital bed. I couldn't do that—I got my reputation to think of.'

'Mr Coker, your reputation smells like one of those stiffs you got tucked away in the back room,' I told him, and he smiled at me blandly from behind his gold-rimmed spectacles, but he was right of course, it would be a long time still before I could take *Dancer* out after the big billfish.

'Now don't you fuss yourself, Mister Harry. Soon as you better I will arrange a few lucrative charters for you.'

He was talking about the night run again, his commission on a single run could go as high as seven hundred and fifty dollars. I could handle that even in my present beaten-up condition, it involved merely conning *Dancer* in and out again—just as long as we didn't run into trouble.

'Forget it, Mr Coker. I told you from now on I fish, that's all,' and he nodded and smiled and went on as though I had not spoken.

'Had persistent inquiries from one of your old clients.'

'Body? Box?' I demanded. Body was the illegal carrying to or from the African mainland of human beings, fleeing politicians with the goon squad after them—or on the other hand aspiring politicians trying for radical change in the regime. Boxes usually contained lethal hardware and it was a one-way traffic. In the old days they called it gun-running.

Coker shook his head and said, 'Five, six,'—from the old nursery rhyme: 'Five, six. Pick up sticks.' In this context sticks were tusks of ivory. A massive, highly organized poaching operation was systematically wiping out the African elephant from the game reserves and tribal lands of East Africa. The Orient was an insatiable and high-priced market for the ivory. A fast boat and a good skipper were needed to get the valuable cargo out of an estuary mouth, through the dangerous inshore waters, out to where one of the big ocean-going dhows waited on the stream of the Mozambique.

'Mr Coker,' I told him wearily. 'I'm sure your mother never even knew your father's name.'

'It was Edward, Mister Harry,' he smiled carefully. 'I told the client that the going rate was up. What with inflation and the price of diesel fuel.'

'How much?'

'Seven thousand dollars a trip,' which was not as much as it sounds after Coker had clouted fifteen per cent, then Inspector Peter Daly had to be slipped the same again to dim his eyesight and cloud his hearing. On top of that Chubby and Angelo always earned a danger money bonus of five hundred each for a night run.

'Forget it, Mr Coker,' I said unconvincingly. 'You just fix a couple of fishing parties.' But he knew I couldn't fight it.

'Just as soon as you fit enough to fish, we'll fix that. Meantime, when do you want to do the first night run? Shall I tell them ten days from today? That will be high spring tide and a good moon.'

'All right,' I agreed with resignation. 'Ten days' time.'

With a positive decision made, it seemed that my recovery from the wounds was hastened. I had been in peak physical condition which contributed, and the gaping holes in my arm and back began to shrink miraculously.

I reached a milestone in my convalescence on the sixth day. Sister May was giving me a bed bath, with a basin of suds and a face cloth, when there was a monumental demonstration of my physical well-being. Even I, who was no stranger to the phenomenon, was impressed, while Sister May was so overcome that her voice became a husky little whisper.

'Lord!' she said. 'You've sure got your strength back.'

'Sister May, do you think we should waste that?' I asked, and she shook her head vehemently.

* * *

From then onwards I began to take a more cheerful view of my circumstances, and not surprisingly the canvas-wrapped secret off Big Gull Island began to nag me. I felt my good resolutions weakening.

'I'll just take a look,' I told myself. 'When I am sure the dust has really settled.'

They were allowing me up for a few hours at a time now, and I felt restless and anxious to get on with it. Not even Sister May's devoted efforts could blunt the edge of my awakening energy. Mac-Nab was impressed.

'You heal well, Harry old chap. Closing up nicely—another week.'

'A week, hell!' I told him determinedly. Seven days from now I was making the night run. Coker had set it up without trouble—and I was just about stony broke. I needed that run pretty badly.

My crew came up to visit me every evening, and to report progress on the repairs to *Dancer*. One evening Angelo arrived earlier than usual, he was dressed in his courting gear—rodeo boots and all—but he was strangely subdued and not alone.

The lass with him was the young nursery grade teacher from the government school down near the fort. I knew her well enough to exchange smiles on the street. Missus Eddy had summed up her character for me once.

'She's a good girl, that Judith. Not all flighty and flirty like some others. Going to make some lucky fellow a good wife.'

She was also good-looking with a tall willowy figure, neatly and conservatively dressed, and she greeted me shyly.

'How do, Mister Harry.'

'Hello, Judith. Good of you to come,' and I looked at Angelo, unable to hide my grin. He couldn't meet my eye, colouring up as he hunted for words.

'Me and Judith planning to marry up,' he blurted at last. 'Wanted you to know that, boss.'

'Think you can keep him under control, Judith?' I laughed delightedly.

'You just watch me,' she said with a flash of dark eyes that made the question superfluous.

'That's great—I'll make a speech at your wedding,' I assured them. 'You going to let Angelo go on crewing for me?'

'Wouldn't ever try to stop him,' she assured me. 'It's good work he's got with you.'

They stayed for another hour and when they left I felt a small prickle of envy. It must be a good feeling to have someone—apart from yourself. I thought some day if I ever found the right person I might try it. Then I dismissed the thought, raising my guard again. There were a hell of a lot of women—and no guarantee you will pick right.

MacNab discharged me with two days to spare. My clothes hung on my bony frame, I had lost more than twenty-five pounds and my tan had faded to a dirty yellow brown, there were big blue smears under my eyes and I still felt weak as a baby. The arm was in a sling and the wounds were still open, but I could change the dressing myself.

Angelo brought the pick-up to the hospital and waited while I said goodbye to Sister May on the steps.

'Nice getting to know you, Mister Harry.'

'Come out to the shack some time soon. I'll grill you a mess of crayfish, and we'll drink a little wine.'

'My contract ends next week. I'll be going home to England then.'

'You be happy, hear,' I told her.

Angelo drove me down to Admiralty, and with Chubby we spent an hour going over *Dancer*'s repairs.

Her decks were snowy white, and they had replaced all the woodwork in the saloon bulkhead, a beautiful piece of joinery with which even I could find no fault.

We took her down the channel as far as Mutton Point and it was good to feel her riding lightly under my feet and hear the sweet burble of her engines. We came home in the dusk to tie up at moorings and sit out on the bridge in the dark, drinking beer out of the can and talking.

I told them that we had a run set for the following night, and they asked where to and what the cargo was. That was all—it was set, there was no argument.

'Time to go,' Angelo said at last. 'Going to pick Judith up from night school,' and we rowed ashore in the dinghy.

63

There was a police Land-Rover parked beside my old pick-up at the back of the pineapple sheds and Wally, the young constable, climbed out as we approached. He greeted his uncle, and then turned to me.

'Sorry to worry you, Mister Harry, but Inspector Daly wants to see you up at the fort. He says it's urgent.'

'God,' I growled. 'It can wait until tomorrow.'

'He says it can't, Mister Harry.' Wally was apologetic, and for his sake I went along.

'Okay, I'll follow you in the pick-up—but we got to drop Chubby and Angelo off first.'

I thought it was probably that Daly wanted to haggle about his payoff. Usually Fred Coker fixed that, but I guessed that Daly was raising the price of his honour.

Driving one-handed and holding the steering wheel with a knee while I shifted gear with my good hand, I followed the red tail lights of Wally's Land-Rover rattling over the drawbridge and parked beside it in the courtyard of the fort.

The massive stone walls had been built by slave labour in the mid-eighteenth century and from the wide ramparts the long thirty-six pounder cannon ranged the channel and the entrance to Grand Harbour.

One wing was used as the island police headquarters, jail and armoury—the rest of it was government offices and the Presidential and State apartments.

We climbed the front steps to the charge office and Wally led me through a side door, and along a corridor, down steps, another corridor, more stone steps.

I had never been down here before and I was intrigued. The stone walls here must have been twenty feet thick, the old powder store probably. I half expected the Frankenstein monster to be lurking behind the thick oak door, iron studded and weathered, at the end of the last passage. We went through.

It wasn't Frankenstein, but next best. Inspector Daly waited for us with another of his constables. I noticed immediately they both wore sidearms. The room was empty except for a wooden table and four P.W.D. type chairs. The walls were unpainted stonework and the floor was paved.

At the back of the room an arched doorway led to a row of cells. The lights were bare hundred-watt bulbs hanging on black electrical

64

cable that ran exposed across the beamed roof. They cast hard black shadows in the angles of the irregularly shaped room.

On the table lay my FN carbine. I stared at it uncomprehendingly.

Behind me Wally closed the oak door.

'Mr Fletcher, is this your firearm?'

'You know damn well it is,' I said angrily. 'Just what the hell are you playing at, Daly?'

'Harold Delville Fletcher, I am placing you under arrest for the unlawful possession of Category A firearms. To wit, one unlicensed automatic rifle type Fabrique Nationale Serial No. 4163215.'

'You're off your head,' I said, and laughed. He didn't like that laugh. The weak little lips below his moustache puckered up like those of a sulky child and he nodded at his constables. They had been briefed, and they went out through the oak door.

I heard the bolts shoot home, and Daly and I were alone. He was standing well away from me across the room—and the flap of his holster was unbuttoned.

'Does his excellency know about this, Daly?' I asked, still smiling.

'His excellency left St Mary's at four o'clock this afternoon to attend the conference of Commonwealth heads in London. He won't be back for two weeks.'

I stopped smiling. I knew it was true. 'In the meantime I have reason to believe the security of the State is endangered.'

He smiled now, thinly and with the mouth only. 'Before we go any further I want you to be sure I am serious.'

'I believe you,' I said.

'I have two weeks with you alone, here, Fletcher. These walls are pretty thick, you can make as much noise as you like.'

'You are a monstrous little turd, you really are.'

'There is only one of two ways you are going to leave here. Either you and I come to an arrangement—or I'll get Fred Coker to come and fetch you in a box.'

'Let's hear your deal, little man.'

'I want to know exactly—and I mean exactly—where your charter carried out their diving operations before the shoot-out.'

'I told you—somewhere off Rastafa Point. I couldn't give you the exact spot.'

'Fletcher, you know the spot to within inches. I'm willing to stake *your* life on that. You wouldn't miss a chance like that. You know it.

65

I know it—and they knew it. That's why they tried to sign you off.'

'Inspector, go screw,' I said.

'What is more it was nowhere near Rastafa Point. You were working north of here, towards the mainland. I was interested—I had some reports of your movements.'

'It was somewhere off Rastafa Point,' I repeated doggedly.

'Very well,' he nodded. 'I hope you aren't as tough as you put out, Fletcher, otherwise this is going to be a long messy business. Before we start though, don't waste our time with false data. I'm going to keep you here while I check it out—I've got two weeks.'

We stared at each other, and my flesh began to crawl. Peter Daly was going to enjoy this, I realized. There was a gloating expression on those thin lips and a smoky glaze to his eyes.

'I had a great deal of experience in interrogation in Malaya, you know. Fascinating subject. So many aspects to it. So often it's the tough, strong ones that pop first—and the little runts that hang on for ever—'

This was for kicks, I saw clearly that he was aroused by the prospect of inflicting pain. His breathing had changed, faster and deeper, there was fresh colour in his cheeks.

'—of course, you are at a physical low ebb right now, Fletcher. Probably your threshold of pain is much lowered after your recent misadventures. I don't think it will take long—'

He seemed to regret that. I gathered myself, tightening up for an attempt.

'No,' he snapped. 'Don't do it, Fletcher.' He placed his hand on the butt of the pistol. He was fifteen feet away. I was one-armed, weak, there was a locked door behind me, two armed constables—my shoulders sagged as I relaxed.

'That's better.' He smiled again. 'Now I think we will handcuff you to the bars of a cell, and we can get to work. When you have had enough you have merely to say so. I think you will find my little electrical set-up simple but effective. It's merely a twelve-volt car battery—and I clip the terminals on to interesting parts of the body—'

He reached behind him—and for the first time I noticed the button of an electric bell set on the wall. He pressed it and I heard the bell ring faintly beyond the oaken door.

The bolts shot back and the two constables came back in.

'Take him through to the cells,' Daly ordered, and the constables hesitated. I guessed they were strangers to this type of operation.

'Come on,' snapped Daly, and they stepped up on either side of me. Wally laid a hand lightly on my injured arm, and I allowed myself to be led forward towards the cells—and Daly.

I wanted to have a chance at him, just one chance.

'How's your mom, Wally?' I asked casually.

'She's all right, Mister Harry,' he muttered embarrassedly.

'She get the present I sent up for her birthday?'

'Yeah, she got it.' He was distracted as I intended.

We had come level with Daly, he was standing by the doorway to the cells, waiting for us to go through, slapping the malacca swagger stick against his thigh.

The constables were holding me respectfully, loosely, unsure of themselves, and I stepped to one side pushing Wally slightly off balance—then I spun back, breaking free.

Not one of them was ready for it, and I covered the three paces to Daly before they had realized what I was doing—and I put my right knee into him with my full body weight behind it. It thumped into the crotch of his legs, a marvellously solid blow. Whatever the price I was going to have to pay for the pleasure, it was cheap.

Daly was lifted off his feet, a full eighteen inches in the air, and he flew backwards to crash against the bars. Then he doubled up, both hands pressed into his lower body, screaming thinly—a sound like steam from a boiling kettle. As he went over I lined up for another shot at his face, I wanted to take his teeth out with a kick in the mouth—but the constables recovered their wits and leaped forward to drag me away. They were rough now, twisting the arm.

'You didn't ought to do that, Mister Harry,' Wally shouted angrily. His fingers bit into my bicep and I gritted my teeth.

'The President himself cleared me, Wally. You know that,' I shouted back at him, and Daly straightened up, his face twisted with agony, still holding himself.

'This is a frame up.' I knew I had only a few seconds to talk, Daly was reeling towards me, brandishing the swagger stick, his mouth wide open as he tried to find his voice.

'If he gets me in that cell he's going to kill me, Wally—'

'Shut up!' screeched Daly.

'He wouldn't dare try this if the President—'

'Shut up! Shut up!' He swung the swagger stick, a side-arm cut, that hissed like a cobra. He had gone for my wounds deliberately, and the supple cane snapped around me like a pistol shot.

67

The pain of it was beyond belief, and I convulsed, bucking involuntarily in their grip. They held me.

'Shut up!' Daly was hysterical with pain and rage. He swung again, and the cane cut deeply into half-healed flesh. This time I screamed.

'I'll kill you, you bastard.' Daly staggered back, still hunched with pain, and he fumbled with his holstered pistol.

What I had hoped for now happened. Wally released me and jumped forward.

'No,' he shouted. 'Not that.'

He towered over Daly's slim crouching form and with one massive brown hand he blocked Daly's draw.

'Get out of my way. That's an order,' shouted Daly, but Wally unclipped the lanyard from the pistol's butt and disarmed him, stepping back with the pistol in his hand.

'I'll break you for this,' snarled Daly. 'It's your duty—'

'I know my duty, Inspector,' Wally spoke with a simple dignity, 'and it's not to murder prisoners.' Then he turned to me. 'Mister Harry, you'd best get out of here.'

'You're freeing a prisoner—' Daly gasped. 'Man, I'm going to break you.'

'Didn't see no warrant,' Wally cut in. 'Soon as the President signs a warrant, we'll fetch Mister Harry right back in again.'

'You black bastard,' Daly panted at him, and Wally turned to me. 'Get!' he said. 'Quickly.'

❊   ❊   ❊

It was a long ride out to the shack, every bump in the track hit me in the chest. One thing I had learned from the evening's jollifications was that my original thoughts were correct—whatever that bundle off Big Gull Island contained, it could get a peace-loving gentleman like myself into plenty of trouble.

I was not so trusting as to believe that Inspector Daly had made his last attempt at interrogating me. Just as soon as he recovered from the kick in his multiplication machinery which I had given him, he was going to make another attempt to connect me up to the lighting system. I wondered if Daly was acting on his own, or if he had partners—and I guessed he was alone, taking opportunity as it presented itself.

I parked the pick-up in the yard and went through on to the veranda of my shack. Missus Chubby had been out to sweep and tidy while I was away. There were fresh flowers in a jam-jar on the dining-room table—but more important there was eggs and bacon, bread and butter in the icebox.

I stripped off my blood-stained shirt and dressing. There were thick raised welts around my chest that the cane had left, and the wounds were a mess.

I showered and strapped on a fresh dressing, then, standing naked over the stove, I scrambled a pan full of eggs with bacon and while it cooked, I poured a very dark whisky and took it like medicine.

I was too tired to climb between the sheets, and as I fell across the bed I wondered if I would be fit enough to work the night run on schedule. It was my last thought before sun-up.

And after I had showered again and swallowed two Doloxene pain-killers with a glass of cold pineapple juice and eaten another panful of eggs for breakfast I thought the answer was yes. I was stiff and sore, but I could work. At noon I drove into town, stopped off at Missus Eddy's store for supplies and then went on down to Admiralty.

Chubby and Angelo were on board already, and *Dancer* lay against the wharf.

'I filled the auxiliary tanks, Harry,' Chubby told me. 'She's good for a thousand miles.'

'Did you break out the cargo nets?' I asked, and he nodded.

'They are stowed in the main sail locker.' We would use the nets to deck load the bulky ivory cargo.

'Don't forget to bring a coat—it will be cold out on the stream with this wind blowing.'

'Don't worry, Harry. You the one should watch it. Man, you look bad as you were ten days ago. You look real sick.'

'I feel beautiful, Chubby.'

'Yeah,' he grunted, 'like my mother-in-law,' then he changed the subject. 'What happened to your carbine, man?'

'The police are holding it.'

'You mean we going out there without a piece on board?'

'We never needed it yet.'

'There is always a first time,' he grunted. 'I'm going to feel mighty naked without it.'

Chubby's obsession with armaments always amused me.

Despite all the evidence that I presented to the contrary, Chubby could never quite shake off the belief that the velocity and range of a bullet depended upon how hard one pulled the trigger—and Chubby intended that his bullets go very fast and very far indeed.

The savage strength with which he sent them on their way would have buckled a less robust weapon than the FN. He also suffered from a complete inability to keep his eyes open at the moment of firing.

I have seen him miss a fifteen-foot tiger shark at a range of ten feet with a full magazine of twenty rounds. Chubby Andrews was never going to make even a fair shot, but he just naturally loved firearms and things that went bang.

'It will be a milk run, a high old pleasure cruise, Chubby, you'll see,' and he crossed his fingers to avert the hex, and shuffled off to work on *Dancer's* already brilliant brasswork, while I went ashore.

The front office of Fred Coker's travel agency was deserted and I rang the bell on the desk. He stuck his head through from the back room.

'Welcome, Mister Harry.' He had removed his coat and tie and had rolled up his shirt sleeves, about his waist he wore a red rubber apron. 'Lock the front door, please, and come through.'

The back room was in contrast to the front office with its gaudy wallpaper and bright travel posters. It was a long, gloomy barn. Along one wall were piled cheap pine coffins. The hearse was parked inside the double doors at the far end. Behind a grimy canvas screen in one corner was a marble slab table with guttering around the edges and a spout to direct fluid from the guttering into a bucket on the floor.

'Come in, sit down. There is a chair. Excuse me if I carry on working while we talk. I have to have this ready for four o'clock this afternoon.'

I took one look at the frail naked corpse on the slab. It was a little girl of about six years of age with long dark hair. One look was enough and I moved the chair behind the screen so I could see only Fred Coker's bald head, and I lit a cheroot. There was a heavy smell of embalming fluid in the room, and it caught in my throat.

'You get used to it, Mister Harry.' Fred Coker had noticed my distaste.

'Did you set it up?' I didn't want to discuss his gruesome trade.

'It's fixed,' he assured me.

'Did you square our friend at the fort?'

'It's all fixed.'

'When did you see him?' I persisted. I wanted to know about Daly. I was very interested in how Daly felt.

'I saw him this morning, Mister Harry.'

'How was he?'

'He seemed all right.' Coker paused in his grisly task and looked at me questioningly.

'Was he standing up, walking around, dancing a jig, singing, putting the cat out?'

'No. He was sitting down, and he was not in a very good mood.'

'It figures.' I laughed and my own injuries felt better. 'But he took the payoff?'

'Yes, he took it.'

'Good, then we have still got a deal.'

'Like I told you, it's all fixed.'

'Lay it on me, Mr Coker.'

'The pick up is at the mouth of the Salsa stream where it enters the south channel of the main Duza estuary.' I nodded, that was acceptable. There was a good channel and the holding ground off the Salsa was satisfactory.

'The recognition signal will be two lanterns—one over the other, placed on the bank nearest the mouth. You will flash twice, repeated at thirty-second intervals and when the lower lantern is extinguished you can anchor. Got that?'

'Good.' It was all satisfactory.

'They will provide labour to load from the lighters.'

I nodded, then asked, 'They know that slack water is three o'clock —and I must be out of the channel before that?'

'Yes, Mister Harry. I told them they must finish loading before two hundred hours.'

'All right then—what about the drop-off?'

'Your drop-off will be twenty-five miles due east of Rastafa Point.'

'Fine.' I could check my bearings off the lighthouse at Rastafa. It was good and simple.

'You will drop off to a dhow-rigged schooner, a big one. Your recognition signal will be the same. Two lanterns on the mast, you will flash twice at thirty seconds, and the lower lamp will extinguish. You can then offload. They will provide labour and will put down an oil slick for you to ride in. I think that is all.'

71

'Except for the money.'

'Except for the money, of course.' He produced an envelope from the front pocket of his apron. I took it gingerly between thumb and forefinger and glanced at his calculations scribbled in ballpoint on the envelope.

'Half up front, as usual, the rest on delivery,' he pointed out.

That was thirty-five hundred, less twenty-one hundred for Coker's commission and Daly's payoff. It left fourteen hundred, out of which I had to find bonus for Chubby and Angelo—a thousand dollars—not much over.

I grimaced. 'I'll be waiting outside your office at nine o'clock tomorrow morning, Mr Coker.'

'I'll have a cup of coffee ready for you, Mister Harry.'

'That had better not be all,' I told him, and he laughed and stooped once more over the marble slab.

*　*　*

We cleared Grand Harbour in the late afternoon, and I made a fake run down the channel towards Mutton Point for the benefit of a possible watcher with binoculars on Coolie Peak. As darkness fell, I came around on to my true heading, and we went in through the inshore channel and the islands towards the wide tidal mouth of the Duva River.

There was no moon but the stars were big and the break of surf flared with phosphorescence, ghostly green in the afterglow of the setting sun.

I ran *Dancer* in fast, picking up my marks successively—the loom of an atoll in the starlight, the break of a reef, the very run and chop of the water guided me through the channels and warned of shoals and shallows.

Angelo and Chubby huddled beside me at the bridge rail. Occasionally one of them would go below to brew more of the powerful black coffee, and we sipped at the steaming mugs, staring out into the night watching for a flash of paleness that was not breaking water but the hull of a patrol boat.

Once Chubby broke the silence. 'Hear from Wally you had some trouble up at the fort last night.'

'Some,' I agreed.

'Wally had to take him up to the hospital afterwards.'

72

'Wally still got his job?' I asked.

'Only just. The man wanted to lock him up but Wally was too big.'

Angelo joined in. 'Judith was up at the airport at lunchtime. Went up to fetch a crate of school books, and she saw him going out on the plane to the mainland.'

'Who?' I asked.

'Inspector Daly, he went across on the noon plane.'

'Why didn't you tell me before?'

'Didn't think it was important, Harry.'

'No,' I agreed. 'Perhaps it isn't.'

There were a dozen reasons why Daly might go out to the mainland, none of them remotely connected with my business. Yet it made me feel uneasy—I didn't like that kind of animal prowling around in the undergrowth when I was taking a risk.

'Wish you'd brought that piece of yours, Harry,' Chubby repeated mournfully, and I said nothing but wished the same.

The flow of the tide had smoothed the usual turmoil at the entrance to the southern channel of the Duza and I groped blindly for it in the dark. The mud banks on each side were latticed with standing fish traps laid by the tribal fishermen, and they helped to define the channel at last.

When I was sure we were in the correct entrance, I killed both engines and we drifted silently on the incoming tide. All of us listened with complete concentration for the engine beat of a patrol boat, but there was only the cry of a night heron and the splash of mullet leaping in the shallows.

Ghost silent, we were swept up the channel; on each side the dark masses of mangrove trees hedged us in and the smell of the mud swamps was rank and fetid on the moisture-laden air.

The starlight danced in spots of light on the dark agitated surface of the channel, and once a long narrow dugout canoe slid past us like a crocodile, the phosphorescence gleaming on the paddles of the two fishermen returning from the mouth. They paused to watch us for a moment and then drove on without calling a greeting, disappearing swiftly into the gloom.

'That was bad,' said Angelo.

'We will be drinking a lager in the Lord Nelson before they could tell anyone who matters.' I knew that most of the fishermen on this coast kept their own secrets, close with words like most of their kind. I was not perturbed by the sighting.

73

Looking ahead I saw the first bend coming up, and the current began to push *Dancer* out towards the far bank. I hit the starter buttons, the engines murmured into life, and I edged back into the deep water.

We worked our way up the snaking channel, coming out at last into the broad placid reach where the mangrove ended and firm ground rose gently on each side.

A mile ahead I saw the tributary mouth of the Salsa as a dark break in the bank, screened by tall stands of fluffy headed reeds. Beyond it the twin signal lanterns glowed yellow and soft, one upon the other.

'What did I tell you, Chubby, a milk run.'

'We aren't home yet.' Chubby the eternal optimist.

'Okay, Angelo. Get up on the bows. I'll tell you when to drop the hook.'

We crept on down the channel and I found the words of the nursery rhyme running through my mind as I locked the wheel and took the hand spotlight from the locker below the rail.

'Three, Four, knock at the door, Five, Six, pick up sticks.'

I thought briefly of the hundreds of great grey beasts that had died for the sake of their teeth—and I felt a draught of guilt blow coldly along my spine at my complicity in the slaughter. But I turned my mind away from it by lifting the spotlight and aiming the agreed signal upstream at the burning lanterns.

Three times I flashed the recognition code but I was level with the signal lanterns before the bottom one was abruptly extinguished.

'Okay, Angelo. Let her go,' I called softly as I killed the engines. The anchor splashed over and the chain ran noisily in the silence. *Dancer* snubbed up, and swung around at the restraint of the anchor, facing back down the channel.

Chubby went to break out the cargo nets for loading, but I paused by the rail, peering across at the signal lantern. The silence was complete, except for the clink and croak of the swamp frogs in the reed banks of the Salsa.

In that silence I felt more than heard the beat like that of a giant's heart. It came in through the soles of my feet rather than my ears.

There is no mistaking the beat of an Allison marine diesel. I knew that the old Second World War Rolls-Royce marines had been stripped out of the Zinballa crash boats and replaced by Allisons, and right now the sound I was feeling was the idling note of an Allison marine.

'Angelo,' I tried to keep my voice low, but at the same time transmit my urgency. 'Slip the anchor. For Christ's sake! Quick as you can.'

For just such an emergency I had a shackle pin in the chain, and I thanked the Lord for that as I dived for the controls.

As I started engines, I heard the thump of the four-pound hammer as Angelo drove out the pin. Three times he struck, and then I heard the end of the chain splash overboard.

'She's gone, Harry,' Angelo called, and I threw *Dancer* in to drive and pushed open the throttles. She bellowed angrily and the wash of her propellers spewed whitely from below her counter as she sprang forward.

Although we were facing downstream, *Dancer* had a five-knot current running into her teeth and she did not jump away handily enough.

Even above our own engines I heard the Allisons give tongue, and from out of the reed-screened mouth of the Salsa tore a long deadly shape.

Even by starlight, I recognized her immediately, the widely flared bows, and the lovely thrusting lines, greyhound waisted and the square chopped-off stern—one of the Royal Navy crash boats who had spent her best days in the Channel and now was mouldering into senility on this fever coast.

The darkness was kind to her, covering the rust stains and the streaky paintwork, but she was an old woman now. Stripped of her marvellous Rolls marines—and underpowered with the more economical Allisons. In a fair run *Dancer* would toy with her—but this was no fair run and she had all the speed and power she needed as she charged into the channel to cut us off, and when she switched on her battle lights they hit us like something solid. Two glaring white beams, blinding in their intensity so I had to throw up my hand to protect my eyes.

She was dead ahead now, blocking the channel, and on her foredeck I could see the shadowy figures of the gun crew crouching around the three-pounder on its wide traversing plate. The muzzle seemed to be looking directly into my left nostril—and I felt a wild and desperate despair.

It was a meticulously planned and executed ambush. I thought of ramming her, she had a marine ply wooden hull, probably badly rotted, and *Dancer*'s fibreglass bows might stand the shock—but with the current against her *Dancer* was not making sufficient speed through the water.

Then suddenly a bull-horn bellowed electronically from the dark behind the dazzling battle lights.

'Heave to, Mr Fletcher. Or I shall be forced to fire upon you.'

One shell from the three-pounder would chop us down, and she was a quick firer. At this range they would smash us into a blazing wreck within ten seconds.

I closed down the throttles.

'A wise decision, Mr Fletcher—now kindly anchor where you are,' the bull-horn squawked.

'Okay, Angelo,' I called wearily, and waited while he rigged and dropped the spare anchor. Suddenly my arm was very painful again —for the last few hours I had forgotten about it.

'I said we should have brought that piece,' Chubby muttered beside me.

'Yeah, I'd love to see you shooting it out with that dirty great cannon, Chubby. That would be a lot of laughs.'

The crash boat manoeuvred alongside inexpertly, with gun and lights still trained on us. We stood helplessly in the blinding illumination of the battle lights and waited. I didn't want to think, I tried to feel nothing—but a spiteful inner voice sneered at me.

'Say goodbye to *Dancer*, Harry old sport, this is where the two of you part company.'

There was more than a good chance that I would be facing a firing squad in the near future—but that didn't worry me as much as the thought of losing my boat. With *Dancer* I was Mister Harry, the damnedest fellow on St Mary's and one of the top billfish men in the whole cock-eyed world. Without her, I was just another punk trying to scratch his next meal together. I'd prefer to be dead.

The crash boat careered into our side, bending the rail and scraping off a yard of our paint before they could hook on to us.

'Motherless bastards,' growled Chubby, as half a dozen armed and uniformed figures poured over our side, in a chattering undisciplined rabble. They wore navy blue bell bottoms and bum-freezers with white flaps down the back of the neck, white and blue striped T-shirts, and white berets with red pom-poms on the top—but the cut of the uniform was Chinese and they brandished long AK47 automatic assault rifles with forward-curved magazines and wooden butts.

Fighting amongst themselves for a chance to get in a kick or a shove with a gun butt, they drove the three of us down into the saloon, and knocked us into the bench seat against the for'ard bulkhead. We sat there shoulder to shoulder while two guards stood over us with machine-guns a few inches from our noses, and fingers curved hopefully around the triggers.

'Now I know why you paid me that five hundred dollars, boss,' Angelo tried to make a joke of it, and a guard screamed at him and hit him in the face with the gun butt. He wiped his mouth, smearing blood across his chin, and none of us joked again.

The other armed seamen began to tear *Dancer* to pieces. I suppose it was meant to be a search, but they raged through her accommodation wantonly smashing open lockers or shattering the panelling.

One of them discovered the liquor cabinet, and although there were only one or two bottles, there was a roar of approval. They squabbled noisily as seagulls over a scrap of offal, then went on to loot the galley stores with appropriate hilarity and abandon. Even when their commanding officer was assisted by four of his crew to make the hazardous journey across the six inches of open space that separated the crash boat from *Dancer*, there was no diminution in the volume of shouting and laughter and the crash of shattering woodwork and breaking glass.

The commander wheezed heavily across the cockpit and stooped to enter the saloon. He paused there to regain his breath.

He was one of the biggest men I had ever seen, not less than six feet six tall and enormously gross—a huge swollen body with a belly like a barrage balloon beneath the white uniform jacket. The jacket strained at its brass buttons and sweat had soaked through at the armpits. Across his breast he wore a glittering burst of stars and medals, and amongst them I recognized the American Naval Cross and the 1918 Victory Star.

His head was the shape and colour of a polished black iron pot, the type they traditionally use for cooking missionaries, and a naval cap, thick with gold braid, rode at a jaunty angle upon it. His face ran with rivers of glistening sweat, as he struggled noisily with his breathing and mopped at the sweat, staring at me with bulging eyes.

Slowly his body began to inflate, swelling even larger, like a great bullfrog, until I grew alarmed—expecting him to burst.

The purple-black lips, thick as tractor tyres, parted and an unbelievable volume of sound issued from the pink cavern of his mouth.

'Shut up!' he roared. Instantly his crew of wreckers froze into silence, one of them with his gun butt still raised to attack the panelling behind the bar.

The huge officer trundled forward, seeming to fill the entire saloon with his bulk. Slowly he sank into the padded leather seat. Once more he mopped at his face, then he looked at me again and slowly his whole face lit up into the most wonderfully friendly smile, like an enormous chubby and lovable baby; his teeth were big and flawlessly white and his eyes nearly disappeared in the rolls of smiling black flesh.

'Mr Fletcher, I can't tell you what a great pleasure this is for me.' His voice was deep and soft and friendly, the accent was British upper class—almost certainly acquired at some higher seat of learning. His English was better than mine.

'I have looked forward to meeting you for a number of years.'

'That's very decent of you to say so, Admiral.' With that uniform he could not rank less.

'Admiral,' he repeated with delight, 'I like that,' and he laughed. It began with a vast shaking of belly and ended with a gasping and straining for breath. 'Alas, Mr Fletcher, you are deceived by appearances,' and he preened a little, touching the medals and adjusting the peak of his cap. 'I am only a humble Lieutenant Commander.'

'That's really tough, Commander.'

'No. No, Mr Fletcher—do not waste your sympathy on me. I wield all the authority I could wish for.' He paused for deep breathing exercises and to wipe away the fresh ooze of sweat. 'I hold the powers of life and death, believe me.'

'I believe you, sir,' I told him earnestly. 'Please don't feel you have to prove your point.'

He shouted with laughter again, nearly choked, coughed up something large and yellow, spat it on to the floor and then told me, 'I like you, Mr Fletcher, I really do. I think a sense of humour is very important. I think you and I could become very close friends.' I doubted it, but I smiled encouragingly.

78

'As a mark of my esteem you may use the familiar form when addressing me—Suleiman Dada.'

'I appreciate that—I really do, Suleiman Dada, and you may call me Harry.'

'Harry,' he said. 'Let's have a dram of whisky together.' At that moment another man entered the saloon. A slim boyish figure, dressed not in his usual colonial police uniform but in a lightweight silk suit and lemon-coloured silk shirt and matching tie, with alligator-skin shoes on his feet.

The light blond hair was carefully combed forward into a cowlick, and the fluffy moustache was trim as ever, but he walked carefully, seeming to favour an injury. I grinned at him.

'So, how does the old ball-bag feel now, Daly?' I asked kindly, but he did not answer and went to sit across from Lieutenant Commander Suleiman Dada.

Dada reached out a huge black paw and relieved one of his men of the scotch whisky bottle he carried, part of my previous stock, and he gestured to another to bring glasses from the shattered liquor cabinet.

When we all had half a tumbler of scotch in our hands, Dada gave us the toast.

'To lasting friendship, and mutual prosperity.' We drank, Daly and I cautiously, Dada deeply and with evident pleasure. While his head was tilted back and his eyes closed, the crew man attempted to retrieve the bottle of scotch from the table in front of him.

Without lowering the glass Dada hit him a mighty open-handed clout across the side of the head, a blow that snapped his head back and hurled him across the saloon to crash into the shattered liquor cabinet. He slid down the bulkhead and sat stunned on the deck, shaking his head dazedly. Suleiman Dada, despite his bulk, was a quick and fearsomely powerful man, I realized.

He emptied the glass, set it down, and refilled it. He looked at me now, and his expression changed. The clown had disappeared, despite the ballooning rolls of flesh, I was confronting a shrewd, dangerous and utterly ruthless opponent.

'Harry, I understand that you and Inspector Daly were interrupted in the course of a recent discussion,' and I shrugged.

'All of us here are reasonable men, Harry, of that I am certain.' I said nothing, but studied the whisky in my glass with deep attention. 'This is very fortunate—for let us consider what might happen to an unreasonable man in your position.' He paused, gargled a little with a sip of whisky. Sweat had formed like a rash of little white blisters on his nose and chin. He wiped it away. 'First of all, an unreasonable man might watch while his crew were taken out one at a time and executed. We use pickaxe handles here. It is a gruelling business, and Inspector Daly assures me that you have a special relationship with these two men.' Beside me Chubby and Angelo shifted uneasily in their seats. 'Then an unreasonable man would have his boat taken in to Zinballa Bay. Once that happened there would be no way in which it would ever be returned to him. It would be officially confiscated, out of my humble hands.' He paused, and showed me the humble hands, stretching them towards me. They would have fitted a bull gorilla. We both stared at them for a moment. 'Then the unreasonable man might find himself in Zinballa jail—which, as you are probably aware, is a maximum security political prison.'

I had heard of Zinballa prison, as had everyone on the coast. Those who came out of it were either dead or broken in body and spirit. They called it the 'Lion Cage.'

'Suleiman Dada, I want you to know that I am one of nature's original reasonable men,' I assured him, and he laughed again.

'I was certain of it,' he said. 'I can tell one a mile off,' then again he was serious. 'If we leave here immediately, before the turn of the tide we can be out of the inshore channel before midnight.'

'Yes,' I agreed, 'that we could.'

'Then you could lead us to this place of interest, wait while we satisfy ourselves as to your good faith—which I for one do not doubt one moment—you and your crew will then be free to sail away in your magnificent boat and you could sleep tomorrow night in your own bed.'

'Suleiman Dada—you are a generous and cultivated man. I also have no reason to doubt your good faith,'—no more than that of Materson and Guthrie, I silently qualified the statement—'and I have a peculiarly intense desire to sleep tomorrow night in my own bed.'

Daly spoke for the first time, snarling quietly under his little moustache. 'I think you should know that a turtle fisherman saw your boat anchored in the lagoon across the channel from the Old Men and Gunfire Reef on the night before the shooting incident—we will expect to be taken that way.'

'I have nothing against a man who takes a bribe, Daly—God knows I have done so myself—but then where is the honour among thieves that the poet sings of?' I was very disappointed in Daly, but he ignored my recriminations.

'Don't try any more of your tricks,' he warned me.

'You really are a champion turd, Daly. I could win prizes with you.'

'Please, gentlemen.' Dada held up his hands to halt my flow of rhetoric. 'Let us all be friends. Another small glass of whisky—and then Harry will take us all on a tour of interest.' Dada topped up our glasses, and paused before drinking again. 'I think I should warn you, Harry—I do not like rough water. It does not agree with me. If you take me into rough water I shall be very very angry. Do we understand each other?'

'Just for you I shall command the waters to stand still, Suleiman Dada,' I assured him, and he nodded solemnly, as though it was the very least he expected.

*　　*　　*

The dawn was like a lovely woman rising from the couch of the sea, soft flesh tones and pearly light, the cloud strands like her hair tresses flowing and tousled, gilded blonde by the early sunlight.

We ran northwards, hugging the quieter waters of the inshore channel. Our order of sailing placed *Wave Dancer* in the van, she ambled along like a blood filly mouthing the snaffle, while half a mile astern the crash boat waddled and wallowed, as the Allisons tried to push her up on to the plane. We were headed for the Old Men and Gunfire Reef.

On board *Dancer* I had the con, standing alone at the wheel upon the open bridge. Behind me stood Peter Daly, and an armed seaman from the crash boat.

In the saloon below us, Chubby and Angelo still sat on the bench seat and three more seamen, armed with assault rifles, kept them there.

Dancer had been looted of all her galley stores, so none of us had breakfasted, not even a cup of coffee.

The first paralysing despair of capture had passed—and I was now thinking frenetically, trying to plot my way out of the maze in which I was trapped.

I knew that if I showed Daly and Dada the Break at Gunfire Reef they would either explore it and find nothing—which was the most

81

likely for whatever had been there was now packaged and deposited at Big Gull Island—or they would find some other evidence at the Break. In both cases I was in for unpleasantness—if they found nothing Daly would have the very great pleasure of connecting me up to the electrical system in an attempt to make me talk. If they found something definite my presence would become superfluous—and a dozen eager seamen would vie for job of executioner. I didn't like the sound of pick-handles—it promised to be a messy business.

Yet the chances of escape seemed remote. Although she was half a mile astern the three-pounder of the foredeck of Dada's crash boat kept us on an effective leash, and we had aboard Daly and four members of the goon squad.

I lit my first cheroot of the day and its effect was miraculous, almost immediately I seemed to see a pin-prick of light at the end of the long dark tunnel. I thought about it a little longer, puffing quietly on the black tobacco, and it seemed worth a try—but first I had to talk to Chubby.

'Daly,' I turned to speak over my shoulder. 'You had better get Chubby up here to take the wheel, I have got to go below.'

'Why?' he demanded suspiciously. 'What are you going to do?'

'Let's just say that whatever it is happens every morning at this time, and nobody else can do it for me. If you make me say more, I shall blush.'

'You should have been on the stage, Fletcher. You really slay me.'

'Funny you should mention that. It had crossed my mind.'

He sent the guard to fetch Chubby from the saloon, and I handed the con to him.

'Stick around, I want to talk to you later,' I muttered out of the side of my mouth and clambered down into the cockpit. Angelo brightened a little when I entered the saloon, and flashed a good imitation of the old bright grin, but the three guards, clearly bored, turned their weapons on me enthusiastically and I raised my hands hurriedly.

'Easy, boys, easy,' I soothed them and sidled past them down the companionway. However, two of them followed me. When I reached the heads they would have entered with me and kept me company. 'Gentlemen,' I protested, 'if you continue to point those things at me during the next few critical moments you will probably pioneer the sovereign cure for constipation.' They scowled at me uncertainly and as I closed the door firmly upon them I added, 'But you really don't want a Nobel prize—do you?'

When I opened it again they were waiting in exactly the same attitudes, as though they had not moved. With a conspiratory gesture I beckoned them to follow. Immediately they showed interest, and I led them to the master cabin. Below the big double bunk I had spent many hours building in a concealed locker. It was about the size of a coffin, and was ventilated. It would accommodate a man lying prone. During the time when I was running human cargo it had been a hidey hole in case of a search—but now I used it as a store for valuables and illicit or dangerous cargo. It contained at the present time five hundred rounds of ammunition for the FN, a wooden crate of hand grenades, and two cases of Chivas Regal scotch whisky.

With exclamations of delight the two guards slung their machine-guns on their shoulder straps and dragged out the whisky cases. They had forgotten about me and I slipped away and returned to the bridge. I stood next to Chubby, delaying the moment of take-over.

'You took your time,' growled Daly.

'Never rush a good thing,' I explained, and he lost interest and strolled back to stare across our wake at the following gunboat.

'Chubby,' I whispered. 'Gunfire Break. You told me once there was a passage through the reef from the landward side.'

'At high springs, for a whaleboat and a good man with a steady nerve,' he agreed. 'I did it when I was a crazy kid.'

'It's high spring in three hours. Could I run *Dancer* through?' I asked.

Chubby's expression changed. 'Jesus!' he whispered, and turned to stare at me in disbelief.

'Could I do it?' I insisted quietly, and he sucked his teeth noisily, looking away at the sunrise, scratching the bristles of his chin.

Then suddenly he reached an opinion, and spat over the side. 'You might, Harry—but nobody else I know could.'

'Give me the bearings, Chubby, quickly.'

'It was a long time ago, but,' sketchily he described the approach, and the passage of the Break, 'there are three turns in the passage, left, right, then left again, then there is a narrow neck, brain coral on each hand—*Dancer* might just get through but she'll leave some paint behind. Then you are into the big pool at the back of the main reef. There is room to circle there and wait for the right sea before you shoot the gap out into the open water.'

'Thanks, Chubby,' I whispered. 'Now go below. I let the guards have the spare whisky. By the time I start my run for the Break they will be blasted right out through the top of their skulls. I will signal three stamps on the deck, then it will be up to you and Angelo to get those pieces away from them and wrap them up tightly.'

The sun was well up, and the triple-peaked silhouette of the Old Men was rising only a few miles dead ahead when I heard the first raucous shout of laughter and crash of breaking furniture below. Daly ignored it and we ran on over the quiet inshore waters towards the reverse side of Gunfire Reef. Already I could see the jagged line of the reef, like the black teeth of an ancient shark. Beyond it the tall oceanic surf flashed whitely as it burst, and beyond that lay the open sea.

I edged in towards the reef, and eased open the throttles a fraction. *Dancer's* engine beat changed, but not enough to alert Daly. He lounged against the rail, bored and unshaven and probably missing his breakfast. I could distinctly hear the boom of the surf on coral now, and from below, the sounds of revelry became continuous. Daly noticed at last, frowned and told the other guard to go below and investigate. The guard, also bored, disappeared below with alacrity and never returned.

I glanced astern. My increase in speed was slowly opening the gap between *Dancer* and the crash boat, and steadily we edged in closer to the reef.

I was looking ahead anxiously, trying to pick up the marks and bearings that Chubby had described to me. Gently I touched the throttles, opening them another notch. The crash boat fell a little farther astern.

Suddenly I saw the entrance to Gunfire Break a thousand yards ahead. Two pinnacles of old weathered coral marked it, and I could see the colour difference of clear sea water pouring through the gap in the coral barrier.

Below there was another screech of wild laughter, and one of the guards reeled drunkenly into the cockpit. He reached the rail only just in time and vomited copiously into the wake. Then his legs gave way and he collapsed on to the deck and lay in an abandoned huddle.

Daly let out an angry exclamation and raced down the ladder. I took the opportunity to push the throttles open another two notches.

I stared ahead, gathering myself for the effort. I must try and open the gap between *Dancer* and her escort a little more, every inch would help to confound her gunners.

I planned to come up level with the channel, and then commit *Dancer* to it under full power, risking the submerged coral fangs rather than test the aim of the gunners aboard the crash boat. It was half a mile of narrow, tortuous channel through the coral before we reached the open sea. For most of it, *Dancer* would be partially screened by coral outcrops, and the weaving of the channel would help to confuse the range of the three-pounder. I was hoping also that the surf working through the gap would give *Dancer* plenty of up-and-down movement, so that she would heave and weave unpredictably like one of those little ducks in a shooting gallery.

One thing was certain: that intrepid mariner, Lieutenant Commander Suleiman Dada, would not risk pursuit through the channel, so I could give his gun layer a rapidly increasing range to contend with.

I ignored the alcoholic din from below, and I watched the mouth of the channel approach rapidly. I found myself hoping that the seamanship of the crash boat's crew and commander was a faithful indication of their marksmanship.

Suddenly Peter Daly flew up the ladder to confront me. His face was pink with anger and his moustache tried to bristle its silky hairs. His mouth worked for a moment before he could speak.

'You gave them the liquor, Fletcher. Oh, you crafty bastard.'

'Me?' I asked indignantly. 'I wouldn't do a thing like that.'

'They're drunk as pigs—all of them,' he shouted, then he turned and looked over the stern. The crash boat was a mile behind us, and the distance was increasing.

'You are up to something,' he shrilled at me, and groped in the side pocket of his silk jacket. At that moment we came level with the entrance to the channel.

I hit both throttles wide open, and *Dancer* bellowed and hurled herself forward.

Still groping in his pocket, Daly was thrown off balance. He staggered backwards, still shouting.

I spun the wheel to full right lock, and *Dancer* whirled like a ballet dancer. Daly changed the direction of his stagger, thrown wildly across the deck he came up hard against the side rail as

Dancer leaned over steeply in her turn. At that moment Daly dragged a small nickelled-silver automatic from his side pocket. It looked like a .25, the type ladies carry in their handbags.

I left *Dancer's* wheel for an instant. Stooping, I got my hand on Daly's ankles and lifted sharply. 'Leave us now, comrade,' I said as he went backwards over the rail, falling twelve feet, striking the lower deck rail a glancing blow and then splashing untidily into the water alongside.

I darted back to the wheel, catching *Dancer's* head before she could pay off, and at the same time stamping three times on the deck.

As I lined *Dancer* up for the entrance I heard the shouts of conflict in the saloon below, and winced as a machine-gun fired with a sound like ripping cloth—Barrapp—and bullets exploded out through the deck behind me, leaving a jagged hole edged with white splinters. At least they were fired at the roof, and were unlikely to have hit either Angelo or Chubby.

Just before I entered the coral portals, I glanced back once more. The crash boat still lumbered along a mile behind, while Daly's head bobbed in the churning white wake. I wondered if they would reach him before the sharks did.

Then there was no more time for idle speculation. As *Dancer* dashed headlong into the channel I was appalled by the task I had set her.

I could have leant over and touched coral outcrops on each hand, and I could see the sinister shape of more coral lurking below the shallow turbulent waters ahead. The waters had expended most of their savagery on the long twisting run through the channel, but the farther in we went the wilder they would become, making *Dancer's* response to the helm just that much more unpredictable.

The first bend in the channel showed ahead, and I put *Dancer* to it. She came around willingly, swishing her bottom, and with only a trifling yaw that pushed her outwards towards the menacing coral.

As I straightened her into the next stretch, Chubby came swarming up the ladder. He was grinning hugely. Only two things put him into that sort of mood—and one of them was a good punch up. He had skinned his right knuckle.

'All quiet below, Harry. Angelo's looking after them.' He glanced around. 'Where's the policeman?'

'He went for a swim.' I did not take my attention from the channel. 'Where is the crash boat? What are they doing?'

Chubby peered across at her. 'No change. It doesn't seem to have sunk in yet—hold on, though—' his voice changed, '—yes, there they go. They are manning the deck gun.'

We drove on swiftly down the channel, and I risked a quick glance backwards. At that instant I saw the long streak of white cordite smoke blow like a feather from the three-pounder, and an instant later there was the sharp crack of shot passing high overhead, followed immediately by the flat report of the shot.

'Ready for it now, Harry. Left-hander coming up.'

We swept into the next turn, and the next round fell short, bursting in a shower of fragment and blue smoke on one of the coral heads fifty yards off our beam.

I coaxed *Dancer* smoothly into the turn, and as we went into it another shell fell in our wake, lifting a tall and graceful column of white water high above the bridge. The following wind blew the spray over us.

We were halfway through now, and the waves that rushed to meet us were six feet high and angry with the restraint enforced upon them by the walls of coral.

The gun crew of the crash boat were making alarmingly erratic practice. A round burst five hundred yards astern, then the next went between Chubby and me, a stunning blaze of passing shot that sent me reeling in the backwash of disrupted air.

'Here's the neck now,' Chubby called anxiously and my spirit quailed as I saw how the channel narrowed and how bridge-high buttresses of coral guarded it.

It seemed impossible that *Dancer* would pass through so narrow an opening.

'Here we go, Chubby, cross your fingers,' and, still under full throttle, I put *Dancer* at the neck. I could see him grasping the rail with both hands, and I expected the stainless steel to bend with the strength of his grip.

We were halfway through when we hit, with a jarring rending crash. *Dancer* lurched and hesitated.

At the same moment another shell burst alongside. It showered the bridge with coral chips and humming steel fragments, but I hardly noticed it as I tried to ease *Dancer* through the gap.

I sheered off the wall, and the tearing scraping sound ran along our starboard side. For a moment we jammed solidly, then another big green wave raced down on us, lifting us free of the coral teeth and we were through the neck. Dancer lunged ahead.

'Go below, Chubby,' I shouted. 'Check if we holed the hull.' Blood was dripping from a fragment scratch on his chin, but he dived down the ladder.

With another stretch of open water ahead, I could glance back at the crash boat. She was almost obscured by an intervening block of coral, but she was still firing rapidly and wildly. She seemed to have heaved to at the entrance to the channel, probably to pick up Daly— but I knew she would not attempt to follow us now. It would take her four hours to work her way round to the main channel beyond the Old Men.

The last turn in the channel came up ahead, and again Dancer's hull touched coral; the sound of it seemed to tear into my own soul. Then at last we burst out into the deep pool in the back of the main reef, a circular arena of deep water three hundred yards across, fenced in by coral walls and open only through the Gunfire Break to the wild surf of the Indian Ocean.

Chubby appeared at my shoulder once more. 'Tight as a mouse's ear, Harry. Not taking on a drop.' Silently I applauded my darling.

Now for the first time we were in full view of the gun crew half a mile away across the reef, and my turn into the pool presented Dancer to them broadside. As though they sensed that this was their last chance they poured shot after shot at us.

It fell about us in great leaping spouts, too close to allow me any latitude of decision. I swung Dancer again, aimed her at the narrow break, and let her race for the gap in Gunfire Reef.

I committed her and when we had passed the point of no return, I felt my belly cramp up with horror as I looked ahead through the gap to the open sea. It seemed as though the whole ocean was rearing up ahead of me, gathering itself to hurl down upon the frail little vessel like some rampaging monster.

'Chubby,' I called hollowly. 'Will you look at that.'

'Harry,' he whispered, 'this a good time to pray.'

And Dancer ran out bravely to meet this freak Goliath of the sea.

It came up, humping monstrous shoulders as it charged, higher and higher still it rose, a glassy green wall and I could hear it rustling—like wildfire in dry grass.

Another shot passed close overhead but I hardly noticed it, as

Dancer threw up her head and began to climb that mountainous wave.

It was turning pale green along the crest high above, beginning to curl, and *Dancer* went up as though she were on an elevator.

The deck canted steeply, and we clung helplessly to the rail.

'She's going over backwards,' Chubby shouted, as she began to stand on her tail. 'She's turtling, man!'

'Go through her,' I called to *Dancer*. 'Cut through the green!' and as though she heard me she lunged with her sharp prow into the curl of the wave an instant before it could fall upon us and crush the hull.

It came aboard us in a roaring green horror, solid sheets of it swept *Dancer* from bows to stern, six feet deep, and she lurched as though to a mortal blow.

Then suddenly we burst out through the back of the wave, and below us was a gaping valley, a yawning abyss into which *Dancer* hurled herself, falling free, a gut-swooping drop down into the trough.

We hit with a sickening crash that seemed to stun her, and which threw Chubby and me to the deck. But as I dragged myself up again, *Dancer* shook herself free of the tons of water that had come aboard, and she ran on to meet the next wave.

It was smaller, and *Dancer* beat the curl and porpoised over her.

'That's my darling,' I shouted to her and she picked up speed, taking the third wave like a steeple-chaser.

Somewhere close another three-pound shell cracked the sky, but then we were out and running for the long horizon of the ocean and I never heard another shot.

The guard who had passed out in the cockpit from an excess of scotch whisky must have been washed overboard by the giant wave, for we never saw him again. The other three we left on a small island thirty miles north of St Mary's where I knew there was water in a brackish well, and which would certainly be visited by fishermen from the mainland.

They had sobered by that time, and were all inflicted with nasty hangovers. They made three forlorn figures on the beach as we ran southwards into the dusk. It was dark when we crept into Grand Harbour. I picked up moorings, not tying up to the wharf at Admiralty. I did not want *Dancer*'s glaring injuries to become a subject of speculation around the island.

Chubby and Angelo went ashore in the dinghy—but I was too exhausted to make the effort, and dinnerless I collapsed across the double bunk in the master cabin and slept without moving until Judith woke me after nine in the morning. Angelo had sent her down with a dinner pail of fish cakes and bacon.

'Chubby and Angelo gone up to Missus Eddy's to buy some stores they need to repair the boat,' she told me. 'They'll be down soon now.'

I wolfed the breakfast and went to shave and shower. When I returned she was still there, sitting on the edge of the bunk. She clearly had something to discuss.

She brushed away my clumsy efforts at dressing my wound, and had me sit while she worked on it.

'Mister Harry, you aren't going to get my Angelo killed or jailed, are you?' she demanded. 'If you go on like this, I'm going to make him come ashore.'

'That's great, Judith.' I laughed at her concern. 'Why don't you send him across to Rawano for three years, while you sit here.'

'That's not kind, Mister Harry.'

'Life is not very kind, Judith,' I told her more gently. 'Angelo and I are both doing the best we can. Just to keep my boat afloat, I've got to take a few chances. Some with Angelo. He told me that he's saved enough to buy you a nice little house up near the church. He got the money by running with me.'

She was silent while she finished the dressing, and when she would have turned to go I took her hand and drew her back. She would not look at me, until I took her chin and lifted her face. She was a lovely child, with great smoky eyes and a smoothly silken skin.

'Don't fuss yourself, Judith. Angelo is like a kid brother to me. I'll look after him.'

She studied my face a long moment. 'You really mean that, don't you?' she asked.

'I really do.'

'I believe you,' she said at last, and she smiled. Her teeth were very white against the golden amber skin. 'I trust you.'

Women are always saying that to me. 'I trust you.' So much for feminine intuition.

'You name one of your kids for me, hear?'

'The first one, Mister Harry.' Her smile blazed and her dark eyes flashed. 'That's a promise.'

'They do say that when you fall from a horse you should immediately ride him again—so as not to lose your nerve, Mister Harry.' Fred Coker sat at his desk in the travel agency, behind him a poster of a beefeater and Big Ben—'England Swings,' it said. We had just discussed at great length our mutual concern at Inspector Peter Daly's perfidious conduct, though I suspected that Fred Coker's concern was considerably less than mine. He had collected his commission in advance and nobody had put his head in a noose, nor had they almost wrecked his boat. We were now discussing the subject of whether or not our business arrangement should continue.

'They also say, Mr Coker, that a man with his buttocks hanging out of the holes in his trousers should not be too fussy,' I said, and Coker's spectacles glittered with satisfaction. He nodded his head.

'And that, Mister Harry, is probably the wiser of the two sayings,' he agreed.

'I'll take anything, Mr Coker. Body, box or sticks. Just one thing, the cost of dying has gone up to ten thousand dollars a run—all in advance.'

'Even at that price, we'll find work for you,' he promised, and I realized I had been working cheaply before.

'Soon,' I insisted.

'Very soon,' he agreed. 'You are fortunate. I do not think that Inspector Daly will be returning to St Mary's now. You will save the commission usually payable there.'

'He owes me that at least,' I agreed.

I made three night runs in the next six weeks. Two body carries, and a box job—all below the river into Portuguese waters. The bodies were both singles, silent black men dressed in jungle fatigues, and I took them far south, deep penetrations. They waded ashore on remote beaches and I wondered briefly upon what unholy missions they travelled—how much pain and death would arise from those secret landings.

The box job involved eighteen long wooden crates with Chinese markings. We picked up from a submarine out in the channel, and dropped off in a river-mouth, unloading into pairs of dugout canoes lashed together for stability. We spoke to no one and nobody challenged us.

They were milk runs and I cleared eighteen thousand dollars—

enough to carry me and my crew through the off-season in the style to which we were accustomed. More important, the intervals of quiet and rest were sufficient to heal my wounds and give me back my strength. At first I lay for hours in the hammock under the palms, reading or sleeping. Then as it came back to me, I swam and fished and sun-baked, went for oysters and crayfish—until I was hard and lean and sunbrowned again.

The wound healed into a thickened and irregular cicatrice, tribute to MacNab's surgical skills, it curled around my chest and on to my back like an angry purple dragon. In one thing he had been correct, the massive damage to my upper left arm left it stiff and weakened. I could not lift my elbow above shoulder-level, and I lost my title in Indian wrestling to Chubby in the bar of the Lord Nelson. However, I hoped that swimming and regular exercise would strengthen it.

As my strength returned so did my curiosity and sense of adventure. I began dreaming about the canvas-wrapped package off Big Gull Island. In one dream I swam down and opened the package—it contained a tiny feminine figure, the size of a Dresden doll, a golden mermaid with Sister May's lovely face and a truly startling bosom, the tail was the graceful sickle shape of a marlin's. The little mermaid smiled shyly and held out her hand to me. On her palm lay a shiny silver shilling.

'Sex, money and billfish—' I thought when I woke, '—good old uncomplicated Harry, real Freud food.' I knew then that pretty soon I would be going for Big Gull Island.

It was very late in the season before I could prevail on Fred Coker to arrange a straight fishing charter for me, and it turned sour as cheap wine. The party consisted of two overweight, flabby German industrialists with fat bejewelled wives. I worked hard for them, and put both men into fish.

The first was a good black marlin, but the party screwed down on his stardrag, freezing the reel while the fish was still green and crazy to run. It lifted the German's huge backside out of the seat, and before I could release the stardrag for him, it had my three hundred dollar rod down on the gunwale. The fibreglass rod snapped like a matchstick.

The other member of the party, after losing two decent fish, panted and sweated three hours over a baby blue marlin. When he finally brought it to the gaff, I could hardly bring myself to put the steel in, and I was too ashamed to hang it on Admiralty. We took the photographs on board *Dancer* and I smuggled it ashore wrapped in a tarpaulin. Like Fred Coker I also have a reputation to preserve. The German industrialist, however, was so delighted by his prowess that he slipped an extra five hundred dollars into my avaricious little paw. I told him it was a truly magnificent fish, which was a thousand-dollar lie. I always give good value. Then the wind backed into the south, the temperature of the water in the channel dropped four degrees and the fish were gone. For ten days we hunted far north but it was over, another season was past.

We stripped and cleaned all the billfish equipment and laid it away in thick yellow grease. I pulled *Dancer* up on to the slip at the fuelling basin and we went over her hull, cleaning it down, re-working the temporary patches I had put on the injuries she had received at Gunfire Reef.

Then we painted her until she glistened, sleek and lovely, before we refloated her and took her out to moorings. There we worked lackadaisically on her upper works, stripping varnish, sand-papering, re-varnishing, checking out the electrical system, re-soldering a connection here, replacing wiring there.

I was in no hurry. It would be three weeks before my next charter arrived—an expedition of marine biologists from a Canadian university.

In the meantime the days were cooler, and I was feeling the old glow of good health and bodily well-being again. I dined at Government House, sometimes as often as once a week, and each time I had to tell the full story of the shoot-out with Guthrie and Materson. President Biddle knew the story by heart and corrected me if I omitted a single detail. It always ended with the President crying excitedly, 'Show them your scar, Mister Harry,' and I had to open the starched front of my dress shirt at the dinner table.

They were good lazy days. The island life drifted placidly by. Peter Daly never returned to St Mary's—and at the end of six weeks, Wally Andrews was promoted to acting Inspector and commanding officer of the police force. One of his first acts was to return to me my FN carbine.

This quiet time was spiced by the secret tingle of anticipation which I felt. I knew that one day soon I was going back to Big Gull Island and the piece of unfinished business that lay there in the shallow limpid waters—and I teased myself with the knowledge.

Then one Friday evening I was rounding out the week with my

crew in the bar of the Lord Nelson. Judith was with us, having replaced the flock that had previously gathered around Angelo on Friday nights. She was good for him, he no longer drank to the morbid stage.

Chubby and I had just begun the first duet of the evening and were keeping within a few beats of each other when Marion slipped into the seat beside me.

I put one arm around her shoulders and held my tankard to her lips while she drank thirstily, but the distraction caused me to forge even farther ahead of Chubby in the song.

Marion worked on the switchboard at the Hilton Hotel. She was a pretty little thing with a sexy pugface and long straight black hair. It was she whom Mike Guthrie had used for a punch-bag so long ago.

When Chubby and I straggled to the end of the chorus, Marion told me, 'There is a lady asking for you, Mister Harry.'

'What lady?'

'At the hotel, one of the guests, she came in on this morning's plane. She knew your name and everything. She wants to see you. I told her I would see you tonight and give you the message.'

'What is she like?' I asked Marion with interest.

'She's beautiful, Mister Harry. Such a lady too.'

'Sounds like my type,' I agreed, and ordered a pint for Marion.

'Aren't you going to see her now?'

'With you beside me, Marion, all the beautiful ladies of the world can wait until tomorrow.'

'Oh, Mister Harry, you are a real devil man,' she giggled, and snuggled a little closer.

'Harry,' said Chubby on my other side, 'I'm going to tell you now what I never told you before.' He took a long swallow from his tankard, then went on with sentimental tears swimming in his eyes. 'Harry, I love you, man. I love you better than my own brother.'

* * *

I went up to the Hilton a few minutes before midday. Marion came through from her cubicle behind the reception desk. She still had her earphones around her neck.

'She's waiting for you on the terrace.' She pointed across the vast reception area with its *ersatz* Hawaiian décor. 'The blonde lady in the yellow bikini.'

94

She was reading a magazine, lying on her belly on one of the reclining sun couches, and she had her back to me so my first impression was of masses of blonde hair, thick and shiny, teased up like the mane of a lion, then falling in a slick golden cascade.

She heard my footsteps on the paving. She glanced around, pushed her sunglasses up on top of her head, then she stood up to face me, and I realized that she was tiny, seeming to reach not much higher than my chest. The bikini also was tiny and showed a flat smooth belly with a deep navel, firm shoulders lightly tanned, small breasts, and a trim waist. Her legs had lovely lines and her neat little feet were thrust into open sandals, the nails painted clear red to match her long fingernails. Her hands as she pushed at her hair were small and shapely.

She wore heavy make-up, but wore it with rare skill, so that her skin had a soft pearly lustre and colour glowed subtly on her cheeks and lips. Her eyes had long dark artificial lashes, and the eyelids were touched with colour and line to give them an exotic oriental cast.

'Duck, Harry!' Something deep inside me shouted a warning, and I almost obeyed. I knew this type well, there had been others like her—small and purringly feline—I had scars to prove it, scars both physical and spiritual. However, one thing nobody can say about old Harry is that he runs for cover when trouble walks in.

Courageously I stepped forward, crinkling my eyes and twisting my mouth into the naughty small boy grin that usually dynamites them.

'Hello,' I said, 'I'm Harry Fletcher.'

She looked at me, starting at my feet and going up six feet four to the top where her gaze lingered speculatively and she pouted her lower lip.

'Hello,' she answered, her voice was husky, breathless-sounding—and carefully rehearsed. 'I'm Sherry North, Jimmy North's sister.'

* * *

We were on the veranda of the shack in the evening. It was cool and the sunset was a spectacular display of pyrotechnics that flamed and faded above the palms.

She was drinking a Pimms No. 1 filled with fruit and ice—one of my seduction specials—and she wore a kaftan of light floating stuff

95

through which her body showed in shadowy outline as she stood against the rail backlit by the sunset. I could not be certain as to whether or not she wore anything beneath the kaftan—this and the tinkle of ice in her glass distracted me from the letter I was reading. She had showed it to me as part of her credentials. It was a letter from Jimmy North written a few days before his death. I recognized the handwriting and the turn of phrase was typical of that bright and eager lad. As I read on, I forgot the sister's presence in the memory of the past. It was a long bubbling letter, written as though to a loving friend, with veiled references to the mission and its successful outcome, the promise of a future in which there would be wealth and laughter and all good things.

I felt a pang of regret and personal loss for the boy in his lonely sea grave, for the lost dreams that drifted with him like rotting seaweed.

Then suddenly my own name leapt from that page at me, '—you can't help liking him, Sherry. He's big and tough-looking, all scarred and beat up like an old tom cat that's been out alley-fighting every night. But under it, I swear he is really a softy. He seems to have taken a shine to me. Even gives me fatherly advice!—'

There was more in the same vein that embarrassed me so that my throat closed up and I took a swallow of whisky, which made my eyes water and the words swim, while I finished the letter and refolded it.

I handed it to Sherry, and walked away to the end of the veranda. I stood there for a while looking out over the bay. The sun slid below the horizon and suddenly it was dark and chill.

I went back and lit the lamp, setting it up high so the glare did not fall in our eyes. She watched me in silence until I had poured another scotch and settled in my cane-backed chair.

'Okay,' I said, 'you're Jimmy's sister. You've come to St Mary's to see me. Why?'

'You liked him, didn't you?' she asked, as she left the rail and came to sit beside me.

'I like a lot of people. It's a weakness of mine.'

'Did he die—I mean, was it like they said in the newspapers?'

'Yes,' I said. 'It was like that.'

'Did he ever tell you what they were doing out here?'

I shook my head. 'They were very cagey—and I don't ask questions.'

96

It was starting to make some sort of sense at last.

'How does Jimmy fit into this?'

She made an impatient gesture. 'Wait,' she said, then went on. 'Do you have any idea what the value of that cargo might be in the open market?'

'I should imagine you could write your own cheque—give or take a couple of million dollars.' And old bad Harry came to attention, he had been getting exercise lately and growing stronger.

Sherry nodded. 'The test pilot of the "pogo stick" was a Commander in the U. S. Navy named William Bryce. The aircraft developed a fault at fifty thousand feet, just before he came out through the top of the weather. He fought her all the way down, he was a conscientious officer, but at five hundred feet he knew he wasn't going to make it. He ejected and watched the aircraft go in.'

She was speaking carefully, and her choice of words was odd, too technical for a woman. She had learned all this, I was certain—from Jimmy? Or from somebody else?

Listen and learn, Harry, I told myself.

'Billy Bryce was three days on a rubber raft on the ocean in a typhoon before the rescue helicopter from Rawano found him. He had time to do some thinking. One of the things he thought about was the value of that cargo—and he compared it to the salary of a Commander. His evidence at the court of inquiry omitted the fact that the "pogo stick" had gone down within sight of land, and that Bryce had been able to take a fix on a recognizable land feature before he was blown out to sea by the typhoon.'

I could not see any weakness in her story—it looked all right—and very interesting.

'The court of inquiry gave a verdict of "pilot error" and Bryce resigned his commission. His career was destroyed by that verdict. He decided to earn his own retirement annuity and also to clear his reputation. He was going to force the U. S. Navy to buy back its "killer whale" missiles and to accept the evidence of the flight recorder.'

I was going to ask a question, but again Sherry stopped me with a gesture. She did not want her recital interrupted.

'Jimmy had done some work for the U. S. Navy—a hull inspection of one of their carriers—and he had met Bryce at that time. They had become friends, and so Billy Bryce naturally came to Jimmy. Between them they had not sufficient capital for the expedition they needed to mount, so they planned to find financial backers. It isn't the kind of thing you can advertise in the *Times*, and they were working on it when Billy Bryce was killed in his Thunderbird on the M4 near the Heathrow turn-off.'

'There seems to be some sort of curse on this thing,' I said.

'Are you superstitious, Harry?' she asked, looking at me through those slanted tiger eyes.

'I don't knock it,' I admitted, and she nodded, seeming to file the information away before she went on.

'After Billy was dead, Jimmy went on with the project. He found backers. He wouldn't tell me who, but I guessed they were unsavoury. He came out here with them—and you know the rest.'

'I know the rest,' I agreed, and instinctively massaged the thickened scar tissue through the silk of my shirt. 'Except of course the site of the crash.'

We stared at each other.

'Did he tell you?' I asked, and she shook her head.

'Well, it was an interesting story.' I grinned at her. 'It's a pity we can't check out the truth of it.'

She stood up abruptly and went to the veranda rail. She hugged her arms and she was so angry that if she'd had a tail she would have switched it like a lioness.

I waited for her to recover, and the moment came when she shrugged her shoulders and turned back to me. Her smile was light.

'Well, that's that! I thought I was entitled to some of the rewards. Jimmy was my brother—and I came a long way to find you because he liked and trusted you. I thought we could work together—but I guess if you want it all, there's not much I can do about it.'

She shook out her hair, and it rippled and shone in the lamplight. I stood up.

'I'll take you home now,' I said, and touched her arm. She reached up with both arms, and her fingers locked in the thick curly hair at the back of my neck.

'It's a long way home,' she whispered, and pulled my head down, standing on her tiptoes.

Her lips were very soft and moist, and her tongue was thrusting and restless. After a while she drew back and smiled up at me, her eyes were unfocused and her breath was short and fast.

'Perhaps it wasn't a wasted journey, after all?'

I picked her up, and she was light as a child, hugging my neck, pressing her cheek to mine as I carried her into the shack. I learned long ago to eat hearty whenever there was food, because you never know when the famine is going to hit.

Even the soft light of dawn was cruel to her as she lay sprawled in sleep beneath the mosquito net on the big double bed. Her make-up had smeared and caked, and she slept with her mouth open. The mane of blonde hair was a tangled bush and it did not match the triangle of thick dark curls at the base of her belly. I felt repelled by her this morning, for I had learned during the night that Miss Sherry was a raving sadist.

I slipped out of the bed and stood over her a few moments, searching her sleeping face in vain for a resemblance to Jimmy North. I left her, and, still naked, walked out of the shack and down to the beach.

The tide was in and I plunged into the cool clear water and swam out to the entrance to the bay. I swam fast, driving hard in an Australian crawl, and the salt water stung the deep scratches in my back.

It was one of my lucky mornings, old friends were waiting for me beyond the reef, a school of big bottle-nosed porpoise, who came flashing to meet me, their tall fins cutting the dark surface as they steeplechased over the swells. They circled me, whistling and snorting, the blowholes in the tops of their heads gulping like tiny mouths and their own huge mouths fixed in idiotic grins of pleasure.

They teased me for ten minutes before one of the big old bulls allowed me to get a grip on his dorsal fin and gave me a tow. It was a thrilling sleigh ride that had the water creaming wildly about my chest and head. He took me half a mile offshore before the force of water tore me from his back.

It was a long swim back, with the bull dolphin circling me and giving me an occasional friendly prod in the backside, inviting me aboard for another ride. At the reef they whistled farewell and slid gracefully away, and I was happy when I waded ashore. The arm ached a little, but it was the healthy ache of healing and growing strength.

The bed was empty, and the bathroom door was locked. She was probably shaving her armpits with my razor, I thought. I felt a flare of annoyance, an old dog like me doesn't like his routine disturbed. I used the guest shower to sluice off the salt and my annoyance receded under the rush of hot water. Then fresh but unshaven and hungry as a python, I went through to the kitchen. I was frying ham with pineapple and buttering thick cuts of toast when Sherry came into the kitchen.

She was once more immaculate. She must have carried a complete cosmetic counter in the Gucci handbag, and her hair was dressed and lacquered into its mane and fall.

Her smile was brilliant. 'Good morning, lover,' she said and came to kiss me lingeringly. I was now well disposed towards the world and all its creatures. I no longer felt repelled by this glittering woman. The fine mood of the dolphins had returned and my gaiety must have been infectious. We laughed a lot over the meal and afterwards I took the coffee pot out on to the veranda.

'When are we going to find the pogo stick?' she asked suddenly, and I poured another mug of strong black coffee without answering. Sherry North had evidently decided that a night of her company had made me her slave for life. Now I may not be a connoisseur of women, but on the other hand I have had some little experience—I mean I'm not exactly a virgin—and I didn't rate Sherry North's charms as worth four killer whale missiles and the flight recorder of a secret strike aircraft.

'Just as soon as you show me the way,' I answered carefully. It is an old-fashioned feminine conceit that if a man pleasures them with skill and aplomb, then he must be made to pay for it. I have long believed that it should be the other way around.

She reached across and held my wrist, the tiger's eyes were suddenly big and soulful.

'After last night,' she whispered huskily, 'I know that there is a lot ahead of us, Harry. You and I, together.'

I had lain awake for hours during the night and reached my decision. Whatever lay in the package was not an entire aircraft, but probably some small part of it—something that identified it clearly. It was almost certainly not either the flight recorder or one of the missiles. Jimmy North would not have had sufficient time to remove the recorder from the fuselage, even if he had known where it was situated and had the proper tools. On the other hand the package was the wrong shape and size for a missile, it was a squat round object, not aerodynamically designed.

It was almost certainly some fairly innocuous object. If I took Sherry North with me to recover it, I would be playing only a minor card from my hand—although it would look like a major trump.

I would be giving nothing away, not the site of the crash at Gunfire Reef, nor any of the valuable objects associated with it.

On the other hand, I would be beating the tall grass for tigers. It would be very instructive to see exactly how Mademoiselle North reacted, once she thought she knew the site of the crash.

'Harry,' she whispered again. 'Please,' and she leaned closer. 'You must believe me. I have never felt like this before. From the first moment I saw you—I just knew—'

I roused myself from my calculations and leaned towards her, assuming an expression of simple-minded passion and lust.

'Darling—' I began but my voice choked up, and I enfolded her in a bear hug, feeling her stiffen irritably as I smeared her lipstick and ruffled the meticulously dressed hairstyle. I could sense the effort it required for her to respond with equal passion.

'Do you feel the same way?' she asked from the depths of my embrace, smothered against my chest, and for the fun of watching her play the role she had assigned herself, I picked her up again and carried her through to the frowsy rumpled bed.

'I will show you how I feel for you,' I muttered hoarsely.

'Darling,' she protested desperately, 'not now.'

'Why not?'

'We have so much to do. There will be time later—all the time in the world.' With a show of reluctance I set her down, although truthfully I was thankful for I knew that on top of a huge breakfast of ham and three cups of coffee, it would have given me heartburn.

* * *

It was a few minutes after noon when I cleared Grand Harbour, and swung away south and east. I had told my crew to take a day ashore, I would not be fishing.

Chubby looked down at Sherry North, sprawled bikini-clad on the cockpit deck, and scowled noncommittally, but Angelo rolled his eyes expressively and asked, 'Pleasure cruise?' with a certain inflection.

'You've got a filthy mind,' I scolded him and he laughed delightedly, as though I had paid him the nicest compliment, and the two of them walked away up the wharf.

Dancer romped down the necklace of atolls and islands until, a little after three o'clock, I ran the deep-water passage between Little Gull Island and Big Gull Island, and rounded into the shallow open water between the east shore of Big Gull and the blue water of the Mozambique.

There was enough breeze to make the day pleasantly cool, and to kick up a white flecky chop off the surface.

I manoeuvred carefully, squinting over at Big Gull as I put *Dancer* in position. When I hit the marks I pushed a little upwind to allow for *Dancer's* fall-back. Then I cut the engines and hurried down to the foredeck to drop the hook.

Dancer came around and settled down like a well-behaved lady.

'Is this the place?' Sherry had watched everything I did with her disconcerting feline stare.

'This is it,' and I risked overplaying my part as the besotted lover by pointing out the marks to her.

'I lined up those two palms, the ones leaning over, with that single palm right up on the skyline, see it?'

She nodded silently, again I caught that look as though the information was being carefully filed and remembered.

'Now what do we do?' she asked.

'This is where Jimmy dived,' I explained. 'When he came back on board he was very excited. He spoke secretly with the others—Materson and Guthrie—and they seemed to catch his excitement. Jimmy went down again with rope and a tarpaulin. He was down a long time—and when he came up again, it started, the shooting.'

'Yes,' she nodded eagerly, the reference to her brother's death seemed to leave her unmoved. 'We should go now, before someone else sees us here.'

'Go?' I asked, looking at her. 'I thought we were going to have a look?'

She recognized her mistake. 'We should organize it properly, come back when we are prepared, when we have made arrangements to pick up and transport—'

'Lover,' I grinned, 'I didn't come all this way not to take at least one quick look.'

'I don't think you should, Harry,' she called after me, but already I was opening the engine-room hatch.

'Let's come back another time,' she persisted, but I went down the ladder to the rack which held the air bottles and took down a

Draeger twin set. I fitted the breathing valve and tested the seal, sucking air out of the rubber mouthpiece.

Glancing quickly up at the hatch to make sure she was not watching me, I reached across and threw the concealed cut-out switch on the electrical system. Now nobody could start *Dancer*'s engines while I was overboard.

I swung the diving ladder over the stern and then dressed in the cockpit—short-sleeved neoprene wet suit and hood, weight belt and knife, Nemrod wrap-around face-plate and fins.

I slung the scuba set on my back and picked up a coil of light nylon rope and hooked it on to my belt.

'What happens if you don't come back?' Sherry asked, showing apprehension for the first time. 'I mean what happens to me?'

'You'll pine to death,' I told her, and went over the side, not in a showy back flip but a simple use of the steps, more in keeping with my age and dignity.

The water was transparent as mountain air, and as I went head down I could see every detail of the bottom fifty feet below.

It was a coral landscape, lit with dappled light and wondrous colour. I drifted down to it, and the sculptured shapes of the coral were softened and blurred with sea growth and restless with the sparkling jewels of myriad tropical fish. There were deep gullies and standing towers of coral, fields of eel grass between, and open stretches of blinding white coral sand.

My marks had been remarkably accurate, considering the fact that I had been only just conscious from blood loss. I had dropped the anchor almost directly on top of the canvas package. It lay on one of the open spaces of coral sand, looking like some horrible sea monster, green and squat with the loose ropes floating about it like tentacles.

I crouched beside it, and shoals of tiny fish, zebra-striped in gold and black, gathered around me in such numbers that I had to blow bubbles at them and shoo them off, before I could get on with the job.

I unclipped the nylon rope from my belt, and lashed one end securely to the package with a series of half-hitches. Then I rose to the surface slowly paying out the line. I surfaced thirty feet astern of *Dancer*, swam to the ladder, and clambered into the cockpit. I made the end of the line fast to the arm of the fighting chair.

'What did you find?' Sherry demanded anxiously.

'I don't know yet,' I told her. I had resisted the temptation to open the package on the bottom. I hoped it might be worth the sacrifice to watch her expression as I opened the canvas.

I stripped my diving gear and washed it off with fresh water before stowing it all carefully away. I wanted the tension to eat into her a little longer.

'Damn you, Harry. Let's get it up,' she burst out at last.

I remembered the package as being as heavy as all creation, but then my strength had been almost gone. Now I braced myself against the gunwale and began recovering line. It was heavy, but not impossibly so, and I coiled the wet line as it came in with the old tunny fisherman's wrist action.

The green canvas broke the surface alongside, sodden and gushing water. I reached over and got a purchase on the knotted rope, with a single heave I lifted it over the side and it clunked weightily on to the deck of the cockpit—metal against wood.

'Open it,' ordered Sherry impatiently.

'Right away, madam,' I said, and drew the bait-knife from the sheath on my belt. It was razor sharp, and I cut the ropes with a single stroke for each.

Sherry was leaning forward eagerly as I drew the stiff wet folds of canvas aside, and I was watching her face.

The greedy, anticipatory expression flared suddenly into triumph as she recognized the object. She recognized it before I did, and then instantly she dropped a curtain of uncertainty over her eyes and face.

It was nicely done, she was an actress of skill. Had I not been watching carefully for it, I would have missed the quick play of emotion.

I looked down at the humble object for which already so many men had been killed or mutilated, and I was torn with surprise and puzzlement—and disappointment. It was not what I had expected.

Half of it was badly eaten away as though by a sand-blasting machine, the bronze was raw and shiny and deeply etched. The upper half of it was intact, but tarnished heavily with a thick skin of greenish verdigris, but the lug for the shackle was intact and the ornamentation was still clear through the corrosion—a heraldic crest—or part of it—and lettering in a flowery antique style. The lettering was fragmentary, most of it had been etched away in an irregular flowing line, leaving the bright worn metal.

It was a ship's bell, cast in massive bronze, it must have weighed close to a hundred pounds, with a domed and lugged top and a wide flared mouth.

Curiously I rolled it over. The clapper had corroded solidly, and barnacle and other shellfish had encrusted the interior. I was intrigued by the pattern of wear and corrosion on the outside, until suddenly the solution occurred to me. I had seen other metal objects marked like this after long submersion. The bell had been half buried on the sandy bottom, the exposed portion had been subjected to the tidal rush of Gunfire Break, and the fine grains of coral sand had abrased away a quarter of an inch of the outer skin of the metal.

However, the portion that had been buried was protected, and now I examined the remaining lettering more closely.

'VVN L'

There was an extended 'V' or a broken 'W' followed immediately by a perfect 'N'—then a gap and a whole 'L'; beyond that the lettering had been obliterated again.

The coat of arms worked into the metal on the opposite side of the barrel was an intricate design with two rampant beasts—probably lions—supporting a shield and a mailed head. It seemed vaguely familiar, and I wondered where I had seen it before.

I rocked back on my heels and looked at Sherry North. She was unable to meet my gaze.

'Funny thing,' I mused. 'A jet aircraft with a bloody great brass bell hanging on its nose.'

'I don't understand it,' she said.

'No more do I.' I stood up and went to get a cheroot from the saloon. I lit it and sat back in the fighting chair.

'Okay. Let's hear your theory.'

'I don't know, Harry. Truly I don't.'

'Let's try some guesses,' I suggested. 'I'll begin.'

She turned away to the rail.

'The jet aircraft turned into a pumpkin,' I hazarded. 'How about that one?'

She turned back to me. 'Harry, I don't feel well. I think I'm going to be sick.'

'So, what must I do?'

'Let's go back now.'

'I was thinking of another dive—look around a bit more.'

'No,' she said quickly. 'Please, not now. I don't feel up to it. Let's go. We can come back if we have to.'

I studied her face for evidence of her sickness: she looked like an ad for health food.

'All right,' I agreed; there was not really much point in another dive, but only I knew that. 'Let's go home and try and work it out.'

I stood up and began rewrapping the brass bell.

'What are you going to do with that?' she asked anxiously.

'Redeposit it,' I told her. 'I am certainly not going to take it back to St Mary's and display it in the market place. Like you said, we can always come back.'

'Yes,' she agreed immediately. 'You are right, of course.'

I dropped the package over the side once more and went to haul the hook.

On the homeward run I found Sherry North's presence on the bridge irritated me. There was a lot of hard thinking I had to do. I sent her down to make coffee.

'Strong,' I told her, 'and with four spoons of sugar. It will be good for your seasickness.'

She reappeared on the bridge within two minutes.

'The stove won't light,' she complained.

'You have to open the main gas cylinders first.' I explained where to find the taps. 'And don't forget to close them when you finish, or you'll turn the boat into a bomb.'

She made lousy coffee.

* * *

It was late evening when I picked up moorings in Grand Harbour, and dark by the time I dropped Sherry at the entrance of the hotel. She didn't even invite me in for a drink, but kissed me on the cheek and said, 'Darling, let me be alone tonight. I am exhausted. I am going to bed now. Let me think about all this, and when I feel better we can plan more clearly.'

'I'll pick you up here—what time?'

'No,' she said. 'I'll meet you at the boat. Early. Eight o'clock. Wait for me there—we can talk in private. Just the two of us, no one else—all right?'

'I'll bring *Dancer* to the wharf at eight,' I promised her.

It had been a thirsty day, and on the way home I stopped off at the Lord Nelson.

Angelo and Judith were with a noisy party of their own age in one of the booths. They called me over and made room for me between two of the girls.

I brought them each a pint, and Angelo leaned over confidentially. 'Hey, skipper, are you using the pick-up tonight?'

'Yes,' I said. 'To get me home.' I knew what was coming, of course. Angelo acted as though he had shares in the vehicle.

'There's a big party down at South Point tonight, boss,' suddenly he was very free with the 'boss' and 'skipper,' 'I thought if I run you out to Turtle Bay, then you'd let us have the truck. I'd pick you up early tomorrow, promise.'

I took a swallow at my tankard and they were all watching me with eager hopeful faces.

'It's a big party, Mister Harry,' said Judith. 'Please.'

'You pick me up seven o'clock sharp, Angelo, hear?' and there was a spontaneous burst of relieved laughter. They all chipped in to buy me another pint.

* * *

I had a disturbed night, with restless sleep interspersed with periods of wakefulness. I had the dream again, when I dived to the canvas package. Once more it contained a tiny Dresden mermaid, but this time she had Sherry North's face and she offered me the model of a jet fighter aircraft that changed into a golden pumpkin as I reached for it. The pumpkin was etched with the letters:

'VVN L'

It rained after midnight, solid sheets of water, that poured off the eaves, and the lightning silhouetted the palm fronds against the night sky.

It was still raining when I went down to the beach, and the heavy drops exploded in minute bomb bursts of spray upon my naked body. The sea was black in the bad light, and the rain squalls reached to the horizon. I swam alone, far out beyond the reef, but when I came back to the beach the excursion had not provided the usual lift to my spirits. My body was blue and shivering with the cold, and a vague but pervading sense of trouble and depression pressed heavily upon me.

I had finished breakfast when the pick-up came down the track through the palm plantation, splashing through the puddles, splattered with mud and with headlights still burning.

In the yard Angelo hooted and shouted, 'You ready, Harry?' and I ran out with a sou'-wester held over my head.

Angelo smelled of beer and he was garrulous and slightly bleary of eye.

'I'll drive,' I told him, and as we crossed the island he gave me a blow-by-blow description of the great party—from what he told me it seemed there might be an epidemic of births on St Mary's in nine months' time.

I was only half listening to him, for as we approached the town so my sense of disquiet mounted.

'Hey, Harry, the kids said to thank you for the loan of the pick-up.'

'That's okay, Angelo.'

'I sent Judith out to the boat—she's going to tidy up, Harry, and get the coffee going for you.'

'She shouldn't have worried,' I said.

'She wanted to do that specially—sort of thank you, you know.'

'She's a good girl.'

'Sure is, Harry. I love that girl,' and Angelo burst into song, 'Devil Woman' in the style of Mick Jagger.

When we crossed the ridge and started down into the valley I had a sudden impulse. Instead of continuing straight down Frobisher Street to the harbour, I swung left on to the circular drive above the fort and hospital and went up the avenue of banyan trees to the Hilton Hotel. I parked the pick-up under the canopy and went through to the reception lobby.

There was nobody behind the desk this early in the morning, but I leaned across the counter and peered into Marion's cubicle. She was at her switchboard and when she saw me her face lit up in a wide grin and she lifted off her earphones.

'Hello, Mister Harry.'

'Hello, Marion, love,' I returned the grin. 'Is Miss North in her room?'

Her expression changed. 'Oh no,' she said, 'she left over an hour ago.'

'Left?' I stared at her.

'Yes. She went out to the airport with the hotel bus. She was catching the seven-thirty plane.' Marion glanced at the cheap Japanese watch on her wrist. 'They would have taken off ten minutes ago.'

I was taken completely off-balance, of all things I had least expected this. It didn't make sense for many seconds—and then suddenly and sickeningly it did.

'Oh Jesus Christ,' I said. 'Judith!' and I ran for the pick-up. Angelo saw my face as I came and he sat up straight in the seat and stopped singing.

I jumped into the driver's seat and started the engine, thrusting the pedal down hard and swinging in a roaring two-wheeled turn.

'What is it, Harry?' Angelo demanded.

'Judith?' I asked grimly. 'You sent her down to the boat, when?'

'When I left to fetch you.'

'Did she go right away?'

'No, she'd have to bathe and dress first.' He was telling it straight, not hiding the fact they had slept together. He sensed the urgency of the situation. 'Then she'd have to walk down the valley from the farm.' Angelo had lodgings with a peasant family up near the spring, it was a three-mile walk.

'God, let us be in time,' I whispered. The truck was bellowing down the avenue, and I hit the gears in a racing change as we went out through the gates in a screaming broadside, and I slammed down hard again on the accelerator, pulling her out of the skid by main strength.

'What the hell is it, Harry?' he demanded once again.

'We've got to stop her going aboard *Dancer*,' I told him grimly as we roared down the circular drive above the town. Past the fort a vista of Grand Harbour opened beneath us. He did not waste time with inane questions. We had worked together too long for that and if I said so then he accepted it as so.

Dancer was still at her moorings amongst the other island craft, and halfway out to her from the wharf Judith was rowing the dinghy. Even at this distance I could make out the tiny feminine figure on the thwart, and recognize the short businesslike oarstrokes. She was an island girl, and rowed like a man.

'We aren't going to make it,' said Angelo. 'She'll get there before we reach Admiralty.'

At the top of Frobisher Street I put the heel of my left hand on the horn ring, and blowing a continuous blast I tried to clear the road. But it was a Saturday morning, market day, and already the streets were filling. The country folk had come to town in their bullocks, carts and ancient jalopies. Cursing with a terrible frustration, I hooted and forced my way through them.

It took us three minutes to cover the half mile from the top of the street down to Admiralty Wharf.

'Oh God,' I said, leaning forward in the seat as I shot through the mesh gates, and crossed the railway tracks.

The dinghy was tied up alongside *Wave Dancer,* and Judith was climbing over the side. She wore an emerald green shirt and short denim pants. Her hair was in a long braid down her back.

I skidded the truck to a halt beside the pineapple sheds, and both Angelo and I hit the wharf at a run.

'Judith!' I yelled, but my voice did not carry out across the harbour.

Without looking back, Judith disappeared into the saloon. Angelo and I raced down to the end of the jetty. Both of us were screaming wildly, but the wind was in our faces and *Dancer* was five hundred yards out across the water.

'There's a dinghy!' Angelo caught my arm. It was an ancient clinker-built mackerel boat, but it was chained to a ring in the stone wharf.

We jumped into it, leaping the eight foot drop and falling in a heap together over the thwart. I scrambled to the mooring chain. It had quarter-inch galvanized steel links, and a heavy brass padlock secured it to the ring.

I took two twists of chain around my wrist, braced one foot against the wharf and heaved. The padlock exploded, and I fell backwards into the bottom of the dinghy.

Angelo already had the oars in the rowlocks.

'Row,' I shouted at him. 'Row like a mad bastard.'

I was in the bows cupping my hands to my mouth as I hailed Judith, trying to make my voice carry above the wind.

Angelo was rowing in a dedicated frenzy, swinging the oar blades flat and low on the back reach and then throwing his weight upon them when they bit. His breathing exploded in a harsh grunt at each stroke.

Halfway out to *Dancer* another rain squall enveloped us, shrouding the whole of Grand Harbour in eddying sheets of grey water. It stung my face, so I had to screw up my eyes.

Dancer's outline was blurred by grey rain, but we were coming

111

close now. I was beginning to hope that Judith would sweep and tidy the cabins before she struck a match to the gas ring in the galley. I was also beginning to hope that I was wrong—that Sherry North had not left a farewell present for me.

Yet still I could hear my own voice speaking to Sherry North the previous day. 'You have to open the main gas cylinders first—and don't forget to close them when you finish, or you'll turn the boat into a bomb.'

Closer still we came to *Dancer* and she seemed to hang on tendrils of rain, ghostly white and insubstantial in the swirling mist.

'Judith,' I shouted, she must hear me now—we were that close. There were two fifty-pound cylinders of Butane gas on board, enough to destroy a large brickbuilt house. The gas was heavier than air, once it escaped it would slump down, filling *Dancer*'s hull with a murderously explosive mixture of gas and air. It needed just one spark from battery or match.

I prayed that I was wrong and yelled again. Then suddenly *Dancer* blew.

It was flash explosion, a fearsome blue light that shot through her. It split her hull with a mighty hammer stroke, and blew her superstructure open, lifting it like a lid.

Dancer reared to the mortal blow, and the blast hit us like a storm wind. Immediately I smelled the electric stench of the blast, acrid as an air-sizzling strike of lightning against ironstone.

Dancer died as I watched, a terrible violent death, and then her torn and lifeless hull fell back and the cold grey waters rushed into her. The heavy engines pulled her swiftly down, and she was gone into the grey waters of Grand Harbour.

Angelo and I were frozen with horror, crouching in the violently rocking dinghy, staring at the agitated water that was strewn with loose wreckage—all that remained of a beautiful boat and a lovely young girl. I felt a vast desolation descend upon me, I wanted to cry aloud in my anguish, but I was paralysed.

Angelo moved first. He leapt upright with a sound in his throat like a wounded beast. He tried to throw himself over the side, but I caught and held him.

'Leave me,' he screamed. 'I must go to her.'

'No.' I fought with him in the crazily rocking dinghy. 'It's no good, Angelo.'

Even if he could get down through the forty feet of water in which *Dancer*'s torn hull now lay, what he would find might drive him mad. Judith had stood at the centre of that blast, and she would have been subjected to all the terrible trauma of massive flash explosion at close range.

'Leave me, damn you.' Angelo got one arm free and hit me in the face, but I saw it coming and rolled my head. It grazed the skin from my cheek, and I knew I had to get him quieted down.

The dinghy was on the point of capsizing. Though he was forty pounds lighter than me, Angelo fought with maniac strength. He was calling her name now.

'Judith, Judith,' on an hysterical rising inflection. I released my grip on his shoulder with my right hand, and swung him slightly away from me, lining him up carefully. I hit him with a right chop, my fist moving not more than four inches. I hit him cleanly on the point below his left ear, and he dropped instantly, gone cold. I lowered him to the floorboards and laid him out comfortably. I rowed back to the wharf without looking back. I felt completely numbed and drained.

I carried Angelo down the wharf and I hardly felt his weight in my arms. I drove him up to the hospital and MacNab was on duty.

'Give him something to keep him muzzy and in bed for the next twenty-four hours,' I told MacNab, and he began to argue.

'Listen, you broken-down old whisky vat,' I told him quietly, 'I'd love an excuse to beat your head in.'

He paled until the broken veins in his nose and cheeks stood out boldly.

'Now listen—Harry old man,' he began. I took a step towards him, and he sent the duty sister to the drug cupboard.

I found Chubby at breakfast and it took only a minute to explain what had happened. We went up to the fort in the pick-up, and Wally Andrews responded quickly. He waived the filing of statements and other police procedure and instead we piled the police diving equipment into the truck and by the time we reached the harbour, half of St Mary's had formed a silent worried crowd along the wharf. Some had seen it and all of them had heard the explosion.

An occasional voice called condolences to me as we carried the diving equipment to the mackerel boat.

'Somebody find Fred Coker,' I told them. 'Tell him to get down here with a bag and basket,' and there was a buzz of comment.

'Hey, Mister Harry, was there somebody aboard?'

'Just get Fred Coker,' I told them, and we rowed out to *Dancer's* moorings.

While Wally kept the dinghy on station above us, Chubby and I went down through the murky harbour water.

Dancer lay on her back in forty-five feet, she must have rolled as she sank—but there was no need to worry about access to her interior, for her hull had been torn open along the keel. She was far past any hope of refloating.

Chubby waited at the hole in the hull while I went in.

What remained of the galley was filled with swirling excited shoals of fish. They were in a feeding frenzy and I choked and gagged into the mouthpiece of my scuba when I saw what they were feeding upon.

The only way I knew it was Judith was the tatters of green cloth clinging to the fragments of flesh. We got her out in three main pieces, and placed her in the canvas bag that Fred Coker provided.

I dived again immediately, and worked my way through the shattered hull to the compartment below the galley where the two long iron gas cylinders were still bolted to their beds. Both taps were wide open, and somebody had disconnected the hoses to allow the gas to escape freely.

I have never experienced anger so intense as I felt then. It was that strong for it fed upon my loss. *Dancer* was gone—and *Dancer* had been half my life. I closed the taps and reconnected the gas hose. It was a private thing—I would deal with it personally.

When I walked back along the wharf to the pick-up, all that gave me comfort was the knowledge that *Dancer* had been insured. There would be another boat—not as beautiful or as well beloved as *Dancer*—but a boat nevertheless.

In the crowd I noticed the shiny black face of Hambone Williams —the harbour ferryman. For forty years he had plied his old dinghy back and forth at threepence a hire.

'Hambone,' I called him over. 'Did you take anybody out to *Dancer* last night?'

'No, sir, Mister Harry.'

'Nobody at all?'

'Only your party. She left her watch in the cabin. I took her out to fetch it.'

'The lady?'

'Yes, the lady with the yellow hair.'

'What time, Hambone?'

'About nine o'clock—did I do wrong, Mister Harry?'

'No, it's all right. Just forget it.'

We buried Judith next day before noon. I managed to get the plot beside her mother and father for her. Angelo liked that. He said he did not want her to be lonely up there on the hill. Angelo was still half doped, and he was quiet and dreamy eyed at the graveside.

The next morning the three of us began salvage work on *Dancer*. We worked hard for ten days and we stripped her completely of anything that had a possible value—from the big-game fishing reels and the FN carbine to the twin bronze propellers. The hull and superstructure were so badly broken up as to be of no value.

At the end of that time *Wave Dancer* had become a memory only. I have had many women, and now they are just a pleasant thought when I hear a certain song or smell a particular perfume. Like them, already *Dancer* was beginning to recede into the past.

❊   ❊   ❊

On the tenth day I went up to see Fred Coker—and the moment I entered his office I knew there was something very wrong. He was shiny with nervous sweat, his eyes moved shiftily behind the glittering spectacles and his hands scampered about like frightened mice— running over his blotter or leaping up to adjust the knot of his necktie or smooth down the thin strands of hair on his polished cranium. He knew I'd come to talk insurance.

'Now don't get excited please, Mister Harry,' he advised me. Whenever people tell me that, I become very excited indeed.

'What is it, Coker? Come on! Come on!' I slammed one fist on the desk top, and he leapt in his chair so the gold-rimmed spectacles slid down his nose.

'Mister Harry, please—'

'Come on! You miserable little grave worm—'

'Mister Harry—it's about the premiums on *Dancer*.' I stared at him.

'You see—you had never made a claim before—it seemed such a waste to—'

I found words. 'You pocketed the premiums,' I whispered, my voice failing me suddenly. 'You didn't pay them over to the company.'

'You understand,' Fred Coker nodded. 'I knew you'd understand.'

I tried to go over the desk to save time, but I tripped and fell. Fred Coker leapt from his chair, slipping through my outstretched groping fingers. He ran through the back door, slamming it behind him.

I ran straight through the door, tearing off the lock, and leaving it hanging on broken hinges.

Fred Coker ran as though all the dark angels pursued him, which would have been better for him. I caught him at the big doors into the alley and lifted him by the throat, holding him with one hand, pressing his back against a pile of cheap pine coffins.

He had lost his spectacles, and he was weeping with fright, big slow tears welling out of the helpless short-sighted eyes.

'You know I'm going to kill you,' I whispered, and he moaned, his feet dancing six inches above the floor.

I pulled back my right fist and braced myself solidly on the balls of my feet. It would have taken his head off. I couldn't do it—but I had to hit something. I drove my fist into the coffin beside his right ear. The panelling shattered, stove in along its full length. Fred Coker shrieked like an hysterical girl at a rock concert, and I let him drop. His legs could not hold him and he sank to the concrete floor.

I left him lying there moaning and blubbering with terror—and I walked out into the street as near to bankrupt as I'd been in the last ten years.

Mister Harry transformed in a single stroke into Fletcher, wharf rat and land-bound bum. It was a classic case of reversion to type— before I reached the Lord Nelson I was thinking the same way I had ten years before. Already I was calculating the percentages, seeking the main chance once more.

Chubby and Angelo were the only customers in the public bar so early in the afternoon. I told them, and they were quiet. There wasn't anything to say.

We drank the first one in silence, then I asked Chubby, 'What will you do now?' and he shrugged.

'I've still got the old whaleboat—' It was a twenty-footer, admiralty design, open-decked, but sea-kindly. 'I'll go for stump again, I reckon.' Stump were the big reef crayfish. There was good money in the frozen tails. It was how Chubby had earned his bread before *Dancer* and I came to St Mary's.

'You'll need new engines, those old Sea Gulls of yours are shot.'

We drank another pint, while I worked out my finances—what the hell, a couple of thousand dollars was not going to make much difference to me. 'I'll buy two new twenty horse Evinrudes for the boat, Chubby,' I volunteered.

'Won't let you do it, Harry.' He frowned indignantly and shook his head. 'I got enough saved up working for you,' and he was adamant.

'What about you, Angelo?' I asked.

'Guess I'll go sell my soul on a Rawano contract.'

'No,' Chubby scowled at the thought. 'I'll need crew for the stump-boat.'

They were all settled then. I was relieved, for I felt responsible for them both. I was particularly glad that Chubby would be there to care for Angelo. The boy had taken Judith's death very badly. He was quiet and withdrawn, no longer the flashing Romeo. I had kept him working hard on the salvage of *Dancer*, that alone seemed to have given him the time he needed to recover from the wound.

Nevertheless he began drinking hard now, chasing tots of cheap brandy with pints of bitter. This is the most destroying way to take in alcohol, short of drinking meths, that I know of.

Chubby and I took it nice and slow, lingering over our tankards, yet under our jocularity was a knowledge that we had reached a crossroads and from tomorrow we would no longer be travelling together. It gave the evening the fine poignancy of impending loss.

There was a South African trawler in harbour that night that had come in for bunkers and repairs. When at last Angelo passed out cold, Chubby and I began our singing. Six of the trawler's beefy crew members voiced their disapproval in the most slanderous terms. Chubby and I could not allow insults of that nature to pass unchallenged. We all went out to discuss it in the backyard.

It was a glorious discussion, and when Wally Andrews arrived with the riot squad he arrested all of us, even those who had fallen in the fray.

'My own flesh and blood—' Chubby kept repeating as he and I staggered arm and arm into the cells. 'He turned on me. My own sister's son—'

Wally was human enough to send one of his constables down to the Lord Nelson for something to make our durance less vile. Chubby and I became very friendly with the trawler-men in the next cell, passing the bottle back and forth between the bars.

When we were released next morning, Wally Andrews declining to press charges, I drove out to Turtle Bay to begin closing up the shack. I made sure the crockery was clean, threw a few handfuls of mothballs in the cupboards and did not bother to lock the doors. There is no such thing as burglary on St Mary's.

For the last time I swam out beyond the reef, and for half an hour hoped that the dolphins might come. They did not and I swam back, showered and changed, picked up my old canvas and leather campaign bag from the bed and went out to where the pick-up was parked in the yard. I didn't look back as I drove up through the palm plantation, but I made myself a promise that I'd be coming this way again.

I parked in the front lot of the hotel and lit a cheroot. When Marion finished her shift at noon she came out the front entrance and set off down the drive with her cheeky little bottom swinging under the mini-skirt.

I whistled and she saw me. She slipped into the passenger's seat beside me.

'Mister Harry, I'm so sorry about your boat—' We talked for a few minutes until I could ask the question.

'Miss North, while she was staying at the hotel, did she make any phone calls or send a cable?'

'I don't remember, Mister Harry, but I could check for you.'

'Now?'

'Sure,' she agreed.

'One other thing, could you also check with Dicky if he got a shot of her?' Dicky was the roving hotel photographer, it was a good chance that he had a print of Sherry North in his file.

Marion was gone for nearly three-quarters of an hour, but she returned with a triumphant smile.

'She sent a cable on the night before she left.' Marion handed me a flimsy copy. 'You can keep this copy,' she told me as I read the message.

It was addressed to: 'MANSON FLAT 5 CURZON STREET 97 LONDON W.1.' and the message read: 'CONTRACT SIGNED RETURNING HEATHROW BOAC FLIGHT 316 SATURDAY.' There was no signature.

'Dicky had to go through all his files—but he found one.' She handed me a six-by-four glossy print. It was of Sherry North reclining on a sun couch on the hotel terrace. She wore her bikini and sunglasses, but it was a good likeness.

'Thanks, Marion.' I gave her a five-pound note.

'Gee, Mister Harry,' she grinned at me as she tucked it into the front of her bra. 'For that price you can take what you fancy.'

'I've got a plane to catch, love.' I kissed her on the little snub nose, and slapped her bottom as she climbed out of the cab.

Chubby and Angelo came out to the airport. Chubby was to take care of the pick-up for me. We were all subdued, and shook hands awkwardly at the departure gate. There wasn't much to say, we had said it all the night before.

As the piston-engined aircraft took off for the mainland, I glimpsed the two of them standing together at the perimeter fence.

I stopped over three hours at Nairobi before catching the BOAC flight on to London. I did not sleep during the long night flight. It was many years since I had returned to my native land—and I was coming back now on a grim mission of vengeance. I wanted very much to talk to Sherry North.

*　　*　　*

When you are flat broke, that is the time to buy a new car and a hundred-guinea suit. Look brave and prosperous, and people will believe you are.

I shaved and changed at the airport and instead of a Hillman I hired a Chrysler from the Hertz Depot at Heathrow, slung my bag in the trunk and drove to the nearest Courage pub.

I had a double portion of ham and egg pie, washed down with a pint of Courage while I studied the road map. It was all so long ago that I was unsure of my directions.

The lush and cultivated English countryside was too tame and green after Malaya and Africa, and the autumn sunshine was pale gold when I was used to a brighter fiercer sun—but it was a pleasant drive over the downs and into Brighton.

I parked the Chrysler on the promenade opposite the Grand Hotel and dived into the warren of The Lanes. They were filled with tourists even this late in the season.

Pavilion Arcade was the address I had read so long ago on Jimmy North's underwater sledge, and it took me nearly an hour to find it.

It was tucked away at the back of a cobbled yard, and most of the windows and doors were shuttered and closed.

'North's Underwater World' had a ten-foot frontage on to the lane. It was also closed, and a blind was drawn across the single window. I tried without success to peer round the edge of the blind, but the interior was darkened, so I hammered on the door. There was no sound from within, and I was about to turn away when I noticed a square piece of cardboard that had once been stuck on to the bottom of the window but had fallen to the floor inside. By twisting my head acrobatically, I could read the handwritten message which had fortunately fallen face up: Enquiries to Seaview, Downers Lane, Falmer, Sussex. I went back to the car and took the road map out of the glove compartment.

✳   ✳   ✳

It began to rain as I pushed the Chrysler through narrow lanes. The windscreen wipers flogged sullenly at the spattering drops and I peered into the premature gloom of early evening.

Twice I lost my way but finally I pulled up outside a gate in a thick hedge. The sign nailed to the gate read: NORTH SEAVIEW, and I believed that it might be possible to look southwards on a clear day and see the Atlantic.

I drove down between hedges, and came into the paved yard of an old double-storied red-brick farmhouse, with oak beams set into the walls and green moss growing on the wood-shingle roof. There was a light burning downstairs.

I parked the Chrysler and crossed the yard to the kitchen door, turning up my collar against the wind and rain. I beat on the door, and heard somebody moving around inside. The bolts were shot back and the top half of the stable door opened on a chain. A girl looked out at me.

I was not immediately impressed by her for she wore a baggy blue fisherman's jersey and she was a tall girl with a swimmer's shoulders. I thought her plain—in a striking manner.

Her brow was pale and broad, her nose was large but not bony or beaked, and below it her mouth was wide and friendly. She wore no make-up at all, so her lips were pale pink and there was a peppering of fine freckles on her nose and cheeks.

Her hair was drawn back severely from her face into a thick braid behind her neck. Her hair was black, shimmering iridescent black in the lamplight, and her eyebrows were black also, black and boldly arched over eyes that seemed also to be black until the light caught them and I realized they were the same dark haunted blue as the Mozambique current when the noon sun strikes directly into it.

Despite the pallor of her skin, there was an aura of good and glowing health about her. The pale skin had a lustre and plasticity to it, a quality that was somehow luminous so that when you studied her closely—as I was now doing—it seemed that you could see down through the surface to the flush of clean blood rising warmly to her cheeks and neck. She touched the tendril of silky dark hair that escaped the braid and floated lightly on her temple. It was an appealing gesture, that betrayed her nervousness and belied the serene expression in the dark blue eyes.

Suddenly I realized that she was an unusually handsome woman, for, although she was only in her mid-twenties, I knew she was no longer girl—but full woman. There was a strength and maturity about her, a deep sense of calm that I found intriguing.

Usually the women I choose are more obvious, I do not like to tie up too much of my energy in the pursuit. This was something beyond my experience and for the first time in years I felt unsure of myself.

We had been staring at each other for many seconds, neither of us speaking or moving.

'You're Harry Fletcher,' she said at last, and her voice was low and gently modulated, a cultivated and educated voice. I gaped at her.

'How the hell did you know that?' I demanded.

'Come in.' She slipped the chain and opened the bottom of the stable door, and I obeyed. The kitchen was warm and welcoming and filled with the smell of good food cooking.

'How did you know my name?' I asked again.

'Your picture was in the newspaper—with Jimmy's,' she explained. We were silent again, once more studying each other.

She was taller even than I had thought at first, reaching to my shoulder, with long legs clad in dark blue pants and the tops thrust into black leather boots. Now I could see the narrow waist and the promise of good breasts beneath the thick jersey.

At first I had thought her plain, ten seconds later I had reckoned her handsome, now I doubted I had ever seen a more beautiful woman. It took time for the full effect to sink in.

'You have me at a disadvantage,' I said at last. 'I don't know your name.'

'I'm Sherry North,' she answered, and I stared at her for a moment before I recovered from the shock. She was a very different person from the other Sherry North I had known.

'Did you know that there is a whole tribe of you?' I asked at last.

'I don't understand.' She frowned at me. Her eyes were enchantingly blue under the lowered brows.

'It's a long story.'

'I'm sorry.' For the first time she seemed to become aware that we were standing facing each other in the centre of the kitchen. 'Won't you sit down. Can I get you a beer?'

Sherry took a couple of cans of Carlsberg lager from the cupboard and sat opposite me across the kitchen table.

'You were going to tell me a long story.' She popped the tabs on the cans, and slid one across to me, then looked at me expectantly.

I began to tell her the carefully edited version of my experiences since Jimmy North arrived at St Mary's. She was very easy to talk to, like being with an old and interested friend. Suddenly I wanted to tell her everything, the entire unblemished truth. It was important that from the very beginning it should be right, with no reservations.

She was a complete stranger, and yet I was placing trust in her beyond any person I had ever known. I told her everything exactly as it had happened.

She fed me after dark had fallen, a savoury casserole out of an earthenware pot which we ate with homemade bread and farm butter. I was still talking but no longer about the recent events on St Mary's, and she listened quietly. At last I had found another human being with whom I could talk without reserve.

I went back in my life, in a complete catharsis I told her of the early days, even of the dubious manner in which I had earned the money to buy *Wave Dancer,* and how my good resolutions since then had wavered.

It was after midnight when at last she said: 'I can hardly believe all you've told me. You don't look like that—you look so,' she seemed to search for the word, 'wholesome.' But you could see it was not the word she wanted.

'I work hard at being that. But sometimes my halo falls over my eyes. You see, appearances are deceptive,' I said, and she nodded.

'Yes, they are,' and there was a significance in the way she said it, a warning perhaps. 'Why have you told me all this? It is not really very wise, you know.'

'It was just time that somebody knew about me, I suppose. Sorry, you were elected.'

She smiled. 'You can sleep in Jimmy's room tonight,' she said. 'I can't risk you rushing out and telling anybody else.'

I hadn't slept the night before and suddenly I was exhausted. I felt as though I did not have the strength to climb the stairs to the bedroom—but I had one question still to ask.

'Why did Jimmy come to St Mary's? What was he looking for?' I asked. 'Do you know who he was working with, who they were?'

'I don't know.' She shook her head, and I knew it was the truth. She wouldn't lie to me now, not after I had placed such trust in her.

'Will you help me find out? Will you help me find them?'

'Yes, I'll help you,' she said, and stood up from the table. 'We'll talk again in the morning.'

Jimmy's room was under the eaves, the pitch of the roof giving it an irregular shape. The walls were lined with photographs and packed bookshelves, silver sporting trophies and the treasured *bric-à-brac* of boyhood.

The bed was high and the mattress soft.

I went to fetch my bag from the Chrysler while Sherry put clean sheets upon the bed. Then she showed me the bathroom and left me.

I lay and listened to the rain on the roof for only a few minutes before I slept. I woke in the night and heard the soft whisper of her voice somewhere in the quiet house.

Barefooted and in my underpants I opened the bedroom door and crept silently down the passage to the stairs. I looked down into the hall. There was a light burning and Sherry North stood at the wall-hung telephone. She was speaking so quietly into the receiver, cupping her hands to her mouth, that I could not catch the words. The light was behind her. She wore a flimsy nightdress, and her body showed through the thin stuff as though she was naked.

I found myself staring like a peeping Tom. The lamplight glowed on the ivory sheen of her skin, and there were intriguing secret hollows and shadows beneath the transparent cloth.

With an effort I pulled my eyes off her and went back to my bed. I thought about Sherry's telephone call and felt a vague disquiet, but soon sleep overtook me once more.

*   *   *

In the morning the rain had stopped but the ground was slushy and the grass heavy and wet when I went out for a breath of cold morning air.

I expected to feel awkward with Sherry after the previous night's outpourings of the soul, but it was not so. We talked easily at breakfast, and afterwards she said, 'I promised I'd help you; what can I do?'

'Answer a few questions.'

'All right, ask me.'

Jimmy North had been very secretive, she did not know he was going to St Mary's. He had told her he had a contract to install some electronic underwater equipment at the Cabora-Bassa Dam in Portuguese Mozambique. She had taken him up to the airport with all his equipment. As far as she knew he was travelling alone. The police had come to the shop in Brighton to tell her of his murder. She had read the newspaper reports, and that was all.

'No letters from Jimmy?'

'No, nothing.' I nodded, the wolf pack must have intercepted his mail. The letter I had been shown by Sherry's impostor was certainly genuine.

'I don't understand anything about this. Am I being stupid?'

'No.' I took out a cheroot, and almost lit it before I stopped myself. 'Okay if I smoke one of these?'

'It doesn't bother me,' she said, and I was glad, for it would have been hell giving them up. I lit it and drew in the fragrant smoke.

'It looks as though Jimmy stumbled on something big. He needed backing and he went to the wrong people. As soon as they thought they knew where it was, they killed him and tried to kill me. When that didn't work they sent out someone impersonating you. When she thought she knew the location of this object, she set a trap for me and went home. Their next move will be a return to the area off Big Gull Island, where they are due for another disappointment.'

She refilled the coffee cups, and I noticed that she had applied make-up this morning—but so lightly that the freckles still showed. I reconsidered the previous night's judgement—and confirmed that she was one of the most beautiful women I had ever met, even in the early morning.

She was frowning thoughtfully, staring into her coffee cup and I wanted to touch one of her slim strong-looking hands that lay on the tablecloth near my own.

'What were they after, Harry? And who are these people who killed him?' she asked at last.

'Two excellent questions. I have leads to both—but we will tackle the questions in the order you asked them. Firstly, what was Jimmy after? When we know that we can go after his murderers.'

'I have no idea at all what it could be.' She looked up at me. The blue of her eyes was lighter than it had been last night, it was the colour of a good sapphire. 'What clues have you?'

'The ship's bell. The design upon it.'

'What does it signify?'

'I don't know, but it shouldn't be too hard to find out.' I could no longer resist the temptation. I placed my hand over hers. It felt as firm and strong as it looked and her flesh was warm. 'But first I should like to check the shop in Brighton and Jimmy's room here. There might be something we can use.'

She had not withdrawn her hand. 'All right, shall we go to the shop first? The police have already been through it all, but they might have overlooked something.'

'Fine. I'll buy you lunch.' I squeezed her hand, and she turned it in my grasp and squeezed back.

'I'll take you up on that,' she said, and I was too astonished by my own reaction to her grip to find a light reply. My throat was dry and my pulse beat as though I'd run a mile. Gently she removed her hand and stood up.

'Let's do the breakfast dishes.'

If the girls of St Mary's could only have seen Mister Harry drying dishes, my reputation would have shattered into a thousand pieces.

She let us into the shop the back way, through a tiny enclosed yard which was almost filled with unusual objects, all of them associated with diving and the underwater world—discarded air bottles and a portable compressor, brass portholes and other salvage from wrecked ships, even the jawbone of a killer whale with all its teeth intact.

'I haven't been in for a long time,' Sherry apologized as she unlocked the back door of the shop. 'Without Jimmy—' she shrugged and then went on, '—I must really get down to selling up all this junk

125

and closing the shop down. I could re-sell the lease, I suppose.'

'I'm going to look round, okay?'

'Fine, I'll get the kettle going.'

I started in the yard, searching quickly but thoroughly through the piles of junk. There was nothing that had significance as far as I could see. I went into the shop and poked around among the seashells and sharks' teeth on the shelves and in the display case. Finally I saw a desk in the corner and began going through the drawers.

Sherry brought me a cup of tea and perched on the corner of the desk while I piled old invoices, rubber bands and paper clips on the top. I read every scrap of paper and even rifled through Jimmy's notebook of charges for equipment and services.

'Nothing?' Sherry asked.

'Nothing,' I agreed and glanced at my watch. 'Lunchtime,' I told her.

She locked up the shop and by good fortune we stumbled on English's restaurant. They gave us a secluded table in the back room and I ordered a bottle of Pouilly Fuissé to go with the lobster. Once I recovered from the shock of the price, we laughed a lot during the meal, and it wasn't just the wine. The feeling between us was good and growing stronger.

After lunch we drove back to Seaview and we went up to Jimmy's room.

'This is our best bet,' I guessed. 'If he was keeping secrets, this is where they would be.' But I knew I had a long job ahead of me. There were hundreds of books and piles of magazines—mostly *American Argosy, Trident, The Diver* and other diving publications. There was also a complete shelf of springback files at the foot of the bed.

'I'll leave you to it,' Sherry said, and went.

I took down the contents of a shelf, sat at the reading table and began to skim through the publications. Immediately I saw it was an even bigger task than I had thought. Jimmy had been one of those people who read with a pencil in one hand. There were notes pencilled in the margin, comments, queries and exclamation marks, and anything that interested him was underlined.

I read doggedly, looking for something that could remotely be linked to St Mary's.

Around eight o'clock I began on the shelf that held the springback files. The first two were filled with newspaper clippings on shipwrecks or other marine phenomena. The third of them had an unlabelled, black imitation leather cover. It held a thin sheath of papers, and I saw immediately that they were out of the ordinary.

They were a series of letters filed with their envelopes and stamps still attached. There were sixteen of them in all, addressed to Messrs Parker and Wilton in Fenchurch Street.

Every letter was in a different hand, but all were executed in the elegant penmanship of the last century.

The envelopes were sent from different parts of the old Empire—Canada, South Africa, India—and the nineteenth century postage stamps alone must have been of considerable value.

After I had read the first two letters, it was clear that Messrs Parker and Wilton were agents and factors, and they had acted for a number of distinguished clients in the service of Queen Victoria. The letters were instructions to deal with estates, moneys and securities.

All the letters were dated during the period from August 1857 to July 1858 and must have been offered by a dealer or an antique auctioneer as a lot.

I glanced through them quickly, but the contents were really very dull. However, something on the single page of the tenth letter caught my eye and I felt my nerves jump.

Two words had been underlined in pencil and in the margin was a notation in Jimmy North's handwriting.

'B. Mus. E.6914(8).'

However, it was the words themselves that held me.

'Dawn Light.'

I had heard those words before. I wasn't sure when, but they were significant.

Quickly I began at the top of the page. The sender's address was a laconic 'Bombay,' and it was dated 16th Sept. 1857.

My Dear Wilton,

I charge you most strictly with the proper care and safe storage of five pieces of luggage consigned in my name to your London address aboard the Hon. Company's ship *Dawn Light*. Due out of this port before the 25th instant and bound for the Company's wharf in the Port of London.

Please acknowledge safe receipt of same with all despatch.
I remain yours faithfully,
Colonel Sir Roger Goodchild.
Officer Commanding 101st Regiment
Queens Own India Rifles.
Delivery by kind favour of Captain commanding Her
Majesty's Frigate *Panther*.

The paper rustled and I realized that my hand was shaking with
excitement. I knew I was on to it now. This was the key. I laid the
letter carefully on the reading table and placed a silver paper knife
upon it to weight it down.

I began to read it again slowly, but there was a distraction. I
heard the engine noise of an automobile coming down the lane from
the gate. Headlights flashed across the window and then rounded
the corner of the house.

I sat up straight, listening. The engine noise died, and car doors
slammed shut.

There was a long silence then before I heard the murmur and
growl of voices—men's voices. I began to stand up from the table.

Then Sherry screamed. It rang clearly through the old house, and
cut into my brain like a lance. It aroused in me a protective instinct
so fierce that I was down the stairs and into the hall before I realized
I had moved.

The door to the kitchen was open and I paused in the doorway.
There were two men with Sherry. The heavier and elder of the two
wore a beige camelhair topcoat and a tweed cap. He had a greyish,
heavy lined face and deep-sunk eyes. His lips were thin and
colourless.

He had Sherry's left hand twisted up between her shoulder blades,
and was holding her jammed against the wall beside the gas stove.

The other man was younger, and he was slim and pale,
bareheaded with long straw-yellow hair falling to the shoulders of
his leather jacket. He was grinning gleefully as he held Sherry's
other hand over the blue flames of the gas ring, bringing it down
slowly.

She was struggling desperately, but they held her and her hair
had come loose as she fought.

'Slowly, lad,' the man in the cap spoke in a thick strangled voice.
'Give her time to think about it.'

Sherry screamed again as her fingers were forced down remorselessly towards the hissing blue flames.

'Go ahead, luv, shout your head off,' laughed the blond. 'There isn't anybody to hear you.'

'Only me,' I said, and they spun to face me, with expressions of comical amazement.

'Who—' asked the blond, releasing Sherry's arm and reaching quickly for his back pocket.

I hit him twice, left in the body and right in the head, and although neither shot pleased me particularly—there was not the right solidness at impact—the man went down, falling heavily over a chair and crashing into the cupboard. I had no more time for him, and I went for the one in the cloth cap.

He was still holding Sherry in front of him, and as I started forward he hurled her at me. It took me off-balance and I was forced to grab her, to save both of us from falling.

The man turned and darted out of the door behind him. It took me a few seconds to disentangle myself from Sherry and cross the kitchen. As I barged out into the yard he was halfway to an elderly Triumph sports car, and he glanced over his shoulder.

I could almost see him make the calculation. He wasn't going to be able to get into the car and turn it to face the lane before I caught him. He swerved to the left and sprinted into the dark mouth of the lane with the skirts of the camelhair coat billowing behind him. I raced after him.

The surface was greasy with wet clay, and he was making heavy going of it. He slid and almost fell, and I was right behind him, coming up swiftly when he turned and I heard the snap of the knife and saw the flash of the blade as it jumped out. He dropped into a crouch with the knife extended and I ran straight in without a check.

He didn't expect that, the glint of steel will stop most men dead. He went for my belly, a low underhand stroke, but he was shaky and breathless and it lacked fire. I blocked on the wrist and at the same time hit the pressure point in his forearm. The knife dropped out of his hand and I threw him over my hip. He fell heavily on his back, and although the mud softened the impact I dropped on one knee into his belly. It had two hundred and ten pounds of body weight behind it and it drove the air out of his lungs in a loud whoosh. He doubled up like a foetus in the womb, wheezing for breath, and I flipped him over on to his face. The cloth cap fell off his head and I found that he had a thick shock of dark hair shot through with strands of silver. I took a good handful of it, sat on his shoulders and pushed his face deep into the yellow mud.

'I don't like little boys who bully girls,' I told him conversationally, and behind me the engine of the Triumph roared into life. The headlights blazed out and then swung in a wide arc until they burned directly up the narrow lane.

I knew I hadn't taken the blond out properly, it had been a hurried botchy job. I left the man in the mud and ran back down the lane. The wheels of the Triumph spun on the paving of the barnyard and, with its headlights blazing dazzlingly into my eyes, it jumped forward, slewing and skidding as it left the paving and entered the muddy lane. The driver met the skid and came straight at me.

I fell flat and rolled into the cold ooze of a narrow open drain that carried run-off water through the tall hedge.

The Triumph hit the side a glancing blow and the hedge pushed it slightly off its line. The nearside wheels spun viciously on the edge of the stone coping of the drain inches from my face, and mud and a shower of twigs fell on me. Then it was past.

It checked as it came level with the man in the muddy camelhair coat. He was kneeling on the verge of the road and now he dragged himself into the passenger seat of the Triumph. Just as I crawled out of the drain and ran up behind the sports car it pulled away again, mud spraying from the spinning rear wheels. In vain I raced after it, but it gathered speed and tore away up the slope.

I gave up, turned and ran back down the lane, groping for the keys of the Chrysler in my sodden trouser pockets, and realized I had left them on the table in Jimmy's room.

Sherry was leaning in the open doorway of the kitchen. She held her burned hand to her chest and her hair was in tangled disarray. The sleeve of her jersey was torn loose from the shoulder.

'I couldn't stop him, Harry,' she gasped. 'I tried.'

'How bad is it?' I asked her, abandoning all thought of chasing the sports car when I saw her distress.

'Slightly singed.'

'I'll take you to a doctor.'

'No. It doesn't need it,' but her smile was lopsided with pain. I went up to Jimmy's room and from my travelling medicine kit I took a Doloxene for the pain and Mogadon to let her sleep.

'I don't need it,' she protested.

'Do I have to hold your nose and force them down?' I asked, and she grinned, shook her head and swallowed them.

'You'd better take a bath,' she said, 'you are soaked,' and suddenly I realized I was sodden and cold. When I came back to the kitchen, glowing from the bath, she was already woozy with the pills, but she had made coffee for us and strengthened it with a tot of whisky. We drank it sitting opposite each other.

'What did they want?' I asked. 'What did they say?'

'They thought I knew why Jimmy had gone to St Mary's. They wanted to know.'

I thought about that. Something didn't make sense, it worried me.

'I think—' Sherry's voice was unsteady and she staggered slightly as she tried to stand. 'Wow! What did you give me?'

I picked her up and she protested weakly, but I carried her up to her room. It was chintzy and girlish, with rose-patterned wallpaper. I laid her on the bed, pulled off her shoes and covered her with the quilt.

She sighed and closed her eyes. 'I think I'll keep you around,' she whispered. 'You're very useful.'

Thus encouraged, I sat on the edge of the bed and gentled her to sleep, smoothing her hair off her temples and stroking the broad forehead; her skin felt like warm velvet. She was asleep within a minute. I switched off the light, and was about to leave when I thought better of it.

I slipped off my own shoes and crept in under the quilt. In her sleep she rolled quite naturally into my arms, and I held her close.

It was a good feeling and soon I slept also. I woke in the dawn. Her face was pressed into my neck, one leg and arm were thrown over me and her hair was soft and tickling against my cheek.

Without waking her, I gently disengaged myself, kissed her forehead, picked up my shoes and went back to my own room. It was the first time I had spent an entire night with a beautiful woman in my arms, and done nothing but sleep. I felt puffed up with virtue.

* * *

The letter lay upon the reading table in Jimmy's room where I had left it and I read it through again before I went to the bathroom. The pencilled note in the margin 'B. Mus. E.6914(8)' puzzled me and I fretted over it while I shaved.

The rain had stopped and the clouds were breaking up when I went down into the yard to examine the scene of the previous night's encounter. The knife lay in the mud and I picked it up and tossed it over the hedge. I went into the kitchen, stamping my feet and rubbing my hands in the cold.

Sherry had started breakfast.

'How's the hand?'

'Sore,' she admitted.

'We'll find a doctor on the way up to London.'

'What makes you think I'm going to London?' she asked carefully, as she buttered toast.

'Two things. You can't stay here. The wolf pack will be back.' She looked up at me quickly but was silent. 'The other is that you promised to help me—and the trail leads to London.'

She was unconvinced, so while we ate I showed her the letter I had found in Jimmy's file.

'I don't see the connection,' she said at last, and I admitted frankly, 'It's not clear to me even.' I lit my first cheroot of the day as I spoke, and the effect was almost magical. 'But as soon as I saw the words *Dawn Light* something went click—' I stopped. 'My God!' I breathed. 'That's it. The *Dawn Light!*' I remembered the scraps of conversation carried to the bridge of *Wave Dancer* through the ventilator from the cabin below.

'To get the dawn light then we will have to—' Jimmy's voice, clear and tight with anticipation. 'If the dawn light is where—' Again the words repeated had puzzled me at the time. They had stuck like burrs in my memory.

I began to explain to Sherry, but I was so excited that it came tumbling out in a rush of words. She laughed, catching my excitement but not understanding the explanations.

'Hey!' she protested. 'You are not making sense.'

I began again, but halfway through I stopped and stared at her silently.

'Now what is it?' She was half amused, half exasperated. 'This is driving me crazy, also.'

I snatched up my fork. 'The bell. You remember the bell I told you about. The one Jimmy pulled up at Gunfire Reef?'

'Yes, of course.'

'I told you it had lettering on it, half eaten away by sand.'

'Yes, go on.'

With the fork I scratched on the butter, using it as a slate.
'—VV N L—'
I drew in the lettering that had been chased into the bronze.
'That was it,' I said. 'It didn't mean anything then—but now—'
Quickly I completed the letters, 'DAWN LIGHT.'
And she stared at it, nodding slowly as it fitted together.
'We have to find out about this ship, the *Dawn Light.*'
'How?'
'It should be easy. We know she was an East Indiaman—there
must be records—Lloyd's—the Board of Trade?'
She took the letter from my hand and read it again. 'The gallant
colonel's luggage probably contained dirty socks and old shirts.' She
pulled a face and handed it back to me.
'I'm short of socks,' I said.

*   *   *

Sherry packed a case, and I was relieved to see that she had the
rare virtue of being able to travel light. She went down to speak to
the tenant farmer while I packed the bags into the Chrysler. He
would keep an eye on the cottage during her absence, and when she
came back she merely locked the kitchen door and climbed into the
Chrysler beside me.
'Funny,' she said. 'This feels like the beginning of a long journey.'
'I have my plans,' I warned and leered at her.
'Once I thought you looked wholesome,' she said sorrowfully, 'but
when you do that—'
'Sexy, isn't it?' I agreed, and took the Chrysler up the lane.
I found a doctor in Haywards Heath. Sherry's hand had now blis-
tered badly, fat white bags of fluid hung from her fingers like sickly
grapes. He drained them, and rebandaged the hand.
'Feels worse now,' she murmured as we drove on northwards, and
she was pale and silent with the pain of it. I respected her silence,
until we were into the suburbs of the city.
'We had better find some place to stay,' I suggested. 'Something
comfortable and central.'
She looked across at me quizzically.
'It would probably be a lot more comfortable and cheaper if we
got a double room somewhere, wouldn't it?'
I felt something turn over in my belly, something warm and excit-

ing. 'Funny you should say that, I was just about to suggest the same.'

'I know you were,' she laughed for the first time in two hours. 'I saved you the trouble.' She shook her head, still laughing. 'I'll stay with my uncle. He's got a spare room in his apartment in Pimlico, and there is a little pub around the corner. It's friendly and clean—you could do worse.'

'I am crazy about your sense of humour,' I muttered.

She phoned the uncle from a pay phone, while I waited in the car. 'It's fixed up,' she told me, as she climbed into the passenger seat. 'He's at home.'

It was a ground-floor apartment in a quiet street near the river. I carried Sherry's bag for her as she led the way, and rang the doorbell.

The man that opened the door was small and lightly built. He was sixtyish and he wore a grey cardigan, darned at the elbows. His feet were thrust into carpet slippers. The homely attire was somehow incongruous, for his iron-grey hair was neatly cropped as was the short stiff moustache. His skin was clear and ruddy, but it was the fierce predatory glint of the eye and the military set of the shoulders that warned me. This man was aware.

'My uncle, Dan Wheeler.' Sherry stood aside to introduce us. 'Uncle Dan, this is Harry Fletcher.'

'The young man you were telling me about,' he nodded abruptly. His hand was bony and dry and his gaze stung like nettles. 'Come in. Come in, both of you.'

'I won't bother you, sir—' it was quite natural to call him that, an echo of my military training from so long ago, 'I want to find a room myself.'

Uncle Dan and Sherry exchanged glances and I thought she shook her head almost imperceptibly, but I was looking beyond them into the apartment. It was monastic, completely masculine in the severity and economy of furniture and ornaments. Somehow that room seemed to confirm my first impressions of the man. I wanted as little to do with him as I could arrange while seeing as much of Sherry as I possibly could.

'I'll pick you up in an hour for lunch, Sherry,' and when she agreed I left them and returned to the Chrysler. The pub that Sherry recommended was the Windsor Arms, and when I mentioned the uncle's name as she suggested, they put me in a quiet back room with a fine view of sky and television aerials. I lay on the bed fully clothed, and considered the North family and its relatives while I waited for the hour to run by. Of one thing only was I certain—that Sherry North the Second was not going to pass me silently in the night. I was going to keep pretty close station upon her, and yet there was much about her that still puzzled me. I suspected that she was a more complicated person than her serene and lovely face suggested. It was going to be interesting finding out. I put the thought aside, sat up and reached for the telephone. I made three phone calls in the next twenty minutes. One to Lloyd's Register of Shipping in Fenchurch Street, another to the National Maritime Museum at Greenwich and the last to the India Office Library in Blackfriars Road. I left the Chrysler in the private parking lot behind the pub, a car is more trouble than it is worth in London, and I walked back to the uncle's apartment. Sherry answered the door herself, and she was ready to leave. I liked that about her, she was punctual.

'You didn't like Uncle Dan, did you?' she challenged me over the lunch table and I ducked.

'I made some phone calls. The place that we are looking for is in Blackfriars Road. It's in Westminster. The India Office Library. We will go down there after we've eaten.'

'He really is very sweet when you get to know him.'

'Look, darling girl, he's your uncle. You keep him.'

'But why, Harry? It interests me.'

'What does he do for a living—army, navy?'

She stared at me. 'How did you know that?'

'I can pick them out of a crowd.'

'He's army, but retired—why should that make a difference?'

'What are you going to try?' I waved the menu at her. 'If you take the roast beef, I'll go for the duck,' and she accepted the decoy, and concentrated on the food.

The India Office Archives were housed in one of those square modern blocks of greenish glass and Air Force-blue steel panels.

Sherry and I armed ourselves with visitor's passes and signed the book. We made our way first to the Catalogue Room and thence to the marine section of the archives. These were presided over by a neatly dressed but stern-faced lady with greying hair and steel-rimmed spectacles.

I handed her a requisition slip for the dossier which would

include material on the Honourable Company's ship *Dawn Light* and she disappeared amongst the laden ceiling-high tiers of steel shelving.

It was twenty minutes before she returned and placed a bulky dossier on the counter top before me.

'You'll have to sign here,' she told me, indicating a column on the stiff cardboard folder. 'Funny!' she remarked. 'You are the second one who has asked for this file in less than a year.'

I stared at the signature J. A. North in the last space. We were following closely in Jimmy's footsteps, I thought, as I signed 'RICHARD SMITH' below his name.

'You can use one of the desks over there, dear.' She pointed across the room. 'Please try and keep the file tidy, won't you, then.'

Sherry and I sat down at the desk shoulder to shoulder, and I untied the tape that secured the file.

The *Dawn Light* was of the type known as the Blackwall Frigate, characteristically built at the Blackwall yards in the early nineteenth century. The type was very similar to the naval frigates of that period.

She had been built at Sunderland for the Honourable English East India Company, and she was of 1330 net register tons. At the waterline her dimensions were 226 feet with a beam of twenty-six feet. Such a narrow beam would have made her very fast but uncomfortable in a stiff blow.

She had been launched in 1832, just the year before the Company lost its China monopoly, and this stroke of ill-fortune seemed to have dogged her whole career.

Also in the file were a whole series of reports of the proceedings of various courts of inquiry. Her first master gloried in the name of Hogge and on her maiden voyage he piled the *Dawn Light* on to the bank at Diamond Harbour in Hooghly River. He was found by the Court of Inquiry to be under the influence of strong drink at the time and stripped of his command.

'Made a pig of himself,' I observed to Sherry, and she groaned softly and rolled her eyes at my wit.

The trail of misfortune continued. In 1840 while making passage in the South Atlantic the elderly mate who had the dog watch let her come up, and away went her masts. Wallowing helpless with her top hamper dragging alongside, she was found by a Dutchman. They cut away the wreckage and she was dragged into Table Bay. The Salvage Court made an award of £12,000.

In 1846 while half her crew were ashore on the wild coast of New Guinea they were set upon by the cannibals and slaughtered to a man. Sixty-three of her crew died.

Then on the 23rd September, 1857, she sailed from Bombay, outward bound for St Mary's, the Cape of Good Hope, St Helena and the Pool of London.

'The date.' I placed my finger on the line. 'This is the voyage that Goodchild talks of in the letter.'

Sherry nodded without reply, I had learned in the last few minutes that she read faster than I did. I had to restrain her from turning each page when I was only three-quarters finished. Now her eyes darted across each line, her colour was up, a soft flush upon her pale cheeks, and she was biting her underlip.

'Come on,' she urged me. 'Hurry up!' and I had to hold her wrist.

The *Dawn Light* never reached St Mary's—she disappeared. Three months later, she was considered lost at sea with all hands and the underwriters were ordered by Lloyd's to make good their assurances to the owners and shippers.

The manifest of her cargo was impressive for such a small ship for she had loaded out of China and India a cargo that consisted of:

364 chests of tea 494 half-chests of tea	72 tons on behalf of Messrs Dunbar and Green.
101 chests of tea 618 half-chests of tea	65 tons on behalf of Messrs Simpson, Wyllie & Livingstone.
577 bales of silk	82 tons on behalf of Messrs Elder and Company.
5 cases goods	4 tons on behalf of Col. Sir Roger Goodchild.
16 cases goods	6 tons on behalf of Major John Cotton.
10 cases goods	2 tons on behalf of Lord Elton.
26 boxes various spices	2 tons on behalf of Messrs Paulson and Company.

Wordlessly I laid my finger on the fourth item of the manifest, and again Sherry nodded, with her eyes shining like sapphires. The claim had been settled and the matter appeared closed until, four months later in April, 1858, the East Indiaman *Walmer Castle* arrived in England, carrying aboard the survivors from the *Dawn Light*.

There were six of them. The first mate, Andrew Barlow, a boatswain's mate, and three topmast men. There was also a young woman of twenty-two years, a Miss Charlotte Cotton, who had been a passenger making the homeward passage with her father, a Major in the 40th Foot.

The mate, Andrew Barlow, gave his evidence to the Court of Inquiry, and beneath the dry narrative and the ponderous questions and guarded replies lay an exciting and romantic story of the sea, an epic of shipwreck and survival.

As we read I saw the meagre scraps of knowledge I had scraped together fit neatly into the story.

Fourteen days out from Bombay, the *Dawn Light* was set upon by a furious storm out of the south-east. For seven days the savagery of the storm raged unabated, driving the ship before her. I could imagine it clearly, one of those great cyclones that had torn the roof from my own shack at Turtle Bay.

Once again *Dawn Light* was dismasted, no spars were left standing except the fore lower mast, mizzen lower mast, and bowsprit. The rest had carried away on the tempest and there was no opportunity to set up a jury mainmast or send yards aloft in the mountainous seas.

Thus when land was sighted to leeward, there was no chance that the ship might avoid her fate. A conspiracy of wind and current hurled her down into the throat of a funnel-shaped reef upon which the storm surf burst like the thunder of the heavens.

The ship struck and held, and Andrew Barlow was able with the help of twelve members of his crew to launch one of the boats. Four passengers including Miss Charlotte Cotton left the stricken ship with them, and Barlow, with an unlikely combination of good fortune and seamanship, was able to find a passage through the wild sea and murderous reefs into the quieter waters of the inshore channel.

Finally they ran the boat ashore on the spindrift-smothered beach of an island. Here the survivors huddled for four days while the cyclone blew itself out.

Barlow alone climbed to the summit of the southernmost of the treble peaks of the island. The description was completely clear. It was the Old Men and Gunfire Reef. There was no doubt of it. This then was how Jimmy North had known what he was looking for—the island with three peaks and a barrier of coral reef.

Barlow took bearings off the sea-battered hull of the *Dawn Light* as she lay in the jaws of the reef, swept by each successive wave. On the second day the ship's hull began to break up, and while Barlow watched from the peak, the front half of her was carried up over the reef to disappear into a dark gaping hole in the coral. The stern fell back into the sea and was smashed to matchwood.

When at last the skies cleared and the wind dropped, Andrew Barlow discovered that his small party were all that survived from a ship's company of 149 souls. The others had perished in the wild sea.

To the west, low against the horizon, he descried a low land mass which he hoped was the African mainland. He embarked his party in the ship's boat once more and they made the crossing of the inshore channel. His hopes were fulfilled, it was Africa—but as always she was hostile and cruel.

The seventeen lost beings began a long and dangerous journey southwards, and three months later only Barlow, four seamen and Miss Charlotte Cotton reached the island port of Zanzibar. Fever, wild animals, wild men and misfortune had whittled away their numbers—and even those who survived were starved to gaunt living skeletons, yellowed with fever and riddled with dysentery from foul water.

The Court of Inquiry had highly commended Andrew Barlow, and the Hon. Company had made him an award of £500 for meritorious service.

When I finished reading, I looked up at Sherry. She was watching me.

'Wow!' she said, and I also felt drained by the magnitude of the old drama.

'It all fits, Sherry,' I said. 'It's all there.'

'Yes,' she said.

'We must see if they have the drawings here.'

The Prints and Drawings Room was on the third floor and a quick search by an earnest assistant soon revealed the *Dawn Light* in all her splendour.

She was a graceful three-masted ship with a long low profile. She had no crossjack or mizzen course. Instead she carried a large spanker and a full set of studding sails. The long poop gave space for several passenger cabins, and she carried her boats on top of her deckhouse aft.

She was heavily armed, with thirteen black-painted gunports aside, from which she could run out her long eighteen-pounder cannon to defend herself, in those hostile seas east of the Cape of Good Hope across which she plied to China and India.

'I need a drink,' I said, and picked up the drawings of the *Dawn Light*. 'I'll get them to make copies of these for us.'

'What for?' Sherry wanted to know.

The assistant emerged from her lair amongst the piled trays of old prints and sucked in her cheeks at my request for copies.

'I'll have to charge you seventy-five pence,' she tried to discourage me.

'That's reasonable,' I said.

'And we won't have them ready until next week,' she added inexorably.

'Oh dear,' said I, and gave her the smile. 'I did need them tomorrow afternoon.'

The smile crushed her, she lost the air of purpose and tried to tuck her straying wisps of hair into the side frames of her glasses.

'Well, I'll see what I can do then,' she relented.

'That's very sweet of you, really it is,' and we left her looking confused, but pleased.

* * *

My sense of direction was returning and I found my way to El Vino's without trouble. The evening flood of journalists from Fleet Street had not yet swamped it and we found a table at the back. I ordered two vermouths and we saluted each other over the glasses.

'You know, Harry, Jimmy had a hundred schemes. His whole life was one great treasure hunt. Every week he had found, almost found, the location of a treasure ship from the Armada or a sunken Aztec city, a buccaneer wreck—' she shrugged. 'I have a built-in resistance to believing any of it. But this one—' She sipped the wine.

'Let's go over what we have,' I suggested. 'We know that Goodchild was very concerned that his agent receive five cases of luggage and put it into safe keeping. We know that he was going to ship it aboard *Dawn Light* and he sent advance notice, probably through a personal friend, the captain of the naval frigate *Panther*.'

'Good,' she agreed.

'We know that those cases were listed on the ship's manifest. That the ship was lost, presumably with them still on board. We know the exact location of the wreck. We have had it confirmed by the ship's bell.'

'Still good.'

'We only do not know what those cases contained.'

'Dirty socks,' she said.

'Four tons of dirty socks?' I asked, and her expression changed. The weight of the cargo had not meant anything to her.

'Ah,' I grinned at her, 'it went over your head. I thought so. You read so fast you only take in half of it.'

She pulled a face at me.

'Four tons, my darling girl, is a great deal of something—whatever it is.'

'All right,' she agreed. 'Figures don't mean much to me, I admit. But it sounds a lot.'

'Say the same weight as a new Rolls Royce—to put it in terms you might understand,' and her eyes widened and turned a darker blue.

'That *is* a lot.'

'Jimmy obviously knew what it was, and had proof sufficient to convince some very hard-headed backers. They took it seriously.'

'Seriously enough to—' and she stopped herself. For an instant I saw the old grief for Jimmy's death in her eyes. I was embarrassed by it, and I looked away, making a show of taking the letter out of my inner pocket.

Carefully I spread it on the table top between us. When I looked at her, she had recovered her composure once more.

The pencilled note in the margin engaged my attention again. 'B. Mus. E.6914(8).' I read it aloud. 'Any ideas?'

'Bachelor of Music.'

'Oh, that's great,' I applauded.

'You do better,' she challenged, and I folded the letter away with dignity and ordered two more drinks.

'Well, that was a good run on that scent,' I said when I had paid the waiter. 'We have an idea what it was all about. Now, we can go on my other lead.'

She sat forward and encouraged me silently.

'I told you about your impostor, the blonde Sherry North?' and she nodded. 'On the night before she left the island she sent a cable to London.' I produced the flimsy from my wallet and handed it to Sherry. While she read it, I went on: 'This was clearly an okay to her principal, Manson. He must be the big man behind this. I am going to start moving in on him now.' I finished my vermouth. 'I'll drop you back with your martial uncle, and contact you again tomorrow.'

Her lips set in a line of stubbornness which I had not seen before and there was a glint in her eyes like the blue of gun-metal.

'Harry Fletcher, if you think you are going to ditch me just when things start livening up, you must be off your tiny head.'

The cab dropped us in Berkeley Square and I led her into Curzon Street.

'Take my arm quickly,' I muttered, glancing over my shoulder in a secretive manner. Instantly she obeyed, and we had gone fifty yards before she whispered, 'Why?'

'Because I like the feel of it,' I grinned at her and spoke in a natural voice.

'Oh, you!' She made as if to pull away, but I held her and she capitulated. We sauntered up the street towards Shepherd Market, stopping now and then to window-shop like a pair of tourists.

No. 97 Curzon Street was one of those astronomically expensive apartment blocks, six storeys of brick facing, and an ornate street door of bronze and glass beyond which was a marbled foyer guarded by a uniformed doorman. We went on past it, up as far as the White Elephant Club and there we crossed the street and wandered back on the opposite pavement.

'I could go and ask the doorman if Mr Manson occupied Flat No. 5,' Sherry volunteered.

'Great,' I said. 'Then he says "yes", what do you do then? Tell him Harry Fletcher says hello?'

'You are really very droll,' she said, and once more she tried to take her hand away.

'There is a restaurant diagonally opposite No. 97.' I prevented her withdrawal. 'Let's get a table in the front window, drink some coffee, and watch for a while.'

It was a little past three o'clock when we settled at the window seat with a good view across the street, and the next hour passed pleasantly. I found it not a difficult task to keep Sherry amused, we shared a similar sense of humour and I liked to hear her laugh.

I was in the middle of a long, complicated story when I was interrupted by the arrival outside No. 97 of a Silver Wraith Rolls Royce. It pulled to the curb and a chauffeur in a smart dove-grey uniform left the car and entered the foyer. He and the doorman fell into conversation, and I resumed my story.

Ten minutes later, there was sudden activity opposite. The elevator began a series of rapid ascents and descents, each time discharging a load of matching crocodile-skin luggage. This was carried out by the doorman and chauffeur and packed into the Rolls. It seemed endless, and Sherry remarked, 'Somebody is off on a long holiday.' She sighed wistfully.

'How do you fancy a tropical island with blue water and white sands, a thatched shack amongst the palms—'

'Stop it,' she said. 'On an autumn day in old London, I just can't bear the thought.'

I was about to move into a stronger position when the footman and chauffeur stood to attention and once more the glass doors of the elevator opened and a man and woman stepped out of it.

The woman wore a full-length honey mink and her blonde hair was piled high on her head in an elaborate lacquered Grecian style. Anger struck me like a fist in the guts as I recognized her.

It was Sherry North, the First. The nice lady who had blown Judith and *Wave Dancer* to the bottom of Grand Harbour.

With her was a man of medium height with soft brown hair fashionably long and curly over his ears. He had a light tan, probably from a sun lamp, and he was dressed too well. Very expensively, but as flamboyantly as an entertainment personality.

He had a heavy jaw and a long fleshy nose with soft gazelle eyes, but his mouth was pinched and hungry. A greedy mouth that I remembered so well.

'Manson!' I said. 'Jesus! Manson Resnick—Manny Resnick.' He would be just the one Jimmy North would find his way to with his outrageous proposition. In exactly the same way that so long ago I had gone to him with my plans for the gold heist at Rome Airport. Manny was an underworld entrepreneur, and he had clearly climbed a long way up the ladder since our last meeting.

He was keeping great style now, I thought, as he crossed the pavement and entered the back seat of the Rolls, settling down next to the mink-clad blonde.

'Wait here,' I told Sherry urgently, as the Rolls pulled away towards Park Lane.

I ran out on to the pavement and searched wildly for a cab to follow them. There were none and I ran after the Rolls praying desperately for the sight of a big black cab with its top light burning, but ahead of me the Rolls swung right into South Audley Street and accelerated smoothly away.

I stopped at the corner and it was already far ahead, infiltrating the traffic towards Grosvenor Square.

I turned and ambled disappointedly back to where Sherry waited. I knew that Sherry had been correct. Manny and the blonde were off on a long journey. There was no point in hanging around No. 97 Curzon Street any longer.

Sherry was waiting for me outside the restaurant.

'What was that all about?' she demanded and I took her arm. As we walked back towards Berkeley Square, I told her.

'That man is probably the one who ordered Jimmy murdered, who was responsible for having half my chest shot away, who had them to roast your lovely pinkies—in short, the big man.'

'You know him?'

'I did business with him a long time ago.'

'Nice friends you have.'

'I'm trying for a better class lately,' I said, and squeezed her arm. She ignored my gallantry.

'And the woman. Is she the one from St Mary's, the one who blew up your boat and the young girl?'

I experienced a violent return of the anger which had gripped me a few minutes earlier when I had seen that sleek, meticulously polished predator dressed in mink.

Beside me Sherry gasped, 'Harry, you are hurting me!'

'Sorry.' I relaxed my grip on her arm.

'I guess that answers my question,' she muttered ruefully, and massaged her upper arm.

The private bar of the Windsor Arms was all dark oak panels and antique mirrors. It was crowded by the time Sherry and I returned. Outside darkness had fallen and there was an icy wind stirring the fallen leaves in the gutters.

The warmth of the pub was welcome. We found seats in a corner, but the crowd pushed us together, forcing me to place an arm around Sherry's shoulders, and our heads were close so we could hold a very private conversation in this public place.

'I can guess where Manny Resnick and his friend are headed,' I said.

'Big Gull Island?' Sherry asked, and when I nodded she went on, 'He'll need a boat and divers.'

'Don't worry, Manny will get them.'

'And what will we do?'

'We?' I asked.

'A form of speech,' she corrected herself primly. 'What will you do?'

'I have a choice. I can forget about it all—or I can go back to Gunfire Reef and try to find out what the hell was in Colonel Goodchild's five cases.'

'You'll need equipment.'

'It might not be as elaborate as Manny Resnick's will be, but I could get enough together.'

'How are you for money, or is that a rude question?'

'The answer is the same. I could get enough together.'

'Blue water and white sand,' she murmured dreamily.

'—and the palm fronds clattering in the trade winds.'

'Stop it, Harry.'

'Fat crayfish grilling on the coals, and me beside you singing in the wilderness,' I went on remorselessly.

'Pig,' she said.

'If you stay here, you'll never know if it was dirty socks,' I pressed her.

'You'd write and tell me,' she pleaded.

'No, I wouldn't.'

'I'll have to come with you,' she said at last.

'Good girl.' I squeezed her shoulder.

'But I insist on paying my own way, I refuse to become a kept woman.' She had guessed how hard pressed I was financially.

'I should hate to erode your principles,' I told her happily, and my wallet sighed with relief. It was going to be a near-run thing to mount an expedition to Gunfire Reef on what I had left.

There was much we had to discuss now that the decision had been made. It seemed only minutes later that the landlord was calling, 'Time, gentlemen.'

145

'The streets are dangerous at night,' I warned Sherry. 'I don't think we should chance it. Upstairs I have a very comfortable room with a fine view—'

'Come on, Fletcher.' Sherry stood up. 'You had better walk me home, or I shall set my uncle on to you.'

As we walked the half block to her uncle's apartment, we agreed to meet for lunch next day. I had a list of errands to perform in the morning including making the airline reservations, while Sherry had to have her passport renewed and pick up the photostat drawings of the *Dawn Light*.

At the door of the apartment we faced each other, suddenly both of us were shy. It was so terribly corny that I almost laughed. We were like a pair of old-fashioned teenagers at the end of our first date —but sometimes corny feels good.

'Good night, Harry,' she said, and with the age-old artistry of womankind she showed me in some indefinable manner that she was ready for kissing.

Her lips were soft and warm, and the kiss went on for a long time.

'My goodness,' she whispered throatily, and drew away at last.

'Are you sure you won't change your mind—it is a beautiful room, hot and cold water, carpets on the floor, T.V.—'

She laughed shakily and pushed me gently backwards. 'Good night, dear Harry,' she repeated, and left me.

I went out into the street and strolled back towards my pub. The wind had dropped but I could smell the damp emanating from the river close by. The street was deserted but the curb was lined with parked vehicles, bumper to bumper they reached to the corner.

I sauntered along the pavement, in no hurry for bed, even toying with the idea of a stroll down the Embankment first. My hands were thrust deep into the pockets of my car coat, and I was feeling relaxed and happy as I thought about this woman.

There was a lot to think about Sherry North, much that was unclear or not yet explained, but mainly I cherished the thought that perhaps here at last was something that might last longer than a night, a week, or a month—something that was already strong and that would not be like the others, diminishing with the passage of time, but instead would grow ever stronger.

Suddenly a voice beside me said, 'Harry!' It was a man's voice, a strange voice, and I turned instinctively towards it. As I did so I knew that it was a mistake.

The speaker was sitting in the back seat of one of the parked cars. It was a black Rover. The window was open and his face was merely a pale blob in the darkness of the interior.

Desperately I tried to pull my hands out of my pockets and turn to face the direction from which I knew the attack would come. As I turned I ducked and twisted, and something whirred past my ear and struck my shoulder a numbing blow.

I struck backwards with both elbows, connecting solidly and hearing the gasp of pain. Then my hands were clear and I was around, moving fast, weaving, for I knew they would use the cosh again.

They were just midnight shapes, menacing and huge, dressed in dark clothing. It seemed there were a legion of them, but there were only four—and one in the car. They were all big men, and the one had the cosh up to strike again. I hit him under the chin with the palm of my hand, snapping his head backwards and I thought I might have broken his neck, for he went down hard on the pavement.

A knee drove for my groin, but I turned and caught it on the thigh, using the impetus of the turn to counter-punch. It was a good one, jolting me to the shoulder, and the man took it in the chest, and was thrown backwards, but immediately one of them was hugging the arm, smothering it and a fist caught me in the cheek under the eye. I felt the skin tear open.

Another one was on my back, an arm around my throat throttling me, but I heaved and pushed. In a tight knot, locked together, we surged around the pavement.

'Hold him still,' another voice called, low and urgent. 'Let me get a shot at him.'

'What the bloody hell you think we are trying to do?' panted another, and we fell against the side of the Rover. I was pinned there, and I saw the one with the cosh was on his feet. He swung again, and I tried to roll my head, but it caught me in the temple. It did not put me out completely, but it knocked all the fight out of me. I was instantly weak as a child, hardly able to support my own weight.

'That's it, get him into the back.' They hustled me into the centre seat in the back of the Rover and one of them crowded in on each side of me. The doors slammed, the engine whirred and caught and we pulled away swiftly.

My brain cleared, but the side of my head was numb and felt like

147

a balloon. There were three of them in the front seat, one on each side of me in the back. All of them were breathing heavily, and the one next to the driver was massaging his neck and jaw tenderly. The one on my right had been eating garlic, and he panted heavily as he searched me for weapons.

'I think you should know that something died in your mouth a long time ago, and it's still there,' I told him, with a thickened tongue and an ache in my head, but the effort was not worth it. He showed no sign of having heard, but continued doggedly with this task. At last he was satisfied and I readjusted my clothing.

We drove in silence for five minutes, following the river towards Hammersmith, before they had all recovered their breath and tended their wounds, then the driver spoke.

'Listen, Manny wants to talk to you, but he said it's no big thing. He was merely curious. He said also that if you gave us a hard time, not to go to no trouble, just to sign you off and toss you in the river.'

'Charming chap, Manny,' I said.

'Shut up!' said the driver. 'So you see, it's up to you. Behave yourself and you get to live a little longer. I heard you used to be a sharp operator, Harry. We been expecting you to show up, ever since Lorna missed you on the island—but sure as hell we didn't expect you to parade up and down Curzon Street like a brass band. Manny couldn't believe it. He said, "That can't be Harry. He must have gone soft." It made him sad. "How are the mighty fallen. Tell it not in the streets of Ashkelon," he said.'

'That's Shakespeare,' said the one with the garlic breath.

'Shut up,' said the driver and then went on. 'Manny was sad but not that sad that he cried or anything, you understand.'

'I understand,' I mumbled.

'Shut up,' said the driver. 'Manny said, "Don't do it here. Just follow him to a nice quiet place and pick him up. If he comes quietly you bring him to talk to me—if he cuts up rough then toss him in the river."'

'That sounds like my boy, Manny. He always was a soft-hearted little devil.'

'Shut up,' said the driver.

'I look forward to seeing him again.'

'You just stay good and quiet and you might get lucky.'

I stayed that way through the night as we picked up the M4 and rushed westwards. It was two in the morning when we entered Bristol, skirting the city centre as we followed the A4 down to Avonmouth.

Amongst the other craft in the yacht basin was a big motor yacht. She was moored to the wharf and she had her gangplank down. Her name painted on the stern and bows was *Mandrake*. She was an ocean-goer, steel-hulled painted blue and white, with pleasing lines. I judged her fast and sea-kindly, probably with sufficient range to take her anywhere in the world. A rich man's toy. There were figures on her bridge, lights burning in most of her portholes, and she seemed ready for sea.

They crowded me as we crossed the narrow space to the gangplank. The Rover backed and turned and drove away as we climbed to the *Mandrake*'s deck.

The saloon was too tastefully fitted out for Manny Resnick's style, it had either been done by the previous owners or a professional decorator. There were forest-green wall-to-wall carpets and matching velvet curtains, the furniture was dark teak and polished leather and the pictures were choice oils toned to the general décor.

This was half a million pounds worth of vessel, and I guessed it was a charter. Manny had probably taken her for six months and put in his own crew—for Manny Resnick had never struck me as a bluewater man.

As we waited in the centre of the wall-to-wall carpeting, a grimly silent group, I heard the unmistakable sounds of the gangplank being taken in, and the moorings cast off. The tremble of her engines became a steady beat, and the harbour lights slid past the saloon portholes as we left the entrance and thrust out into the tidal waters of the River Severn.

I recognized the lighthouses at Portishead Point and Red Cliff Bay as *Mandrake* came around for the run down-river past Weston-super-Mare and Berry for the open sea.

Manny came at last, he wore a blue silk gown and his face was still crumpled from sleep, but his curls were neatly combed and his smile was white and hungry.

'Harry,' he said, 'I told you that you would be back.'

'Hello, Manny. I can't say it's any great pleasure.'

He laughed lightly and turned to the woman as she followed him into the saloon. She was carefully made up and every hair of the elaborate hairstyle was in its place. She wore a long white housegown with lace at throat and cuffs.

149

'You have met Lorna, I believe, Lorna Page.'

'Next time you send somebody to hustle me, Manny, try for a little better class. I'm getting fussy in my old age.'

Her eyes slanted wickedly, but she smiled.

'How's your boat, Harry? Your lovely boat?'

'It makes a lousy coffin.' I turned back to Manny. 'What's it going to be, Manny, can we work out a deal?'

He shook his head sorrowfully. 'I don't think so, Harry. I would like to—truly I would, if just for old times' sake. But I can't see it. Firstly, you haven't anything to trade—and that makes for a lousy deal. Secondly, I know you are too sentimental. You'd louse up any deal we did make for purely emotional reasons. I couldn't trust you, Harry, all the time you'd be thinking about Jimmy North and your boat, you'd be thinking about the little island girl that got in the way,' and about Jimmy North's sister who we had to get rid of—' I took a mild pleasure in the fact that Manny had obviously not heard what had happened to the goon squad he had sent to take care of Sherry North, and that she was still very much alive. I tried to make my voice sincere and my manner convincing.

'Listen, Manny, I'm a survivor. I can forget anything, if I have to.'

He laughed again. 'If I didn't know you better, I'd believe you, Harry.' He shook his head again. 'Sorry, Harry, no deal.'

'Why did you go to all the trouble to bring me down here, then?'

'I sent others to do the job twice before, Harry. Both times they missed you. This time I want to make sure. We will be cruising over some deep water on the way to Cape Town, and I'm going to hang some really heavy weights on to you.'

'Cape Town?' I asked. 'So you are going after the *Dawn Light* in person. What is so fascinating about that old wreck?'

'Come on, Harry. If you didn't know, you wouldn't be giving me such a hard time.' He laughed, and I thought it best not to let them know my ignorance.

'You think you can find your way back?' I asked the blonde. 'It's a big sea and a lot of islands look the same. I think you should keep me as insurance,' I insisted.

'Sorry, Harry.' Manny crossed to the teak and brass bar. 'Drink?' he asked.

'Scotch,' I said, and he half filled a glass with the liquor and brought it to me.

'To be entirely truthful with you, part of this is for Lorna's benefit.

150

You made the girl bitter, Harry, I don't know why—but she wanted especially to be there when we say goodbye. She enjoys that sort of thing, don't you, darling, it turns her on.'

I drained the glass. 'She needs turning on—as you and I both know, she's a lousy lay without it,' I observed, and Manny hit me in the mouth, crushing my lips and the whisky stung the raw flesh.

'Lock him up,' he said softly. As they hustled me out of the saloon, and along the deck towards the bows, I took pleasure in knowing that Lorna would have painful questions to answer. On either hand the shore lights moved steadily past us in the night, and the river was black and wide.

* * *

Forward of the bridge there was a low deckhouse above the forecastle, and a louvred companionway opened on to a deck ladder that descended to a small lobby. This was obviously the crew's quarters, doors opened off the lobby into cabins and a communal mess.

In the bows was a steel door and a stencilled sign upon it read 'FORECASTLE STORE'. They shoved me through the doorway and slammed the heavy door. The lock turned and I was alone in a steel cubicle probably six by four. Both bulkheads were lined with storage lockers, and the air was damp and musty.

My first concern was to find some sort of weapon. The cupboards were all of them locked and I saw that the planking was inch-thick oak. I would need an axe to hack them open, nevertheless I tried. I attempted to break in the doors using my shoulder as a ram, but the space was too confined and I could not work up sufficient momentum.

However, the noise attracted attention. The door swung open and one of the crew stood well back with a big ugly .41 Rueger Magnum in his hand.

'Cut it out,' he said. 'There ain't anything in there,' and he gestured to the pile of old life-jackets against the far wall. 'You just sit there nice and quiet or I'll call some of the boys to help me work you over.' He slammed the door and I sank down on to the life-jackets.

There was clearly a guard posted at the door full-time. The others would be within easy call. I hadn't expected him to open the door and I had been off-balance. I had to get him to do it again—but this time I would have a go. It was a poor chance, I realized. All he had to do was point that cannon into the storeroom and pull the trigger. He could hardly miss.

I needed some sort of distraction, some sort of cover to get close enough. I looked longingly at the lockers again, then turned my attention to my own pockets. They had cleaned me out, my lighter and cheroots, car keys, penknife were all gone. But they had left my handkerchief, three five-pound notes folded into my hip pocket they had overlooked and I had my wristwatch.

I looked down at the pile of life-jackets, and stood again to pull them aside. Beneath them was a small wooden fruit box, it contained discarded cleaning materials. A nylon floorbrush, cleaning rags, a tin of Brasso, half a cake of yellow soap, and a brandy bottle half filled with clear fluid. I unscrewed the cap and sniffed it. It was benzine.

I sat down again and reassessed my position, trying to find a percentage in it without much success.

The light switch was outside the doorway and the light overhead was in a thick glass cover. I stood up and climbed halfway up the lockers, wedging myself there while I unscrewed the light cover and examined the bulb. It gave me a little hope.

I climbed down again and selected one of the heavy canvas life-jackets. The clasp of the steel strap on my wristwatch made a blunt blade and I sawed and hacked at the canvas, tearing a hole large enough to get my forefinger in. I ripped the canvas open and pulled out handfuls of the white kapok stuffing. I piled it on the floor, tearing open more life-jackets until I had a considerable heap.

I soaked the cotton waste with benzine from the bottle and took a handful of it with me when I climbed again to the light fitting. I removed the bulb and was plunged instantly into darkness. Working by sense of touch alone, I pressed the benzine-soaked stuffing close to the electricity terminals. I had nothing to use as insulation so I held the steel strap of my wristwatch in my bare hands and used it to dead-short the terminals.

There was a sizzling blue flash, the benzine ignited instantly and 180 volts hit me like a charge of buckshot, knocking me off my perch. I fell in a heap on to the deck with a ball of flaming kapok in my hands.

Outside I heard faint shouts of annoyance and anger. I had succeeded in shorting the entire lighting system of the forecastle. Quickly I tossed the burning kapok on to the prepared pile, and it burned up fiercely. I brushed the sparks from my hands, wrapped the handkerchief around my mouth and nose, snatched up one of the undamaged life-belts and went to stand against the steel door.

In seconds the benzine burned away and the cotton began to smoulder, fiercely pouring out thick black smoke that smelled vile. It filled the store, and my eyes began to stream with tears. I tried to breathe shallowly but the smoke tore my lungs and I coughed violently.

There was another shout beyond the door.

'Something is burning.' And it was answered, 'For Chrissake, get those lights on.'

It was my cue, I began beating on the steel door and screaming at the top of my voice. 'Fire! The ship is on fire!' It was not all acting. The smoke in my prison was thick and solid, and more boiled off the burning cotton kapok. I realized that if nobody opened that door within the next sixty seconds I would suffocate and my screams must have carried conviction. The guard swung the door open, he carried the big Rueger revolver and shone a flashlight into the storeroom.

I had time only to notice those details and to see that the ship's lights were still dead, shadowy figures milled about in the gloom, some with flashlights—then a solid black cloud of smoke boiled out of the storeroom.

I came out with the smoke like a fighting bull from its pen, desperate for clean air and terrified at how close I had come to suffocating. It gave strength to my efforts.

The guard went sprawling under my rush and the Rueger fired as he went down. The muzzle flame was bright as a flashbulb, lighting the whole area and allowing me to get my bearings on the companion ladder to the deck.

The blast of the shot was so deafening in the confined space that it seemed to paralyse the other shadowy figures. I was halfway to the ladder before one of them leaped to intercept me. I drove my shoulder into his chest and heard the wind go out of him like a punctured football.

There were shouts of concern now, and another big dark figure blocked the foot of the ladder. I had gathered speed across the lobby and I put that and all my weight into a kick that slogged into his belly, doubling him over and dropping him to his knees. As he went over a flashlight lit his face and I saw it was my friend with the garlicky breath. It gave me a lift of pleasure to light me on my way, and I put one foot on his shoulder and used it as a springboard to leap halfway up the ladder.

Hands clutched at my ankle but I kicked them away, and dragged myself to the deck level. I had only one foot on the rungs, and I was clinging with one hand to the life-jacket and with the other to the brass handrail. In that helpless moment, the doorway to the deck was blocked by yet another dark figure—and the lights went on. A sudden blinding blaze of light.

The man above me was the lad with the cosh, and I saw his savage delight as he raised it over my helpless head. The only way to avoid it was to let go the handrail and drop back into the forecastle, which was filled with surging angry goons.

I looked back and was actually opening my grip when behind me, the gunman with the Rueger Magnum sat up groggily, lifted the weapon, tried to brace himself against the ship's movement and fired at me. The heavy bullet cracked past my ear, almost splitting my ear drum and it hit the coshman in the centre of his chest. It picked him up and hurled him backwards across the deck. He hung in the rigging of the foremast with his arms spread like those of a derelict scarecrow, and with a desperate lunge I followed him out on to the deck and rolled to my feet still clutching the life-jacket.

Behind me the Rueger roared again and I heard the bullet splinter the coping of the hatch. Three running strides carried me to the rail and I dived over the side in a gut-swooping drop until I hit the black water flat, but I was dragged deep as the boil of the propellers caught me and swirled me under.

The water was shockingly cold, it seemed to drive in the walls of my lungs and probe with icy lances into the marrow of my bones.

The life-jacket helped pull me to the surface at last and I looked wildly about me. The lights of the coast seemed clear and very bright, twinkling whitely across the black water. Out here in the seaway there was a chop and swell to the surface, alternately lifting and dropping me.

Mandrake slid steadily onwards towards the black void of the open sea. With all her lights blazing she looked as festive as a cruise ship as she sailed away from me.

Awkwardly I rid myself of my shoes and jacket, then I managed to get my arms into the sleeves of the life-jacket. When I looked again *Mandrake* was a mile away, but suddenly she began to turn and from her bridge the long white beam of a spotlight leaped out and began to probe lightly and dance across the surface of the dark sea.

Quickly I looked again towards the land, seeking and finding the riding lights of the buoy at English Ground and relating it to the lighthouse on Flatholm. Within seconds the relative bearing of the two lights had altered slightly, the tide was ebbing and the current was setting westerly. I turned with it and began to swim.

The *Mandrake* had slowed and was creeping back towards me. The spotlight turned and flared, swept and searched, and steadily it came down towards me.

I pushed with the current, using a long side stroke so as not to break the surface and show white water, restraining myself from going into an overarm stroke as the brightly lit ship crept closer. The beam of the spotlight was searching the open water on the far side of *Mandrake* as she drew level with me.

The current had pushed me out of her track, and the *Mandrake* was as close as she would come on this leg—about one hundred and fifty yards off—but I could see the men on her bridge. Manny Resnick's blue silk gown glowed like a butterfly's wing in the bridge lights and I could hear his voice raised angrily, but could not make out the words.

The beam reached towards me like the long cold white finger of an accuser. It quartered the sea in a tight search pattern, back and across, back and across, the next pass must catch me. It reached the end of its traverse, swung out and came back. I lay full in the path of the swinging beam, but at the instant it swept over me, a chance push of the sea lifted a swell of dark water and I dropped into the trough. The light washed over me, diffused by the crest of the swell, and it did not check. It swept onwards in the relentless search pattern.

They had missed me. They were going on, back towards the mouth of the Severn. I lay in the harsh embrace of the canvas lifejacket and watched them bear away and I felt sick and nauseated with relief and the reaction from violence. But I was free. All I had to worry about now was how long it would take to freeze to death.

* * *

I began swimming again, watching *Mandrake*'s lights dwindle and lose themselves against the spangled backdrop of the shore.

I had left my wristwatch in the forecastle so I did not know how long it was before I lost all sense of feeling in my arms and legs. I tried to keep swimming but I was not sure if my limbs were responding.

I began to feel a wonderful floating sense of release. The lights of the land faded out, and I seemed to be wrapped in warmth and soft white clouds. I thought that if this was dying it wasn't as bad as its propaganda, and I giggled, lying sodden and helpless in the life-jacket.

I wondered with interest why my vision had gone, it wasn't the way I had heard it told. Then suddenly I realized that the sea fog had come down in the dawn, and it was this that had blinded me. However, the morning light was growing in strength, I could see clearly twenty feet into the eddying fog banks.

I closed my eyes and fell asleep; my last thought was that this was probably my last thought. It made me giggle again as darkness swept over me.

Voices woke me, voices very clear and close in the fog, the rich and lovely Welsh accents roused me. I tried to shout, and with a sense of great achievement it came out like the squawk of a gull.

Out of the fog loomed the dark ungainly shape of an ancient lobster boat. It was on the drift, setting pots, and two men hung over the side, intent on their labours.

I squawked again and one of the men looked up. I had an impression of pale blue eyes in a weathered and heavily lined ruddy face, cloth cap and an old briar pipe gripped in broken yellow teeth.

'Good morning,' I croaked.

'Jesus!' said the lobster man around the stem of his pipe.

I sat in the tiny wheelhouse wrapped in a filthy old blanket, and drank steaming unsweetened tea from a chipped enamel mug—shivering so violently that the mug leaped and twitched in my cupped hands.

My whole body was a lovely shade of blue, and returning circulation was excruciating agony in my joints. My two rescuers were taciturn men, with a marvellous sense of other people's privacy, probably bred into them by a long line of buccaneers and smugglers.

By the time they had set their pots and cleared for the homeward run it was after noon and I had thawed out. My clothes had dried over the stove in the miniature galley and I had a belly full of brown bread and smoked mackerel sandwiches.

We went into Port Talbot, and when I tried to pay them with my rumpled fivers for their help, the older of the two lobster men turned a blue and frosty eye upon me.

'Any time I win a man back from the sea, I'm paid in full, mister. Keep your money.'

* * *

The journey back to London was a nightmare of country buses and night trains. When I stumbled out of Paddington Station at ten o'clock the next morning I understood why a pair of bobbies paused in their majestic pacing to study my face. I must have looked like an escaped convict.

The cabby ran a world-weary eye over my two days' growth of dark stiff beard, the swollen lip and the bruised eye. 'Did her husband come home early, mate?' he asked, and I groaned weakly.

Sherry North opened the door to her uncle's apartment and stared at me with huge startled blue eyes.

'Oh my God, Harry! What on earth happened to you? You look terrible.'

'Thanks,' I said. 'That really cheers me up.'

She caught my arm and drew me into the apartment. 'I've been going out of my mind. Two days. I've even called the police, the hospitals—everywhere I could think of.'

The uncle was hovering in the background and his presence set my nerves on edge. I refused the offer of a bath and clean clothes—and instead I took Sherry back with me to the Windsor Arms.

I left the door to the bathroom open while I shaved and bathed so that we could talk, and although she kept out of direct line of sight while I was in the tub, I thought it was developing a useful sense of intimacy between us.

I told her in detail of my abduction by Manny Resnick's trained gorillas, and of my escape—making no attempt to play down my own heroic role—and she listened in a silence that I could only believe was fascinated admiration.

I emerged from the bath with a towel wound round my waist and sat on the bed to finish the tale while Sherry doctored my cuts and abrasions.

'You'll have to go to the police now, Harry,' she said at last. 'They tried to murder you.'

'Sherry, my darling girl, please don't keep talking about the police. You make me nervous.'

'But, Harry—'

'Forget about the police, and order some food for us. I haven't eaten since I can remember.'

The hotel kitchen sent up a fine grilling of bacon and tomatoes, fried eggs, toast and tea. While I ate, I tried to relate the recent rapid turn of events to our previous knowledge, and alter our plans to fit in.

'By the way, you were on the list of expendables. They didn't intend merely holding a barbecue with your fingers. Manny Resnick was convinced that his boys had killed you—' and a queasy expression passed over her lovely face. 'They were apparently getting rid of anyone who knew anything at all about the *Dawn Light*.'

I took another mouthful of egg and bacon and chewed in silence.

'At least we have a timetable now. Manny's charter—which is incidentally called *Mandrake*—looks very fast and powerful, but it's still going to take him three or four weeks to get out to the islands. It gives us time.'

She poured tea for me, milk last the way I like it.

'Thanks, Sherry, you are an angel of mercy.' She stuck out her tongue at me, and I went on, 'Whatever it is we are looking for, it just has to be something extraordinary. That motor yacht Manny has hired himself looks like the Royal Yacht. He must be laying out close to a hundred thousand pounds on this little lark. God, I wish we knew what those five cases contain. I tried to sound Manny out—but he laughed at me. Told me I knew or I wouldn't be taking so much trouble—'

'Oh, Harry.' Sherry's face lit up. 'You've given us the bad news—now stand by for the good.'

'I could stand a little.'

'You know Jimmy's note on the letter—B. Mus.?'

I nodded. 'Bachelor of Music?'

'No, idiot—British Museum.'

'I'm afraid you just lost me.'

'I was discussing it with Uncle Dan. He recognized it immediately. It's a reference to a work in the library of the British Museum. He holds a reader's card. He's researching a book, and works there often.'

'Could we get in there?'

'We'll give it a college try.'

*   *   *

I waited almost two hours beneath the vast golden and blue dome of the Reading Room at the British Museum, and the craving for a cheroot was like a vice around my chest.

I did not know what to expect—I had simply filled in the withdrawals form with Jimmy North's reference number—so when at last the attendant laid a thick volume before me, I seized it eagerly.

It was a Secker and Warburg edition, first published in 1963. The author was a Doctor P. A. Ready and the title was printed in gold on the spine: LEGENDARY AND LOST TREASURES OF THE WORLD.

I lingered over the closed book, teasing myself a little, and I wondered what chain of coincidence and luck had allowed Jimmy North to follow this paperchase of ancient clues. Had he read this book first in his burning obsession with wrecks and sea treasure and had he then stumbled on the batch of old letters? I would never know.

There were forty-nine chapters, each listing a separate item. I read carefully down the list.

There were Aztec treasures of gold, the plate and bullion of Panama, buccaneer hoards, a lost goldmine in the Rockies of North America, a valley of diamonds in South Africa, treasure ships of the Armada, the *Lutine* bullion ship from which the famous *Lutine* Bell at Lloyd's had been recovered, Alexander the Great's chariot of gold, more treasure ships—both ancient and modern—from the Second World War to the sack of Troy, treasures of Mussolini, Prester John, Darius, Roman generals, privateers and pirates of Barbary and Coromandel. It was a vast profusion of fact and fancy, history and conjecture. The treasures of lost cities and forgotten civilizations, from Atlantis to the fabulous golden city of the Kalahari Desert— there was so much of it, and I did not know where to look.

With a sigh I turned to the first page, ducking the introduction and preface. I began to read.

By five o'clock I had skimmed through sixteen chapters which could not possibly relate to the *Dawn Light* and had read five others in depth and by this time I understood how Jimmy North could have been bitten by the romance and excitement of the treasure hunter. It was making me itchy also—these stories of great riches, abandoned, waiting merely to be gathered up by someone with the luck and fortitude to ferret them out.

I glanced at the new Japanese watch with which I'd replaced my Omega, and hurried out of the massive stone portals of the museum and crossed Great Russell Street to my rendezvous with Sherry. She was waiting in the crowded saloon bar of the Running Stag.

'Sorry,' I said, 'I forgot the time.'

'Come on.' She grabbed my arm. 'I'm dying of thirst and curiosity.'

I gave her a pint of bitter for her thirst, but could only inflame her curiosity with the title of the book. She wanted to send me back to the library, before I had finished my supper of ham and turkey from the carvery behind the bar, but I held out and managed to smoke half a cheroot before she drove me out into the cold.

I gave her the key to my room at the Windsor Arms, placed her in a cab and told her to wait for me there. Then I hurried back to the Reading Room.

The next chapter of the book was entitled 'THE GREAT MOGUL AND THE TIGER THRONE OF INDIA.'

It began with a brief historical introduction describing how Babur, descendant of Timur and Genghis Khan, the two infamous scourges of the ancient world, crossed the mountains into northern India and established the Mogul Empire. I recognized immediately that this fell within the area of my interest, the *Dawn Light* had been outward bound from that ancient continent.

The history covered the period of Babur's illustrious successors, Muslim rulers who rose to great power and influence, who built mighty cities and left behind such monuments to man's sense of beauty as the Taj Mahal. Finally it described the decline of the dynasty, and its destruction in the first year of the Indian mutiny when the avenging British forces stormed and sacked the ancient citadel and fortress at Delhi—shooting the Mogul princes out of hand and throwing the old emperor Bahadur Shah into captivity.

Then abruptly the author switched his attention from the vast sweep of history.

In 1665 Jean Baptiste Tavernier, a French traveller and jeweller, visited the court of the Mogul Emperor Aurangzeb. Five years later he published in Paris his celebrated *Travels in the Orient*. He seems to have won special favour from the Muslim

Emperor, for he was allowed to enter the fabled treasure chambers of the citadel and to catalogue various items of special interest. Amongst these was a diamond which he named the 'Great Mogul.' Tavernier weighed this stone and listed its bulk at 280 carats. He described this paragon as possessing extraordinary fire and a colour as clear and white 'as the great North Star of the heavens.'

Tavernier's host informed him that the stone had been recovered from the famed Golconda Mines in about 1650 and that the rough stone had been a monstrous 787 carats.

The cut of the stone was a distinctive rounded rose, but was not symmetrical—being proud on the one side. The stone has been unrecorded since that time and many believe that Tavernier actually saw the Koh-i-noor or the Orloff. However, it is highly improbable that such a trained observer and craftsman as Tavernier could have erred so widely in his weights and descriptions. The Koh-i-noor before it was recut in London weighed a mere 191 carats, and was certainly not a rose cut. The Orloff, although rose cut, was and is a symmetrical gem stone and weighs 199 carats. The descriptions simply cannot be mated with that of Tavernier, and all the evidence points to the existence of a huge white diamond that has dropped out of the known world.

In 1739 when Nadir Shah of Persia entered India and captured Delhi, he made no attempt to hold his conquest, but contented himself with vast booty, which included the Koh-i-noor diamond and the peacock throne of Shah Jehan. It seems probable that the Great Mogul diamond was overlooked by the rapacious Persian and that after his withdrawal, Mohammed Shah the incumbent Mogul Emperor, deprived of his traditional throne, ordered the construction of a substitute. However, the existence of this new treasure was veiled in secrecy and although there are references to its existence in the native accounts, only one European reference can be cited.

The journal of the English Ambassador to the Court of Delhi during the year of 1747, Sir Thomas Jenning, describes an audience granted by the Mogul Emperor at which he was 'clad in precious silks and bedecked with flowers and jewels, seated upon a great throne of gold. The shape of the throne was as of a fierce tiger, with gaping jaws and a single glittering cyclopean eye. The body of the tiger was amazingly worked with all manner of precious stones. His majesty was gracious enough to allow me to approach the throne closely and to examine the eye of the tiger which he assured me was a great diamond descended from the reign of his ancestor Aurangzeb.'

Was this Tavernier's 'Great Mogul' now incorporated into the 'Tiger Throne of India'? If it was, then credence is given to a strange set of circumstances which must end our study of this lost treasure.

In 1857 on the 16th September, desperate street fighting filled the streets of Delhi with heaps of dead and wounded, and the outcome of the struggle hung in the balance as the British forces and loyal native troops fought to clear the city of the mutinous sepoys and seized the ancient fortress that dominated the city.

While the fighting raged within, a force of loyal native troops from 101st regiment under two European officers was ordered to cross the river and encircle the walls to seize the road to the north. This was in order to prevent members of the Mogul royal family or rebel leaders from escaping the doomed city.

The two European officers were Captain Matthew Long and Colonel Sir Roger Goodchild—

The name leapt out of the page at me not only because someone had underlined it in pencil. In the margin, also in pencil, was one of Jimmy North's characteristic exclamation marks. Master James's disrespect for books included those belonging to such a venerable institution as the British Museum. I found I was shaking again, and my cheeks felt hot with excitement. This was the last fragment missing from the puzzle. It was all here now and my eyes raced on across the page.

No one will ever know now what happened on that night on a lonely road through the Indian jungle—but six months later, Captain Long and the Indian Subahdar, Ram Panat, gave evidence at the court martial of Colonel Goodchild.

They described how they had intercepted a party of Indian nobles fleeing the burning city. The party included three Muslim priests and two princes of the royal blood. In the presence of Captain Long one of the princes attempted to buy their freedom by offering to lead the British officers to a great

162

treasure, a golden throne shaped like a tiger and with a single diamond eye.

The officers agreed, and the princes led them into the forest to a jungle mosque. In the courtyard of the mosque were six bullock carts. The drivers had deserted, and when the British officers dismounted and examined the contents of these vehicles they proved indeed to contain a golden throne statue of a tiger. The throne had been broken down into four separate parts to facilitate transportation—hindquarters, trunk, forequarters and head. In the light of the lanterns these fragments nestled in beds of straw, blazing with gold and encrusted with precious and semi-precious stones.

Colonel Roger Goodchild then ordered that the princes and priests should be executed out of hand. They were lined up against the outer wall of the mosque and despatched with a volley of musketry. The Colonel himself walked amongst the fallen noblemen administering the *coup-de-grâce* with his service revolver. The corpses were afterwards thrown into a well outside the walls of the mosque.

The two officers now separated, Captain Long with most of the native troops returning to the patrol of the city walls, while the Colonel, Subahdar Ram Panat and fifteen sepoys rode off with the bullock carts.

The Indian Subahdar's evidence at the court martial described how they had taken the precious cargo westwards passing through the British lines by the Colonel's authority. They camped three days at a small native village. Here the local carpenter and his two sons laboured under the Colonel's direction to manufacture four sturdy wooden crates to hold the four parts of the throne. The Colonel in the meantime set about removing from the statue the stones and jewels that were set into the metal. The position of each was carefully noted on a diagram prepared by Goodchild and the stones were numbered and packed into an iron chest of the type used by army paymasters for the safekeeping of coin and specie in the field.

Once the throne and the stones had been packed into the four crates and iron chest, they were loaded once more on to the bullock carts and the journey towards the railhead at Allahabad was continued.

The luckless carpenter and his sons were obliged to join the convoy. The Subahdar recalled that when the road entered an area of dense forest, the Colonel dismounted and led the three craftsmen amongst the trees. Six pistol shots rang out and the Colonel returned alone.

I broke off my reading for a few moments to reflect on the character of the gallant Colonel. I should have liked to introduce him to Manny Resnick, they would have had much in common. I grinned at the thought and read on.

The convoy reached Allahabad on the sixth day and the Colonel claimed military priority to place his five crates upon a troop train returning to Bombay. Having done this he and his small command rejoined the regiment at Delhi.

Six months later, Captain Long supported by the Indian Petty Officer, Ram Panat, brought charges against the commanding officer. We can believe that thieves had fallen out, Colonel Goodchild had perhaps decided that one share was better than three. Be that as it may, nothing has since given a clue to the whereabouts of the treasure.

The trial conducted in Bombay was a *cause célèbre* and was widely reported in India and at home. However, the weakness of the prosecution's case was that there was no booty to show, and dead men tell no tales.

The Colonel was found not guilty. However, the pressure of the scandal left him no choice but to resign his commission and return to London. If he managed somehow to take with him the Great Mogul diamond and the golden tiger throne, his subsequent career gave no evidence of his possessing great wealth. In partnership with a notorious lady of the town he opened a gaming house in the Bayswater Road which soon acquired an unsavoury reputation. Colonel Sir Roger Goodchild died in 1871, probably from tertiary syphilis contracted during his remarkable career in India. His death revived stories of the fabulous throne, but these soon subsided for lack of hard facts and the secret passed on with that sporting gentleman.

Perhaps we should have headed this chapter—'The Treasure That Never Was'.

'Not on your life, fellow,' I thought happily. 'It was—and is.' And I began once more at the beginning of the story, but this time I made careful notes for Sherry's benefit.

*　*　*

She was waiting for me when I returned, sitting wakefully in the armchair by the window, and she flew at me when I entered.

'Where have you been?' she demanded, 'I've been sitting here all evening eating my heart out with curiosity.'

'You are not going to believe it,' I told her, and I thought she might do me a violence.

'Harry Fletcher, you've got ten seconds to cut out the introductory speeches and give me the goodies—after that I scratch your eyes out.'

We talked until long after midnight, and by then we had the floor strewn with papers over which we pored on knees and elbows. There was an Admiralty Chart of the St Mary's Archipelago, the copies of the drawings of the *Dawn Light*, the notes I had made of the mate's description of the wreck, and those I had made in the Reading Room of the British Museum.

I had out my silver travelling flask and we drank Chivas Regal from the plastic tooth mug as we argued and schemed—trying to guess in what section of the *Dawn Light*'s hull the five crates had been stowed, guessing also how she had broken up on the reef, what part of her had been washed into the break and what part had fallen to the seaward side.

I had made sketches of a dozen eventualities, and I had opened a running list of my minimum equipment requirements for a expedition, to which I added, as various items came to mind, or as Sherry made intelligent suggestions.

I had forgotten that she must be a first rate scuba diver, but I was reminded of this as we talked. I was aware now that she would not be a passenger on this expedition, my feelings towards her were becoming tinged with professional respect, and the mood of exhilaration mixed with camaraderie was building to a crescendo of physical tension.

Sherry's pale smooth cheeks were flushed with excitement, and we were shoulder to shoulder as we knelt on the carpeted floor. She turned to say something, she was chuckling and the blue lights in her eyes were teasing and inviting, only inches from mine.

Suddenly all the golden thrones and legendary diamonds in this world must wait their turn. We both recognized the moment, and we turned to each other with unashamed eagerness. We were in a consuming fever of urgency, and we became lovers without rising from the floor, right on top of the drawings of the *Dawn Light*— which was probably the happiest thing that had ever happened to that ill-starred vessel.

When at last I lifted her to the bed and we twined our bodies together beneath the quilt, I knew that all the brief amorous acrobatics that had preceded my meeting with this woman were meaningless. What I had just experienced transcended the flesh and became a thing of the spirit—and if it was not loving, then it was the nearest thing to it that I would ever know.

My voice was husky and unsteady with wonder as I tried to explain it to her. She lay quietly against my chest, listening to the words I had never spoken to another woman, and she squeezed me when I stopped talking—which was clearly a command to continue. I think I was still talking when we both fell asleep.

*　　*　　*

From the air, St Mary's has the shape of one of those strange fish from the ocean's abysmal depths, a squat misshapen body with stubby body fins and tailfins in unusual places, and a huge mouth many sizes too big for the rest of it.

The mouth was Grand Harbour and the town nestled in the hinge of the jaws. The iron roofs flashed like signal mirrors from the dark green cloak of vegetation. The aircraft circled the island, treating the passengers to a vista of snowy white beaches and water so clear that each detail of the reefs and deeps was whorled and smeared below the surface like some vast surrealistic painting.

Sherry pressed her face to the round perspex window and exclaimed with delight as the Fokker Friendship sank down over the pineapple fields where the women paused in their labours to look up at us. We touched down and taxied to the single tiny airport building on which a billboard announced 'St Mary's Island—Pearl of the Indian Ocean' and below the sign stood two other pearls of great price.

I had cabled Chubby and he had brought Angelo with him to welcome us. Angelo rushed to the barrier to embrace me and grab my bag, and I introduced him to Sherry.

Angelo's whole manner underwent a profound change. On the island there is one mark of beauty that is esteemed above all else. A girl might have buck teeth and a squint, but if she possessed a 'clear' complexion she would have suitors forming squadrons around her. A clear complexion did not mean that she was free of acne, it was rather a gauge of the colour of the skin—and Sherry must have had one of the clearest complexions ever to land on the island.

Angelo stared at her in a semi-catatonic state as she shook his hand. Then he roused himself, handed me back my bag and instead took hers from her hand. He then fell in a few paces behind her, like a faithful hound, staring at her solemnly and only breaking into his flashing smile whenever she glanced in his direction. He was her slave from the first moment.

Chubby trundled forward to meet us with more dignity, as big and timeless as a cliff of dark granite, and his face was contorted in a frown of even greater ferocity than usual as he took my hand in a huge horny fist and muttered something to the effect that it was good to see me back.

He stared at Sherry and she quailed a little beneath the ferocity of his gaze, but then something happened that I had never seen before. Chubby lifted his battered old sea cap from his head, exposing the gleaming polished brown dome of his pate in an unheard-of display of gallantry, and he smiled so widely that we could see the pink plastic gums of his artificial teeth. He pushed Angelo aside when Sherry's bags were brought out of the hold, picked up one in each hand and led her to the pick-up. Angelo followed her devotedly and I struggled along in the rear under the weight of my own luggage. It was fairly obvious that my crew approved of my choice, for once.

We sat in the kitchen of Chubby's house and Mrs Chubby fed us on banana cake and coffee while Chubby and I worked out a business deal. For a hard-bargained fee, he would charter his stump boat with its two spanking new Evinrude motors for an indefinite period. He and Angelo would crew it at the old wages, and there would be a large 'billfish bonus' at the end of the charter, if it were successful. I went into no detail as to the object of the expedition, but merely let them know that we would be camping on the outer islands of the group and that Sherry and I would be working underwater.

By the time we had agreed and slapped hands on the bargain, the traditional island rite of agreement, it was mid-afternoon and the island fever had already started to reassert its hold on my constitution. Island fever prevents the sufferer from doing today what can reasonably be put off until the morrow, so we left Chubby and Angelo to begin their preparations while Sherry and I stopped only briefly at Missus Eddy's for provisions before pushing the pick-up over the ridge and down through the palms to Turtle Bay.

'It's story book,' murmured Sherry, as she stood under the thatch on the wide veranda of the shack. 'It's make-believe.' She shook her head at the sway-boled palm trees and the aching white sands beyond.

I went to stand behind her, placing my arms around her middle and drawing her to me. She leaned back against me, crossing her own arms over mine and squeezing my hands.

'Oh, Harry, I didn't think it would be like this.' There was a change taking place within her, I could sense it clearly. She was like a winter plant, too long denied the sun, but there were reserves in her that I could not fathom and they troubled me. She was not a simple person, nor easily understood. There were barriers, conflicts within her that showed only as dark shadows in the depths of her ocean-blue eyes, shadows like those of killer sharks swimming deep. More than once when she believed herself unobserved I had caught her looking at me in a manner which seemed at once calculating and hostile—as though she hated me.

That had been before we came to the island, and now it seemed that, like the winter plant, she was blooming in the sun; as though here she could cast aside some restraint of the soul which had curbed her spirit before.

She kicked off her shoes, and barefooted turned within my encircling arms to stand upon tiptoe to kiss me.

'Thank you, Harry. Thank you for bringing me here.'

Mrs Chubby had swept the floors and aired the linen, placed flowers in the jars and charged the refrigerator. We walked through the shack hand in hand—and though Sherry murmured admiration for the utilitarian décor and solid masculine furnishings, yet I thought I detected that gleam in her eye which a woman gets just before she starts pushing the furniture around and throwing out the lovingly accumulated but humble treasures of a man's lifetime.

As she paused to rearrange the bowl of flowers that Mrs Chubby had placed upon the broad camphor-wood refectory table, I knew we were going to see some changes at Turtle Bay—but strangely the thought did not perturb me. I realized suddenly that I was sick to death of being my own cook and housekeeper.

We changed into swimsuits in the main bedroom—for I had found in the very few hours since we had become lovers that Sherry had an overdeveloped sense of personal modesty, and I knew it would take time before I could wean her to the standard casual Turtle Bay swimming attire. However, it was some compensation for my temporary overdress to see Sherry North in a bikini.

It was the first time I had really had an opportunity to look at her openly. The most striking single thing about her was the texture and lustre of her skin. She was tall, and if her shoulders were too wide and her hips a little too narrow, her waist was tiny and her belly was flat with a small delicately chiselled navel. I have always thought that the Turks were right in considering the navel as a highly erotic portion of a woman's anatomy—Sherry's would have launched a thousand ships.

She didn't like me staring at it. 'Oh, Grandma—what big eyes you've got,' she said, and wrapped a towel around her waist like a sarong. But she walked barefooted through the sand with an unconscious push and sway of buttock and breast that I watched with uninhibited pleasure.

We left our towels above the high water mark and ran down over the hard wet sand to the edge of the clear warm sea. She swam with a deceptively slow and easy stroke, that drove her through the water so swiftly that I had to reach out myself and drive hard to catch and hold her.

Beyond the reef we trod water and she was puffing a little. 'Out of training,' she panted.

While we rested I looked out to sea and at that moment a line of black fins broke the surface together in line abreast, bearing down on us swiftly and I could not restrain my delight.

'You are an honoured guest,' I told her. 'This is a special welcome.' The dolphins circled us, like a pack of excited puppies, gambolling and squeaking while they looked Sherry over carefully. I have known them to sheer away from most strangers, and it was a rarity for them to allow themselves to be touched on a first meeting and then only after assiduous wooing. However, with Sherry it was love at first sight, almost of the calibre that Chubby and Angelo had demonstrated.

Within fifteen minutes they were dragging her on the Nantucket sleigh ride while she squealed with glee. The instant she fell off the back of one, there was another prodding her with his snout, competing fiercely for her attention.

When at last they had exhausted us both and we swam in wearily to the beach, one of the big bull dolphins followed Sherry into water so shallow it reached to her waist. There he rolled on his back while she scratched his belly with handfuls of coarse white sand and he grinned that fixed idiotic dolphin grin.

After dark, while we sat on the veranda and drank whisky together, we could still hear the old bull whistling and slapping the water with his tail, in an attempt to seduce her into the sea again.

* * *

The next morning I gamely fought off a fresh onslaught of island fever, and the temptation to linger in bed, especially as Sherry awoke beside me with the pink glossy look of a little girl, and her eyes were clear, her breath sweet and her lips languorous.

We had to check through the equipment we had salvaged from *Wave Dancer,* and we needed an engine to drive the compressor. Chubby was sent off with a fistful of banknotes and returned with a motor that required much loving attention. As that occupied me for the rest of the day, Sherry was sent off to Missus Eddy's for camping equipment and provisions. We had set a three-day deadline for our departure and our schedule was tight.

It was still dark when we took our places in the boat, Chubby and Angelo at the motors in the stern and Sherry and I perched like sparrows on top of the load.

The dawn was a flaming glory of gold and hot red, promise of another fiery day, as Chubby took us northwards on a course possible only for a small boat and a good skipper. We ran close in on island and reef, sometimes with only eighteen inches of water between our keel and the fierce coral fangs.

All of us were in a mood of anticipation. I truly do not believe it was the prospect of vast wealth that excited me then—all I really needed in my life was another good boat like *Wave Dancer*—rather it was the thought of rare and exquisite treasure, and the chance to win it back from the sea. If what we sought had been merely bullion in bars or coin I do not think it would have intrigued me half as much. The sea was the adversary and once more we were pitted against each other.

The blazing colours of the dawn faded into the hard hot blue of the sky as the sun rose out of the sea, and Sherry North stood up in the bows to strip off her denim jacket and jeans. Under them she wore her bikini and now she folded the clothes away into her canvas duffle bag and produced a tube of sun lotion with which she began to anoint her fine pale body.

Chubby and Angelo reacted with undisguised horror. They held a hurried and scandalized consultation after which Angelo was sent forward with a sheet of canvas to rig a sun shelter for Sherry. There followed a heated exchange between Angelo and Sherry.

'You will damage your skin, Miss Sherry,' Angelo protested, but she drove him in defeat back to the stern.

There the two of them sat like mourners at a wake, Chubby's whole face creased into a huge brown scowl and Angelo openly wringing his hands in anxiety. Finally, they could stand it no longer and after another whispered discussion Angelo was elected as emissary once more and he crawled forward over the cargo to enlist my support.

'You can't let her do it, Mister Harry,' Angelo pleaded. 'She will go *dark*.'

'I think that's the idea, Angelo,' I told him. However, I did warn Sherry to take care of the sun at noon. Obediently she covered herself when we ran ashore on a sandy beach to eat our midday meal.

It was the middle of the afternoon when we raised the triple peaks of the Old Men and Sherry exclaimed, 'Just as the old mate described them.'

We approached the island from the sea side, through the narrow stretch of calm water between the island and the reef. When we passed the entrance to the channel through which I had taken *Wave Dancer* to escape from the Zinballa crash boat, Chubby and I grinned at each other in fond recollection, then I turned to Sherry and pointed it out to her.

'I plan to set up our base camp on the island, and we will use the gap to reach the area of the wreck.'

'It looks a little risky.' She eyed the narrow channel with reserve.

'It will save us a round journey of nearly twenty miles each day—and it isn't as bad as it looks. Once I took my big fifty-foot cruiser through there at full throttle.'

'You must be crazy.' She pushed her dark glasses up on top of her head to look at me.

'By now you should be a good judge of that.' I grinned at her, and she grinned back.

'I am an expert already,' she boasted. The sun had darkened the freckles on her nose and cheeks and given her skin a glow. She had one of those rare skins that do not redden and become angry when exposed to sunlight. Instead, it was the kind that quickly turned a golden honey brown.

It was high tide when we rounded the northern tip of the island into a protected cove and Chubby ran the whaleboat on to the sand only twenty yards from the first line of palm trees.

We offloaded the cargo, carrying it up amongst the palms well above the high-water mark and once again covered it with tarpaulins to protect it from the ubiquitous sea salt.

It was late by the time we had finished. The heat had gone out of the sun, and the long shadows of the palms barred the earth as we trudged inland, carrying only our personal gear and a five-gallon container of fresh water. In the back of the most northerly peak, generations of visiting fishermen had scratched out a series of shallow caves in the steep slope.

I selected a large cave to act as our equipment store, and a smaller one as living quarters for Sherry and me. Chubby and Angelo chose another for themselves, about a hundred yards along the slope and screened from us by a patch of scrub.

I left Sherry to sweep out our new quarters with a brush improvised from a palm frond, and to lay out our sleeping bags on the inflatable mattress while I took my cast net and went back to the cove.

It was dark when I returned with a string of a dozen big striped mullet. Angelo had the fire burning and the kettle bubbling. We ate in contented silence, and afterwards Sherry and I lay together in our cave and listened to the big fiddler crabs clicking and scratching amongst the palms.

'It's primeval,' Sherry whispered, 'as though we are the first man and woman in the world.'

'Me Tarzan, you Jane,' I agreed, and she chuckled and drew closer to me.

* * *

172

In the dawn Chubby set off alone in the whaleboat on the long return journey to St Mary's. He would return next day with a full load of gasoline and fresh water in jerry-cans. Sufficient to last us for two weeks or so.

While we waited for him to return, Angelo and I took on the wearying task of carrying all the equipment and stores up to the caves. I set up the compressor, charged the empty air bottles and checked the diving gear, and Sherry arranged hanging space for our clothes and generally made our quarters comfortable.

The next day, she and I roamed the island, climbing the peaks and exploring the valleys and beaches between. I had hoped to find water, a spring or well overlooked by the other visitors—but naturally there was none. Those canny old fishermen overlooked nothing.

The south end of the island, farthest from our camp, was impenetrable with salt marsh between the peak and the sea. We skirted the acres of evil-smelling mud and thick swamp grass. The air was rank and heavy with rotted vegetation and dead fish.

Colonies of red and purple crabs had covered the mudflats with their holes from which they peered stalk-eyed as we passed. In the mangroves, the herons were breeding, perched long-legged upon their huge shaggy nests, and once I heard a splash and saw the swirl of something in one of the swamp pools that could only have been a crocodile. We left the fever swamps and we climbed to the higher ground, then we picked our way through the thickets of shrub growth towards the southernmost peak.

Sherry decided we must climb this one also. I tried to dissuade her for it was the tallest and steepest. My protests went completely unnoticed, and even after we had made our way on to a narrow ledge below the southern cliff of the peak, she pressed on determinedly.

'If the mate of the *Dawn Light* found a way to the top—then I'm going up there too,' she announced.

'You'll get the same view from there as from the other peaks,' I pointed out.

'That's not the point.'

'What is the point, then?' I asked, and she gave me the pitying look usually reserved for small children and half-wits, refused to dignify the question with an answer, and continued her cautious sideways shuffle along the ledge.

There was a drop of at least two hundred feet below us, and if there is one deficiency in my formidable arsenal of talent and courage, it is that I have no head for heights. However, I would rather have balanced on one leg atop St Paul's Cathedral than admit this to Miss North, and so with great reluctance I followed her.

Fortunately it was only a few paces farther that she uttered a cry of triumph and turned off the ledge into a narrow vertical crack that split the cliff-face. The fracturing of the rock had formed a stepped and readily climbable chimney to the summit, into which I followed her with relief. Almost immediately Sherry cried out again.

'Oh dear God, Harry, look!' and she pointed to a protected area of the wall, in the back of the dark recess. Somebody long ago had patiently chipped an inscription into the flat stone surface.

A. BARLOW.
WRECKED ON THIS PLACE
14th OCT. 1858.

As we stared at it, I felt her hand grope for mine and squeeze for comfort. No longer the intrepid mountaineer, her expression was half fearful as she studied the writing.

'It's creepy,' she whispered. 'It looks as though it was written yesterday—not all those years ago.'

Indeed, the letters had been protected from weathering so that they seemed fresh cut and I glanced around almost as though I expected to see the old seaman watching us.

When at last we climbed the steep chimney to the summit we were still subdued by that message from the remote past. We sat there for almost two hours watching the surf break in long white lines upon Gunfire Reef. The gap in the reef and the great dark pool of the Break showed very clearly from our vantage point, while it was just possible to make out the course of the narrow channel through the coral. From here Arthur Barlow had watched the *Dawn Light* in her death throes, watched her broken up by the high surf.

'Time is running against us now, Sherry,' I told her, as the holiday mood of the last few days evaporated. 'It's fourteen days since Manny Resnick sailed in the *Mandrake*. He will not be far from Cape Town by now. We will know when he reaches there.'

'How?'

'I have an old friend who lives there. He is a member of the Yacht Club—and he will watch the traffic and cable me the moment *Mandrake* docks.'

I looked down the back slope of the peak, and for the first time no-

174

ticed the blue haze of smoke spreading through the tops of the palms from Angelo's cooking fire.

'I have been a little half-arsed on this trip,' I muttered, 'we have been behaving like a group of school kids on a picnic. From now on we will have to tighten up the security—just across the channel there is my old friend Suleiman Dada, and *Mandrake* will be in these waters sooner than I'd like. We will have to keep a nice low silhouette from now on.'

'How long will we need, do you think?' Sherry asked.

'I don't know, my sweeting—but be sure that it will be longer than we think possible. We are shackled by the need to ferry all our water and gasoline from St Mary's—we will only be able to work in the pool during a few hours of each tide when the condition and the height of the water will let us. Who knows what we are going to find in there once we start, and finally we may discover that the Colonel's parcels were stowed in the rear hold of the *Dawn Light*—that part of the ship that was carried out into the open water. If it was, then you can kiss it all goodbye.'

'We've been over that part of it before, you dreadful old pessimist,' Sherry rebuked me. 'Think happy thoughts.'

So we thought happy thoughts and did happy things until at last I made out the tiny dark speck, like a water beetle on the brazen surface of the sea, as Chubby returned from St Mary's in the whaleboat.

We climbed down the peak and hurried back through the palm groves to meet him. He was just rounding the point and entering the cove as we came out on the beach. The whaleboat was low in the water under her heavy cargo of fuel and drinking water. And Chubby stood in the stern as big and solid and as eternal as a great rock. When we waved and shouted he inclined his head gravely in acknowledgement.

Mrs Chubby had sent a banana cake for me and for Sherry a large sunhat of woven palm fronds. Chubby had obviously reported Sherry's behaviour, and his expression was more than normally lugubrious when he saw that the damage was already being done. Sherry was toasted to an edible medium rare.

* * *

It was after dark by the time we had carried fifty jerry-cans up to the cave. Then we gathered about the fire where Angelo was cook-

175

ing an island chowder of clams that he had gathered from the lagoon that afternoon. It was time to tell my crew the true reason for our expedition. Chubby I could trust to say nothing, even under torture—but I had waited to get Angelo into the isolation of the island before telling him. He has been known to commit the most monstrous indiscretions—usually in an attempt to impress one of his young ladies.

They listened in silence to my explanation, and remained silent after I had finished. Angelo was waiting for a lead from Chubby—and that gentleman was not one to charge his fences. He sat scowling into the fire, and his face looked like one of those copper masks from an Aztec temple. When he had created the correct atmosphere of theatrical suspense he reached into his back pocket and produced a purse, so old and well handled that the leather was almost worn through.

'When I was a boy and fished the pool at Gunfire Break, I took a big old Daddy grouper fish. When I open his belly pouch I found this in him.' From the purse he took out a round disc. 'I kept it since then, like a good luck charm, even though I was offered ten pounds for it by an officer on one of my ships.'

He handed me the disc and I examined it in the firelight. It was a gold coin, the size of a shilling. The reverse side was covered with oriental characters which I could not read—but the obverse face bore a crest of two rampant lions supporting a shield and an armoured head. The same design as I had last seen on the bronze ship's bell at Big Gull Island. The legend below the shield read: 'AUS: REGIS & SENAT: ANGLIA.' while the rim was struck with the bold title 'ENGLISH EAST INDIA COMPANY.'

'I always promised me that I would go back to Gunfire Break—looks like this is the time,' Chubby went on, as I examined the coin minutely. There was no date on it, but I had no doubt that it was a gold mohur of the company. I had read of the coin but never seen one before.

'You got this out of a fish's gut, Chubby?' I asked, and he nodded.

'Guess that old grouper seen it shine and took a snap at it. Must have stuck in his belly until I pulled him out.'

I handed the coin back to him. 'Well then, Chubby, that goes to show there is some truth in my story.'

'Guess it does, Harry,' he admitted, and I went to the cave to fetch the drawings of the *Dawn Light* and a gas lantern. We pored over the drawings. Chubby's grandfather had sailed as a topmastman in an East Indiaman, which made Chubby something of an expert. He was of the opinion that all passengers' luggage and other small pieces would be stowed in the forehold beside the forecastle—I wasn't going to argue with him. Never hex yourself, as Chubby had warned me so often.

When I produced my tide tables and began calculating the time differences for our latitude, Chubby actually smiled. Although it was hard to recognize it as such. It looked much more like a sneer, for Chubby had no faith in rows of printed figures in pamphlets. He preferred to judge the tides by the sea clock in his own head. I have known him to call the tides accurately for a week ahead without reference to any other source.

'I reckon we will have a high tide at one-forty tomorrow,' I announced.

'Man, you got it right for once,' Chubby agreed.

* * *

Without the enormous loads that had been forced on her recently, the whaleboat seemed to run with a new lightness and eagerness. The twin Evinrudes put her up on the plane, and she flew at the narrow channel through the reef like a ferret into a rabbit-hole.

Angelo stood in the bows, using hand signals to indicate underwater snags to Chubby in the stern. We had picked good water to come in on, and Chubby met the dying surf with confidence. The little whaleboat tossed up her head and kicked her heels over the swells, splattering us with spray.

The passage was more exhilarating than dangerous, and Sherry whooped and laughed with the thrill of it.

Chubby shot us through the narrow neck between the coral cliffs with feet to spare on each side, for the whaleboat had half of *Wave Dancer*'s beam, then we zigzagged through the twisted gut of the channel beyond and at last burst out into the pool.

'No good trying to anchor,' Chubby growled, 'it's deep here. The reef goes down sheer. We got twenty fathoms under us here and the bottom is foul.'

'How you going to hold?' I asked.

'Somebody got to sit at the motor and keep her there with power.'

'That's going to chew fuel, Chubby.'

'Don't I know it,' he growled.

With a tide only half made, the occasional wave was coming in over the reef. Not yet with much force, just a frothing spill that cascaded into the pool, turning the surface to ginger beer with bubbles. However, as the tide mounted so the surf would come over stronger. Soon it would be unsafe in the pool and we would have to run for it. We had about two hours in which to work, depending on the stage of neap and spring tides. It was a cycle of too little or too much. At low tide there was insufficient water to negotiate the entrance channel—and at high tide the surf breaking over the reef might overwhelm the open whaleboat. Each of our moves had to be finely judged.

Now every minute was precious. Sherry and I were already dressed in our wet suits with face-plates on our foreheads, and it was necessary only for Angelo to lift the heavy scuba sets on to our backs and to clinch the webbing harness.

'Ready, Sherry?' I asked, and she nodded, the ungainly mouthpiece already stuffed into her pretty mouth.

'Let's go.'

We dropped over the side, and sank down together beneath the cigar-shaped hull of the whaleboat. The surface was a moving sheet of quicksilver above us, and the spill over the reef charged the upper layer of water with a rash of champagne bubbles.

I checked with Sherry. She was comfortable, and breathing in the slow rhythm of the experienced diver that conserves air and ventilates the body effectively. She grinned at me, her lips distorted by the mouthpiece and her eyes enormously enlarged by the glass face-plate, and she gave me the high sign with both thumbs.

I pointed my head straight for the bottom and began pedalling with my swimming fins, going down fast, reluctant to waste air on a slow descent.

The pool was a dark hole below us. The surrounding walls of coral shut out much of the light, and gave it an ominous appearance. The water was cold and gloomy, I felt a prickle of almost superstitious awe. There was something sinister about this place, as though some evil and malignant force lurked in the sombre depths.

I crossed my fingers at my sides, and went on down, following the sheer coral cliff. The coral was riddled with dark caves and ledges that overhung the lower walls. Coral of a hundred different sorts, outcropped in weird and lovely shapes, tinted with the complete spectrum of colour. Weeds and marine growth waved and tossed in the movement of water, like the hands of supplicating beggars, or the dark manes of wild horses.

I looked back at Sherry. She was close behind me and she smiled again. Clearly she felt nothing of my own sense of awe. We went on down.

From secret ledges protruded the long yellow antennae of giant crayfish, gently they moved, sensing our presence in the disturbed water. Clouds of multi-coloured coral fish floated along the cliff-face; they sparkled like gemstones in the fading blue light that penetrated into the depths of the pool.

Sherry tapped my shoulder and we paused to peer into a deep black cave. Two great owl eyes peered back at us, and as my eyes became accustomed to the light I made out the gargantuan head of a grouper. It was speckled like a plover's egg, splotches of brown and black on a beige-grey ground and the mouth was a wide slash between thick rubbery lips. As we watched, the huge fish assumed a defensive attitude. It blew itself out, increasing its already impressive girth, spread the gill covers, enlarged the head and finally it opened its mouth in a gape that could have swallowed a man whole —a cavernous maw, lined with spiked teeth. Sherry seized my hand. We drew away from the cave, and the fish closed its mouth and subsided. Any time I wanted to claim a world record grouper I knew where to come looking. Even allowing for the magnifying effect of water I judged that he was close to a thousand pounds in weight.

We went on down the coral wall, and all around us was the wondrous marine world seething with life and beauty, death and danger. Lovely little damsel fish nestled in the venomous arms of giant sea anemone, immune to the deadly darts; a moray eel slid like a long black battle pennant along the coral wall, reached its lair and turned to threaten us with dreadful ragged teeth and glittering snakelike eyes.

Down we went, pedalling with our fins, and now at last I saw the bottom. It was a dark jungle of sea growth, dense stands of sea bamboo and petrified coral trees thrust out of the smothering marine foliage, while mounds and hillocks of coral were worked and riven into shapes that teased the imagination and covered I knew not what.

We hung above this impenetrable jungle and I checked my time-elapse wristwatch and depth gauge. I had one hundred and twenty-eight feet, and time elapsed was five minutes forty seconds.

I gave Sherry the hand signal to remain where she was and I sank down to the tops of the marine jungle and gingerly parted the cold slimy foliage. I worked my way down through it and emerged into a relatively open area below. It was a twilight area roofed in by the bamboo and peopled with strange new tribes of fish and marine animals.

I knew at once that it would not be a simple task to search the floor of the pool. Visibility here was ten feet or less, and the total area we must cover was two or three acres in extent.

I decided to bring Sherry down with me and for a start we would make a sweep along the base of the cliff, keeping in line abreast and within sight of each other.

I inflated my lungs and used the buoyancy to rise from the bottom, out through the thick belt of foliage into the clear.

I did not see Sherry at first, and I felt a quick dart of concern stab me. Then I saw the silver stream of her bubbles rising against the black wall of coral. She had moved away, ignoring my instruction, and I was annoyed. I finned towards her and was twenty feet from her when I saw what she was doing. My annoyance gave way instantly to shock and horror.

The long series of accidents and mishaps that were to haunt us in Gunfire Break had begun.

Growing out of the coral cliff was a lovely fernlike structure, graceful sweeps, branching and rebranching, pale pink shading to crimson.

Sherry had broken off a large branch of it. She held it in her bare hands and even as I raced towards her I saw her legs brush lightly against the red arms of the dreaded fire coral.

I seized her wrists and dragged her off the cruel and beautiful plant. I dug my thumbs into her flesh, shaking her hands viciously, forcing her to drop her fearsome burden. I was frantic in the knowledge that from their cells in the coral branches tens of thousands of minute polyps were firing their barbed poison darts into her flesh.

She was staring at me with great stricken eyes, aware that something bad had happened, but not yet sure what it was. I held her and began the ascent immediately. Even in my anxiety I was careful to obey the elementary rules of ascent, never overtaking my own bubbles but rising steadily with them.

I checked my watch—eight minutes thirty seconds elapsed. That was three minutes at one hundred and thirty feet. Quickly I calculated my decompression stops, but I was caught between the devil of diver's bends and the deep blue sea of Sherry's coming agony.

It hit her before we were halfway to the surface, her face contorted and her breathing went into the shallow ragged panting of deep distress until I feared she might beat the mechanical efficiency of her demand valve, jamming it so that it could no longer feed her with air.

She began to writhe in my grip and the palms of her hands blushed angrily, the livid red weals rose like whiplashes across her thighs—and I thanked God for the protection her suit had given to her torso.

When I held her at a decompression stop fifteen feet below the surface she fought me wildly, kicking and twisting in my grip. I cut the stop fine as I dared, and took her to the surface.

The instant our heads broke clear I spat out my mouthpiece and yelled: 'Chubby! Quick!'

The whaleboat was fifty yards away, but the motor was ticking over steadily and Chubby spun her on her own tail. The instant she was pointed at us, he gave the con to Angelo and scrambled up into the bows. Coming down on us like a great brown colossus.

'It's fire coral, Chubby,' I shouted. 'She's hit hard. Get her out!'

Chubby leaned out and took hold of webbing harness at the back of her neck and he lifted her bodily from the water; she dangled from his big brown fists like a drowning kitten.

I ditched my scuba set in the water for Angelo to recover, shrugging out of the harness, and when I scrambled over the side, Chubby had laid her on the floorboards and he was leaning over her, folding her in his arms to quieten her struggles and still her moans and sobs of agony.

I found my medical kit under a pile of loose equipment in the bows, and my fingers were clumsy with haste as I heard Sherry's sobs behind me. I snapped the head of an ampoule of morphine and filled a disposable syringe with the clear fluid. Now I was angry as well as concerned.

'You stupid broad,' I snarled at her. 'What made you do a crazy, half-witted thing like that?'

She could not answer me, her lips were shaking and blue, flecked with spittle. I took a pinch of skin on her thigh and thrust the needle into it as I expelled the fluid into her flesh. I went on angrily.

'Fire coral—my God, you aren't an effing conchologist's backside. Isn't a kid on the island that stupid.'

'I didn't think, Harry,' she panted wildly.

'Didn't think—' I repeated, her pain was goading me to new excesses of anger. 'I don't think you've got anything in your head to think with, you stupid little bird-brain.'

I withdrew the needle, and ransacked the medicine box for the anti-histamine spray.

'I should put you over my knee, you—'

Chubby looked up at me. 'Harry, you talk to Miss Sherry just one more word like that and, man—I'm going to have to break your head, hear?'

With only mild surprise I realized that he meant it. I had seen him break heads before, and knew it was something to avoid, so I told him,

'Instead of making speeches—how about you get us the hell out of here and back to the island.'

'You just treat her gentle, man, otherwise I'm going to roast your arse so you wish you'd been the one that sat on a bunch of fire coral instead of her, hear?'

I ignored this mutinous outburst and sprayed the ugly scarlet weals, coating them with a protective and soothing skin, and then I lifted her into my arms and held her like that while the morphine smoothed out the fearful burning agony of the stings and Chubby ran us back to the island.

When I carried Sherry up to the cave she was already half comatose from the drug. All that night I stayed by her side, helping her through the shivering and sweating fever produced by the virulent poison. Once she moaned and whispered half in delirium, 'I'm sorry, Harry. I didn't know. It's the first time I've dived in coral water. I didn't recognize it.'

Chubby and Angelo did not sleep either. I heard the murmur of their voices from the fireside and every hour one of them would cough outside the cave entrance and then inquire anxiously,

'How's she doing, Harry?'

By the morning Sherry had fought off the worst effects of the poisoning, and the stings had subsided into an ugly rash of blisters. However, it was another thirty-six hours before any of us could raise the enthusiasm to tackle the pool again, then the tides were wrong. We had to wait another day.

The precious hours were slipping away. I could imagine the *Mandrake* making fair passage, she had looked a fast and powerful vessel and each day wasted whittled away the lead I had counted upon.

On the third day, we ran out again to the pool. It was midafternoon and we took a chance with the water in the channel, scraping through early in the flood with inches to spare over the sharp coral snags.

Sherry was still in mild disgrace and, with her hands wrapped in acriflavine bandages, she was left in the whaleboat to keep Angelo company. Chubby and I dived together, going down fast and pausing above the swaying bamboo tops only long enough to drop the first marker buoy. I had decided it was necessary to search the pool bottom systematically. I was marking off the whole area into squares, anchoring inflatable buoys above the marine forest on thin nylon line.

We worked for an hour and found nothing that was obviously wreckage, although there were masses of coral covered with marine growth that would bear closer investigation. I marked these on the underwater slate attached to my thigh.

At the end of that hour, our air reserves in the double ninety-cubic-foot bottles were uncomfortably low. Chubby used more air than I did, for he was a much bigger man and his technique lacked finesse, so I regularly checked his pressure gauge.

I took him up and was especially careful on the decompression periods, although Chubby showed his usual impatience. He had never seen as I had, a diver come up too fast so the blood in his veins starts fizzing like champagne. The resultant agonies can cripple a man and an air bubble lodged in the brain can do permanent damage.

'Any luck?' Sherry called as soon as we surfaced, and I gave her the thumbs down as we swam to the whaleboat. We drank a cup of coffee from the Thermos and I smoked an island cheroot while we rested and chatted. I think we were all mildly disappointed that success had not been immediate, but I kept their spirits up by anticipating the first find.

Chubby and I changed our demand valves on to freshly charged bottles and down we went again. This time I would only allow forty-five minutes working at 130 feet, for the effects of gas absorption into the blood are cumulative, and repeated deep diving greatly increases the danger.

We worked carefully through the forests of bamboo stems and over the tumbled coral blocks, exploring the gullies and cracks between them, pausing every few minutes to map the locations of interesting features, then going on, back and forth on the legs of a search pattern between my marker buoys.

Time elapse was forty-three minutes, and I glanced across at Chubby. None of our wet suits would fit him, so he dived naked except for an ancient black woollen bathing costume. He looked like one of my friendly dolphins—only not as graceful—as he forced his way through the thickets. I grinned at the thought and was about to turn away when a chance ray of light pierced the canopy above us and glinted upon something white on the floor below Chubby. I finned in quickly, and examined the white object. At first I thought it was a piece of clam shell, but then I noticed that it was too thick and regular in shape. I sank down closer to it and saw that it was embedded in a decaying sheet of coelenterate coral. I groped for the small jenny bar on my webbing belt, drew it from its sheath and prised off the lump of coral containing the white object. The lump weighed about five pounds and I slipped it into my netting carrybag.

Chubby was watching me and I gave him the signal for the ascent.

'Anything?' Sherry called immediately we surfaced. Her confinement to the whaleboat was obviously playing the devil with her nerves. She was irritable and impatient—but I was not letting her dive until the ugly, suppurating lesions on her hands and thighs had healed. I knew how easily secondary infection could attack those open sores under these conditions, and I was feeding her antibiotics and trying to keep her quiet.

'I don't know,' I answered, as we swam to the boat and I handed the net bag up to her. She took it eagerly, and while we climbed aboard and stripped our equipment she was examining it closely, turning it over in her hands.

Already the surf was breaking heavily on the reef, boiling into the pool and the whaleboat was swinging and bobbing in the disturbance. Angelo was having difficulty holding her on station—and it was time to go. We had spent as much time underwater as I considered safe for one day, and soon now the heavy oceanic surf would begin leaping the coral barrier and sweeping the pool.

'Take us home, Chubby,' I called and he went to the motors. All our attention was focused on the wild ride back through the channel. With the flood of the tide the swells came up under our stern, surfing us, coming through under our hull so fast that our relative speed was reversed and the whaleboat's steering was inverted so we threatened to broach to and tumble broadside on to the coral walls of the channel. However, Chubby's seamanship never faltered, and at last we shot out into the protected waters behind the reef and turned for the island.

Now I could give my attention to the object I had recovered from the pool. With Sherry giving me a great deal of advice that I did not really need, and cautioning me to exercise care, I placed the lump of dead coral on the thwart and gave it a smart crack with the jenny bar. It split into three pieces and revealed a number of articles that had been ingested and protected by the living coral polyps.

There were three round grey objects the size of marbles and I picked one out of the coral bed and weighed it in my hand. It was heavy. I handed it to Sherry.

'Guesses?' I asked.

'Musket balls,' she said without hesitation.

'Of course,' I agreed. I should have recognized it and I made amends by identifying the next object.

'A small brass key.'

'Genius!' she said with irony, and I ignored her as I worked delicately to free the white object which had first caught my attention. It came away at last and I turned it over to examine the blue design worked on one side.

It was a segment of white glazed porcelain, a chip from the rim of a plate which had been ornamented by a coat of arms. Half of the design was missing but I recognized the rampant lion immediately, and the words 'Senat. ANGELIA.' It was the device of John Company again, part of a set of ship's plate.

I passed it to Sherry and suddenly I saw how it must have been. I told her my vision and she listened quietly, fondling the chip of porcelain. 'When at last the surf broke her back and the coral tore her in half, she would have gone down by the middle, and all her heavy cargo and gear would have shifted—tearing out her inner bulkhead. It would all have poured out of her, cannon and shot,

185

plate and silver, flask and cup, coin and pistol—it would have littered the floor of the pool, a rich sowing of man-made articles and the coral has sucked it up and absorbed it.'

'The treasure crates?' Sherry demanded. 'Would they have fallen out of the hull?'

'I don't know,' I admitted, and Chubby, who had been listening intently, spat over the side and growled.

'The forehold was always double-skinned, three-inch oak planks, to hold the cargo from shifting in a storm. Anything was in there then, is still in there now.'

'And that opinion would have cost you ten guineas in Harley Street,' I told Sherry, and winked at her. She laughed and turned to Chubby.

'I don't know what we would do without you, Chubby dear,' and Chubby scowled murderously and suddenly found something of engrossing interest out on the distant horizon.

It was only later, after Sherry and I had taken our swim on one of the secluded beaches and had changed into fresh clothes and were sitting around the fire drinking Chivas Regal and eating fresh prawns netted in the lagoon, that the elation of our first minor finds wore off—and I began soberly to consider the implications of the *Dawn Light* broken up and scattered across the marine hothouse of the pool.

If Chubby were wrong and the treasure crates, with their enormous weight of gold, had smashed through the sides of the hold and fallen free, then it would be an endless task searching for them. I had seen two hundred blocks and mounds of coral that day—any one of which could have concealed a part of the tiger throne of India.

If he were correct and the hold had retained its cargo, then the coral polyps would have spread over the entire front section of the vessel as it lay on the bottom, covering the woodwork with layer upon layer of calcified stone, until it had become an armoured repository for the treasure, disguised with a growth of marine plants.

We discussed it in detail, all of us beginning to appreciate the magnitude of the task we had set ourselves, and we agreed that it fell into two separate parts.

First we had to locate and identify the treasure cases, and then we had to wrest them from the stubborn embrace of the coral.

'You know what we are going to need, don't you, Chubby?' I asked, and he nodded.

'You still got those two cases?' I felt ashamed to mention the word gelignite in front of Sherry. It reminded me too vividly of the project for which Chubby and I had found it necessary to lay in large stocks of high explosive. That had been three years ago, during a lean season when I had been desperate for ready cash to keep myself and *Wave Dancer* aloft. Not even by stretching the letter of the law could our project have been considered legal, and I would rather have closed that chapter and forgotten it—but we needed gelignite now.

Chubby shook his head. 'Man, that stuff began sweating like a stevedore in a heatwave. If you belched within fifty feet of it—it would have blown the top off the island.'

'What did you do with it?'

'Angelo and I took it out into the Mozambique Channel and gave it a deep six.'

'We will need at least a couple of cases. It will take a full shot to break up those big chunks down there.'

'I'll speak to Mister Coker again—he should be able to fix it.'

'Do that, Chubby. Next time you go back to St Mary's you tell Fred Coker to get us three cases.'

'What about the pineapples we saved from *Wave Dancer?*' Chubby asked.

'No good,' I told him. I did not want my obituary to read, 'The man who tried to fuse MK VII hand-grenades in 130 feet of water.'

* * *

I was wakened the next morning by the unnatural hush, and the static charged heat of the air. I lay awake listening, but even the fiddler crabs were silent and the perpetual rattle of the palm fronds was stilled. The only sound was the low and gentle breathing of the woman beside me. I kissed her lightly on the cheek and managed to withdraw my bad arm from under her head without waking her. Sherry boasted that she never used a pillow, it was bad for the spine she told me with an air of rectitude, but this didn't prevent her from using any convenient portion of my anatomy as a substitute.

I ambled out of the cave trying to restore the circulation to my limb by massage, and while I made a libation to my favourite palm tree I studied the sky.

It was a sickly dawn, smeared with a dark haze that dimmed the stars. The heated air lay heavy and languorous against the earth, with no breeze to stir it, and my skin prickled in the charged atmosphere.

Chubby was feeding twigs to the fire and blowing life into it, when I returned. He looked up at me and confirmed my diagnosis.

'Weather going to break.'

'What is coming, Chubby?' and he shrugged. 'Glass is down to 28·2, but we'll know by noon,' and he went back to huffing and puffing over the fire.

The weather had affected Sherry also. The hair at her temples was damp with perspiration and she snapped at me peevishly as I changed her dressings, but minutes later she came up behind me as I dressed, and laid her cheek against my naked back.

'Sorry, Harry, it's just so sticky and close this morning,' and she ran her lips across my back, touching the thick raised cicatrice of the bullet scar with her tongue.

'Forgive?' she asked.

Chubby and I dived into the pool at eleven o'clock that morning. We had been down thirty-eight minutes without making any further significant discovery when I heard the tinny clink! clink! clink!—transmitted through the water. I paused and listened, noticing that Chubby had stopped also. It came again, thrice repeated.

On the surface, Angelo had immersed half of a three-foot length of iron rail into the water and was beating out the recall signal upon it with a hammer from the tool kit.

I gave Chubby the open-handed 'wash out' sign and we began the ascent at once.

As we climbed into the boat I asked impatiently, 'What is it, Angelo?' and in reply he pointed out to seaward over the jagged and irregular back of the reef.

I pulled off my mask and blinked my eyes, refocusing after the limited horizons of the marine world.

It lay low and black against the sea, a thin dark smear as though some playful god had drawn a charcoal line across the horizon—but even as I watched, it seemed to grow—spreading wider into the paler blue of the sky, darker and still darker it rose out of the sea. Chubby whistled softly and shook his head.

'Here comes Lady C and, man, she is in a big hurry.'

The speed of that low dark front was uncanny. It lifted up, drawing a funereal curtain across the sky and as Chubby gunned the motors and ran for the channel the first racing streamers of cloud spread across the sun.

Sherry came to sit beside me on the thwart and help me strip the clinging wet rubber suit.

'What is it, Harry?' she asked.

'Lady C,' I told her. 'It's the cyclone, the same one that killed the *Dawn Light*. She's out hunting again,' and Angelo fetched the lifebelts from the forepeak and handed one to each of us. We tied them on and sat close together and watched it come on in awesome grandeur, overwhelming the sun, changing the sky from a high pure blue dome into a low grey roof of filthy scudding cloud.

We were running hard before her, leaving the channel and flying across the inner waters to the shelter of the cove. All our faces were turned to watch it, all our hearts quailed at the sense of our own frailty before such force and power.

The cloud front passed over our heads as we ran into the bay, and immediately we were plunged into a twilight world, fraught with the fury to come. The cloud dragged a skirt of cold damp air beneath it. It passed over us, and we shivered in the sudden drop in temperature. With a shriek, the wind was upon us, turning the air into a mixture of sand and driven spray.

'The motors,' Chubby bellowed at me, as the whaleboat touched the beach. Those two new Evinrudes represented half the savings of a lifetime and I understood his concern.

'We'll take them with us.'

'And the boat?' Chubby persisted.

'Sink it. There's a firm bottom of sand for it to lie on.'

As Chubby and I freed the motors, Angelo and Sherry lashed the folds of the tarpaulin over the open deck to secure the equipment, and then used the nylon diving lines to tie down the irreplaceable scuba sets and the waterproof cases that contained my medical kit and tools.

Then, while Chubby and I hefted the two heavy Evinrudes, Angelo allowed the wind to push the whaleboat out into the bay where he pulled the drainplugs and she filled immediately with water. The steep wind-maddened sea poured in over the side, and she went down swiftly in twenty feet of water.

Angelo returned to the beach using a dogged sidestroke with the waves breaking over his head. By this time, Sherry and I had almost reached the line of palm trees.

Doubled under my load, I glanced back. Chubby was lumbering after us. He was similarly burdened by the second motor, doubled also under the dead weight of metal and wading through the waist-high torrent of blown white sand. Angelo emerged from the water and followed him.

They were close behind us as we ran into the trees. If I had hoped to find shelter here, then I was a fool, for we found ourselves transferred from an exposed position of acute discomfort into one of real and deadly danger.

The great winds of the cyclone had thrashed the palms into a lunatic frenzy. The sound of it was a deafening clattering roar that was stunning in its intensity. The long graceful stems of the palms whipped about wildly, and the wind clawed loose the fronds and sent them flying off into the haze of sand and spray like huge misshapen birds.

We ran in single file along one of the ill-defined footpaths, Sherry leading us, covering her head with both hands, while I was for the first time grateful for the scanty cover given me by the big white motor on my shoulder for all of us were exposed to the double threat of danger.

The whipping of the tall palms flung from the fifty-foot-high heads their clusters of iron-hard nuts. Big as a cannon-ball and almost as dangerous, these projectiles bombarded us as we ran. One of them struck the motor I carried, a blow that made me stagger, another fell beside the path and on the second bounce hit Sherry on the lower leg. Even though most of its power was spent, still it knocked her down and rolled her in the sand like a running springbok hit by a high-powered rifle. When she regained her feet she was limping heavily—but she ran on through the lethal hail of coconuts.

We had almost reached the saddle of the hills when the wind increased the power of its assault. I heard its shrieking overhead on a higher angrier note, and coming in across the treetops roaring like a wild beast.

It hurled a new curtain of sand at us, and as I glanced ahead I saw the first palm tree begin to go.

I saw it lean out wearily, exhausted by its efforts to resist the wind, the earth around its base heaved upwards as the root system was torn from the sandy soil. As it came down so it gathered speed; swinging in a terrible arc, like the axe of the headsman, it fell towards us. Sherry was fifteen paces ahead of me, just beginning the ascent of the saddle and she had her face turned downwards, watching her own feet, her hands still held to her head.

She was running into the path of the falling tree, and she seemed so small and fragile beneath that solid bole of descending timber. It would crush her with a single gargantuan blow.

I screamed at her, but although she was so close she could not hear me. The roaring of the wind seemed to swamp all our senses. Down swung the long limber stem of the palm tree, and Sherry ran on into its path. I dropped the motor, shrugging it from my shoulder and I ran forward. Even then I saw I could not reach her in time, and I dived belly down, reaching out to the full stretch of my right arm and I hit Sherry's back foot, slapping it across the other as she swung it forward. The ankle tap of the football field, and it tripped her. She fell flat on her face in the sand. As the two of us lay outstretched the palm tree descended. The fury of its stroke rushed through the air even above the sound of the wind and it struck with a blow that was transmitted through the earth into my body, jarring me and rattling the teeth in my skull.

Instantly I was up and dragging Sherry to her feet. The palm tree had missed her by eighteen inches and she was stunned and terrified. I hugged her for a few moments, trying to give her comfort and strength. Then I lifted her over the palm stem that blocked the path, pointed her at the saddle and gave her a shove.

'Run!' I shouted and she staggered onwards. Angelo helped me lift the motor on to my shoulder once more. We clambered over the tree and toiled on up the slope after Sherry's running figure.

All around us in the palm groves I could hear the thud and crash of other trees falling and I tried to run with my face upturned to catch the next threat before it developed, but another flying coconut hit me a glancing blow on the temple, dimming my vision for a moment and I staggered on blindly, taking my chances amongst the monstrous guillotines of the falling palms.

I reached the crest of the saddle without realizing it, and I was unprepared for the full unbroken force of the wind in my back. It hurled me forward, the ground fell away from under my feet as I was thrown over the saddle, my knees gave way and the motor and I rolled headlong down the reverse slope. On the way down we caught up with Sherry North, taking her in the back of the legs. She collapsed on top of me and joined the motor and me on our hurried descent.

One moment I was on top and the next Miss North was seated between my shoulder blades, then the motor was on top of both of us.

When we reached the bottom of the steepest pitch and lay together in a battered and weary heap, we were protected by the saddle from the direct fury of the wind so it was possible to hear what Sherry was saying. It was immediately obvious that she bitterly resented what she considered to be an unprovoked assault, and she was loudly casting doubt on my parentage, character and breeding. Even in my own desperate straits her anger was suddenly terribly comical, and I began to laugh. I saw that she was trying to find sufficient strength to hit me so I decided to distract her.

'—Jack and Jill went up the hill
They each had a dollar and a quarter—'

I croaked at her,

'—Jill came down with half a crown
They didn't go up for water.'

She stared at me for a moment as though I had started frothing at the mouth, then she started to laugh also, but the laughter had a wild hysterical note to it.

'Oh you swine!' she sobbed with laughter, tears streaming down her cheeks and her sodden sand-caked hair dangling in thick dark snakes about her face.

Angelo thought she was weeping when he reached us and he drew her tenderly to her feet and helped her down the last few hundred yards to the caves, leaving me to hoist the motor once more to my bruised shoulder and follow them.

Our cave was well placed to weather the cyclone winds, probably chosen by the old fishermen with that in mind. I retrieved the canvas fly leaf from where it was wrapped around the bole of a palm tree and used it to screen the entrance, piling stones upon the trailing end to hold it down and we had a dimly lit haven into which we crept like two wounded animals.

I had left my motor with Chubby in his cave. I felt at that moment that if I never saw it again it would be too soon, but I knew Chubby would treat it with all the loving care of a mother for her sickly infant and that when the cyclone passed on, it would once more be ready for sea.

Once I had rigged the tarpaulin to screen the cave and keep out the wind, Sherry and I could strip and clean ourselves of the salt and sand. We used a basinful of the precious fresh water for this purpose, each of us taking it in turn to stand in the basin and be sponged down by the other.

I was a mass of scratches and bruises from my long battle with the motor, and although my medical kit was still in the boat at the bottom of the bay, I found a large bottle of mercurochrome in my bag. Sherry began a convincing imitation of Florence Nightingale, with the antiseptic and a roll of cotton wool she anointed my wounds, murmuring condolences and sympathetic sounds.

I rather enjoy being fussed over, and I stood there in a semi-hypnotic state lifting an arm or moving a leg as I was bidden. The first hint that I received that Miss North was not treating my crippling injuries with the true gravity they deserved was when she suddenly emitted a hoot of glee and daubed my most delicate extremity with a scarlet splash of mercurochrome.

'Rudolph the red-nosed reindeer,' she chortled, and I roused myself to protest bitterly.

'Hey! That stuff doesn't wash off.'

'Good!' she cried. 'I'll be able to find you now if you ever get lost in a crowd.' I was shocked by such unseeming levity. I gathered about me my dignity and went to find a pair of dry pants.

Sherry reclined on the mattress and watched me scratching in my bag.

'How long is this going to last?' she asked.

'Five days,' I told her, as I paused to listen to the unabated roar of the wind.

'How do you know?'

'It always lasts five days,' I explained, as I stepped into my shorts and hoisted them.

'That's going to give us a little time to get to know each other.'

* * *

We were caged by the cyclone, locked together in the confined few square feet of the cave, and it was a strange experience.

Any venture out into the open forced upon us by nature, or to check how Chubby and Angelo were faring, was fraught with discomfort and danger. Although the trees were stripped of most of their fruit during the first twelve hours and the weaker trees fell during that period also—yet there was still the occasional tree that came crashing down, and the loose trash and fronds flew like arrows on

193

the wind with sufficient force to blind a person or inflict other injury.

Chubby and Angelo worked away quietly on the motors, stripping them down and cleaning them of salt water. They had something to keep them busy.

In our cave, once the initial novelty had passed there developed some crisis of will and decision which I did not properly understand, but which I sensed was critical.

I had never pretended to understand Sherry North in any depth, there were too many unanswered questions, too many areas of reserve, barriers of privacy beyond which I was not allowed to pass. She had not to this time made any declaration of her feelings, there was never any discussion of the future. This was strange, for any other woman I had ever known expected—nay demanded—declarations of love and passion. I sensed also that this indecision was causing her as much distress as it was me. She was caught up in something against which she struggled, and in the process her emotions were being badly mauled.

However, with Sherry there was nothing spoken of—for I had accepted the tacit agreement and we did not discuss any of our feelings for each other. I found this restricting, for I am a lover with a florid turn of speech. If I have not yet succeeded in talking a bird down out of a tree—it is probably because I have never seriously made the attempt. I could make this adjustment without too much pain, however, it was the lack of a future that chafed at me.

It seemed that Sherry did not look for our relationship to last longer than the setting of the sun, yet I knew that she could not feel this way, for in the moments of warmth that interspersed those of gloom, there could be no doubts.

Once when I started to speak of my plans for when we had raised the treasure—how I would have another boat built to my design, a boat that incorporated all the best features of the beloved *Wave Dancer*—how I would build a new dwelling at Turtle Bay that would not deserve the title of shack—how I would furnish it and people it—she took no part in the discussion. When I ran out of words, she turned away from me on the mattress and pretended to sleep although I could feel the tension in her body without touching her.

At another time I found her watching me with that hostile, hating look. While an hour later she was in a frenzy of physical passion which was in diametric contrast.

She sorted and mended my clothing from the bag, sitting cross-legged on the mattress and working with neat businesslike stitches. When I thanked her, she became caustic and derisive, and we ended up in a blazing row until she flung herself out of the cave and ran through the raging wind to Chubby's cave. She did not return until after dark, with Chubby escorting her and holding a lantern to light her way.

Chubby regarded me with an expression that would have melted a lesser man and frostily refused my invitation to drink whisky, which meant that he was either very sick or very disapproving, then he disappeared again into the storm muttering darkly.

By the fourth day my nerves were in a jangling mess, but I had considered the problem of Sherry's strange behaviour from every angle and I reached my conclusions.

Cooped up with me in that tiny cave she was being forced at last to consider her feelings for me. She was falling in love, probably for the first time in her life, and her fiercely independent spirit was hating the experience. I cannot say in truthfulness that I was enjoying it very much either—or rather I enjoyed the short periods of repentance and loving between each new tantrum—but I looked forward fervently to the moment when she accepted the inevitable and succumbed completely.

I was still awaiting that happy moment when I awoke in the dawn of the fifth day. The island was in a grip of a stillness that was almost numbing after the uproar of the cyclone. I lay and listened to the silence without opening my eyes, but when I felt movement beside me I rolled my head and looked into her face.

'The storm is over,' she said softly, and rose from the bed.

We walked out side by side into the early morning sunlight, blinking around us at the devastation which the storm had created. The island looked like the photographs of a World War II battlefield. The palms were stripped of their foliage, the bare masts pointed pathetically at the sky and the earth below was littered thickly with palm fronds and coconuts. The stillness hung over it all, no breath of wind, and the sky was pale milky blue, still filled with a haze of sand and sea.

From their cave Chubby and Angelo emerged, like big bear and little bear, at the end of winter. They too stood and looked about them uncertainly.

Suddenly Angelo let out a Comanche whoop and leaped four feet in the air. After five days of forced confinement his animal spirits could no longer be suppressed. He took off through the palm trees like a greyhound.

'Last one in the water is a fascist,' he shouted, and Sherry was the first to accept the challenge. She was ten paces behind him when they hit the beach but they dived simultaneously into the lagoon, fully clad, and began immediately pelting each other with handfuls of wet sand. Chubby and I followed at a sedate pace more in keeping with our years. Still wearing his vividly striped pyjamas, Chubby lowered his massive hams into the sea.

'I got to tell you, man, that feels good,' he admitted gravely. I drew deeply on my cheroot as I sat beside him waist deep, then I handed him the butt.

'We lost five days, Chubby,' I said, and immediately he scowled.

'Let's get busy,' he growled, sitting in the lagoon in yellow and purple striped pyjamas, cheroot in his mouth, like a big brown bullfrog.

*　　*　　*

From the peak we looked down into the shallow waters of the lagoon and although they were still a little murky with spindrift and churned sand, yet the whaleboat was clearly visible. She had drifted sideways in the bay and was lying on the bottom in twenty feet of water with the yellow tarpaulin still covering her deck.

We raised the whaleboat with air bags and once her gunwales broke the surface we were able to bale her out and row her into the beach. The rest of that day was needed to unload the waterlogged cargo, clean and dry it, pump the air bottles, get the motors aboard and prepare for the next visit to Gunfire Reef.

I was beginning to become seriously concerned by the delays which had left us sitting on the island, day after day, while Manny Resnick and his merry men cut away the lead we had started with.

That evening we discussed it around the campfire, and agreed that we had made almost no progress in ten days other than to confirm that part of the *Dawn Light*'s wreckage had fallen into the pool.

However, the tides were set fair for an early start in the morning and Chubby ran us through the channel with hardly sufficient light to recognize the coral snags, and when we took up our station in the back of the reef the sun was only just showing its blazing upper rim above the horizon.

During the five days we had lain ashore, Sherry's hands had almost entirely healed, and although I suggested tactfully that she should allow Chubby to accompany me for the next few days, my tact and concern were wasted. Sherry North was suited and finned and Chubby sat in the stern beside the motors holding us on station.

Sherry and I went down fast, and entered the forest of sea bamboo, picking up position from the markers that Chubby and I had left on our last dive.

We were working in close to the base of the coral cliff and I placed Sherry on the inside berth where it would be easier to hold position in the search pattern while she oriented herself.

We had hardly begun the first leg and had swum fifty feet from the last marker when Sherry tapped urgently on her bottles to attract my attention and I pushed my way through the bamboo to her.

She was hanging against the side of the coral cliff upside down like a bat, closely examining a fall of coral and debris that had slid down to the floor of the pool. She was in deep shade under the loom of dark coral so I was at her side before I saw what had attracted her.

Propped against the cliff, its bottom end lying in the mound of debris and weed, was a long cylindrical object which itself was heavily infested with marine growth and had already been partially ingested by the living coral.

Yet its size and regular shape indicated that it was man-made—for it was nine feet long and twenty inches thick, perfectly rounded and slightly tapered.

Sherry was studying it with interest and when I came up she turned to meet me and made signs of incomprehension.

I had recognized what it was immediately and the skin of my forearms and at the nape of my neck felt prickly with excitement. I made a pistol of my thumb and forefinger and mimed the act of firing it, but she did not understand and shook her head so I scribbled quickly on the underwater slate and showed it to her.

'Cannon.'

She nodded vigorously, rolled her eyes and blew bubbles to register triumph before turning back to the cannon.

It was about the correct size to be one of the long nine-pounders that had formed part of the *Dawn Light*'s armament but there was no chance that I should be able to read any inscription upon it, for the surface was crocodile-skinned with growth and corrosion. Unlike the bronze bell that Jimmy North had recovered, it had not been buried in the sand to protect it.

I floated down along the massive barrel examining it closely and almost immediately found another cannon in the deeper gloom nearer the cliff. However, three-quarters of this weapon had been incorporated into the cliff, built into it by the living coral polyps.

I swam in closer, ducking under the first barrel and went into the jumble of debris and fallen coral blocks. I was within two feet of this amorphous mass when with a shock which constricted my breathing and flushed warmly through my blood I recognized what I was looking at.

Quickly and excitedly I finned over the mound of debris, finding where it ended and the unbroken coral began, forcing my way up through the sea bamboo to estimate its size, and pausing to examine any opening or irregularity in it.

The total mass of debris was the size of a couple of railway pullman coaches, but it was only when I pushed aside a larger floating clump of weed and peered into the squared opening of a gunport, from which the muzzle of a cannon still protruded and which had not been completely altered in shape by the encroaching coral, that I was certain that what we had discovered was the entire forward section of the frigate *Dawn Light*, broken off just behind the main mast.

I looked around wildly for Sherry and saw her finned feet protruding from another portion of the wreckage. I pulled her out, removed her mouthpiece and kissed her lustily before replacing it. She was laughing with excitement and when I signalled her that we were ascending, she shook her head vehemently and shot away from me to continue her explorations. It was fully fifteen minutes later that I was able to drag her away and take her up to the whaleboat.

We both began talking at once the moment we had the rubber mouthpieces out of the way. My voice is louder than hers, but she is more persistent. It took me some minutes to assert my rights as expedition leader and I could begin to describe it to Chubby.

'It's the *Dawn Light* sure enough. The weight of her armament and cargo must have pulled her down the instant she was clear of the reef. She went down like a stone, and she is lying against the foot of the cliff. Some of her cannons have fallen out of the hull, and they're lying jumbled around it—'

'We didn't recognize it at first,' Sherry chimed in again, just when I had her quieted down. 'It's like a rubbish dump. Just an enormous heap.'

'From what I could judge she must have broken her back abaft the main mast, but she's been smashed up badly for most of her length. The cannon must have torn up her gundeck and it's only the two ports nearest the bows that are intact—'

'How does she lie?' Chubby demanded, coming immediately to the pith of the matter.

'She's bottom up,' I admitted. 'She must have rolled as she went down.'

'That makes it a real problem, unless you can get in at a gunport or under the waist,' Chubby growled.

'I had a good look,' I told him, 'but I couldn't find a point at which we could penetrate the hull. Even the gunports are solid with growth.'

Chubby shook his head mournfully. 'Man, looks like this place is badly hexed,' and immediately all three of us made the cross-fingered sign against it.

Angelo told him primly, 'You talking up a storm. Shouldn't say that, hear?' but Chubby shook his head again, and his face collapsed into pessimistic folds.

I slapped him on his back and asked him, 'Is it true that you pass iced water—even in hot weather?' and my attempt at humour made him look as cheerful as an unemployed undertaker.

'Oh, leave Chubby alone,' Sherry came to his rescue. 'Let's go down again and try and find a break in the hull.'

'We'll take half an hour's rest,' I said, 'a smoke and a mug of coffee —then we'll go take another look.'

We stayed down so long on the second dive that Chubby had to sound the triple recall signal—and when we surfaced the pool was boiling. The cyclone had left a legacy of high surf, and on the rising tide it was coming in heavily across the reef and pounding in through the gap, higher in the channel than we had ever known it.

We clung to the thwarts in silence as Chubby took us home on a wild ride, and it was only when we entered the quieter waters of the lagoon that we could continue the discussion.

'She's as tight as the Chatwood lock on the national safe deposit,' I told them. 'The one gunport is blocked by the cannon, and I got into the other about four feet before I ran into part of the bulkhead which must have collapsed. It's the den of a big old moray eel that looks like a python—he's got teeth on him like a bulldog and he and I aren't friends.'

'What about the waist?' Chubby demanded.

'No,' I said, 'she's settled down heavily, and the coral has closed her up.'

Chubby put on an expression which meant that he had told us so. I could have beaten him over the head with a spanner, he was so smug—but I ignored him and showed them the piece of woodwork that I had prised off the hull with a crowbar.

'The coral has closed everything up solid. It's like those old forests that have been petrified into stone. The *Dawn Light* is a ship of stone, armour-plated with coral. There is only one way we will get into her—and that is to pop her open.'

Chubby nodded, 'That's the way to do it,' and Sherry wanted to know:

'But if you use explosive, won't it just blow everything to bits?'

'We won't use an atomic bomb,' I told her. 'We'll start with half a stick in the forward gunport. Just enough to kick out a chunk of that coral plating,' and I turned back to Chubby. 'We need that gelignite right away, every hour is precious now, Chubby. We've got a good moon. Can you take us back to St Mary's tonight?' and Chubby did not bother to answer such a superfluous question. It was an indirect slur on his seamanship.

There was a horned moon, with a pale halo around it. The atmosphere was still full of dust from the big winds. The stars also were misty and very far away, but the cyclone had blown great masses of oceanic plankton into the channel so that the sea was a glowing phosphorescent mass wherever it was disturbed.

Our wake glowed green and long, spread behind us like a peacock's tail, and the movement of fish beneath the surface shone like meteors. Sherry dipped her hand over the side and brought it out burning with a weird and liquid flame, and she cooed with wonder.

Later when she was sleepy she lay against my chest under the tarpaulin I had spread to keep off the damp and we listened to the booming of the giant manta rays out in the open water as they leaped high and fell to smack the surface of the sea with their flat bellies and tons of dead weight.

It was long after midnight when we raised the lights of St Mary's like a diamond necklace around the throat of the island.

The streets were utterly deserted as we left the whaleboat at her moorings and walked up to Chubby's house. Missus Chubby opened to us in a dressing-gown that made Chubby's pyjamas look conservative. She had her hair in large pink plastic curlers. I had never seen her without a hat before and I was surprised that she was not as bald as her spouse. They looked so alike in every other way.

She gave us coffee before Sherry and I climbed into the pick-up and drove to Turtle Bay. The bedclothes were damp and needed airing but neither of us complained.

I stopped at the Post Office in the early morning and my box was half filled, mostly with fishing equipment catalogues and junk mail, but there were a few letters from old clients inquiring for charter—that gave me a pang—and one of the buff cable envelopes which I opened last. Cables have always borne bad news for me. Whenever I see one of those envelopes with my name peering out of the window like a long-term prisoner I have this queasy feeling in my stomach.

The message read: 'MANDRAKE SAILED CAPETOWN OUTWARD BOUND ZANZIBAR 12.00 HOURS FRIDAY 16TH. STEVE.'

My premonitions of evil were confirmed. *Mandrake* had left Cape Town six days ago. She had made a faster passage than I would have believed possible. I felt like rushing to the top of Coolie Peak to search the horizon. Instead I passed the cable to Sherry and drove down to Frobisher Street.

Fred Coker was just opening the street door of his travel agency as I parked outside Missus Eddy's store and sent Sherry in with a shopping list while I walked on down the street to the Agency.

Fred Coker had not seen me since I had dropped him moaning on the floor of his own morgue, and now he was sitting at his desk in a white shark-skin suit and wearing a necktie which depicted a hula girl on a palm-lined beach and the legend 'Welcome to St Mary's! Pearl of the Indian Ocean.'

He looked up with a smile that went well with the tie, but the moment he recognized me his expression changed to utter dismay.

He let out a bleat like an orphan lamb and shot out of his chair, heading for the back room.

I blocked his escape and he backed away before me, his gold-rimmed glasses glittering like the sheen of nervous sweat that covered his face until the chair caught him in the back of his knees and he collapsed into it. Only then did I give him my big friendly grin—and I thought he would faint with relief.

'How are you, Mister Coker?' He tried to answer but his voice failed him. Instead he nodded his head so rapidly that I understood he was very well.

'I want you to do me a favour.'

'Anything,' he gabbled, suddenly recovering the power of speech. 'Anything, Mister Harry, you have only to ask.'

Despite his protestations it took him only a few minutes to recover his courage and wits. He listened to my very reasonable request for three cases of high explosive, and went into a pantomime to impress me with the utter impossibility of compliance. He rolled his eyes, sucked in his cheeks and made clucking noises with his tongue.

'I want it by noon tomorrow—latest,' and he clasped his forehead as if in agony.

'And if it's not here by twelve o'clock precisely, you and I will continue our discussion on the insurance premiums—'

He dropped his hand and sat upright, his expression once more willing and intelligent.

'That's not necessary, Mister Harry. I can get what you ask—but it will cost a great deal of money. Three hundred dollars a case.'

'Put it on the slate,' I told him.

'Mister Harry!' he cried, 'you know I cannot extend credit.'

I was silent, but I slitted my eyes, clenched my jaws and began to breathe deeply.

'Very well,' he said hurriedly. 'Until the end of the month, then.'

'That's very decent of you, Mister Coker.'

'It's a pleasure, Mister Harry,' he assured me. 'A very great pleasure.'

'There is just one other thing, Mr Coker,' and I could see him mentally quail at my next request, but he braced himself like a hero.

'In the near future I expect to be exporting a small consignment to Zürich in Switzerland.' He sat a little forward in his seat. 'I do not wish to be bothered with customs formalities—you understand?'

'I understand, Mister Harry.'

'Do you ever have requests to send the body of one of your customers back to the near and dear?'

'I beg your pardon?' He looked confused.

'If a tourist were to pass away on the island—say of a heart attack — you would be called on to embalm his corpse for posterity and to ship it out in a casket. Am I correct?'

'It has happened before,' he agreed. 'On three occasions.'

'Good, so you are familiar with the procedure?'

'I am, Mister Harry.'

'Mister Coker, lay in a casket and get yourself a pile of the correct forms. I'll be shipping soon.'

'May I ask what you intend to export—in lieu of a cadaver?' He phrased the question delicately.

'You may well ask, Mister Coker.'

I drove down to the fort and spoke to the President's secretary. He was in a meeting, but he would see me at one o'clock if I would care to lunch with him in his office. I accepted the invitation and, to pass the hours until then, I drove up the track to Coolie Peak as far as the pick-up would take me. There I parked it and walked on to the ruins of the old lookout and signal station. I sat on the parapet looking out across a vista of sea and green islands while I smoked a cheroot and did my last bit of careful planning and decision-making, glad of this opportunity to make certain of my plans before committing myself to them.

I thought of what I wanted from life, and decided it was three things—Turtle Bay, *Wave Dancer II* and Sherry North, not necessarily in that order of preference.

To stay on at Turtle Bay, I had to keep a clean pair of hands in St Mary's, to have *Wave Dancer II* I needed cash and plenty of it, and Sherry North—well, that took plenty of hard thought, and at the end of it my cheroot had burned to a stub and I ground it out on the stone parapet. I took a deep breath and squared my shoulders.

'Courage, Harry me lad,' I said and drove down to the fort.

The President was delighted to see me, coming out into the reception room to welcome me and rising on tip-toe to place an arm around my shoulders and lead me into his office.

It was a room like a baronial hall with a beamed ceiling, panelled walls and English landscapes in massive ornate frames and dark smoky looking oils. The diamond-paned window rose from the floor to the ceiling and looked out over the harbour, and the floor was lush with oriental carpets.

Luncheon was spread on the oaken conference table below the windows—smoked fish, cheese and fruit with a bottle of Château Lafite '62 from which the cork had been drawn.

The President poured two crystal glasses of the deep red wine, offered one to me and then plopped two cubes of ice into his own glass. He grinned impishly as he saw my startled expression. 'Sacrilege, isn't it?' He raised the glass of rare wine and ice cubes to me. 'But, Harry, I know what I like. What is suitable on the Rue Royale isn't necessarily suitable on St Mary's.'

'Right on, sir!' I grinned back at him and we drank.

'Now, my boy, what did you want to talk to me about?'

* * *

I found a message that Sherry had gone to visit Missus Chubby when I arrived back at the shack, so I went out on to the veranda with a cold beer. I went over my meeting with President Biddle, reviewing it word for word, and found myself satisfied. I thought I had covered all the openings—except the ones I might need to escape through.

* * *

Three wooden cases marked 'Canned Fish. Produce of Norway' arrived on the ten o'clock plane from the mainland addressed to Coker's Travel Agency.

'Eat your liver, Alfred Nobel,' I thought when I saw the legend as Fred Coker unloaded them from the hearse at Turtle Bay and I placed them in the rear of the pick-up under the canvas cover.

'Until the end of the month then, Mister Harry,' said Fred Coker, like the leading man from a Shakespearian tragedy.

'Depend upon it, Mister Coker,' I assured him and he drove away through the palms.

Sherry had finished packing away the stores. She looked so different from yesterday's siren, with her hair scraped back, dressed in one of my old shirts, which fitted her like a nightdress, and a pair of faded jeans with raggedy legs cut off below the knees.

I helped her carry the cases out to the pick-up, and we climbed into the cab.

'Next time we come back here we'll be rich,' I said, and started the motor, forgetting to make the sign against the hex.

We ground up through the palm grove, hit the main road below the pineapple fields and climbed up the ridge.

We came out on the crest above the town and the harbour.

'God damn it!' I shouted angrily, and hit the brakes hard, swinging off the road on to the verge so violently that the pineapple truck following us swerved to avoid running into our rear, and the driver hung out of his window to shout abuse as he passed.

'What is it?' Sherry pulled herself off the dashboard where my manoeuvre had thrown her. 'Are you crazy?'

It was a bright and cloudless day, the air so clear that every detail of the lovely white and blue ship stood out like a drawing. She lay at the entrance to Grand Harbour on the moorings usually reserved for visiting cruise ships, or the regular mail ship.

She was flying a festival burst of signal flags and I could see her crew in tropical whites lining the rail and staring at the shore. The harbour tender was running out to her, carrying the harbour-master, the customs inspector and Doctor MacNab.

'*Mandrake?*' Sherry asked.

'*Mandrake* and Manny Resnick,' I agreed, and swung the truck into a U-turn across the road.

'What are you going to do?' she asked.

'One thing I'm not going to do is show myself in St Mary's while Manny and his fly lads are ashore. I've met most of them before in circumstances which are likely to have burned my lovely features clearly into even their rudimentary brains.'

Down the hill at the first bus stop beyond the turn off to Turtle Bay was the small General Dealers' Store which supplied me with eggs, milk, butter and other perishables. The proprietor was delighted to see me and he flourished my outstanding bill like a winning lottery ticket. I paid him, and then closed the door of his back office while I used the telephone.

Chubby did not have a phone, but his next-door neighbour called him to speak to me.

'Chubby,' I told him, 'that big white floating brothel at the mail ship mooring is no friend of ours.'

'What you want me to do, Harry?'

'Move fast. Cover the water cans with stump nets and make like you are going fishing. Get out to sea and come around to Turtle Bay.

We'll load from the beach and run for Gunfire Reef as soon as it's dark.'

'I'll be in the bay in two hours,' he said and hung up.

He was there in one hour forty-five minutes. One of the reasons I liked working with him is that you can put money on his promises.

As soon as the sun set and visibility was down to a hundred yards we slipped out of Turtle Bay, and we were well clear of the island by the time the moon came up.

Huddled under the tarpaulin, sitting on a case of gelignite, Sherry and I discussed the arrival of *Mandrake* in Grand Harbour.

'First thing Manny will do, he will send his lads out with a pocketful of bread to ask a few questions around the shops and bars. "Anyone seen Harry Fletcher?" and they'll be lining up to tell him all about it. How Mister Harry chartered Chubby Andrews' stump boat, and how they been diving looking for seashells. If he gets really lucky somebody will point him in the direction of Frederick Coker Esquire—and Fred will fall over himself to tell all, as long as the price is right.'

'Then what will he do?'

'He will have an attack of the vapours when he hears that I didn't drown in the Severn. When he recovers from that, he will send a team out to ransack and search the shack at Turtle Bay. He will draw a dud card there. Then the lovely Miss Lorna Page will lead them all to the alleged site of the wreck off Big Gull. That will keep them happy and busy for two or three days—until they find they have nothing but the ship's bell.'

'Then?'

'Well, then Manny is going to get mad. I think Lorna is in line for some unpleasantness—but after that I don't know what will happen. All we can do is try to keep out of sight and work like a tribe of beavers to get the Colonel's goodies out of the wreck.'

*　*　*

The next day the state of the tides was such that we could not navigate the channel before the late morning. It gave us time to make preparations. I opened one of the cases of gelignite and took out ten of the waxy yellow sticks. I reclosed the case and buried it with the other two in the sandy soil of the palm grove, well away from the camp.

Then Chubby and I assembled and checked the blasting equipment. It was a home-made contraption, but it had proved its efficiency before. It consisted of two nine-volt transistor batteries in a simple switchbox. We had four reels of light insulated copper wire, and a cigar-box of detonators. Each of the lethal silver tubes was carefully wrapped in cotton wool. There was also a selection of time-delayed detonators of the pencil type in the box.

Chubby and I isolated ourselves while we worked with them, clamping the electric detonators to the hand-made terminals that I had soldered for the purpose.

The use of high explosives is simple in theory, and nerve-racking in practice. Even an idiot can wire it up and hit the button, but in its refined form it becomes an art.

I have seen a medium-sized tree survive a blast of half a case, losing only its leaves and some of its bark—but with half a stick I can drop the same tree neatly across a road to block it effectively, without removing a single leaf. I consider myself something of an artist, and I had taught Chubby all I knew. He was a natural, although he could never be termed an artist—his glee in the proceedings was too frankly childlike. Chubby just naturally loved to blow things up. He hummed happily to himself as he worked with the detonators.

We took up position in the pool a few minutes before noon and I went down alone, armed only with a Nemrod captive air spear gun with a barbed crucifix head I had designed and made myself. The point was needle-sharp, and it was multi-barbed for the first six inches. Twenty-four small sharp barbs, like those used by Batonka tribesmen when they spear catfish in the Zambezi River. Behind the barbs was the crucifix, a four-inch cross-piece which would prevent the victim slipping down the shaft close enough to attack me when I held the reverse end. The line was five hundred pound blue nylon and there was a twenty foot loop of it under the barrel of the spear gun.

I finned down on to the overgrown heap of wreckage and I settled myself comfortably beside the gunport and closed my eyes for a few seconds to accustom them to the gloom, then I peered cautiously into the dark square opening, pushing the barrel of the spear gun ahead of me.

The dark slimy coils of the Moray eel slithered and unwound as it sensed my presence, and it reared threateningly, displaying the fearsome irregular yellow fangs. In the gloom the eyes were black and bright, catching the feeble light like those of a cat.

He was a huge old fellow, thick as my calf and longer than the stretch of both my arms. The waving mane of his dorsal fin was angrily erected as he threatened me.

I lined him up carefully, waiting for him to turn his head and offer a better target. It was a scary few moments, I had one shot and if that was badly placed he would fly at me. I had seen a captive Moray chew mouthfuls out of the woodwork of a dinghy. Those fangs would tear easily through rubber suit and flesh, right down to the bone.

He was weaving slowly, like a flaring cobra, watching me and the range was extreme for accurate shooting. I waited for the moment, and at last he went into the second stage of aggression. He blew up his throat and turned slightly to offer me a profile.

'My God,' I thought, 'I once used to do this for fun,' and I took up the slack in the trigger. The gas hissed viciously and the plunger thudded to the end of its travel as it threw the spear. It flew in a long blur with the line whipping out behind it.

I had aimed for the dark earlike marking at the back of the skull, and I was an inch and a half high and two inches right. The Moray exploded into a spinning, whipping ball of coils that seemed to fill the whole gunport. I dropped the gun and with a push of my fins I shot forward and got a grip of the hilt of the spear. It kicked and thumped in my hands as the eel wound its thick dark body around the shaft. I drew him out of his lair, pinned by a thick bite of skin and rubbery muscle to the barbed head.

His mouth was opened in a silent screech of fury, and he unwound his body and let it fly and writhe like a pennant in a high wind.

The tail slapped into my face, dislodging my mask. Water flooded into my nose and eyes and I had to blow it clear before I could begin the ascent.

Now the eel twisted its head back at an impossible angle and closed the dreadfully gaping jaws on the metal shaft of the spear. I could hear the fangs grinding and squeaking in the steel, and there were bright silver scratches where it had bitten.

I came out through the surface holding aloft my prize. I heard Sherry squeal with horror at the writhing snakelike monster, and Chubby grunted, 'Come to papa, you beauty,' and he leaned out to grasp the spear and lift the eel aboard. He was showing his plastic gums in a happy grin for Moray eel was Chubby's favourite food. He held the neck against the gunwale and, with an expert sweep of his bait-knife, lopped the monstrous head cleanly away, letting it fall into the pool.

'Miss Sherry,' he said, 'you going to love the taste of him.'

'Never!' Sherry shuddered, and drew herself farther away from the bleeding, wriggling carcass.

'Okay, my children, let's have the gelly.' Angelo had the underwater carry-net ready to pass to me, and Sherry slid in over the side prepared to dive. She had the reel of insulated wire and she paid it out smoothly as we went down.

Once again I went directly to the now untenanted gunport and crept into it. The breech of the cannon was jammed solidly against the mass of debris beyond.

I chose two sites to place my shots. I wanted to kick the cannon aside, using it like a giant lever to tear out a slab of the petrified planking. The second shot fired simultaneously would blow into the wall of debris that barred entry to the gundeck.

I wired the shots firmly into place. Sherry passed the end of the line in to me and I snipped and bared the copper wire with the side-cutters before connecting it up to the terminals.

I checked the job once it was finished and then backed out of the port. Sherry was sitting cross-legged on the hull with the reel on her lap and I grinned at her around my mouthpiece and gave her the thumbs up before I retrieved my spear gun from where I had dropped it.

When we climbed over the side of the whaleboat Chubby had the battery switchbox beside him on the thwart and it was wired up. He was scowling with anticipation, as he crouched possessively over the blaster. It would have taken physical force to deprive him of the pleasure of hitting the button.

'Ready to shoot, skipper,' he growled.

'Shoot her then, Chubby.' He fussed with the box a little longer, drawing out the pleasure, then he turned the switch.

The surface of the pool bounced and shivered and we felt the bump come up through the bottom of the boat. Many seconds later there was a surge and frothing of bubbles, as though somebody had dropped a ton of Alka Seltzer into the pool. Slowly it cleared.

'I want you to put the trousers of your suit on, my sweeting,' I told

Sherry, and predictably she took the order as an invitation to debate its correctness.

'Why, the water is warm?'

'Gloves and bootees also,' I said, as I began to pull on my own rubber full-length pants. 'If the hull is open we may penetrate her on this dive. You'll need protection against snags.'

Convinced at last, she did what she should have done without question. I still had a lot of work to do before she was properly trained, I thought, as I assembled the other equipment I needed for this descent.

I took the sealed unit underwater flashlight, the jenny bar and a coil of light nylon line and waited while Sherry completed the major task of wiggling her bottom into the tight rubber pants, assisted faithfully by Angelo. Once she had them hoisted and had buttoned the crotch piece, we were set to go.

When we were halfway down, we came upon the first dead fish floating belly up in the misty blue depths. There were hundreds of them that the explosions had killed or maimed, and they ranged in size from fingerlings to big striped snapper and reef bass as long as my arm. I felt a pang of remorse at the massacre I had perpetrated, but consoled myself with the thought I had killed less than a bluefin tunny would in a single day's feeding.

We went down through this killing ground, and the light caught the eddying and drifting carcasses so they blinked and shone like dying stars in a smoky azure sky.

The bottom of the pool was murky with particles of sand and other material stirred up by the shock of the blast. There was a hole torn in the cover of sea bamboo and we went down into it.

I saw at once that I had achieved my purpose. The explosion had kicked the massive cannon out of the hull, tearing it like a rotten tooth from the black and ancient maw of the gunport. It had fallen to the bed of the pool surrounded by the debris that it had brought away with it.

The upper lip of the gunport had been knocked out, enlarging the opening so that a man might stand almost upright in it. When I flashed the light into the darkness beyond, I saw that it was a turgid fog of suspended dirt and particles which would take time to settle. My impatience would not allow that, however, and as we settled on the hull I checked my time elapse and air reserves. Quickly I calculated our working time, allowing for my two previous descents which would necessitate additional decompression. I reckoned we had seventeen minutes' safe time before beginning the ascent and I set the swivel ring on my wristwatch before preparing for the penetration.

I used the jettisoned cannon as a convenient anchor point on which to fix the end of the nylon line and then rose again to the opening, paying it out behind me as I went.

I had to remove Sherry North from the gunport, in the few seconds while I was busy with the line she had almost disappeared into the hole in the hull. I made angry signs at her to keep clear, and in return she made an unladylike gesture with two fingers which I pretended not to see.

Gingerly I entered the gunport and found that the visibility was down to about three feet in the murky soup.

The shots had only partially moved the blockage beyond the spot where the cannon had lain. There seemed to be a gap beyond but it needed to be enlarged before I could get through. I used the jenny bar to prise a lump of the wreckage away and discovered that it was the heavy gun carriage that was causing most of the blockage.

Working in freshly blasted wreckage is a delicate business, for it is impossible to know how critically balanced the mass may be. Even the slightest disturbance can bring the whole weight of it sliding and crashing down upon the trespasser, pinning and crushing him beneath it.

I worked slowly and deliberately, ignoring the regular thumps on my rump with which Sherry signalled her burning impatience. Once when I emerged with a section of shattered planking, she took my slate and wrote on it 'I am smaller!!' and underlined the 'smaller' twice in case the double exclamation mark was not noticed when she thrust the slate two inches from my nose. I returned her Churchillian salute and went back to my burrowing.

I had now cleared the area sufficiently to see that my only remaining obstacle was the heavy timber bulk of the gun carriage which was hanging at a drunken angle across the entry to the gundeck. The jenny bar was totally ineffective against this mass, and I could abandon the effort and return with another charge of gelignite tomorrow or I could take a chance.

I glanced at my time elapse and saw that I had been busy for twelve minutes. I reckoned that I had probably been using air more wastefully than usual during my recent exertions. Nevertheless, I decided to take a flier.

I passed the flashlight and jenny bar out to Sherry, and worked my way carefully back into the opening. I got my shoulder under the upper end of the gun carriage, and moved my feet around until I had a firm stance. When I was solidly placed, I took a good breath of air and began to lift.

Slowly I increased the strain until I was thrusting upwards with all the strength of my legs and back. I felt my face and throat swelling with pumping blood and my eyes felt ready to jump out of their sockets. Nothing moved, and I took another lungful of air and tried again, but this time throwing all my weight on the timber beam in a single explosive effort.

It gave way, and I felt like Samson who had pulled the temple down on his own head. I lost my balance and tumbled backwards in a storm of falling debris that groaned and grated as it fell, thudding and bumping around me.

When silence had settled, I found myself in utter darkness, a thick pea soup of swirling filth that blotted out the light. I tried to move, and found my leg pinned. Panic rushed through me in an icy wave and I fought frantically to free my leg. It took only half-a-dozen terrified kicks before I realized that I had escaped with great good luck. The gun carriage had missed my foot by a quarter of an inch, and had fallen across the rubber swimming fin. I pulled my foot out of the shoe, abandoning it, and groped my way out into the open.

Sherry was waiting eagerly for news, and I wiped the slate and wrote 'OPEN!!' underlining the word twice. She pointed into the gunport, demanding permission to enter and I checked my time elapse. We had two minutes, so I nodded and led the way in.

Flashing the beam of the flashlight ahead I had visibility of eighteen inches, enough to find the opening I had cleared. There was just sufficient clearance to allow me through without fouling my air bottles or breathing hose.

I paid out the nylon line behind me, like Theseus in the labyrinth of the Minotaur so as not to lose my direction in the *Dawn Light's* warren of decks and companionways.

Sherry followed me along the line. I could feel her hand touch my foot and brush my leg as she groped after me.

Beyond the blockage, the water cleared a little, and we found ourselves in the low wide chamber of the gundeck. It was murky and mysterious, with strange shapes strewn about us in profusion. I saw other gun carriages, cannonballs strewn loosely or in heaps against angles and corners, and other equipment so altered by long immersion as to be unrecognizable.

We moved slowly forward, our fins stirring up fresh whirlpools of dirt and mud. Here also there were dead fish floating about us, although I noticed some of the red reef crayfish scrambling away like monstrous spiders into the depths of the ship. They at least had survived the blast in their armoured carapaces.

I played the beam of the flashlight on the deck above our heads, looking for the entry point to the lower decks and the holds. With the ship lying upside down, I had to keep trying to relate the existing geography of the wreck to the drawing I had studied.

About fifteen feet from our entry point I found the forecastle ladder, another dark square opening above my head, and I rose into it, my bubbles blowing upwards in a silver shower and running like liquid mercury across the bulkheads and decking. The ladder was rotted so that it fell to pieces at my touch, the pieces hanging suspended in the water around my head as I went on into the lower deck.

This was a narrow and crowded alleyway, probably serving the passenger cabins and officers' mess. The claustrophobic atmosphere reminded me of the appalling conditions in which the crew of the frigate must have lived.

I ventured gingerly along this passage, attracted powerfully to the doorways on either hand which promised all manner of fascinating discoveries. I resisted their temptation and finned on down the long deck until it ended abruptly against a heavy timber bulkhead.

This would be the outer wall of the well of the forward hold, where it pierced the deck and went down into the ship's belly.

Satisfied with what we had achieved, I turned the beam of the flashlight on to my wrist and realized with a guilty thrill that we had overrun our working time by four minutes. Every second was taking us closer to the dreaded danger of empty air bottles and uncompleted decompression stops.

I grabbed Sherry's wrist and gave her the cut-throat hand signal for danger before tapping my wristwatch. She understood immediately, and followed me meekly on the long slow journey back through the hull along the guiding line. Already I could feel the stiffening of the demand valve, as it gave me air more reluctantly now that the bottles were almost exhausted.

We came out into the open and I made certain that Sherry was by my side before I looked upwards. What I saw above me made my breathing choke in my throat, and the horror I felt turned to a warm oily liquid sensation in my bowels.

The pool of Gunfire Break had been transformed into a bloody arena. Attracted by the tons of dead fish that had been killed by the blast, the deep-water killer sharks had arrived in their scores. The scent of flesh and blood, together with the excited movements of their fellows transmitted to them through the water, had driven them into that mindless savagery known as the feeding frenzy.

Quickly I drew Sherry back into the gunport and we cowered there, looking up at the huge gliding shapes so clearly silhouetted against the light source of the surface.

Amongst the shoals of smaller sharks there were at least two dozen of the ugly beasts that the islanders called Albacore shark. They were barrel-bodied and swing-bellied, big powerful fish with rounded snouts and wide grinning jaws. They swirled about the pool like some grotesque carousel, with their tails waggling and their mouths opening mechanically to gulp down shreds of flesh. I knew them for greedy but stupid animals, easily discouraged by any aggressive display when not in feeding frenzy. Now that they were in intense excitation they would be dangerous, yet I would have accepted the risk of a decompression ascent if it had been for them alone.

What truly appalled me were two other long lithe shapes that sped silently about the pool, turning with a single powerful flick of the long swallow tail, so that the pointed nose almost touched the tip of the tail, then gliding away again with all the power and grace of an eagle in flight.

When either one of these terrible fish paused to feed, the sickle-moon mouth opened and the multiple rows of teeth came erect like the quills of a porcupine and flared outwards.

They were a matched pair, each about twelve feet in length from nose to tail-tip, with the standing blade of the dorsal fin as long as a man's arm; they were slaty blue across the back and with snowy white bellies and dark tips to tail and fins, they could bite a man in half and swallow the pieces whole.

One of them saw us crouching in the mouth of the gunport, and it turned sharply and came down over us, planing a few feet above us as we cowered back into the gloom so that I could clearly see the long trailing spikes of the male reproductive organs.

These were the dreaded white death sharks, the most vicious fish of all the seas, and I knew that to attempt to ascend in the clear and decompress adequately with limited air and no protection would be certain death.

If I were to get Sherry out alive I would have to take risks that in any other circumstances would be unthinkable.

Quickly I scribbled on the slate: 'STAY!! I am free ascending for air and gun.'

She read the message and immediately shook her head in refusal and made urgent signs to prevent me, but already I had pulled the pin out of the quick release buckle of my harness and I took the last deep, chest-swelling breath before I thrust my scuba set into her hands. I dropped my weight belt to give myself buoyancy and slid down the side of the hull, using the tumble home to cover me as I finned swiftly for the cover of the cliff.

I had left Sherry what remained of my air supplies, perhaps five or six minutes' breathing if she used it sparingly, and now with only the air that I held in my lungs I had to run the gauntlet of the pool and try for the surface.

I reached the cliff and began to go up, close in against the coral, hoping that my dark suit would blend with the shades. I went up with my back to the coral, facing out into the open pool where the great sinister shapes still swirled and milled.

Twenty feet from the bottom and the air in my lungs was expanding rapidly as the pressure of water decreased. I could not hold it in or it would rupture the tissue of my lungs. I let it trickle from my lips, a silver beacon of bubbles that one of the white death sharks noticed immediately.

He rolled and turned, dashing across the pool with slashing strokes of his tail, bearing down upon me.

Desperately I glanced up the cliff and found six feet above me one of the small caves in the rotten coral. I dived into it just as the shark flashed past me, turned and sped back for a second pass as I shrank into my shallow shelter. The shark lost interest and swirled away to pick up the falling-leaf body of a dead snapper, gulping it down convulsively.

My lungs were throbbing and pumping now for the oxygen had

been all absorbed from the air I held, and the carbon-dioxide was building up in my blood. Soon I would begin to black out into anoxia.

I left the shelter of the cave, but, still following the cliff, I drove upwards as hard as I could with the single swimming fin, wishing bitterly for the use of the other still trapped under the gun carriage.

Again I had to release expanding air as I rose, and I knew that in my veins nitrogen was also decompressing too rapidly and soon it would turn to gas and bubble like champagne in my blood.

Above me I saw the silvery moving mirror of the surface and the black cigar shape of the whaleboat's hull suspended upon it. I was coming up fast and I glanced down again. Far below me I could see the shark pack still milling and turning. It looked as though I had escaped their notice.

My lungs burned with the craving for air, and the blood pounded in my temples as I decided that the time had arrived when I must forsake the shelter of the cliff and cross the open pool to the whaleboat.

I kicked out and shot towards the whaleboat where it lay a hundred feet from the reef. Halfway across I glanced down and saw one of the white deaths had seen me and was chasing. It came up from the blue depths with incredible speed, and terror gave me new strength as I drove for the surface and the boat.

I was looking down, watching the shark come. It seemed to swell up in size as it rushed towards me. Every detail was burned into my mind in those frantic seconds. I saw the hog's snout with the two slitted nostrils, the golden eyes with the black pupils like arrowheads, the broad blue back from which stood the tall executioner's blade of the dorsal fin.

I came out through the surface so fast that I broke clear to my waist, and I turned in the air and got my good arm over the gunwale of the boat. With all my strength I swung my body forward and jack-knifed my legs up under my chin.

In that instant the white death struck, the water exploded about me as he burst through the surface, I felt the harsh gritty skin tear across the legs of my suit as he brushed against me, then there was a shuddering crash as he struck the hull of the whaleboat.

I saw Chubby and Angelo's startled faces as the boat heeled over and rocked wildly. My violent contortions had thrown the shark off his run, and he had missed my legs and collided with the hull.

Now with one more desperate kick and heave I tumbled over the gunwale and fell into the bottom of the whaleboat. Again the shark crashed into the hull as I went over, missing me again by inches.

I lay there pumping air into my aching lungs, great sweet gulps of it that made me light-headed and giddy as on strong wine.

Chubby was yelling at me, 'Where is Miss Sherry? That big Johnny Uptail get Miss Sherry?'

I rolled on to my back, panting and sobbing for the precious air. 'Spare lungs,' I gasped. 'Sherry waiting in the wreck. She needs air.'

Chubby leaped into the bows and dragged the canvas sheet off the extra scuba sets stacked there. In a crisis he is the kind of man I like to have covering for me.

'Angelo,' he growled, 'get them Johnny pills.' They were a pack of copper acetate shark repellent pills which I had ordered from an American sports goods catalogue and for which Chubby had professed a deep and abiding scorn. 'Let's see if those fancy things are any bloody good.'

I had breathed enough to drag myself off the floorboards and to tell Chubby: 'We've got problems. The pool is full of big Johnnys, and there are two really mean uptails with them. That one that charged me and another.'

Chubby scowled as he fitted the demand valves to the new sets. 'Did you come straight up, Harry?'

I nodded. 'I left my bottles for Sherry. She's waiting down there.'

'You going to bend, Harry?' He looked up at me and I saw the worry in his eyes.

'Yes,' I nodded, as I dragged myself to my tackle box and lifted the lid. 'I've got to get down again fast—got to put pressure on my blood again before she fizzes.'

I picked out the bandolier of explosive heads for my hand spear. There were twelve of them, and I wished for more as I strapped the bandolier around my thigh. Each head was hand-tapped to screw on to the shaft of a ten-foot stainless steel spear. It contained explosive charge equivalent to that of a 12-gauge shotgun shell and I could fire the charge with a trigger on the handle. It was an effective shark-killer.

Chubby hoisted one of the scuba sets on to my back and clinched the harness, and Angelo knelt before me to strap the shark repellent tablets in their perforated plastic containers to my ankles.

'I'll need another weight belt,' I said, 'and I lost a fin. There is a spare set in—' I did not finish the sentence. Blinding burning agony struck me in the elbow of my bad arm. Agony so fierce that I cried aloud, and my arm snapped closed like the blade of a clasp knife. It was an involuntary reaction, the joint doubling as the pressure of bubbles in the blood pressed on nerve and tendons.

'He's bending,' snarled Chubby. 'Sweet Mary, he's bending.' He leapt to the motors and gunned them, taking me in close to the reef. 'Work fast, Angelo,' Chubby shouted, 'we got to get him down again.'

The pain struck again, a fiery cramping agony in my right leg. The knee doubled under me and I whimpered like an infant. Angelo strapped the weight belt around my waist, and thrust the swimming fin on to my crippled leg.

Chubby cut the motors and we coasted in under the lee of the reef, while Chubby scrambled back to where I crouched on the thwart. He stooped over me to thrust the mouthpiece between my lips and open the cocks on the air bottles.

'Okay?' he asked, and I sucked from the set and nodded.

Chubby leaned over the side and peered down into the pool. 'Okay,' he grunted, 'Johnny Uptail gone somewhere else.'

He lifted me like a child, for I had lost the use of arm and leg, and he lowered me into the water between boat and reef.

Angelo hooked the harness of the extra scuba set for Sherry on to my belt, then he passed me the ten-foot spear and I prayed that I would not drop it.

'You go get Miss Sherry out of there,' said Chubby, and I rolled over in a clumsy one-legged duck dive and went down.

Even in the cramping agony of the bends my first concern was to search for the sinister gliding shapes of the white deaths. I saw one of them, but he was deep down, amongst the pack of lumbering Albacore sharks. Clinging to the shelter of the reef, I kicked and wriggled downwards like a maimed water beetle. Thirty feet under the surface the pain began to recede. Renewed pressure of water was reducing the size of the bubbles in my bloodstream, my limbs straightened and I had use of them.

I went down faster, and the relief was swift and blessed. I felt new courage and confidence flooding away my earlier despair. I had air and a weapon. I had a fighting chance now.

I was ninety feet down, in clear sight of the bottom. I could see

Sherry's bubbles rising from the smoky blue depths, and the sight cheered me. She was still breathing, and I had a fully charged extra scuba set for her. All I had to do was get it to her.

One of the fat ugly Albacore sharks saw me as I slid down the dark cliff face, and he swerved towards me. Already gorged with food, but endlessly hungry, he came in at me grinning horribly and paddling his wide tail.

I backed up and hung in the water against the cliff, facing him. I had the spear with its explosive head extended towards him, and as I finned gently to hold myself ready the streamers of bright blue dye from the shark repellent tablets smoked out in a cloud around me.

The shark came on in, and I lined up to hit him fairly on the snout, but the instant his head and gills encountered clouds of blue dye he spun away, flapping his tail in shock and dismay. The copper acetate had burned his gills and eyes, and he retreated hurriedly.

'Eat your liver, Chubby Andrews,' I thought. 'They work!'

Down again I went, almost to the tops of the bamboo forest, seeing Sherry still crouched in the gunport thirty feet away watching me. She had exhausted her own air bottles and was using mine—but I could tell by the volume and scanty rate of flow of bubbles that she had only seconds of breathing time left to her.

I started towards her, leaving the cliff—and only her frantic hand signals alerted me. I turned and saw the white death coming like a long blue torpedo. He was skimming the tops of the bamboo, and from one corner of his jaws hung a tattered streamer of flesh. He opened that wide maw to gulp down the morsel, and the rows of fangs gleamed whitely, like the petals of some obscene flower.

I faced him as he charged, but at the same time I fell back kicking my fins in his direction and laying a thick smoke-screen of blue dye between us.

With hard slashing strokes of his tail, he arrowed in the last few yards, but then he hit the blue dye and swirled, altering the direction of his charge as he sheered away.

He passed me so close that his tail struck me a heavy blow on the shoulder, sending me tumbling end over end. For seconds I lost my bearings, but as I recovered my balance and looked wildly about me I found the great shark circling.

He swept around me, forty feet away, and in his full length he seemed to my heated eye as long as a battleship and as blue and as vast as a summer sky. It seemed impossible to believe that these fish grew to almost twice this size. This one was still a baby—I was thankful for that.

Suddenly the slim steel spear in which I had placed so much faith seemed futile, and the shark regarded me with a cold yellow eye across which the pale nictitating membrane flicked occasionally in a sardonic wink, and once he opened his jaws in a convulsive gulp, as though in anticipation of the taste of my flesh.

He continued in those wide racing circles, with myself always at the centre, turning with him and paddling frantically with my fins to match his smooth unforced speed.

As I turned, I unhooked the spare lung from my belt and slung it by the harness on my left shoulder like the shield of a Roman legionary, and I tucked the hilt of the spear under my arm and kept the head pointed at the circling monster.

My whole body tingled with the warm flush of adrenalin in the bloodstream, and my senses were enhanced and sharpened by the adrenalin high—the intensely pleasurable sensation of acute fear to which a man can become an addict.

Each detail of the deadly fish was etched indelibly on my memory, from the gentle pulsing of the multiple gill behind the head to the long trailing ribbons of the remora fish holding by their suckers to the smooth snowy expanse of his belly. With a fish of this size, it would only infuriate him further if I went for a hit with the explosive spear on his snout. My only chance was for a hit on the brain.

I recognized the moment when the shark's distaste for the blue mist of repellent was overcome by his hunger and his anger. His tail seemed to stiffen and it gave a series of rapid strokes, driving his speed up sharply.

I braced myself, lifting the spare scuba protectively, and the shark turned hard and fast, breaking the wide circle and coming in directly at me.

I saw the jaws open like a pit, lined with the wedge-shaped fangs, and at the moment of strike I thrust the twin steel bottles of the scuba into it.

The shark closed its jaws on the decoy and it was torn from my grasp, while the impact of the attack tossed me aside like a floating leaf. When I had gathered myself again I looked around frantically and found the white death was twenty feet away, moving only slowly but worrying the steel bottles the way a puppy chews a slipper.

It was shaking its head in the instinctive reaction which tears lumps of flesh from a victim—but which was now inflicting only deep scratches on the painted metal of the scuba.

This was my chance, my one and only chance. Kicking hard, I spurted above the broad blue back, brushing the tall dorsal fin and I sank down over him, coming in on his blind spot like an attacking fighter pilot from high astern.

I reached out with the steel spear and pressed the tip of it firmly on to the curved blue skull, directly between those cold and deadly yellow eyes—and I squeezed the spring-loaded trigger on the hilt of the spear.

The shot fired with a crack that beat in upon my eardrums, and the spear jumped heavily in my grip.

The white death shark reared on its tail like a startled horse, and once again I was tossed lightly aside by his careless bulk, but I recovered to watch him go into a terrible frenzy. The muscles beneath the smooth skin twitched and rippled at random impulse from the damaged brain, and the shark spun and dived, rolling wildly on its back, arrowing downwards to crash snout first into the rocky bottom of the pool, then it stood on its tail and scooted in aimless parabolas through the pale blue waters.

Still watching it, and keeping a respectful distance, I unscrewed the exploded head off the spear and replaced it with a fresh charge.

The white death still had Sherry's air supply clamped in his jaws. I could not leave it. I trailed his violent, unpredictable manoeuvres warily, and when at last he hung stationary for a moment nose down, suspended on the wide flukes of his tail, I shot in again and once more pressed the explosive charge to his skull, holding it firmly against the cartilaginous dome, so that the full shock of the charge would be transmitted directly to the tiny brain.

I fired the shot, cracking painfully in my own ears, and the shark froze rigidly. It never moved again but still in that frozen rigour it rolled over slowly and began to sink towards the floor of the pool. I darted in and wrested the damaged scuba from his jaws.

I saw immediately the air hoses had been torn and shredded by the shark's teeth, but the bottles were only extensively scratched.

Carrying the lung with me I sprinted across the tops of the bamboo towards the wreck. There were no longer air bubbles rising from the gunport, and as I came in sight of her I saw that Sherry had discarded the last empty scuba set. They were empty, and she was dying slowly.

Yet even in the extremes of slow suffocation she had not made the suicidal attempt to rise to the surface. She was waiting for me, dying slowly, but trusting me.

As I came down beside her, I pulled out my own mouthpiece and offered it to her. Her movements were slow and uncoordinated. The mouthpiece slipped from her grasp and floated upwards, spewing out a torrent of air. I grabbed it and forced it into her mouth, holding it there while lowering myself slightly below her level to induce a readier flow of air.

She began to breathe. Her chest rose and fell in long deep draughts of the precious stuff, and almost immediately I saw her regaining strength and purpose. Satisfied I turned my attention to removing a demand valve from one of the abandoned lungs from which the air supply was exhausted and using it to replace the one damaged by the shark.

I breathed off it for half a minute, before strapping it on to Sherry's back and retrieving my own mouthpiece.

We had air now, enough to take us through the long period of slow decompression ahead of us. I knelt facing Sherry in the gunport and she grinned lopsidedly around the mouthpiece and lifted her thumb in a high sign and I returned it. You okay, me okay, I thought, and unscrewed the expended head from the spear and renewed it from the bandolier on my thigh.

Then once more I peered from the safety of the gunport out into the open waters of the pool.

As the supply of dead fish was depleted so the shark pack seemed to have dispersed. I saw one or two of the ungainly dark shapes still searching and sniffing the tainted waters, but their frenzy was reduced. They moved in a more leisurely fashion, and I felt happier about taking Sherry out now.

I reached for her hand and was surprised at how small and cold it felt in mine, but she answered my gesture with a squeeze of her fingers.

I pointed to the surface and she nodded. I led her out of the gunport and we slid down the hull and under cover of the bamboo crossed quickly to the shelter of the reef.

Side by side, still holding hands and with our backs to the cliff, we rose slowly up out of the pool.

The light strengthened and when I looked up I could see the whaleboat high above. My spirits rose.

At sixty feet I stopped for a minute to begin decompressing. A fat old Albacore shark swam past us, blotched and piebald like a pig, but he paid us no attention and I lowered the spear as he drifted away into the hazy distance.

Slowly we rose to the next decompression stop at forty feet, where we stayed for two minutes, allowing the nitrogen in our blood to evaporate out through our lungs gradually. Then up to twenty feet for the next stop.

I peered into Sherry's face-mask and she rolled her eyes at me, clearly she was regaining her courage and cheek. It was all going smoothly now. We were as good as home, and drinking whisky—just another twelve minutes.

The whaleboat was so close it seemed that I could touch it with the spear. I could quite clearly see Chubby's and Angelo's brown faces hanging over the side as they waited anxiously for us to emerge.

I looked away from them, making another careful search of the water about us. At the extreme range of my vision, where the haze of water shaded away to solid blue, I saw something move. It was just a suspicion of a shadow that had come and gone before I had really seen it, but I felt the returning prickle of fear and apprehension.

I hung in the water, completely alert once more, searching and waiting while the last few slow minutes dragged by like crippled insects.

The shadow passed again, this time clearly seen, a swift and deadly movement that left me in no doubt that it was not an Albacore shark. It was the difference between the shape of the prowling hyena in the shadows around the campfire to that of the lion when he hunts.

Suddenly, through the misty blue curtains of water, came the second white death shark. He came swiftly and silently, passing fifty feet away, seeming to ignore us and going on almost to the range of our vision and then turning steeply and returning to pass us again, like a caged animal back and forth along the bars.

Sherry cowered close to me and I disengaged my hand from the death grip in which she had it. I needed both hands now.

On the next pass the shark broke the pattern of its movements and went into the great sweeping circles which always precede attack. Around and around it went, with that pale yellow eye fastened hungrily upon us.

Suddenly my attention was distracted by the slow descent from above of a dozen of the blue plastic shark-repellent containers. Seeing our predicament Chubby must have emptied the entire boxful over the side. One of them passed closely enough for me to snatch it up and hand it to Sherry.

It smoked blue dye in her hand, and I transferred my attention back to the shark. It had sheered off a little from the blue dye, but it was still circling swiftly and grinning loathsomely at us.

I glanced at my watch, three minutes more to be safe, but I could risk sending Sherry out ahead of me. Unlike myself she had not already had a nitrogen fizz in her blood, she would probably be safe in another minute.

The shark tightened its circle, boring in relentlessly on us. Close—so very close that I looked deep into the black spear-headed pupil of his eye, and read his intention there.

I glanced at the watch. It was cutting it fine—very fine, but I decided to send Sherry up. I slapped her shoulder and pointed urgently to the surface. She hesitated, but I slapped her again and repeated my instruction.

She began to rise, going up slowly, the right way, but her legs dangled invitingly. The shark left me and rose slowly in time with her, following her.

She saw it and began to rise faster, smoothly the shark closed in on her. Now I was under them both, and I finned out fast to one side just as the shark went into the stiff-tailed attitude which signalled the instant of his attack.

I was directly under him, as he turned to maul Sherry. I reached up and pressed the spear-head into the softly obscene throat, and I hit the trigger.

I saw the shock kick into the bloated white flesh, and the shark reared away with a convulsive beat of its tail. It shot upwards and went out through the surface, leaping out high and clear, and falling back heavily in a creaming froth of bubbles.

Immediately it began to spin and fly in maddened, crazy circles, as though beset by a swarm of bees. Repeatedly its jaws opened and snapped closed.

Torn with terrible anxiety, I watched Sherry maintain her mental discipline and rise leisurely towards the whaleboat. A pair of huge brown paws were thrust down through the surface to welcome her. As I watched, she came within reach of them. The brown fingers closed on her like steel grab-hooks and she was plucked with miraculous strength from the water.

I could now employ all my attention on the problem of staying alive through the next few minutes before I could follow her. The shark seemed to recover from the shock of the charge, and it exchanged its mindless crazy gyrations for the terrible familiar circling.

It began again on the wide circumference, closing in steadily with each circuit. I glanced at my wristwatch and saw that at last I could begin to rise through the final stage.

I drifted upwards slowly. The agony of the bends was fresh in my memory—but the white death shark was pressing closer and closer.

Ten feet below the whaleboat, I paused again and the shark was suspicious, probably remembering the recent violent explosion in its throat. It ceased its circling and hung motionless in the pale water on the wide pointed wings of his pectoral fins. We stared at each other across a distance of fifteen feet, and I could sense that the great blue beast was gathering himself for the final rush.

I extended the spear to the full reach of my arm, and gently, so as not to trigger him, I finned towards him until the explosive charge was an inch from the nostril slits below the snout.

I hit the trigger and he reared back in shock as the explosive cracked. He whirled away in a wide angry turn and I dropped the spear and shot for the surface.

He was angry as a wounded lion, goaded by the hurts he had received, and he charged for me with his humped back large as a blue mountain and his wide jaws gaping open. I knew there was no turning him this time, nothing short of death would stop him.

As I shot for the surface I saw Chubby's hands waiting for me, the fingers like a bunch of brown bananas, and I loved him at that moment. I lifted my right arm above my head, offering it to Chubby and as the shark flashed across the last few feet that separated us I felt Chubby's fingers close on my wrist.

Then the water exploded about me. I felt the enormous drag on my arm and the powerful disruption of the water as the shark's bulk tore it apart. Then I was lying on my back upon the deck of the whaleboat, dragged from the very jaws of that dreadful animal.

'You got some nice pets, Harry,' said Chubby in a disinterested tone that I knew was forced, and I looked about quickly for Sherry.

'You okay?' I called, as I saw her wet and pale-faced in the stern. She nodded; I doubted she could speak.

I jerked out the quick release pin on my harness, freeing myself of the weight of the scuba.

'Chubby, set up a stick of gelly ready to shoot,' I called, as I rid myself of mask and fins and peered over the side of the whaleboat.

The shark was still with us, circling the whaleboat in a fury of hurt and frustration. He came up to show the full length of his dorsal fin above the surface. I knew he could easily attack and stove in the planking of the whaleboat.

'Oh God, Harry, he's horrible.' Sherry found her voice at last, and I knew how she felt. I hated that loathsome fish with the full force of my recent terror—but I had to distract it from direct attack.

'Angelo, give me that Moray and a bait-knife,' I shouted and he handed me the cold slimy body. I hacked off a ten-pound lump of the dead eel and tossed it into the pool.

The shark swirled and raced for the scrap, gulping it down and scraping the hull of the whaleboat as it passed so close. We rocked violently at its passing.

'Hurry up, Chubby,' I shouted, and fed the shark another lump. It took it as readily as a hungry dog, dashing past under the hull and again bumping the boat so that it swayed unpleasantly and Sherry squeaked and grabbed the gunwale.

'Ready,' said Chubby, and I passed him a two-foot section of the eel with its empty belly cavity hanging open like a pouch.

'Put the stick in there, and tie it up,' I instructed him, and he began to grin.

'Hey, Harry,' he chortled, 'I like it.'

While I fed the monster with scraps of eel, Chubby trussed up the stick of gelignite in a neat parcel of eel flesh, with the insulated copper wire protruding from it. He passed it to me.

'Connect her up,' I instructed, as I coiled a dozen loops of the wire into my left hand.

'Ready to shoot,' grinned Chubby, and I threw the bundle of meat and explosive into the path of the circling shark.

It raced for it, and its glistening blue back broke the surface as it swallowed the offering. Immediately the wire began to stream away over the side and I paid out more from the reel.

'Let him eat it down,' I said and Chubby nodded happily.

'Okay, Chubby, blow the bastard to hell,' I snarled as the fish came to the surface, fin up, and swung around us in another circle, with the copper wire trailing from the corner of the sickle-moon mouth.

Chubby hit the switch, and the shark erupted in a tall burst of pink spray, like a bursting watermelon, as his pale blood mingled with the paler flesh and purple contents of the belly cavity, spurting fifty feet into the air and splattering the pool and whaleboat. The shattered carcass wallowed like a bleeding log upon the surface, then rolled over and began to sink.

'Goodbye, Johnny Uptail,' hooted Angelo, and Chubby grinned like a cherub.

'Let's go home,' I said, for already the oceanic surf was breaking over the reef, and I thought I was going to throw up.

However, my indisposition responded miraculously to a treatment of Chivas Regal whisky, even though taken from an enamel mug, and much later in the cave Sherry said: 'I suppose you want me to thank you for saving my life, and all that crap?'

I grinned at her and opened my arms. 'No, my sweeting, just show me how grateful you are,' which she did, and afterwards there were no ugly dreams to spoil my sleep for I was exhausted in body and spirit.

*　　*　　*

I think all of us were coming to regard the pool at Gunfire Break with a superstitious dread. The series of accidents and mishaps to which we had been subject appeared to be the result of some deliberate malevolent scheme.

It seemed as though each time we returned to the pool it had grown more sinister in its aspect and that an aura of menace was growing about it.

'You know what I think,' Sherry said laughingly, but not completely as a joke. 'I think the spirits of the murdered Mogul princes have followed the treasure to act as guardians—' Even in the bright sunshine of a glorious morning I saw the expressions on the faces of Angelo and Chubby. 'I think the spirits were in those two big

Johnny Uptails that we killed yesterday.' Chubby looked as though he had breakfasted off a dozen rotten oysters, he blanched to a waxy golden brown and I saw him make the sign with his right hand.

'Miss Sherry,' said Angelo severely, 'you must never talk like that.' I could see gooseflesh on his forearms. Both he and Chubby had an attack of the ghostlies.

'Yes, cut it out,' I agreed.

'I was joking,' protested Sherry.

'Good joke,' I said, 'you really slayed us.' And we were all silent during the passage of the channel and until we had taken station in the shelter of the reef.

I was sitting in the bows, and when all three of them looked at me I saw by the expressions on their faces that I had a crisis of morale on my hands.

'I will go down alone,' I announced, and there was a small stir of relief.

'I'll go with you,' Sherry volunteered half-heartedly.

'Later,' I agreed, 'but first I want to check for Johnnies, and recover the equipment we lost yesterday.'

I went down cautiously, hanging just under the boat for five minutes while I scrutinized the depths of the pool for those evil dark shapes, and then finning down quietly.

It was cold and eerie in the deeper shades, but I saw that the night tide had scoured the pool and sucked out to sea all the carrion and blood that had attracted the shark pack the previous day.

There was no sign of the huge white death carcasses, and the only fish I saw were the multitudinous shoals of brilliant coral dwellers. A glint of silver from below led me to the spear I had abandoned in my rush for the boat, and I found the empty scubas and the damaged demand valve where we had left them in the gunport.

I surfaced with my load, and there were smiles amongst my crew for the first time that day when I reported the pool clear.

'All right,' I capitalised on the rise of their spirits, 'today we are going to open up the hold.'

'You going in through the hull?' Chubby asked.

'I thought about that, Chubby, but I reckoned that it would need a couple of heavy charges to get in that way. I've decided to go in through the passenger deck into the well.' I sketched it on my slate for them as I explained. 'The cargo will have shifted, it will be lying in a jumble just beyond that bulkhead and once we pop her open here, we can drag it out item by item into the companionway.'

'It's a long haul from there to the gunport.' Chubby lifted his cap and massaged his bald dome thoughtfully.

'I'll rig a light block and tackle at the gundeck ladder and another at the gunport.'

'A lot of work,' Chubby looked sad.

'The first time you agree with me—I'm going to begin worrying that I may be wrong.'

'I didn't say you were wrong,' said Chubby stiffly, 'I just said it was a lot of work. You can't let Miss Sherry haul on a block and tackle, can you now?'

'No,' I agreed. 'We need somebody with beef,' and I prodded his bulging rock-hard gut.

'That's what I thought,' said Chubby mournfully. 'You want me to get geared up?'

'No.' I stopped him. 'Sherry can come down with me to set the charges now.' I wanted her to test her nerves after the previous day's horrors. 'We will blast the well open and then go home. We aren't going to work again immediately after blasting. We are going to let the tide clean the pool of dead fish before going down. I don't want an action replay of yesterday.'

We crept in through the gunport and followed the nylon guide line we had placed on our first visit, along the gundeck, up through the companion ladder to the passenger deck, and then along the dark forbidding tunnel to the dead-end bulkhead of the forward well.

While Sherry held the light for me, I began to drill a hole through the partition with the brace and bit that I had brought from the surface. It was awkward working without a really firm stance on which to anchor myself, but the first inch and a half was easy going. This layer of wood had rotted to a soft corky consistency, but beyond that I encountered iron hard oak planking and I had to abandon my efforts. I would have been a week at the task.

Unable to place my explosive in prepared shot holes, I would now have to use a larger charge than I really wanted and rely on the tunnel effect of the passageway for a secondary shock to drive the panel inwards. I used six half sticks of gelignite, placed on the corners and in the centre of the bulkhead, and I secured them to bolts driven into the woodwork with a slap hammer.

It took almost half an hour to set up the blast, and afterwards it was a relief to leave the claustrophobic confines of the ancient hull and to rise up through clean clear water to the silver surface, trailing the insulated wires behind us.

Chubby fired the shots while we stripped off our equipment. The shock was cushioned by the hull of the wreck so that it was hardly noticeable to us on the surface.

We left the pool immediately afterwards and ran home with rising spirits to the prospect of a lazy day while we waited for the tide to clean the pool of carrion.

In the afternoon Sherry and I went on a picnic down to the south tip of the island. For provisions we took a wicker-covered two-litre bottle of Portuguese *vinos verde,* but to supplement this we dug out a batch of big sand clams which I wrapped in seaweed and reburied in the sand. Over them I built an open fire of driftwood.

By the time we had almost finished the wine, the sun was setting and the clams were ready to eat. The wine and the food and the glorious sunset had a softening effect on Sherry North. She became doe-eyed and melting, and when the sunset faded at last and made way for a fat yellow lovers' moon, we walked home barefooted on the wet sand.

*   *   *

The next morning Chubby and I worked for half an hour bringing down the equipment we needed from the whaleboat and stacking it on the gundeck of the wreck before we were able to penetrate deeper into the hull.

The heavy charges I had set against the well had wrought the sort of havoc I feared. They had torn out the decking and smashed in the bulkheads of the passenger cabins, blocking the passage for a quarter of its length.

We found a good anchor point for our block and tackle and while Chubby rigged it, I left him and floated back to the nearest cabin. I played my flashlight through the shattered panelling. The interior was, like everything else, smothered in a thick furring of marine growth but I could make out the shape of the simple furniture beneath it.

I eased myself through the gap, and moved slowly across the cluttered deck, fascinated by the objects which I found scattered and heaped about the cabin. There were items of porcelain and china, a shattered washbasin and a magnificent chamber pot with a pink floral design showing through the film of accumulated sediment. There were cosmetic pots and scent bottles, smaller indefinable metal objects and mounds of rotted and amorphous material which may have been clothing, curtaining or mattresses and bed-clothing.

I glanced at my watch and saw that it was time to leave and surface for a change of air bottles. As I turned, a small square object caught my attention and I played the flashlight beam upon it while I gently brushed it clear of the thick layer of muddy filth. It was a wooden box, the size of a portable transistor radio, but the lid was beautifully inlaid with mother-of-pearl and tortoiseshell. I picked it up and tucked it under my arm. Chubby had finished rigging the block and tackle and he was waiting for me beside the gundeck ladder. When we surfaced beside the whaleboat I passed the box up to Angelo before climbing aboard.

While Sherry poured coffee for us and Angelo charged the demand valves to the fresh scuba bottles, I lit a cheroot and examined the box.

It was in a sorry state of deterioration, I saw at once. The inlay was rotten and falling out of its seating, the rosewood was swollen and distorted and the lock and hinges half eaten away.

Sherry came to sit beside me on the thwart and examined my prize with me. She recognized it immediately.

'It's a ladies' jewel box,' she exclaimed. 'Open it, Harry. Let's see what's inside.'

I slipped the blade of a screw-driver under the lock and at the first pressure the hinges snapped and the lid flew off.

'Oh, Harry!' Sherry was first into it, and she came out with a thick gold chain and a heavy locket of the same material. 'This stuff is so in fashion, you'd never believe it.'

Everyone was dipping into the box now. Angelo ripped off a pair of gold and sapphire earrings which immediately replaced the brass pair he habitually wore, while Chubby picked an enormous necklace of garnets which he hung around his neck and preened like a teenage girl.

'For my missus,' he explained.

It was the personal jewellery of a middle-class wife, probably of some minor official or civil servant—none of it of great value, but in its context it was a fascinating collection. Inevitably Miss North acquired the lion's share—but I managed to snatch away a thick plain gold wedding band.

'What do you want with that?' she challenged me, reluctant to yield a single item.

'I'll find a use for it,' I told her, and gave her one of my looks of deep significance, which was completely wasted for she had returned to ransacking the jewel box.

Nevertheless I tucked the ring safely away in the small zip pocket of my canvas gear bag. Chubby by this stage was bedecked with chunky jewellery like a Hindu bride.

'My God, Chubby, you're a dead ringer for Liz Taylor,' I told him and he accepted the compliment with a graceful inclination of his head.

I had a difficult job getting him interested in a return to the wreck, but once we were in the passenger deck again, he worked like a giant amongst the shattered wreckage.

We hauled out the panelling and timber baulks that blocked the passage by use of the block and tackle and our combined strength, and we dragged it down to the gundeck and stacked it out of the way in the recesses of that gloomy gallery.

We had reached the well of the forward hold by the time our air supplies were almost exhausted. The heavy planking had broken up in the explosion and beyond the opening we could make out what appeared to be a solid dark mass of material. I guessed that this was a conglomerate formed by the cargo out of its own weight and pressure.

However, it was afternoon the following day before I found that I was correct. We were at last into the hold, but I had not expected such a Herculean task as awaited us there.

The contents of the hold had been impregnated with sea water for over a century. Ninety per cent of the containers had rotted and collapsed, and the perishable contents had coalesced into a friable dark mass.

Within this solid heap of marine compost, the metal objects, the containers of stronger and impervious material and other imperishable objects, both large and small, were studded like lucky coins in a Christmas pudding. We would have to dig for them.

At this point we encountered our next problem. At the slightest disturbance of this rotted mass the water was immediately filled with a swirling storm of dark particles that blotted out the beams of the flashlights and plunged us into clouds of blinding darkness.

We were forced to work by sense of touch alone. It was painfully slow progress. When we encountered some solid body in the softness we had to drag it clear, manoeuvre it down the passage, lower it to the gundeck and there try to identify it. Sometimes we were obliged to break open what remained of the container, to get at the contents.

If they were of little value or interest, we tucked them away in the depths of the gundeck to keep our working field clear.

At the end of the first day's work we had salvaged only one item which we decided was worth raising. It was a sturdy case of hard wood, covered with what appeared to be leather and with the corners bound in heavy brass. It was the size of a large cabin trunk.

It was so heavy that Chubby and I could not lift it between us. The weight alone gave me high hopes. I believed it could very readily contain part of the golden throne. Although the container did not look like one that had been manufactured by an Indian village carpenter and his sons in the middle of the nineteenth century, yet there was a chance that the throne had been repacked before it was shipped from Bombay.

If it did contain part of the throne, then our task would be simplified. We would know what type of container to look for in the future. Using the block and tackle Chubby and I dragged the case down the gundeck to the gunport and there we shrouded it in a nylon cargo net to prevent it bursting open or breaking during the ascent. To the eyes spliced into the circumference of the net we attached the canvas flotation bags and inflated them from our air bottles.

We went up with the case, controlling its ascent by either spilling air from the bags, or adding more from our bottles. We came out beside the whaleboat and Angelo passed us half a dozen nylon slings with which we secured the case before climbing aboard.

The weight of the case defeated our efforts to lift it over the side, for the whaleboat heeled dangerously when the three of us made the attempt. We had to step the mast and use it as a derrick, only then did our combined efforts suffice and the case swung on board, spouting water from its seams. The moment that it sank to the deck Chubby scrambled back to the motors and ran for the channel. The tide pressed closely on our heels as we went.

The case was too weighty and our curiosity too strong to allow us to carry it up to the caves. We opened it on the beach, prising the lid open with a pair of jenny bars. The elaborate locking device in the lid was of brass and had withstood the ravages of salt sea water. It resisted our efforts bravely, but at last with a rending of woodwork the lid flew back and creaked against the heavily corroded hinges.

My disappointment was immediate, for it was clear that this was no tiger throne. It was only when Sherry lifted out one of the large gleaming discs and turned it curiously in her hands that I began to suspect that we had been awarded an enormous bonus.

It was an entrée plate she held, and my first thought was that it was of solid gold. However, when I snatched a mate from its slot in the cunningly designed rack and turned it to examine the hallmarks, I realized that it was silver and gold gilt.

The gold plating had protected it from the sea so that it was perfectly preserved, a masterpiece of the silversmith's art with a raised coat of arms in the centre and the rim wondrously chased with scenes of woods and deer, of huntsmen and birds.

The plate I held weighed almost two pounds and as I set it aside and examined the rest of the set I saw the weight of the chest fully accounted for.

There were servings for thirty-six guests in the set; soup bowls, fish plates, entrée plates, dessert bowls, side plates and all the cutlery to go with it. There were serving dishes, a magnificent chafing dish, wine coolers, dish covers and a carving dish almost the size of a baby's bath.

Every piece was wrought with the same coat of arms, and the ornamental scenes of wild animals and huntsmen, and the case had been designed to hold this array of plate.

'Ladies and gentlemen,' I said, 'as your chairman, it behoves me to assure you, one and all, that our little venture is now in profit.'

'It's just plates and things,' said Angelo, and I winced theatrically.

'My dear Angelo, this is probably one of the few complete sets of Georgian banquet silverware remaining anywhere in the world—it's priceless.'

'How much?' asked Chubby, doubtfully.

'Good Lord, I don't know. It would depend of course on the maker and the original owner—this coat of arms probably belongs to some noble house. A wealthy nobleman on service in India, an earl, a duke perhaps, even a viceroy.'

Chubby looked at me as though I was trying to sell him a spavined horse.

'How much?' he repeated.

'At Messrs Sothebys on a good day,' I hesitated, 'I don't know, say, a hundred thousand pounds.'

Chubby spat into the sand and shook his head. You couldn't fool old Chubby.

'This fellow Sotheby, does he run a loony house?'

'It's true, Chubby,' Sherry cut in. 'This stuff is worth a fortune. It could be more than that.'

Chubby was now torn between natural scepticism and chivalry. It would be an ungentlemanly act to call Sherry a liar. He compromised by lifting his hat and rubbing his head, spitting once more and saying nothing.

However, he handled the case with new respect when we dragged it up through the palms to the caves. We stored it behind the stack of jerrycans, and I went to fetch a new bottle of whisky.

'Even if there is no tiger throne in the wreck, we aren't going to do too badly out of this,' I told them.

Chubby sipped at his whisky mug and muttered, 'A hundred thousand—they've got to be crazy.'

'We've got to go through that hold and the cabins more carefully. We are going to leave a fortune down there if we don't.'

'Even the little items, less spectacular than the silver plate, they have enormous antique value,' Sherry agreed.

'Trouble is when you touch anything down there it stirs up such a fog you can't see the tip of your nose,' gloomed Chubby, and I refilled his mug with good cheer.

'Listen, Chubby, you know the centrifugal water pump that Arnie Andrews has got out at Monkey Bay?' I asked, and Chubby nodded.

'Will he lend it to us?' Arnie was Chubby's uncle. He owned a small market garden on the southern side of St Mary's Island.

'He might,' Chubby answered warily. 'Why?'

'I want to try and rig a dredge pump,' I explained and sketched it for them in the sand between my feet. 'We set the pump up in the whaleboat, and we use a length of steam hose to reach the wreck—like this.' I roughed it out with my finger. 'Then we use it like a vacuum cleaner in the hold, suck out all that muck and pump it to the surface—'

235

'Hey, that's right,' Angelo burst out enthusiastically. 'When it spills out of the pump we run it through a sieve, and we will be able to pick up all the small stuff.'

'That's right. Only muck and small light items will go up the spout —anything large or heavy will be left behind.'

We discussed it for an hour working out details and refinements on the basic idea. During that time Chubby tried manfully to show no signs of enthusiasm, but finally he could contain himself no longer.

'It might work,' he muttered, which from him was a high accolade.

'Well, you better go fetch that pump then, hadn't you?' I asked.

'I think I will have one more drink,' he procrastinated, and I handed him the bottle.

'Take it with you,' I suggested. 'It will save time.'

He grunted, and went to fetch his overcoat.

*　　*　　*

Sherry and I slept late, gloating on the lazy day ahead and at the feeling of having the island entirely to ourselves. We did not expect Chubby and Angelo to return before noon.

After breakfast we crossed the saddle between the hills and went down to the beach. We were playing in the shallows, and the rumble of the surf on the outer reef and our own splashing and laughter blanketed any other sounds. It was only by chance that I looked up and saw the light aircraft sweeping in from the landward channel.

'Run!' I shouted at Sherry, and she thought I was joking until I pointed urgently at the approaching aircraft.

'Run! Don't let him see us,' and this time she responded quickly. We floundered naked from the water, and went up the beach at the top of our speed.

Now I could hear the buzz of the aircraft engines and I glanced over my shoulder. It was banking low over the southernmost peak of the island and levelling over the long straight beach towards us.

'Faster!' I yelled at Sherry, as she ran long-legged and full-bottomed ahead of me with the wet tresses of her sable hair dangling down her darkly tanned back.

I looked back and the aircraft was headed directly at us, still about a mile distant, but I could see that it was twin-engined. As I watched, it sank lower towards the snowy expanse of coral sands.

236

We snatched up our discarded clothing at full run, and sprinted the last few yards into the palm grove. There was a mound formed by a fallen palm tree and the fronds torn off the trees by the storm. It was a convenient shelter and I grabbed Sherry's arm and dragged her down.

We rolled under the shelter of the dead fronds and lay side by side, panting wildly from the run up the beach.

I saw now that it was a twin-engined Cessna. It came down the beach and swept past our hideaway only twenty feet above the water's edge.

The fuselage was painted a distinctive daisy yellow and was blazoned with the name 'Africair.' I recognized the aircraft. I had seen it before at St Mary's Airport on half a dozen occasions, usually discharging or picking up groups of wealthy tourists. I knew that Africair was a charter company based on the mainland, and that its aircraft were for hire on a mileage tariff. I wondered who was paying for the hire on this trip.

There were two persons in the forward seats of the aircraft, the pilot and a passenger, and their faces were turned towards us as it roared past. However, they were too far from us to make out the features and I could not be sure if I knew either of them. They were both white men, that was all that was certain.

The Cessna turned steeply out over the lagoon and, one wing pointed directly down into the crystal water, it swept around and then levelled for another run down the beach.

This time it passed so closely that for an instant I looked up into the face of the passenger as he peered down into the palm grove. I thought I recognized him, but I could not be certain.

The Cessna then turned away, rising slowly, and set a new course for the mainland. There was something about her going that was complacent, the air of someone having achieved his purpose, a job well done.

Sherry and I crawled from our hiding-place and stood up to brush the sand from our damp bodies.

'Do you think they saw us?' she asked timidly.

'With that bottom of yours flashing like a mirror in the sunlight, they could hardly miss.'

'They might have mistaken us for a couple of native fishermen.'

I looked at her, not at her face, and I grinned: 'Fisherman? With those great beautiful boobs?'

'Harry Fletcher, you are a disgusting beast,' she said. 'But seriously, Harry, what is going to happen now?'

'I wish I knew, my sweeting, I wish I knew,' I answered, but I was glad that Chubby had taken the case of silverware back to St Mary's with him. By now it was probably buried behind the shack at Turtle Bay. We were still in profit—even if we had to run for it soon.

The visit by the aircraft instilled in us all a new sense of urgency. We knew now that our time was strictly rationed, and Chubby brought news with him when he returned that was equally disturbing.

'The *Mandrake* cruised for five days in the south islands. They saw her nearly every day from Coolie Peak, and she was messing about like she didn't know what she was doing,' he reported. 'Then on Monday she anchored again in Grand Harbour. Wally says that the owner and his wife went up to the hotel for lunch, then afterwards they took a taxi and went down to Frobisher Street. They spent an hour with Fred Coker in his office, then he drove them down to Admiralty Wharf and they went back on board *Mandrake*. She weighed and sailed almost immediately.'

'Is that all?'

'Yes,' Chubby nodded, 'except that Fred Coker went straight up to the bank afterwards and put fifteen hundred dollars into his savings account.'

'How do you know that?'

'My sister's third daughter works at the bank.'

I tried to show a cheerful face, although I felt ugly little insects crawling around in my stomach. 'Well,' I said, 'no use moping around. Let's try and get the pump assembled so we can catch tomorrow's tide.'

Later, after we had carried the water pump up to the caves, Chubby returned alone to the whaleboat and when he came back he carried a long canvas-wrapped bundle.

'What have you got there, Chubby?' I demanded, and shyly he opened the canvas cover. It was my FN carbine and a dozen spare magazines of ammunition packed into a small haversack.

'Thought it might come in useful,' he muttered.

I took the weapon down into the grove and buried it beside the cases of gelignite in a shallow grave. Its proximity gave me a little comfort when I returned to assist in assembling the water pump.

We worked on into the night by the light of the gas lanterns, and it was after midnight when we carried the pump and its engine down to the whaleboat and bolted it to a makeshift mounting of heavy timber which we placed squarely amidship. Angelo and I were still working on the pump when we ran out towards the reef in the morning. We had been on station for half an hour before we had it assembled and ready to test.

Three of us dived on the wreck—Chubby, Sherry and myself—and we manhandled the stiff black snake of the hose through the gunport and up into the breach through the well of the hold.

Once it was in position, I slapped Chubby on the shoulder and pointed to the surface. He replied with a high sign and finned away, leaving Sherry and me in the passenger deck.

We had planned this part of the operation carefully and we waited impatiently while Chubby went up, decompressing on his way, and climbed into the whaleboat to prime the pump and start the motor.

We knew he had done so by the faint hum and vibration that was transmitted to us down the hose.

I braced myself in the ragged entrance to the hold, and grasped the end of the hose with both hands. Sherry trained the flashlight beam on to the dark heap of cargo, and I swung the open end of the hose slowly over the rotted cargo.

I saw immediately that it was going to work, small pieces of debris vanished miraculously into the hose, and it caused a small whirlpool as it sucked in water and floating motes of rubbish.

At this depth and with the RPM provided by the petrol engine, the pump was rated to move thirty thousand gallons of water an hour, which was a considerable volume. Within seconds I had cleared the working area and we still had good visibility. I could start probing into the heap with a jenny bar, breaking out larger pieces and pushing them back into the passage behind us.

Once or twice I had to resort to the block and tackle to clear some bulky case or object, but mostly I was able to advance with only the hose and the jenny bar.

We had moved almost fifty cubic feet of cargo before it was time to ascend for a change of air bottle. We left the end of the hose firmly anchored in the passenger deck, and went up to a hero's welcome. Angelo was in transports of delight and even Chubby was smiling.

The water around the whaleboat was clouded and filthy with the thick soup of rubbish we had pumped out of the hold, and Angelo had retrieved almost a bucketful of small items that had come through the outlet of the pump and fallen into the sieve—it was a collection of buttons, nails, small ornaments from women's dresses, brass military insignia, some small copper and silver coins of the period, and odds and ends of metal and glass and bone.

Even I was impatient to return to the task, and Sherry was so insistent that I had to donate my half-smoked cheroot to Chubby and we went down again.

We had been working for fifteen minutes when I came upon the corner of an up-ended crate similar to others that we had already cleared. Although the wood was soft as cork, the seams had been reinforced with strips of hoop iron and iron nails so I struggled with it for some time before I prised out a plank and pushed it back between us. The next plank came free more readily, and the contents seemed to be a mattress of decomposed and matted vegetable fibre.

I pulled out a large hunk of this and it almost jammed the opening of the hose, but eventually disappeared on its way to the surface. I almost lost interest in this box and was about to begin working in another area—but Sherry showed strong signs of disapproval, shaking her head, thumping my shoulder and refusing to direct the beam of the flashlight anywhere but at the unappetizing mess of fibre.

Afterwards I asked her why she had insisted and she fluttered her eyelashes and looked important.

'Female intuition, my dear. You wouldn't understand.'

At her urging, I once more attacked the opening in the case, but scratching smaller chunks of the fibre loose so as not to block the hose opening.

I had removed above six inches of this material when I saw the gleam of metal in the depths of the excavation. I felt the first deep throb of certainty in my belly then, and I tore out another plank with furious impatience. It enlarged the opening so I could work in it more easily.

Slowly I removed the layers of compacted fibre which I realized must have been straw originally used as packing. Like a face materializing in a dream, it was revealed.

The first tiny gleam opened to a golden glory of intricately worked metal and I felt Sherry's grip on my shoulder as she crowded down close beside me.

There was a snout, and lips below that were drawn up in a savage snarl, revealing great golden fangs and an arched tongue. There was a broad deep forehead as wide as my shoulders, and ears flattened down close upon the burnished skull—and there was a single empty eyesocket set fairly in the centre of the wide brow. The lack of an eye gave the animal a blind and tragic expression, like some maimed god from mythology.

I felt an almost religious awe as I stared at the huge, wonderfully fashioned tiger's head we had exposed. Something cold and frightening slithered up my spine, and involuntarily I glanced about me into the dark and forbidding recesses of the hold, almost as if I expected the spirits of the Mogul prince guardians to be lurking there.

Sherry squeezed my shoulder again and I returned my attention to the golden idol, but the sense of awe was so strong upon me that I had to force myself to return to the task of clearing the packing from around it. I worked very carefully for I was fully aware that the slightest scratch or damage would greatly reduce the value and the beauty of this image.

When our working time was exhausted we drew back and stared at the exposed head and shoulders, and the flashlight beam was reflected from the brilliant surface in arrows of golden light that lit the hold like some holy shrine. We turned then and left it to the silence and the dark, while we went up into the sunlight.

Chubby was aware immediately that something significant had happened, but he said nothing until we had climbed aboard and in silence shed our equipment. I lit a cheroot and drew deeply upon it, not bothering to mop the droplets of sea water that ran from my sodden hair down my cheeks. Chubby was watching me but Sherry was withdrawn from us, wrapped in secret thoughts, turned inward upon herself.

'You found it?' Chubby asked at last, and I nodded.

'Yes, Chubby, it's there.' I was surprised to hear that my own voice was husky and unsteady.

Angelo who had not sensed the mood looked up quickly from where he was stacking our equipment. He opened his mouth to say something, but then slowly closed it as he became aware of the charged atmosphere.

We were all silent, moved beyond speech. I had not expected it

241

would be like this, and I looked at Sherry. She met my gaze at last and her dark eyes were haunted.

'Let's go home, Harry,' she said and I nodded at Chubby. He buoyed the hose and dropped it overboard to be retrieved on the following day. Then he threw the motors into gear and swung our bows to face the channel.

Sherry moved across the whaleboat and came to sit beside me on the thwart. I placed my arm about her shoulders but neither of us spoke until the whaleboat slid silently up on to the white beach of the island.

In the sunset Sherry and I climbed to the peak above the camp and we sat close together staring out across the reef, and watching the light fade on the sea and plunge the pool at Gunfire Reef into deeper shadow.

'I feel guilty in a way,' Sherry whispered, 'as though I have committed some dreadful sacrilege.'

'Yes,' I agreed, 'I know what you mean.'

'That thing—it seemed to have a life of its own. It was strange that we should have exposed its head, before any other part of it. Just suddenly to have that face glaring out at one,' she shuddered and was silent for a few moments, 'and yet I felt also a deep satisfaction, a good quiet feeling inside myself. I don't know if I can explain it properly—for the two feelings were so opposite, and yet mingled.'

'I understand. I had the same feelings.'

'What are we going to do with it, Harry, what are we going to do with that fantastic animal?'

Somehow I did not want to talk about money and buyers at that moment—which in itself was a measure of how profound was my involvement with the golden idol.

'Let's go down,' I suggested instead. 'Angelo will be waiting dinner for us.'

Sitting in the firelight with a good meal filling and warming the cold empty place in my belly, and with a mug of whisky in one hand and a cheroot in the other, I felt at last able to tell the others about it.

I explained how we had come upon it, and I described the fearsome golden head. They listened in complete and intent silence.

'We have cleared the head down to the shoulder. I think that is where it ends. It is notched there, probably to fit into the next section. Tomorrow we should be able to lift it clear, but it's going to be ticklish work. We can't just haul it out with the block and tackle. It has to be protected from damage before we can move it.'

Chubby made a suggestion, and for a while we discussed in detail how the head should be handled to minimize the risk of damage.

'We can expect that all five cases containing the treasure were loaded together. I hope to find them in the same part of the hold, probably similarly packed in wooden crates and reinforced with hoop iron—'

'Except for the stones,' Sherry interrupted. 'In the court-martial evidence, the Subahdar described how they were packed in a paymaster's chest.'

'Yes, of course,' I agreed.

'What would that look like?' Sherry asked.

'I saw one on display in the arsenal at Copenhagen which would probably be very similar. It's like a small iron safe—the size of a large cooky tin.' I sketched the size with the spread of my hands like a fisherman boasting of his catch. 'It is ribbed with iron bands and has a locking rod and a pair of head padlocks at each corner.'

'It sounds formidable.'

'After a hundred-odd years in the pool it will probably be soft as chalk—even if it's still in one piece.'

'We'll find out tomorrow,' Sherry announced with confidence.

*　　*　　*

We tramped down to the beach in the morning with rain drumming on our oilskins and cascading from them in sheets. The cloud was right down on the peaks, oily dark banks that rolled steadily in from the sea to loose their bomb loads of moisture upon the island.

The force of the rain lifted a fine pearly spray from the surface of the sea, and the moving grey curtains reduced visibility to a few hundred yards so that the island disappeared in a grey haze as we ran out to the reef.

Everything in the whaleboat was cold and clammy and running with water. Angelo had to bale regularly and we huddled miserably in our oilskins while Chubby stood in the stern and slitted his eyes against the slanting, driving rain as he negotiated the channel.

The fluorescent orange buoy still bobbed close in beside the reef and we picked it up and dragged in the end of the hose and con-

243

nected it to the pump head. It served as an anchor cable and Chubby could cut the motors.

It was a relief to leave the boat, escape from the cold needle lances of the rain and go down into the quiet blue mists of the pool.

After withstanding considerable pressure from Chubby and me, Angelo had at last succumbed to veiled threats and open bribes, and relinquished his ticking mattress stuffed with coconut-fibre. Once the mattress was thoroughly soaked with sea water, it sank readily, and I took it down with me in a neat roll, tied with line.

Only when I had manoeuvred it through the gunport, down the gundeck and into the passenger deck did I cut the line and spread the mattress.

Then Sherry and I returned to the hold where the tiger's head still snarled blindly into the torchlight.

Ten minutes' work was all that was necessary to free the head from its nest. As I suspected, this section ended at shoulder level, and the junction area was neatly flanged—clearly it would mate with the trunk section of the throne, and the flange would engage the female slot to form a joint that would be strong and barely perceivable.

When I rolled the head carefully on to its side I made another discovery. Somehow I had taken it for granted that the idol was made from solid gold, but now I saw that in fact it was a hollow casting.

The actual thickness of metal was only about an inch, and the interior was rough and knobbly to the touch. I realized immediately that a solid idol would have weighed hundreds of tons, and that the cost of such construction would have been prohibitive even to an emperor who could support the construction of a temple as vast as the Taj Mahal.

The thinness of the metal skin had naturally weakened the structure, and I saw immediately when I turned it that the head had already suffered damage.

The rim of the neck cavity was flattened and distorted, probably during its secret journey through the Indian forests in an unsprung cart—or possibly during the wild death struggles of the *Dawn Light* during the cyclone.

Bracing myself in the entrance to the hold, I stooped over it to test its weight, and I cradled the head in my arms like the body of a child. Gradually I increased the strength of my lift and was pleased, but not surprised, when it came up in my arms.

It was, of course, tremendously weighty, and it required all of my strength from a carefully selected stance—but I could lift it. It weighed not much more than three hundred pounds, I thought, as I turned awkwardly under the oppressive load of gleaming gold and laid it gently on the coir mattress that Sherry was holding ready to receive it. Then I straightened up to rest and massage those parts where the sharp edges of metal had bitten into my flesh. While I did so I tried a little mental arithmetic. Three hundred pounds avoirdupois at 16 ounces to the pound was 4800 ounces, at 150 to the ounce was almost three-quarter of a million dollars. That was the intrinsic value of the head alone. There were three other sections to the throne, all were probably heavier and larger—then there was the value of the stones. It was an astronomic total, but could be doubled or even trebled if the artistic and historical value of the hoard were taken into account.

I abandoned my calculations. They were meaningless at this time, and instead I helped Sherry to fold the mattress around the tiger's head and to rope it all into a secure bundle. Then I could use the block and tackle to drag it down to the companion ladder and lower it to the gundeck.

Laboriously we dragged it to the gunport and there we struggled to pass it through the restricted opening, but at last it was accomplished and we could place the nylon cargo net around it and inflate the air bags. Again we had to step the mast to lift it aboard.

But there was no suggestion that the head should remain covered once we had it safely in the whaleboat, and with what ceremony and aplomb I could muster in the streaming tropical rain, I unveiled it for Chubby and Angelo. They were an appreciative audience. Their excitement superseded even the miserable sodden conditions, and they crowded about the head to fondle and examine it amid shouted comment and giddy laughter. It was the festive gaiety which our first discovery of the treasure had lacked. I had taken the precaution of slipping my silver travelling flask into my gearbag, and now I laced the steaming mugs of black coffee with liberal portions of scotch whisky and we toasted each other and the golden tiger in the steaming liquor, laughing while the rain gushed down upon us and rattled on the fabulous treasure at our feet.

At last I swilled out my mug over the side and checked my watch.

'We'll do another dive,' I decided. 'You can start the pump again, Chubby.'

Now we knew where to continue the search, and after I had broken out the remains of the case that had contained the head, I saw, in the opening beyond, the side of a similar crate and I pressed the hose into the area to clear it of dirt before proceeding.

My excavations must have unbalanced the rotting heap of ancient cargo, and it needed only the further disturbance caused by suction of the hose to dislodge a part of it. With a groaning and rumbling it collapsed around us and instantly the swirling clouds of muck defeated the efforts of the hose to clear them and we were plunged into darkness once more.

I groped quickly for Sherry through the darkness, and she must have been searching for me, for our hands met and held. With a squeeze she reassured me that she had not been hit by the sliding cargo, and I could begin to clear out the fouled water with the suction hose.

Within five minutes I could make out the yellow glow of Sherry's torch through the murk, and then her shape and the vague jumble of freshly revealed cargo.

With Sherry beside me, we moved farther into the hold again.

The slide had covered the wooden crate on which I had been working, but in exchange it had exposed something else that I recognized instantly, despite its sorry condition, for it was almost exactly as I had described it to Sherry the previous evening, even down to the detail of the rod that ran through the locking device and the double padlocks. The paymaster's chest was, however, almost eaten through with rust and when I touched it my hand came away smeared with the chalky red of iron oxide.

In each end of the case were heavy iron carrying rings, which had most likely swivelled at one time but were now solidly rusted into the metal side—but still they enabled me to get a firm grip and gently to work the chest out of the clutching bed of muck. It came free in a minor storm of debris, and I was able to lift it fairly easily. I doubt that the total weight exceeded a hundred and fifty pounds, and I felt certain that most of that was made up by the massive iron construction.

After the enormously heavy head in its soft bulky mattress, it was a minor labour to get the smaller lighter chest out of the wreck, and it needed only a single air bag to lift it dangling out of the gunport.

Once again the tide and surf were pouring alarmingly into the pool, and the whaleboat tossed and kicked impatiently as we lifted the chest inboard and laid it on the canvas-covered heap of scuba bottles in the bows.

Then at last Chubby could start the motors and take us out through the channel. We were still all high with excitement, and the silver flask passed from hand to hand.

'What's it feel like to be rich, Chubby?' I called, and he took a swallow from the flask, screwing up his eyes and then coughing at the sting of the liquor before he grinned at me.

'Just like before, man. No change yet.'

'What you going to do with your share?' Sherry insisted.

'It's a little late in the day, Miss Sherry—if only I had it twenty years ago, then I have use for it—and how.' He took another swallow. 'That's the trouble—you never have it when you're young, and when you're old, it's just too damned late.'

'What about you, Angelo?' Sherry turned to him as he perched on the rusted pay chest, with his gipsy curls heavy with rain dangling on to his cheeks and the droplets clinging in the long dark eyelashes. 'You're still young, what will you do?'

'Miss Sherry, I've been sitting here thinking about it—and already I've got a list from here to St Mary's and back.'

It took two trips from the beach to the camp before we had both the head and the chest out of the rain and into the cave we were using as the store room.

Chubby lit two gas lanterns, for the lowering sky had brought on the evening prematurely, and we gathered around the chest, while the golden head snarled down upon us from a place of honour, an earthen ledge hewn into the back of the cave.

With a hacksaw and jenny bar, Chubby and I began work on the locking device and found immediately that the decrepit appearance of the metal was deceptive, clearly it had been hardened and alloyed. We broke three hacksaw blades in the first half hour and Sherry professed to be severely shocked by my language. I sent her to fetch a bottle of Chivas Regal from our cave to keep the workers in good cheer and Chubby and I took the Scottish equivalent of a tea-break.

With renewed vigour we resumed our assault on the case, but it was another twenty minutes before he had sawn through the rod. By that time it was dark outside the cave. The rain was still hissing down steadily, but the soft clatter of the palm fronds heralded the rising westerly wind that would disperse the storm clouds by morning.

With the locking rod sawn through, we started it from its ringbolts with a two-pound hammer from the toolbox. Each blow loosened a soft patter of rust scales from the surface of the metal, and it required a number of goodly blows to drive the rod from the clutching fist of corrosion.

Even when it was cleared, the lid would not lift. Although we hammered it from a dozen different directions and I treated it with a further laying on of abuse, it would not yield.

I called another whisky break to discuss the problem.

'What about a stick of gelly?' Chubby suggested with a gleam in his eye, but reluctantly I had to restrain him.

'We need a welding torch,' Angelo announced.

'Brilliant,' I applauded him ironically, for I was fast losing my patience. 'The nearest welding set is fifty miles away—and you make a remark like that.'

It was Sherry who discovered the secondary locking device, a secret pinning through the lid that hooked into recesses in the body of the chest. It obviously needed a key to release this, but for lack of it I selected a half-inch punch and drove it into the keyhole and by luck I caught the locking arm and snapped it.

Chubby started on the lid again, and this time it came up stiffly on corroded hinges with some of the rotting evil-smelling contents sticking to the inside of it and tearing away from the main body of aged brown cloth. It was woven cotton fabric, a wet solid brick of it, and I guessed that it had been cheap native robes or bolts of cloth used as packing.

I was about to explore further, but suddenly found myself in the second row looking over Sherry North's shoulder.

'You'd better let me do this,' she said. 'You might break something.'

'Come on!' I protested.

'Why don't you get yourself another drink?' she suggested placatingly, as she began lifting off layers of sodden fabric. The suggestion had some merit, I thought, so I refilled my mug and watched Sherry expose a layer of cloth-wrapped parcels.

Each was tied with twine that fell apart at the touch, and the first parcel also disintegrated as she tried to lift it out. Sherry cupped her hand around the decaying mass and scooped it on to a folded tarpaulin placed beside the chest. The parcel contained scores of small nutty objects, varying in size from slightly larger than a match-head to a ripe grape and each had been folded in a wisp of paper, which like the cotton, had completely rotted away.

Sherry picked out one of these lumpy objects and rubbed away the remnants of paper between thumb and forefinger to reveal a large shiny blue stone, cut square and polished on one face.

'Sapphire?' she guessed, and I took it from her and examined it quickly in the lantern light. It was opaque and I contradicted her.

'No, I think it's probably lapis lazuli.' The scrap of paper still adhering to it was faintly discoloured with a blue dye. 'Ink, I should say.' I crumpled it between my fingers. 'At least Roger, the Colonel, took the trouble to identify each stone. He probably wrapped each piece in a numbered slip of paper which related to a master sketch of the throne to enable it to be reassembled.'

'There is no hope of that now,' said Sherry.

'I don't know,' I said. 'It would be a hell of a job, but it would still be possible to put it all together again.'

Amongst our stores was a roll of plastic packets, and I sent Angelo to ferret it out. As we opened each parcel of rotted fabric we superficially cleaned the stones it contained and packed each lot in a separate plastic packet.

It was slow work even though we all contributed and after almost two hours of it we had filled dozens of packets with thousands of semi-precious stones—lapis lazuli, beryl, tiger's eye, garnets, verdite, amethyst, and half a dozen others of whose identity I was uncertain. Each stone had clearly been lovingly cut and exactingly polished to fit into its own niche in the golden throne.

It was only when we had unpacked the chest to its last layer that we came upon the stones of greater value. The old Colonel had obviously selected these first and they had gone into the lowest layer of the chest.

I held a transparent plastic packet of emeralds to the lantern light, and they burned like a bursting green star. We all stared at it as if mesmerized while I turned it slowly to catch the fierce white light.

I laid it aside and Sherry dipped once more into the chest and after a moment's hesitation brought out a smaller parcel. She rubbed away the damp crumbling material, that was wound thick about the single stone it contained.

Then she held up the Great Mogul diamond in the cupped palm

249

of her hand. It was the size of a pullet's egg, cut into a faceted cushion shape, just as Jean Baptiste Tavernier had described it so many hundred years ago.

The glittering array of treasure we had handled before in no way dimmed the glory of this stone, as all the stars of the firmament cannot dull the rising of the sun. They paled and faded away before the brilliance and lustre of the great diamond.

Sherry slowly extended her cupped hand towards Angelo, offering it to him to hold and examine, but he snatched his hands away and clasped them behind his back, still staring at the stone in superstitious awe.

Sherry turned and offered it to Chubby, but with gravity he declined also.

'Give it to Mister Harry. Guess he deserves to be the one.'

I took it from her, and was surprised that such unearthly fire could be so cold to touch. I stood up and I carried it to where the golden tiger's head stood snarling angrily in the unwavering light of the lanterns and I pressed the diamond into the empty eye socket.

It fitted perfectly, and I used my bait-knife to close the golden clasps that held it firmly in place, and which the old Colonel had probably opened with a bayonet a century and a quarter ago.

I stood back then, and I heard the small gasps of wonder. With the eye returned to its socket the golden beast had come to life. It seemed now to survey us with an imperial mien, and at any instant we expected the cave to resound to its crackling wicked snarl of anger.

I went back and took my place in the squatting circle around the rusted chest, and we all stared up at the golden tiger head. We seemed like worshippers in some ancient heathen rite, crouched in awe before the fearsome idol.

'Chubby, my old well beloved and trusted buddy, you will earn yourself an entry on the title page of the book of mercy if you pass me that bottle,' I said, and that broke the spell. They all recovered their voices competing fiercely for a turn to speak—and it wasn't long before I had to send Sherry to fetch another bottle to lubricate dry throats.

We all got more than a little drunk that night, even Sherry North, and she leaned against me for support as we finally made a riotous way through the rain to our own cave.

'You really are corrupting me, Fletcher,' she stumbled into a puddle, and nearly brought me down. 'This is the first time ever I have been stoned.'

'Be of good cheer, my pretty sweeting, your next lesson in corruption follows immediately.'

* * *

When I woke it was still dark and I rose from our bed, careful not to disturb Sherry who was breathing lightly and evenly in the darkness. It was cool so I pulled on shorts and a woollen jersey.

Outside the cave the west wind had broken up the cloud banks. It had stopped raining and the stars were showing in the breaks of the heavens, giving me enough light to read the luminous dial of my wristwatch. It was a little after three o'clock.

As I sought my favourite palm tree, I saw that we had left the lantern burning in the storage cave. I finished what I had to do and went up to the lighted entrance.

The open chest stood where we had left it, as did the priceless golden head with its glittering eye—and suddenly I was struck with the consuming terror that the miser must feel for his hoard. It was so vulnerable.

'—where thieves break in—' I thought, and it was not as though there were any shortage of them in the immediate vicinity.

I had to get it all stowed away safely, and tomorrow would be too late. Despite the pain in my head and the taste of stale whisky in the back of my throat, it must be done now—but I needed help.

Chubby roused to my first soft call at the entrance of his cave, and came out into the starlight, resplendent in his striped pyjamas and as wide awake as if he had drunk nothing more noxious than mother's milk before retiring.

I explained my fears and misgivings. Chubby grunted in agreement and went with me back to the storage cave. The plastic bags of gem stones we repacked casually into the iron chest and I secured the lid with a length of nylon line. The golden head we shrouded carefully in a length of green canvas tarpaulin and we carried both down into the palm grove, before returning for spades and the gas lantern.

By the flat white glare of the lantern we worked side by side, digging two shallow graves in the sandy soil within a few feet of where the gelignite and the FN rifle with its spare ammunition were already buried.

We laid the chest and the golden head away and covered them. Afterwards I brushed the soil over them with a palm frond to wipe out all trace of our labours.

'You happy now, Harry?' Chubby asked at last.

'Yeah, I'm happier, Chubby. You go and get some sleep, hear.'

He went away amongst the palms carrying the lantern and not looking back. I knew I would not be able to sleep again, for the spadework had cleared my head and roused my blood. It would be senseless to return to the cave and try to lie quietly beside Sherry until dawn.

I wanted to find some quiet and secret place where I could think out my next moves in this intricate game of chance in which I was involved. I chose the path that led to the saddle between the lesser peaks and as I climbed it, the last of the clouds were blown aside and revealed a pale yellow moon still a week from full. Its light was strong enough to show me the way to the nearest peak and I left the path and toiled upwards to the summit.

I found a place protected from the wind and settled into it. I wished that I had a cheroot with me for I think better with one of them in my mouth. I also think better without a hangover—but there was nothing I could do about either.

After half an hour I had firmly decided that we must consolidate what we had gained to this point. The miser's fears, which had assailed me earlier, still persisted and I had been given clear warning that the wolf pack was out hunting. As soon as it was light we would take what we had salvaged so far—the head and the chest—and run down the islands to St Mary's to dispose of them in the manner which I had already so carefully planned.

There would be time later to return to Gunfire Reef and recover what remained in the misty depths of the pool. Once the decision had been made I felt a lift of relief, a new lightness of spirit, and I looked forward to the solution of the other major puzzle that had troubled me for so long.

Very soon I would be in a position to call Sherry North's hand and have a sight of those cards which she concealed so carefully from me. I wanted to know what caused those shadows in the blue depths of her eyes, and the answers to many other mysteries that surrounded her. That time would soon come.

There was a paling of the sky at last, dawn's first pearling light spread across from the east and softened the harsh dark plain of the ocean. I rose stiffly from my seat amongst the rocks, and picked my way around the peak into the wicked eye of the west wind. I stood there on the exposed face above the camp with the wind raising a rash of goose bumps along my arms and ruffling my hair.

I looked down into the sheltering arms of the lagoon, and in the feeble glimmer of dawn, the darkened ship that was creeping stealthily into the open arms of the bay looked like some pale phantom.

Even as I stared I saw the splash at her bows as she let go her anchor, and she rounded up into the wind showing her full silhouette so that I could not doubt that she was the *Mandrake*.

Before I had recovered my wits, she had dropped a boat which sped in swiftly towards the beach.

I started to run.

           *   *   *

I fell once on the path, but the force of my headlong descent from the peak carried me on and with a single roll I was on my feet again, still running.

I was panting wildly as I burst into Chubby's cave, and I shouted, 'Move, man, move! They are on the beach already.'

The two of them tumbled from their sleeping bags. Angelo was tousle-haired and blank-eyed from sleep, but Chubby was quick and alert.

'Chubby,' I snapped, 'go get that piece out of the ground. Jump, man, they'll be coming up through the grove in a few minutes.' He had changed while I spoke, pulling on a shirt and belting his denim breeches. He grunted an acknowledgement. 'I'll follow you in a minute,' I called as he ran out into the feeble light of dawn.

'Angelo, snap out of it!' I grabbed his shoulder and shook him. 'I want you to look after Miss Sherry, hear?'

He was dressed now and he nodded owlishly at me.

'Come on.' I half dragged him as we ran across to my cave. I dragged her out of bed and while she dressed I told her.

'Angelo will go with you. I want you to take a can of drinking water and the two of you get the hell down to the south of the island, cross the saddle first though and keep out of sight. Climb the

253

peak and hide out in the chimney where we found the inscription. You know where I mean.'

'Yes, Harry,' she nodded.

'Stay there. Don't go out or show yourself under any circumstances. Understand?'

She nodded as she tucked the tail of her shirt into her breeches.

'Remember, these people are killers. The time for games is over, this is a pack of wolves that we are dealing with.'

'Yes, Harry, I know.'

'Okay then,' I embraced and kissed her quickly. 'Off you go then.' And they went out of the cave, Angelo lugging a five-gallon can of drinking water, and they trotted away into the palm grove.

Quickly I threw a few items into a light haversack, a box of cheroots, matches, binoculars, water bottle and a heavy jersey, a tin of chocolate and of survival rations, a flashlight—and I buckled my belt around my waist with the heavy bait-knife in the sheath. Slinging the strap of the haversack over my shoulder, I also ran from the cave and followed Chubby down into the palm grove towards the beach.

I had run fifty yards when there was the thud, thudding of small-arms fire, a shout and another burst of firing. It was directly ahead of me and very close.

I paused and slipped behind the bole of the palm tree while I peered into the lightening shades of the grove. I saw movement, a figure running towards me and I loosened the bait-knife in its sheath and waited until I was sure, before I called softly, 'Chubby!'

The running figure swerved towards me. He was carrying the FN rifle and the canvas bandolier with spare magazines of ammunition, and he was breathing quickly but lightly as he saw me.

'They spotted me,' he grunted. 'There are hundreds of the bastards.'

At that moment I saw more movement amongst the trees.

'Here they come,' I said. 'Let's go.'

I wanted to give Sherry a clear run, so I did not take the path across the saddle, but turned directly southwards to lead the pursuit off her scent. We headed for the swamps at the southern end of the island.

They saw us as we ran obliquely across their front. I heard a shout, answered immediately by others, and then there were five scattered shots and I saw the muzzle flashes bloom amongst the dark trees. A bullet struck a palm trunk high above our heads, a woody thunk, but we were going fast and within minutes the shouts of pursuit were fading behind us.

I reached the edge of the salt marsh, and swung away inland to avoid the stinking mudflats. On the first gentle slope of the hills I halted to listen and to regain our breath. The light was strengthening swiftly now. Within a short while it would be sunrise and I wanted to be under cover before then.

Suddenly there were distant cries of dismay from the direction of the swamps and I guessed that the pursuit had blundered into the glutinous mud. That would discourage them fairly persuasively, I thought, and grinned.

'Okay, Chubby, let's get on,' I whispered, and as we stood there was a new sound from a different direction.

The sound was muted by distance and by the intervening heights of the ridge, for it came from the seaward side of the island, but it was the unmistakable ripping sound of automatic gunfire.

Chubby and I froze into listening attitudes and the sound was repeated, another long tearing burst of machine-gun fire. Then there was silence, though we listened for three or four minutes.

'Come on,' I said quietly, we could delay no longer and we ran on up the slope towards the southernmost peak.

We climbed quickly in the fast-growing morning light, and I was too preoccupied to feel any qualms as we negotiated the narrow ledge and stepped at last into the deep rock crack where I had arranged to meet Sherry.

The shelter was silent and deserted but I called without hope, 'Sherry! Are you there, love?'

There was no reply from the shadows, and I turned back to Chubby.

'They had a good lead on us. They should have been here,' and only then did that burst of machine-gun fire we had heard earlier take on new meaning.

I removed the binoculars from the haversack and then thrust it away into a crack in the rock.

'They've run into trouble, Chubby,' I told him. 'Come on. Let's go and find out what happened.'

Once we were off the ledge we struck out through the jumble of broken rock towards the seaward side of the island, but even in my haste and dreadful anxiety for Sherry's safety, I moved with stealth and we were careful not to show ourselves to a watcher in the groves or on the beaches below us.

As we crossed the divide of the ridge a new vista opened before us, the curve of the beach and the jagged black sweep of Gunfire Reef.

I halted instantly and pulled Chubby down beside me, as we crouched into cover.

Anchored in a position to command the mouth of the channel through Gunfire Reef was the armed crash boat from Zinballa Bay, flagship of my old friend Suleiman Dada. Returning to it from the beach was a small motor-boat, crowded with tiny figures.

'God damn it,' I muttered, 'they really had it planned. Manny Resnick has teamed up with Suleiman Dada. That's what took him so long to get here. While Manny hit the beach, Dada was covering the channel, so we couldn't make a bolt for it like we did before.

'And he had men on the beach—that was the machine-gun fire. Manny Resnick sailed *Mandrake* into the bay to flush us, and Dada had the back door covered.'

'What about Miss Sherry and Angelo? Do you think they got away? Did Dada's men catch them when they crossed the saddle?'

'Oh God!' I groaned, and cursed myself for not having stayed with her. I stood up and focused the binoculars on the motor-boat as it crawled across the clear waters of the outer lagoon to the anchored crash boat.

'I can't see them.' Even with the aid of the binoculars, the occupants of the dinghy were merely a dark mass, for the morning sun was rising beyond them and the glare off the water dazzled me. I could not make out separate figures, let alone recognize individuals.

'They may have them in the boat—but I can't see.' In my agitation I had left the cover of the rocks, and was seeking a better vantage point, moving about on the sky-line. Out in the open I must have been highlit by the same sun rays that were blinding me.

I saw the familiar flash, and the long white feather of gunsmoke blow from the mounted quick-firer on the bows of the crash boat, and I heard the shell coming with a rushing sound like eagles' wings.

'Get down!' I shouted at Chubby, and threw myself flat amongst the rocks.

The shell burst in very close, with the bright hot glare like the brief opening of a furnace door. Shrapnel and rock fragments trilled and whined around us, and I jumped to my feet.

'Run!' I yelled at Chubby, and we jinked back over the skyline just as the next shell passed over us, making us both flinch our heads at the mighty crack of passing shot.

Chubby was wiping a smear of blood from his forearm as we crouched behind the ridge.

'Okay?' I asked.

'A scratch, that's all. Bit of a rock fragment,' he growled.

'Chubby, I'm going down to find out what happened to the others. No point both of us taking a chance. You wait here.'

'You're wasting time, Harry, I'm coming with you. Let's go.' He hefted the rifle and led the way down the peak. I thought of taking the FN away from him. In his hands it was about as lethal as a slingshot when fired with his closed-eyes technique. Then I left it. It made him feel good.

We moved slowly, hugging any cover there was and searching ahead before moving forward. However, the island was silent except for the sough and clatter of the west wind in the tops of the palms and we saw nobody as we moved up the seaward side of the island.

I cut the spoor left by Angelo and Sherry as they crossed the saddle, above the camp. Their running footsteps had bitten deep into the fluffy soil, Sherry's small slim prints were overlapped by Angelo's broad bare feet.

We followed them down the slope, and suddenly they shied off the track. They had dropped the water-can here and, turning abruptly, had separated slightly, as though they had run side by side for sixty yards.

There we found Angelo, and he was never going to enjoy his share of the spoils. He had been hit by three of the soft heavy-calibre slugs. They had torn through the thin fabric of his shirt, and opened huge dark wounds in his back and chest.

He had bled copiously but the sandy soil had absorbed most of it, and already what was left was drying into a thick black crust. The flies were assembled, crawling gleefully into the bullet holes and swarming on the long dark lashes around his wide open and startled eyes.

Following her tracks I saw where Sherry had run on for twenty paces, and then the little idiot had turned back and gone to kneel beside where Angelo lay. I cursed her for that. She might have been able to escape if she had not indulged in that useless and extravagant gesture.

They had caught her as she knelt beside the body and dragged her down through the palms to the beach. I could see the long slide marks in the sand where she had dug her feet in and tried to resist.

Without leaving the shelter of the trees, I looked down the smooth white sand, following their tracks to where the marks of the motorboat's keel still showed in the sand of the water's edge.

They had taken her out to the crash boat, and I crouched behind a pile of driftwood and dried palm fronds to stare out at the graceful little ship.

Even as I watched she weighed anchor, picked up speed and passed slowly down the length of the island to round the point and enter the inner lagoon where *Mandrake* was still lying at anchor.

I straightened up and slipped back through the grove to where I had left Chubby. He had laid the carbine aside and he sat with Angelo's body in his arms, cradling the head against his shoulder. Chubby was weeping, fat glistening tears slid wearily down the seamed brown cheeks and fell from his jaw to wet the thick dark curls of the boy in his arms.

I picked up the rifle and stood guard over them while Chubby wept for both of us. I envied him the relief of tears, the outpouring of pain that would bring surcease. My own grief was as fierce as Chubby's, for I had loved Angelo as much, but it was down deep inside where it hurt more.

'All right, Chubby,' I said at last. 'Let's go, man.' He stood up with the boy still in his arms and we moved back along the ridge.

In a gully that was choked with rank vegetation we laid Angelo in a shallow grave that we scraped with our hands, and we covered him with a blanket of branches and leaves that I cut with my bait-knife before filling the grave. I could not bring myself to throw sand into his unprotected face, and the leaves made a gentler shroud.

Chubby wiped away his tears with the open palm of his hand and he stood up.

'They got Sherry,' I told him quietly. 'She is aboard the crash boat.'

'Is she hurt?' he asked.

'I don't think so, not yet.'

'What do you want to do now, Harry?' he asked, and the question was answered for me.

Somewhere far off towards the camp, we heard a whistle shrill, and we moved up the ridge to a point where we could see down into the inner lagoon and landward side of the island.

Mandrake lay where I had last seen her and the Zinballa crash boat was anchored a hundred yards closer to the shore. They had seized the whaleboat and were using her to land men on the beach. They were all armed, and uniformed. They set off immediately into the palm trees and the whaleboat ran back to *Mandrake*.

I put the binoculars on to *Mandrake* and saw that there were developments taking place there also. In the field of the glasses I recognized Manny Resnick in a white open-neck shirt and blue slacks as he climbed down into the whaleboat. He was followed by Lorna Page. She wore dark glasses, a yellow scarf around her pale blonde hair and an emerald green slack suit. I felt hatred seethe in my guts as I recognized them.

Now something happened that puzzled me. The luggage that I had seen loaded into the Rolls at Curzon Street was brought out on to the deck by two of Manny's thugs and it also was passed down into the whaleboat.

A uniformed crew member of *Mandrake* saluted from the deck, and Manny waved at him in a gesture of airy dismissal.

The whaleboat left *Mandrake*'s side and moved in towards the crash boat. As Manny, his lady friend, bodyguards and luggage were disembarked on to the deck of the crash boat, *Mandrake* weighed anchor, turned for the entrance of the bay, and set out in a determined fashion for the deep-water channel.

'She's leaving,' muttered Chubby. 'Why is she doing that?'

'Yes, she's leaving,' I agreed. 'Manny Resnick has finished with her. He's got a new ally now, and he doesn't need his own ship. She's probably costing him a thousand pounds a day—and Manny always was a shy man with a buck.'

I turned my glasses on to the crash boat again and saw Manny and his entourage enter the cabin.

'There is probably another reason,' I muttered.

'What's that, Harry?'

'Manny Resnick and Suleiman Dada will want as few witnesses as possible to what they intend doing now.'

'Yeah, I see what you mean,' grunted Chubby.

'I think, my friend, that we are about to be treated to the kind of nastiness that will make what they did to Angelo seem kind, by comparison.'

'We've got to get Miss Sherry off that boat, Harry.' Chubby was coming out of the daze of grief into which Angelo's killing had thrown him. 'We've got to do something, Harry.'

'It's a nice thought, Chubby, I agree. But we aren't going to help her much by getting ourselves killed. My guess is that she will be safe until they get their hands on the treasure.'

His huge brown face creased up like that of a worried bulldog.

'What we going to do, Harry?'

'Right now we are going to run again.'

'What do you mean?'

'Listen,' I told him, and he cocked his head. There was the shrill of the whistle again and then faintly we heard voices carried up to us on the wind.

'Looks like their first effort will be brute strength. They've landed the entire goon squad, and they are going to drive the island and put us up like a brace of cock pheasant.'

'Let's go down and have a go,' Chubby growled, and cocked the FN. 'I got a message for them from Angelo.'

'Don't be a fool, Chubby,' I snapped at him angrily. 'Now listen to me. I want to count how many men they have. Then, if we get a good chance, I want to try and get one of them alone and take his piece off him. Watch for an opportunity, Chubby, but don't have a go yet. Play it very cautious, hear?' I didn't want to refer to his marksmanship in derogatory tones.

'Okay,' Chubby nodded.

'You stay this side of the ridge. Count how many of them come down this side of the island. I'll cross over and do the same on the other side.' He nodded. 'I'll meet you at the spot where the crash boat shelled us in two hours.'

'What about you, Harry?' He made a gesture of handing me the FN—but I didn't have the heart to deprive him.

'I'll be okay,' I told him. 'Off you go, man.'

*　　*　　*

It was a simple task to keep ahead of the line of beaters for they called to each other loudly to keep their spirits up, and they made no pretence at concealment or stealth, but advanced slowly and cautiously in an extended line.

There were nine of them on my side of the ridge, seven of them were blacks in naval uniform, armed with AK47 assault rifles and two of them were Manny Resnick's men. They were dressed in casual tropical gear and carried sidearms. One of them I recognized as the driver of the Rover that night so long ago, and the passenger in the twin-engined Cessna that had spotted Sherry and me on the beach.

Once I had made my head count, I turned my back on them and ran ahead to the curve of the salt marsh. I knew that when the line of beaters ran into this obstacle, it would lose its cohesion and that it was likely that some of its members would become isolated.

I found an advanced neck of swampland with stands of young mangrove and coarse swamp grass in dense shades of fever green. I followed the edge of this thicket and came upon a spot where a fallen palm tree lay across the neck like a bridge—offering escape in two directions. It had collected a dense covering of blown palm fronds and swamp grass which provided a good hide from which to mount an ambush.

I lay in the back of this shaggy mound of dead vegetation and I had the heavy bait-knife in my right hand ready to throw.

The line of the beaters came on steadily, their voices growing louder as they approached the swamp. Soon I could hear the rustle and scrape of branches as one of them came directly down to where I lay.

He paused and called when he was about twenty feet from me, and I pressed my face close to the damp earth and peered under the pile of dead branches. There was an opening there and I saw his feet and his legs below the knees. His trousers were thick blue serge and he wore grubby white sneakers without socks. At each step his naked ankles showed very black African skin.

It was one of the sailors from the crash boat then, and I was pleased. He would be carrying an automatic weapon. I preferred that to a pistol, which was what Manny's boys were armed with.

Slowly I rolled on to my side and cleared my knife arm. The sailor called again so close and so loud that my nerves jumped and I felt the tingling flush of adrenalin in my blood. His call was answered from farther off, and the sailor came on.

I could hear his soft footfalls on the sand, padding towards me.

Suddenly he came into full view, as he rounded the fall of brushwood. He was ten paces from me.

He was in naval uniform, a blue cap on his head with its gay little red pom-pom on the top, but he carried the vicious and brutal-looking machine-gun on his hip. He was a tall lean youngster in his early twenties, smooth faced and sweating nervously so there was a purple black sheen on his skin, against which his eyes were very white.

He saw me and tried to swing the machine-gun on to me, but it was on his right hip and he blocked himself awkwardly in the turn. I aimed for the notch where the two collarbones meet, that was framed by the opening of his uniform at the base of his throat. I threw overhand, snapping my wrist into it at the moment of release so the knife leapt in a silvery blur and thudded precisely into the mark I had chosen. The blade was completely buried and only the dark walnut handle protruded from his throat.

He tried to cry out, but no sound came, for the blade had severed all his vocal chords as I intended. He sank slowly to his knees facing me in a prayerful attitude with his hands dangling at his sides and the machine-gun hanging on its strap.

We stared at each other for a moment that seemed to last for ever. Then he shuddered violently and a thick burst of bubbling blood poured from his mouth and nose, and he pitched face forward to the ground.

Crouched low, I flipped him on to his back and withdrew the knife against the clinging drag of wet flesh, and I cleaned the blade on his sleeve.

Working swiftly I stripped him of his weapon and the spare magazines in the bandolier on his webbing belt, then, still crouching low, I dragged him by his heels into the gluey mud of the creek and knelt on his chest to force him below the surface. The mud flowed over his face as slowly and thickly as molten chocolate, and when he was totally submerged I buckled the webbing belt around my waist, picked up the machine-gun and slipped back quietly through the breach that I had made in the line of beaters.

As I ran doubled over and using all the cover there was, I checked the load on the AK47. I was familiar with the weapon. I had used it in Biafra and I made sure that the magazine was full and that the breech was loaded before I slipped the strap over my right shoulder and held it ready on my hip.

When I had moved back about five hundred yards I paused and took shelter against the trunk of a palm while I listened. Behind me, the line of beaters seemed to have run into trouble against the swamp, and they were trying to sort themselves out. I listened to the shouts and the angry shrill of the whistle. It sounded like a cup final, I thought, and grinned queasily, for the memory of the man I had killed was still nauseatingly fresh.

Now that I had broken through their line I turned and struck directly across the island towards my rendezvous with Chubby on the south peak. Once I was out of the palm groves on to the lower slopes, the vegetation was thicker, and I moved more swiftly through the better cover.

Halfway to the crest I was startled by a fresh burst of gunfire. This time it was the distinctive whipcracking lash of the FN, a sharper slower beat than the storm of AK47 machine-gun fire that answered it immediately.

I judged by the volume and duration of the outburst that all the weapons involved had emptied magazines in a continuous burst. A heavy silence followed.

Chubby was having a go, after all my warnings. Although I was bitterly angry, I was also thoroughly alarmed by what trouble he had gotten himself into. One thing was certain—Chubby had missed whatever he had aimed at.

I broke from a trot into a run, and angled upwards towards the crest, aiming to reach the area from which the gunfire had sounded.

I burst out of a patch of goosebush into a narrow overgrown path that followed the direction I wanted, and I turned into it and went into a full run.

I topped the rise and almost ran into the arms of one of the uniformed seamen coming in the opposite direction, also at a headlong run.

There were six of his comrades with him in Indian file, all making the best possible speed on his heels. Thirty yards farther back was another who had lost his weapon and whose uniform jacket was sodden with fresh blood.

On all their faces were expressions of abandoned terror, and they ran with the single-minded determination of men pursued closely by all the legions of hell.

I knew instantly that this rabble were the survivors of an encounter with Chubby Andrews, and that it had been too much for their nerves. They were hell-bent and homeward-bound—Chubby's shooting must have improved miraculously, and I made him a silent apology.

263

So much were the seamen involved with the devil behind them that they seemed not to notice me for the fleeting instant which it took for me to slip the safety-catch on the machine-gun on my hip, brace myself with knees bent and feet spread.

I swung the weapon in a short kicking traverse aimed low at their knees. With a rate of fire like that of an AK47, you must go for the legs, and rely on another three or four hits in the body as the man drops through the sheet of fire. It also defeats the efforts of the short barrel to ride up under the thrust of the recoil.

They went down in a sprawling shrieking mass, punched backwards into each other by the savage strike of the soft heavy-calibre slugs.

I held the trigger down for the count of four, and then I turned and plunged off the path into the thick wall of goosebush. It hid me instantly and I doubled over as I jinked and dodged under the branches.

Behind me, a machine-gun was firing, and the bullets tore and snapped through the thick foliage. None came near me and I settled back into a quick trot.

I guessed that my sudden and completely unexpected attack would have permanently accounted for two or three of the seamen, and may have wounded one or two others.

However, the effect on their morale would be disastrous—especially coming so soon after Chubby's onslaught. Once they reached the safety of the crash boat, I guessed that the forces of evil would debate long and hard before setting foot on the island again. We had won the second round decisively, but they still had Sherry North. That was the major trump in their hands. As long as they held her they could dictate the course of the game.

Chubby was waiting for me amongst the rocks on the saddle of the peak. The man was indestructible.

'Jesus, Harry, where the hell you been?' he growled. 'I've been waiting here all morning.'

I saw that he had retrieved my haversack from the cleft in the rocks where I had left it. It lay with two captured AK47 rifles and bandoliers of ammunition at his feet.

He handed me the water bottle, and only then did I realize how thirsty I was. The heavily chlorinated water tasted like Veuve Clicquot, but I rationed myself to three swallows.

'I got to apologize to you, Harry. I had a go. Just couldn't help it, man. They were bunched up and standing out in the open like a Sunday-school picnic. Just couldn't help myself, gave them a good old squirt. Dropped two of them and the others run like hens, shooting their pieces straight up in the air as they go.'

'Yeah,' I nodded. 'I met them as they crossed the ridge.'

'Heard the shooting. Just about to come and look for you.'

I sat down on the rock beside him, and found my cheroots in the haversack. We each lit one and smoked in grateful silence for a moment which Chubby spoiled.

'Well, we lit a fire under their tails—don't reckon they'll come back for more. But they have still got Miss Sherry, man. Long as they got her, they are winning.'

'How many were there, Chubby?'

'Ten.' He spat out a scrap of tobacco and inspected the glowing tip of the cheroot. 'But I took out two—and I think I winged another.'

'Yeah,' I agreed. 'I met seven on the ridge. I had a go at them also. Aren't more than four left now—and there are eight more out of my bunch. Say a dozen, plus those left on board—another six or seven. About twenty guns still against us, Chubby.'

'Pretty odds, Harry.'

'Let's work on it, Chubby.'

'Let's do that, Harry.'

I selected the newest and least abused of the three machine-guns and there were five full magazines of ammunition for it. I cached the discarded weapons under a slab of flat rock and loaded and checked the other.

We each had another short drink from the water bottle and then I led the way cautiously along the ridge, keeping off the skyline, back towards the deserted camp.

From the spot at which I had first spotted the approach of the *Mandrake* we surveyed the whole northern end of the island.

As we guessed they would, Manny and Suleiman Dada had taken all their men off the island. Both the whaleboat and the smaller motor-boat were moored alongside the crash boat. There was much confused and meaningless activity on board, and as I watched the scurrying figures I imagined the scenes of terrible wrath and retribution which were taking place in the main cabin.

Suleiman Dada and his new protégé were certainly wreaking a

fearful vengeance on their already badly beaten and demoralized troops.

'I want to go down to the camp, Chubby. See what they left for us,' I said at last, and handed him the binoculars. 'Keep watch for me. Three quick shots as a warning signal.'

'Okay, Harry,' he agreed, but as I stood up there was a renewed outbreak of feverish activity on board the crash boat. I took the glasses back from Chubby and watched Suleiman Dada emerge from the cabin and make a laborious ascent to the open bridge. In his white uniform, bedecked with medals that glittered in the sunlight and attended by a host of helpers he reminded me of a fat white queen termite being moved from its royal cell by swarming worker ants.

The transfer was effected at last and as I watched through the binoculars I saw an electronic bullhorn handed to Suleiman. He faced the shore, lifted the hailer to his mouth and through the powerful lens I saw his lips moving. Seconds later the sound reached us clearly, magnified by the instrument and carried by the wind.

'Harry Fletcher. I hope you can hear me.' The deep well-modulated voice was given a harsher sound by the amplifier. 'I plan to put on a demonstration this evening which will convince you of the necessity of co-operating with me. Please be in a position where you can watch. You will find it fascinating. Nine o'clock this evening on the afterdeck of this ship. It's a date, Harry. Don't miss it.'

He handed the bullhorn to one of his officers and went below.

'They're going to do something to Sherry,' muttered Chubby and fiddled disconsolately with the rifle in his lap.

'We'll know at nine,' I said, and watched the officer with the bullhorn climb from the deck into the motor-boat. They set off on a slow circuit of the island, stopping every half mile to shout a repetition of Suleiman Dada's invitation to me at the silent tree-lined shore. He was very anxious for me to attend.

'All right, Chubby,' I glanced at my watch. 'We have hours yet. I'm going down to the camp. Watch out for me.'

The camp had been ransacked and plundered of most items of value, equipment and stores had been smashed and scattered about the caves—but still some of it had been overlooked.

I found five cans of fuel and hid them along with much other equipment that might be of value. Then I crept cautiously down into the grove, and learned with relief that the hiding-place of the chest and the golden tiger's head and the other stores was undisturbed.

Carrying a five-gallon can of drinking water and three cans of corned beef and mixed vegetables I climbed again to the ridge where Chubby waited. We ate and drank and I said to Chubby: 'Get some sleep if you can. It's going to be a long hard night.'

He grunted and curled up in the grass like a great brown bear. Soon he was snoring softly and regularly.

I smoked three cheroots slowly and thoughtfully, but it was only as the sun was setting that I had my first real stroke of genius. It was so clear and simple, and so delightfully apt that it was immediately suspect and I re-examined it carefully.

The wind had dropped and it was completely dark by the time I was certain of my idea and I sat smiling and nodding contentedly as I thought about it.

The crash boat was brightly lit, all her ports glowed and a pair of floods glared whitely down upon the afterdeck, so it looked like an empty stage.

I woke Chubby and we ate and drank again.

'Let's go down to the beach,' I said. 'We'll have a better view from there.'

'It might be a trap,' Chubby warned me morosely.

'I don't think so. They are all on board, and they are playing from strength. They've still got Sherry. They don't have to try any fancy tricks.'

'Man, if they do anything to that girl—' he stopped himself, and stood up. 'All right, let's go.'

We moved silently and cautiously down through the grove with our weapons cocked and our fingers on the triggers, but the night was still and the grove deserted.

We halted amongst the trees at the top of the beach. The crash boat was only two hundred yards away and I leaned my shoulder against the trunk of a palm and focused my glasses on her. It was so clear and close that I could read the writing on the lid of a packet from which one of the sentries took and lit a cigarette.

We had a front row seat for whatever entertainment Suleiman Dada was planning, and I felt the stir of apprehension and knowledge of coming horror blow like a cold breeze across my skin.

I lowered the glasses and whispered softly to Chubby, 'Change your piece for mine,' and he passed me the long-barrelled FN and took the AK47.

I wanted the accuracy of the FN to command the deck of the crash boat. Naturally there was nothing I could do to intervene while Sherry was unharmed, but if they did anything to her—I would make sure she didn't suffer alone.

I squatted down beside the palm tree, adjusted the peep sights of the rifle, and drew a careful bead on the head of the deck guard. I knew I could put a bullet through his temple from where I sat and when I was satisfied I laid the rifle across my lap and settled down to wait.

The mosquitoes from the swamp whined around our ears but both Chubby and I ignored them and sat quietly. I longed for a cheroot to soothe the tension of my nerves, but I was forced to forgo that comfort.

Time passed very slowly, and new fears came to plague me and make the waiting seem even longer than it was—but finally, a few minutes before the promised hour, there was a renewed stirring and bustle on board the crash boat and once more Suleiman Dada was helped up the ladder by his men and he took his place at the bridge rail looking down over the afterdeck. He was sweating heavily and it had soaked the area around the armpits and across the back of his white uniform jacket. I guessed that he had passed his own period of waiting by frequent recourse to the whisky bottle, probably from my own stock that had been plundered from the cave.

He laughed and joked with the men around him, his vast belly shaking with mirth and his men echoed the laughter slavishly. The sound of it carried across the water to the beach.

Suleiman was followed by Manny Resnick and his blonde lady friend. Manny was well groomed and cool-looking in his expensive casual clothing. He stood slightly apart from the others, his expression aloof and disinterested. He reminded me of an adult at a children's party, seeing out a boring and mildly unpleasant duty.

In contrast, Lorna Page was excited and shiny-eyed as a girl on her first date. She laughed with Suleiman Dada and leaned expectantly over the rail above the deserted deck. Through the powerful glasses I could see the flush on her cheeks which was not rouge.

I was concentrating on her so that it was only when I felt Chubby move suddenly and restlessly, and heard his grunt of alarm that I swung the glasses downwards on to the deck.

Sherry was there, standing between two of the uniformed sailors. They held her arms and she looked small and frail between them.

She still wore the clothes she had thrown on so hurriedly that morning and her hair was dishevelled. Her face was gaunt and her expression strained—but it was only when I studied her carefully that I saw that what looked like sleepless dark rings below her eyes were in fact bruises. With a cold chill of anger, I realized that her lips were swollen and puffed up as though they had been stung by bees. One of her cheeks was also fatly distorted and bruised.

They had beaten her and knocked her about badly. Now that I looked for it I could see dark splotches of dried blood on her blue shirt, and when one of the guards dragged her around roughly to face the shore I saw that one of her hands was bandaged roughly— and that either blood or disinfectant had stained the bandages.

She looked tired and ill, nearly at the end of her strength. My anger threatened to wipe out my reason. I wanted to inflict hurt upon those who had treated Sherry like this, and I had already begun to lift the rifle with hands that shook with the force of my hatred before I could control myself. I closed my eyes tightly and took a long deep breath to steady myself. The time would come—but it was not now.

When I opened my eyes again and refocused the binoculars, Suleiman Dada had the bullhorn to his lips.

'Good evening, Harry, my dear friend. I am sure you recognize this young lady.' He made a wide gesture towards Sherry and she looked up at him wearily. 'After questioning her closely, a procedure which alas caused her a little discomfort, I am at last convinced that she does not know the whereabouts of the property in which my friends and I are interested. She tells me that you have hidden it.' He paused and mopped his streaming face with a towel handed to him by one of his men before he went on.

'She is no longer of any interest to me—except possibly as a medium of exchange.'

He made a gesture, and Sherry was hustled away below. Something cold and slimy moved in my guts at her going. I wondered if I would ever see her again—alive.

On to the deserted deck filed four of Suleiman's men. Each of them had stripped to the waist and the floodlights rippled on their smooth darkly muscled bodies.

Each of them carried the hickory wooden handles of a pickaxe, and silently they formed up at the points of a star about the open deck. Next a man was led into the open centre by two guards. His hands were tied behind his back. They stood on each side of him and slowly forced him to turn in a circle and show himself while Suleiman Dada's voice boomed through the bullhorn.

'I wonder if you recognize him?' I stared at the stooped creature in canvas prison overalls that hung in filthy grey tatters from his gaunt frame. His skin was pale and waxy with deep-set dark eyes, long scraggly blond hair hung in greasy snakes about his face and his half-grown beard was thin and wispy.

He had lost teeth, probably knocked from his mouth with a careless blow.

'Yes, Harry?' Suleiman laughed fruitily over the loud hailer. 'A sojourn in Zinballa prison does wonders for a man, does it not—but the regulation garb is not as smart as that of an Inspector of Police.'

Only then did I recognize ex-Inspector Peter Daly—the man who I had pitched from the deck of *Wave Dancer* into the waters of the outer lagoon just before I had escaped from Suleiman Dada by running the channel at Gunfire Reef.

'Inspector Peter Daly,' Suleiman confirmed with a chuckle, 'a man who let me down badly. I do not like men who let me down, Harry. I really take it very hard. I brought him along for just such an eventuality. It was a wise precaution, for I believe that a graphic demonstration is so much more convincing than mere words.'

Once again he paused to mop his face and to drink deeply from a glass offered him by one of his men. Daly fell to his knees and looked up at the man on the bridge. His expression was of abject terror, and his mouth dribbled saliva as he pleaded for mercy.

'Very well, we can proceed if you are ready, Harry,' he boomed, and one of the guards produced a large black cloth bag which he pulled over Peter Daly's head and secured with a drawn string around his neck. They dragged him roughly to his feet again.

'It's our own variation on the game of blind man's buff.'

Through the glasses I saw the liquid flood soak through the front of Peter Daly's canvas trousers, as his bladder emptied in anguished terror. Obviously he had seen this game played before during his stay in Zinballa prison.

'Harry, I want you to use your imagination. Do not see this snivelling filthy creature—but in his place imagine your lovely young lady friend.' He breathed heavily, but when the man beside him offered him the towel again Suleiman struck him a passionless back-handed blow that sent him sprawling across the bridge, and he continued evenly, 'Imagine her lovely young body, imagine her delicious fear as she stands in darkness not knowing what to expect.'

The two guards began to spin Daly between them, as they do in the children's game, around and around he went and now I could faintly hear his muffled shrieks and cries of fear.

Suddenly the two guards stepped away from him, and left the circle of half-naked men with their pick handles. One of them placed the butt of his weapon in the small of Daly's back and shoved him, reeling and staggering across the circle and the man opposite was waiting to drive the end of his club into Daly's belly.

Back and forth he staggered, driven by the thrust of the clubs. Slowly his tormentors increased the savagery of their attack, until one of them hefted his club and swung it like an axe at a tree. It smashed into Daly's ribs.

It was the signal to end it, and as Peter Daly fell to the deck they crowded about him, the clubs rising and falling in a fearsome rhythm and the blows sounding clearly across the lagoon to where we watched in disgust and revulsion.

One after the other they tired, and stepped back to rest from their grim work and Peter Daly's crumpled and broken body lay in the centre of the deck.

'Crude, you will say, Harry—but then you will not deny that it is effective.'

I was sickened by the barbaric cruelty of it, and Chubby muttered beside me, 'He's a monster—I've never heard of nothing like that before.'

'You have until noon tomorrow, Harry, to come to me unarmed and reasonable. We will talk, we will agree on certain matters, we will make an exchange of assets and we will part friends.'

He stopped speaking to watch while one of his men secured a line to Peter Daly's ankle, and they hoisted him to the masthead of the crash boat where he dangled grotesquely, like some obscene pennant. Lorna Page was looking up at him, her head thrown back so the blonde hair hung down her back and her lips were slightly parted.

'If you refuse to be reasonable, Harry, then at noon tomorrow I shall sail around this island with your lady friend hanging like that—' He pointed up to the corpse whose masked head swung slowly back

271

and forth only a few feet above the deck, '—from the mast. Think about it, Harry. Take your time. Think about it well.'

Suddenly the floodlights were switched off, and Suleiman Dada began his laborious descent to the cabin. Manny Resnick and Lorna Page followed him. Manny was frowning slightly, as though he was pondering a business deal, but I could see that Lorna was enjoying herself.

'I think I'm going to throw up,' muttered Chubby.

'Get it over then,' I said, 'because we have a lot of work to do.'

I stood up and quietly led the way back into the palm grove. We took it in turns to dig while the other stood guard amongst the trees. I would not use a light for fear of attracting attention from the crash boat and we were both exaggeratedly careful to maintain silence and not to let the clank of metal on metal sound through the grove.

We lifted the remaining cases of gelignite and blasting equipment, then we did the same with the rusted pay chest and carried it to a carefully chosen site below the steeply sloping ground of the peak. Fifty yards up the slope was a fold in the ground thickly screened with goosebush and salt grass.

We dug another hole for the chest, going deep into the soft soil until we struck water. Then we repacked the pay chest and reburied it. Chubby climbed up to the hidden fold above us and made his arrangements there.

In the meantime I reloaded the machine-gun and wrapped it lightly in one of my old shirts, the five full magazines placed with it, and I buried the lot under an inch of sand, next to the stem of the nearest palm tree where the recent rain waters had cut a shallow dry runnel down from the slope.

The water-torn trench and the tree were forty paces from the spot where the chest was buried, and I hoped it was far enough. The trench was little more than two feet deep and would provide scanty cover.

The moon came out after midnight and it gave us enough light to check our arrangements. Chubby made sure I was in full view from his hideaway up the slope when I stood beside the shallow runnel. Then I climbed up to him and double-checked him. We lit a cheroot each, sheltering the match and screening the glowing tips with cupped hands, while we went over our planning once again.

I was particularly anxious that there should be no misunderstanding in our timing and signals, and I made Chubby repeat them twice. He did so with long-suffering and theatrical patience, but at last I was satisfied. We dumped the cheroot butts and scraped sand over them and when we went down the slope we both carried palm-frond brooms to sweep out all signs of activity.

The first part of my planning was complete, and we returned to where the golden tiger and the rest of the gelignite was cached. We reburied the tiger and then I prepared a full case of gelignite. It was a massive overdose of explosive, sufficient for a tenfold over-kill—but I have never been a man to stint myself when I have the means to indulge.

I would not be able to use the electric blaster and insulated wire, and I must rely on one of the time-pencil detonators. I have a strong distaste for these temperamental little gadgets. They operate on the principle of acid eating through a thin wire which holds the hammer on a powder cap. When the acid cuts the wire the cap explodes, and the delay in the detonation is governed by the strength of the acid and the thickness of the wire.

There can be a large latitude of error in this timing which on one occasion caused me a nearly fatal embarrassment. However, in this case I had no choice in the matter—and I selected a pencil with a six-hour delay and prepared it for use with the gelignite.

Amongst the equipment overlooked by the looters was my old oxygen rebreathing underwater set. This diving set is almost as dangerous to use as the time pencils. Unlike the aqualung which uses compressed air, the rebreather employs pure oxygen which is filtered and cleansed of carbon dioxide after each breath and then cycled back to the user.

Oxygen breathed at pressures in excess of twice atmospheric becomes as poisonous as carbon monoxide. In other words, if you rebreathe pure oxygen below underwater depths of thirty-three feet, it will kill you. You have to have all your wits together to play around with the stuff—but it has one enormous advantage. It does not blow bubbles on the surface to alarm a sentry and give away your position to him.

Chubby carried the prepared case of gelignite and the rifle when we went back to the beach. It was after three o'clock when I had donned and tested the oxygen set, and then I carried the gelignite down to the water and tested that for buoyancy. It needed a few pounds of lead weights to give it a neutral buoyancy and make it easier to handle in the water.

We had reached the water from the beach around the horn of the bay from the anchored crash boat. The point of sand and palm trees covered us as we worked, and at last I was ready.

It was a long tiring swim. I had to round the point and enter the bay—a distance of almost a mile—and I had to tow the case of explosive with me. It dragged heavily through the water and it took me almost an hour before I could see the lights of the crash boat glimmering above me through the clear water.

Hugging the bottom I crept forward slowly, terribly aware that the moonlight would silhouette me clearly against the white sand of the lagoon bed, for the water was clear as gin and only twenty-five feet deep.

It was a relief to move slowly into the dark shadow cast by the crash boat's hull and to know that I was safe from discovery. I rested for a few minutes, then I unrolled the nylon slings that I had on my belt and secured them to the case of gelignite.

Now I checked the time on my wristwatch, and the luminous hands showed ten minutes past four o'clock.

I crushed the glass ampoule of the time pencil, releasing the acid to begin its slow eroding attack on the wire, and I returned it to its prepared slot in the case of explosive. In six hours, more or less, the whole lot would go up with the force of a two hundred pound aerial bomb.

Now I left the floor of the lagoon and rose slowly to the hull of the crash boat. It was foul with a hanging slimy beard of weed and the hull itself was thick with a rough scale of shellfish and goose-neck mussels.

I moved slowly along the keel, searching for an anchor point—but there was none and at last I was forced to use the shank of the rudder. I bound the case in position with all the nylon rope I had— and when I was finished I was certain that it would resist even the drag of water when the crash boat was travelling at the top of her speed.

Satisfied at last, I sank once more to the bed of the lagoon and moved off quietly on my return. I made much better speed through the water now without the burden of the gelignite case and Chubby was waiting for me on the beach.

'Fixed up?' he asked quietly, as he helped me shed the oxygen set.

'Just as long as that pencil does its job.'

I was so tired now that the walk back through the grove seemed like an eternity and my feet dragged in the loose footing. I had slept little the previous night, and not at all since then.

This time Chubby watched over me while I slept, and when he shook me gently awake it was after seven o'clock and the daylight was growing swiftly.

We ate a breakfast cold from the can, and I finished it with a handful of high-energy glucose tablets from the survival kit and washed them down with a mug of chlorinated water.

I drew the knife from the sheath on my belt and threw it underhand to pin into the trunk of the nearest palm. It stood there shivering with the force of the impact.

'Show off!' muttered Chubby, and I grinned at him, trying to look relaxed and easy.

'Look, just like the man said—no weapons,' and I spread my empty hands.

'You ready?' he asked, and we both stood up and looked at each other awkwardly. Chubby would never wish me good luck—which was the worst of all possible hex to put on someone.

'See you later,' he said.

'Okay, Chubby.' I held out my hand. He took it and squeezed it hard, then he turned away, picked up the FN rifle and plodded off through the grove.

I watched him out of sight, but he never looked back and I turned away myself and walked down unarmed to the beach.

I walked out from amongst the trees and stood at the water's edge, staring across the narrow strip of water at the crash boat. The dangling corpse had been removed from the masthead, I saw with relief.

For many seconds none of the sentries on deck noticed me, so I raised both hands above my head and gave them a loud 'Halloo.' Instantly there was a boil of activity and clamour of shouted orders on board the crash boat. Manny Resnick and Lorna appeared at the rail and stared across at me, while half a dozen armed seamen dropped into the whaleboat and headed for the beach.

As the boat touched, they leaped out on to the sand and surrounded me with the muzzles of the AK47s pressed eagerly into my back and belly. I kept my hands hoisted at half-mast and tried to maintain an expression of disinterest as a petty officer searched me with deliberate thoroughness for any weapon. When he was at last satisfied, he placed his hand between my shoulder blades and gave

275

me a hearty shove towards the whaleboat. One of the more eager of his men took this as a licence and he tried to rupture my kidneys with the butt of his AK47—but the blow landed six inches high.

I made briskly for the whaleboat to forestall any further martial displays and they crowded into the boat around me pressing the muzzles of their fully loaded weapons painfully into various parts of my anatomy.

Manny Resnick watched me come in over the side of the crash boat.

'Hallo again, Harry,' he smiled without mirth.

'The pleasure is all yours, Manny,' I returned the death's head grin, and another blow caught me between the shoulder blades and drove me across the deck. I ground my teeth together to control my anger, and I thought about Sherry North. That helped.

Commander Suleiman Dada was sprawled on a low couch covered with plain canvas cushions. He had removed his uniform jacket and it hung heavy with all the braid and medals from a hook on the bulkhead beside him. He wore only a sweat-soaked and greyish sleeveless undershirt, and even this early in the morning he held a glass of pale brown liquid in his right hand.

'Ah, Harry Fletcher—or should it be Harry Bruce?' he grinned at me like an enormous coal-black baby.

'You take your pick, Suleiman,' I invited him, but I didn't feel like playing word games with him now. I had no illusions about how dangerous was the position in which Sherry and I were placed, and my nerves were painfully tight and fear growled like a caged animal in my belly.

'I have learned so much more about you from my good friends,' he indicated Manny and the blonde Lorna who had followed me into the main cabin. 'Fascinating, Harry. I never dreamed you were a man of such vast talent and formidable achievement.'

'Thanks Suleiman, you really are a brick, but let's not get carried away with compliments. We have important business—don't we?'

'True, Harry, very true.'

'You have raised the tiger throne, Harry, we know that,' Manny cut in, but I shook my head.

'Only part of it. The rest has gone—but we salvaged what there was.'

'All right, I'll buy that,' Manny agreed. 'Just tell us what there is.'

'There is the head of the tiger, about three hundred pounds weight in gold—' Suleiman and Manny glanced at each other.

'Is that all?' Manny asked, and I knew instinctively that Sherry had told them everything she knew during the beating they had given her. I did not hold that against her. I had expected it.

'There is also the jewel chest. The stones removed from the throne were placed in an iron pay chest.'

'The diamond—the Great Mogul?' demanded Manny.

'We've got it,' I said, and they murmured and smiled and nodded at each other. 'But I'm the only one who knows where it is—' I added softly, and immediately they were tense and quiet again.

'This time I've got something to trade, Manny. Are you interested?'

'We are interested, Harry, very interested,' Suleiman Dada spoke for him, and I was aware of the tension growing between my two enemies now that the loot was almost in view.

'I want Sherry North,' I said.

'Sherry North?' Manny stared at me for a moment, and then let out a brief cough of amusement. 'You're a bigger fool than I thought you were, Harry.'

'The girl is of no further interest to us.' Suleiman took a swallow from his glass, and I could smell his sweat in the rising warmth of the cabin. 'You can have her.'

'I want my boat, fuel and water to get me off the island.'

'Reasonable, Harry, very reasonable,' Manny smiled again as if at a secret joke.

'And I want the tiger's head,' and both Manny and Suleiman laughed out loud.

'Harry! Harry!' Suleiman chided me, still laughing.

'Greedy Harry,' Manny stopped laughing.

'You can have the diamond and about fifty pounds' weight of other gem stones—' I tried to sell the idea with all the persuasion I could muster. It was the understandable thing to do for a man in my position, '—in comparison the head is nothing. The diamond is worth a million—the head would just cover my expenses.'

'You are a hard man, Harry,' Suleiman chuckled. 'Too hard.'

'What will I get out of it, then?' I demanded.

'Your life, and be grateful for it,' Manny said softly, and I stared at him. I saw the coldness in his eyes, like those of a reptile and I knew

277

beyond all doubt what his intentions were for me, once I had led them to the treasure.

'How can I trust you?' I went through the motions, however, and Manny shrugged indifferently.

'Harry, how can you not trust us?' Suleiman intervened. 'What could we possibly gain by killing you and your young lady?'

'And what could you possibly lose,' I thought, but I nodded and said, 'Okay. I don't have much choice.'

They relaxed again, smiling at each other and Suleiman lifted his glass in a silent salute.

'Drink, Harry?' he asked.

'It's a little early for me, Suleiman,' I declined, 'but I would like to have the girl with me now.'

Suleiman motioned one of his men to fetch her.

'I want the whaleboat loaded with fuel and water and left on the beach,' I went on doggedly, and Suleiman gave the orders.

'The girl goes with me when we go ashore and after I have shown you the chest and the head, you'll take them and go.' I stared from one to the other. 'You'll leave us on the island unharmed, do we agree?'

'Of course, Harry.' Suleiman spread his hands disarmingly. 'We are all agreed.' I was afraid that they would see the disbelief in my expression—so I turned with relief to Sherry as she was led into the cabin.

My relief faded swiftly as I stared at her.

'Harry,' she whispered through her swollen purple lips. 'You came —oh God, you came.' She took a faltering step towards me.

Her cheek was bruised and swollen horribly, and from the extent of the oedema I thought perhaps the bone was cracked. The bruising under her eyes made her look sick and consumptive, and blood had dried in a black crust on the rims of her nostrils. I didn't want to look at her injuries, so I took her in my arms and held her to my chest.

They were watching the pair of us with amusement and interest, I felt their eyes upon us, but I did not want to face them and let them see the murderous hatred that must show in my eyes.

'All right,' I said, 'let's get it over with.' When at last I turned to face them, I hoped that my expression was under control.

'Unfortunately, I shall not be going with you,' Suleiman made no effort to rise from the couch. 'Climbing in and out of small boats, walking great distances in the sun and through the sand are not my particular pleasures. I shall say farewell to you here, Harry, and my friends—' again he indicated Manny and Lorna, '—will go with you as my representatives. Of course, you will also be accompanied by a dozen of my men—all of them armed and operating under my instructions.' I thought that this warning was not entirely for my benefit alone.

'Goodbye, Suleiman. Perhaps we'll meet again.'

'I doubt it, Harry,' he chuckled. 'But God speed and my blessings go with you.' He dismissed me with one great pink-palmed paw and with the other he raised his glass and drained the last half-inch of liquor.

Sherry sat close beside me in the motor-boat. She leaned against me, and her body seemed to have shrivelled with the pain of her ordeal. I put my arm about her shoulders, and she whispered wearily, 'They are going to kill us, Harry, you know that, don't you.'

I ignored the question and asked softly, 'Your hand,' it was still wrapped in the rough bandage, 'what happened?'

Sherry looked up at the blonde girl beside Manny Resnick, and I felt her shiver briefly against me.

'She did it, Harry.' Lorna Page was chatting animatedly to Manny Resnick. Her carefully lacquered hairstyle resisted the efforts of the breeze to ruffle it, and her face was meticulously made up with expensive cosmetics. Her lipstick was moist and glossy and her eyelids were silvery green, with long mascaraed lashes around the cat's eyes.

'They held me—and she pulled out my fingernails.' She shuddered again, and Lorna Page laughed lightly. Manny cupped his hands around a gold Dunhill lighter for her while she lit a cigarette. 'They kept asking me where the treasure was—and each time I couldn't answer she pulled out a nail with the pliers. They made a tearing sound as they came out.' Sherry broke off and held her injured hand protectively against her stomach. I knew how near she was to breaking completely and I held her close, trying to transmit strength to her by physical contact.

'Gently, baby, gently now,' I whispered, and she pressed a little closer to me. I stroked her hair, and tried once again to control my anger, bearing down hard upon it before it clouded my wits.

The motor-boat ran in and grounded on the beach. We climbed out and stood on the white sands while the guards ringed us with levelled weapons.

'Okay, Harry,' Manny pointed. 'There's your boat all ready for you.' The whaleboat was drawn up on the beach. 'The tanks are full and when you've shown us the goods—you can take off.'

He spoke easily, but the girl beside him looked at us with hot predatory eyes—the way a mongoose looks at a chicken. I wondered what way she had chosen for us. I guessed that Manny had promised us to her for her pleasure without reservations—just as soon as he was through with us.

'I hope we aren't going to play games, Harry. I hope you're going to be sensible—and not waste our time.'

I had noticed that Manny had surrounded himself with his own men. Four of them, all armed with pistols, one of them my old acquaintance who had driven the Rover on our first meeting. To balance them there were ten black seamen under a petty officer, and already I sensed that the opposition was divided into two increasingly hostile parties. Manny further reduced the number of seamen in the party by detailing two of them to stay with the motor-boat. Then he turned to me, 'If you are ready, Harry, you may lead the way.'

I had to help Sherry, holding her elbow and guiding her up through the grove. She was so weak that she stumbled repeatedly and her breathing was distressed and ragged before we reached the caves.

With the mob of armed men following us closely, we went on along the edge of the slope. Surreptitiously I glanced at my watch. It was nine o'clock. One hour to go before the case of gelignite under the crash boat blew. The timing was still within the limits I had set.

I made a small show out of locating the precise spot where the chest was buried, and it was with difficulty that I refrained from glancing up the slope to where the fold of ground was screened by vegetation.

'Tell them to dig here,' I said to Manny, and stepped back. Four seamen handed their weapons to a comrade and assembled the small folding army-type shovels they had brought with them.

The soil was soft and freshly turned so they went down at an alarming speed. They would expose the chest within minutes.

'The girl's hurt,' I said to Manny, 'she must sit down.' He glanced at me, and I saw his mind work swiftly. He knew Sherry could not run far and I think he welcomed the opportunity to distract some of the seamen—for he spoke briefly to the petty officer and I led Sherry to the palm tree and sat her down against the stem.

She sighed with weary relief, and two of the seamen came to stand over us with cocked weapons.

I glanced up the slope, but there was no sign of anything suspicious there, although I knew Chubby must be watching us intently. Apart from the two guards, everyone else was gathered expectantly around the four men who were already knee-deep in the freshly dug hole.

Even our two guards were consumed with curiosity, their attention kept wandering and they glanced repeatedly at the group forty yards away.

I heard quite clearly the clang as a spade struck the metal of the chest—and there was a shout of excitement. They all crowded around the excavation with a babble of rising voices, beginning to pull and elbow each other for the opportunity to look down into it. Our two guards turned their backs on us, and took a step or two in the same direction. It was more than I could have hoped for.

Manny Resnick shoved two seamen aside roughly, and jumped down into the hole beside the diggers. I heard him shouting, 'All right then, bring those ropes and let's lift it out. Carefully, don't damage anything.'

Lorna Page was leaning out over the hole also. It was perfect.

I lifted my right hand and wiped my forehead slowly in the signal I had arranged with Chubby, and as I dropped my hand again, I seized Sherry and rolled swiftly backwards into the shallow rain-washed runnel.

It caught Sherry by surprise, and I had handled her roughly in my anxiety to get under cover. She cried out as I hurt her already painful injuries.

The two guards whirled at the cry, lifting their machine-guns and I knew that they were going to fire—and that the shallow trench provided no cover.

'Now, Chubby, now!' I prayed and threw myself on top of Sherry to shield her from the blast of machine-gun fire and I clapped both hands over her ears to protect them.

At that instant Chubby switched the knob on the electric battery blaster, and the impulse ran down the insulated wire that we had concealed so carefully the night before. There was half a case of gelignite crammed into the iron pay chest—as much explosive as I dared use without destroying Sherry and myself in the blast.

I imagined Chubby's fiendish glee as the case blew. It blew upwards, deflected by the sides of the excavation—but I had packed the sticks of gelignite with sand and handfuls of semi-precious stones to serve as primitive shrapnel and to contain the blast and make it even more vicious.

The group of men around the hole were lifted high in the air, spinning and somersaulting like a troupe of insane acrobats, and a column of sand and dust shot a hundred feet into the air.

The earth jarred under us, slamming into our prone bodies—then the shock wave tore across us. It knocked sprawling the two guards who had been about to fire down on us, ripping their clothing from their bodies.

I thought my eardrums had both burst, I was completely deafened but I knew that I had saved Sherry's ears from damage. Deafened and half blinded by dust, I rolled off Sherry and scratched frantically in the sandy bottom of the trench. My fingers hit the machine-gun buried there and I dragged it out, pulling off the protective rags and coming swiftly to my knees.

Both the guards nearest me were alive, one crawling to his knees and the other sitting up dazedly with blood from a burst eardrum trickling down his cheek.

I killed them with two short bursts that knocked them down in the sand. Then I looked towards the broken heap of humanity around the excavation.

There was small, convulsive movement there and soft moans and whimpering sounds. I stood up shakily from the trench—and I saw Chubby standing up on the slope. He was shouting, but I heard nothing for the ringing buzzing din in my ears.

I stood there, swaying slightly, peering stupidly around me and Sherry rose to her feet beside me. She touched my shoulder, saying something, and with relief I heard her voice as the ringing in my ears subsided slightly.

I looked again towards the area of the explosion and saw a strange and frightening sight. A half-human figure, stripped of clothing and most of its skin, a raw bleeding thing with one arm half torn loose at the shoulder socket and dangling at its side by a shred of flesh rose slowly from beside the excavation like some horrible phantom from the grave.

It stood like that for the long moment which it took me to recognize Manny Resnick. It seemed impossible that he should have survived that holocaust, but more than that he began walking towards me.

He tottered step after step, closer and closer, and I stood frozen, unable to move myself. I saw then that he was blinded, the flying sand had scorched his eyeballs and flayed the skin from his face.

'Oh God! Oh God!' Sherry whispered beside me, and it broke the spell. I lifted the machine-gun and the stream of bullets that tore into Manny Resnick's chest were a mercy.

I was still dazed, staring about me at the shambles we had created when Chubby reached me. He took my arm and I could hear his voice as he shouted, 'Are you okay, Harry?' I nodded and he went on, 'The whaleboat! We have got to make sure of the whaleboat.'

I turned to Sherry. 'Go to the cave. Wait for me there,' and she turned away obediently.

'Make sure of these first,' I mumbled to Chubby, and we went to the heap of bodies about the shattered iron chest. All of them were dead or would soon be so.

Lorna Page lay upon her back. The blast had torn off her outer clothing and the slim pale body was clad only in lacy underwear, with shreds of the green slack suit hanging from her wrists and draped about her torn and still bleeding legs.

Defying even the explosion, her hairstyle retained its lacquered elegance except for the powdering of fine white sand. Death had played a macabre joke upon her—for a lump of blue lapis lazuli from the jewel chest had been driven by the force of the explosion deep into her forehead. It had embedded itself in the bone of her skull like the eye of the tiger from the golden throne.

Her own eyes were closed while the third precious eye of stone glared up at me accusingly.

'They are all dead,' grunted Chubby.

'Yes, they're dead,' I agreed, and tore my eyes away from the mutilated girl. I was surprised that I felt no triumph or satisfaction at her death, nor at the manner of it. Vengeance, far from being sweet, is entirely tasteless, I thought, as I followed Chubby down to the beach.

I was still unsteady from the effects of the explosion, and although my ears had recovered almost entirely, I was hard-pressed to keep up with Chubby. He was light on his feet for such a big man.

I was ten paces behind him as we came out of the trees and stopped at the head of the beach.

The whaleboat lay where we had left her, but the two seamen detailed to guard the motor-boat must have heard the explosion and decided to take no chances.

They were halfway back to the crash boat already, and when they saw Chubby and me, one of them fired his machine-gun in our direction. The range was far beyond the accurate limits of the weapon, and we did not bother to take cover. However, the firing attracted the attention of the crew remaining aboard the crash boat—and I saw three of them run forward to man the quick-firer in the bows.

'Here comes trouble,' I murmured.

The first round was high and wide, cracking into the palms behind us and pitting their stems with the burst of shrapnel.

Chubby and I moved quickly back into the grove and lay flat behind the sandy crest of the beach.

'What now?' Chubby asked.

'Stalemate,' I told him, and the next two rounds from the quick-firer burst in futile fury in the trees above and behind us—but then there was a delay of a few seconds and I saw them training the gun around.

The next shot lifted a tall graceful spout of water from the shallows alongside the whaleboat. Chubby let out a roar of anger, like a lioness whose cub is threatened.

'They are trying to take out the whaleboat!' he bellowed, as the next round tore into the beach in a brief spurt of soft sand.

'Give it to me,' I snapped, and took the FN from him, thrusting the short-barrelled AK47 at him and lifting the strap of the haversack off Chubby's shoulder. His marksmanship was not equal to the finer work that was now necessary.

'Stay here,' I told him, and I jumped up and doubled away around the curve of the bay. I had almost entirely recovered from the effects of the blast now—and as I reached the horn of the bay nearest the anchored crash boat I fell flat on my belly in the sand and pushed forward the long barrel of the FN.

The gun crew were still blazing away at the whaleboat, and spouts of sand and water rose in rapid succession about it. The plate of frontal armour of the gun was aimed diagonally away from me, and the backs and flanks of the gun crew were exposed.

I pushed the rate of fire selector of the FN on to single shot, and drew a few long deep breaths to steady my aim after the long run through the soft sand.

The gun-layer was pedalling the traversing and elevating handles of the gun and had his forehead pressed hard against the pad above the eye-piece of the gunsight.

I picked him up in the peepsight and squeezed off a single shot. It knocked him off his seat and flung him sideways across the breech of the gun. The untended aiming handles spiralled idly and the barrel of the gun lifted lazily towards the sky.

The two gun-loaders looked around in amazement and I squeezed off two more snap shots at them.

Their amazement was altered instantly to panic, and they deserted their posts and sprinted back along the deck, diving into an open hatchway.

I swung my aim across and up to the open bridge of the crash boat. Three shots into the assembled officers and seamen produced a gratifying chorus of yells and the bridge cleared miraculously.

The motor-boat from the beach came alongside, and I hastened the two seamen up the side and into the deckhouse with three more rounds. They neglected to make the boat fast and it drifted away from the side of the crash boat.

I changed the magazine of the FN and then carefully and deliberately I put a single bullet through each porthole on the near side of the boat. I could hear clearly the shattering crack of glass at each shot.

This proved too much provocation for Commander Suleiman Dada. I heard the donkey winch clatter to life and the anchor chain streamed in over the bows, glistening with sea water, and the moment the fluked anchor broke out through the surface, the crash boat's propellers churned a white wash of water under her stern and she swung round towards the opening of the lagoon.

I kept her under fire as she moved slowly past my hiding-place lest she change her mind about leaving. The bridge was screened by a wind shield of dirty white canvas, and I knew the helmsman was lying behind this with his head well down. I fired shot after shot through the canvas, trying to guess his position.

There was no apparent effect so I turned my attention to the portholes again, hoping for a lucky ricochet within the hull.

The crash boat picked up speed rapidly until she was waddling along like an old lady hurrying to catch a bus. She rounded the horn of the bay, and I stood up and brushed off the sand. Then I reloaded the rifle and broke into a trot through the palm grove.

By the time I reached the north tip of the island, and climbed high enough up the slope to look out over the deep-water channel, the crash boat was a mile away, heading resolutely for the distant mainland of Africa, a small white shape against the shaded greens of the sea, and the higher harsher blue of the sky.

I tucked the FN under my arm and found a seat from where I could watch her further progress. My wristwatch showed seven minutes past ten o'clock, and I began to wonder if the case of gelignite below the crash boat's stern had, after all, been torn loose by the drag of the water and the wash of the propellers.

The crash boat was now passing between the submerged outer reefs before entering the open inshore waters. The reefs blew regularly, breathing white foam at each surge of the sea as though a monster lay beneath the surface.

The small white speck of the crash boat seemed ethereal and insubstantial in that wilderness of sea and sky, soon she would merge with the wind-flecked and current-chopped waters of the open sea.

The explosion when it came was without passion, its violence muted by distance and its sound toned by the wind. There was a sudden soft waterspout that enveloped the tiny white boat. It looked like an ostrich feather, soft and blowing on the wind, bending when it reached its full height and then losing its shape and smearing away across the choppy surface.

The sound reached me many seconds later, a single unwarlike thud against my still-tender eardrums, and I thought I felt the flap of the blast like the puff of the wind against my face.

When the spray had blown into nothingness the channel was empty, no sign remained of the tiny vessel and there was no mark of her going upon the wind-blown waters.

I knew that with the tide the big evil-looking Albacore sharks hunted inshore upon the flood. They would be quick to the taint of blood and torn flesh in the water, and I doubted that any of those aboard the crash boat who had survived the blast would long avoid the attentions of those single-minded and voracious killers. Those that found Commander Suleiman Dada would fare well, I thought, unless they recognized a kindred spirit and accorded him professional privilege. It was a grim little joke, and it gave me only fleeting amusement. I stood up and walked down to the caves.

*　　*　　*

I found my medical kit had been broken open and scattered during the previous day's looting, but I retrieved sufficient material to clean and dress Sherry's mutilated fingers. Three of the nails had been torn out. I feared that the roots had been destroyed, and that they would never grow again—but when Sherry expressed the same fears, I denied them stoutly.

Once her injuries were taken care of I made her swallow a couple of Codeine for the pain and made a bed for her in the darkness of the back of the cave.

'Rest,' I told her, kneeling to kiss her tenderly. 'Try and sleep. I will fetch you when we are ready to leave.'

Chubby was already busy with the necessary tasks. He had checked the whaleboat and, apart from a few shrapnel holes, found her in good condition.

We filled the holes with Pratleys putty from the toolchest, and left her on the beach.

The hole in which the chest had been buried served as a communal grave for the dead men and the woman lying about it. We laid them in it like sardines, and covered them with the soft sand.

We exhumed the golden head from its own grave with its glittering eye still in the broad forehead, and staggering under its weight we carried it down to the whaleboat and padded it with the polythene cushions in the bottom of the boat. The plastic packets of sapphires and emeralds I packed into my haversack and laid it beside the head.

Then we returned to the caves and salvaged all the undamaged stores and equipment—the jerrycans of water and petrol, the scuba bottles and the compressor. It was late afternoon before we had packed it all into the whaleboat and I was tired. I laid the FN rifle on top of the load and stood back.

'Okay, Chubby?' I asked, as I lit our cheroots and we took our first break. 'Reckon we can take off now.'

Chubby drew on the cheroot and blew a long flag of blue smoke before he spat on the sand. 'I just want to go up and fetch Angelo,' he muttered, and when I stared at him he went on, 'I'm not going to leave the kid up there. It's too lonely here, he'll want to be with his own people in a Christian grave.'

So while I went back to the caves to fetch Sherry, Chubby selected a bolt of canvas and went off into the gathering darkness.

I woke Sherry and made sure she was warmly dressed in one of my jerseys, then I gave her two more Codeine and took her down towards the beach. It was dark now, and I held the flashlight in one hand and helped Sherry with the other. We reached the beach and I paused uncertainly. There was something wrong, I knew, and I played the flashlight over the loaded vessel.

Then I realized what it was, and I felt a sick little jolt in my belly.

The FN rifle was no longer where I had left it in the whaleboat.

'Sherry,' I whispered urgently, 'get down and stay there until I tell you.'

She sank swiftly to the sand beside the beached hull, and I looked around frantically for a weapon. I thought of the spear-gun, but it was under the jerrycans, my bait-knife was still pegged into a palm tree in the grove—I had forgotten about it until this moment. A spanner from the toolbox, perhaps—but the thought was as far as I got.

'All right, Harry, I've got the gun.' The deep throaty voice spoke out of the darkness close behind me. 'Don't turn around or do anything stupid.'

He must have been lying up in the grove after he had taken the rifle, and now he had come up silently behind me. I froze.

'Without turning around—just toss that flashlight back here. Over your shoulder.'

I did as he ordered and I heard the sand crunch under his feet as he stooped to pick it up.

'All right, turn around—slowly.' As I turned, he shone the powerful beam into my eyes, dazzling me. However, I could still vaguely make out the huge hulking shape of the man beyond the beam.

'Have a good swim, Suleiman?' I asked. I could see that he wore only a pair of short white underpants, and his enormous belly and thick shapeless legs gleamed wetly in the reflected light.

'I am beginning to develop an allergy to your jokes, Harry,' he spoke again in that deep beautifully modulated voice, and I remembered too late how a grossly overweight man becomes light and strong in the supporting salt water of the sea. However, even with the turn of the tide to help him, Suleiman Dada had performed a formidable feat in surviving the explosion and swimming back through almost two miles of choppy water. I doubted any of his men had done as well.

'I think it should be in the belly first,' he spoke again, and I saw that he held the stock of the rifle across his left elbow. With the same

288

hand he aimed the flashlight beam into my face. 'They tell me that is the most painful place to get it.'

We were silent for moments then, Suleiman Dada breathing with his deep asthmatic wheeze and I trying desperately to think of some way in which to distract him long enough to give me a chance to grab the barrel of the FN.

'I don't suppose you'd like to go down on your knees and plead with me?' he asked.

'Go screw, Suleiman,' I answered.

'No, I didn't really think you would. A pity, I would have enjoyed that. But what about the girl, Harry, surely it would be worth a little of your pride—'

We both heard Chubby. He had known there was no way he could cross the open beach undetected, even in the dark. He had tried to rush Suleiman Dada, but I am sure he knew that he would not make it. What he was really doing was giving me the distraction I so desperately needed.

He came fast out of the darkness, running in silently with only the squeak of the treacherous sand beneath his feet to betray him. Even when Suleiman Dada turned the rifle on to him, he did not falter in his charge.

There was the crack of the shot and the long lightning flash of the muzzle blast, but even before that, I was halfway across the distance that separated me from the huge black man. From the corner of my eye I saw Chubby fall, and then Suleiman Dada began to swing the rifle back towards me.

I brushed past the barrel of the FN and crashed shoulder first into his chest. It should have staved his ribs in like the victim of a car smash—instead I found the power of my rush absorbed in the thick padding of dark flesh. It was like running into a feather mattress, and although he reeled back a few paces and lost the rifle, Suleiman Dada remained upright on those two thick tree-trunks of his legs, and before I could recover my own balance I was enfolded in a vast bear hug.

He picked me up off my feet, and pulled me to his mountainously soft chest, trapping both my arms and lifting me so that I could not brace my legs to resist his weight and strength. I experienced a chill of disbelief when I felt the strength of the man, not a hard brutal strength—but something so massive and weighty that there seemed no end to it, almost like the irresistible push and surge of the sea.

I tried with my elbows and knees, kicking and striking to break his hold, but the blows found nothing solid and made no impression upon the man. Instead, the enfolding grip of his arms began to tighten with the slow pulsing power of a giant python. I realized instantly that he was quite capable of literally crushing me to death—and I experienced a sense of panic. I twisted and struggled frantically and unavailingly in his arms, but as he brought more of his immense power to bear upon me, so his breathing wheezed more harshly and he leaned forward, hunching his great shoulders over me and forcing my back into an arc that must soon snap my spine.

I bent back my head, reached up with an open mouth and I locked my teeth into the broad flattened nose. I bit in hard, with all my desperation, and quite clearly I felt my teeth slice through the flesh and gristle of his nose and instantly my mouth filled with the warm salty metallic flood of his blood. Like a dog at a bull-baiting, I worried and tugged at his nose.

The man bellowed a roar of agony and anger and he released his crushing grip from around my body to try and tear my teeth from his face. The instant my arms were free I twisted convulsively and got a purchase with both feet in the firm wet sand, so I could put my hip into him for the throw. He was so busy attempting to dislodge the grip of my teeth from his nose that he could not resist the throw and as he went over backwards my teeth tore loose, cutting away a lump of his living flesh.

I spat out the horrid mouthful but the warm blood streamed down my chin and I resisted the temptation to pause and wipe it clean.

Suleiman Dada was down on his back, stranded like some massive crippled black frog, but he would not remain helpless much longer, I had to take him out cleanly now and there was only one place where he might be vulnerable.

I jumped up high over him and came down to knee-drop into his throat, to drive my one knee with the full weight and momentum of my body into his larynx and crush it.

He was swift as a cobra, throwing up both arms to shield his throat and to catch me as I descended on to him. Once again, I was enmeshed by those thick black arms, and we rolled down the beach, locked chest to chest into the warm shallow water of the lagoon.

In a direct contrast of weight for weight like this, I was outmatched, and he came up over me with blood streaming from his injured nose, still bellowing with anger, and he pinned me into the shallows forcing my head below the surface and bearing down upon my chest and lungs with all his vast weight.

I began to drown. My lungs caught fire, and the need to breathe laced my vision with sparks and whorls of fire. I could feel the strength going out of me and my consciousness receding into blackness.

The shot when it sounded was muted and dull. I did not recognize it for what it was, until I felt Suleiman Dada jerk and stiffen, felt the strength go out of him and his weight slip and fall from me.

I sat up coughing and gasping for air, with water cascading from my hair and streaming into my eyes. In the light of the fallen flashlight I saw Sherry North kneeling on the sand at the edge of the water. She had the rifle still clutched in her bandaged hand and her face was pale and frightened.

Beside me, Suleiman Dada floated face down in the shallow water, his half-naked body glistening blackly like a stranded porpoise. I stood up slowly, water pouring from my clothing and she stared at me, horrified with what she had done.

'Oh God,' she whispered, 'I've killed him. Oh God!'

'Baby,' I gasped. 'That was the best day's work you've ever done,' and I staggered past her to where Chubby lay.

He was trying to sit up, struggling feebly.

'Take it easy, Chubby,' I snapped at him, and picked up the flashlight. There was fresh blood on his shirt and I unbuttoned it and pulled it open around the broad brown chest.

It was low and left, but it was a lung hit. I saw the bubbles frothing from the dark hole at each breath. I have seen enough gunshot wounds to be something of an authority and I knew that this was a bad one.

He watched my face. 'How does it look?' he grunted. 'It's not sore.'

'Lovely,' I answered grimly. 'Every time you drink a beer it will run out of the hole.' He grinned crookedly, and I helped him to sit up. The exit hole was clean and neat, the FN had been loaded with solid ammunition, and it was only slightly larger than the entry hole. The bullet had not mushroomed against bone.

I found a pair of field dressings in the medical chest and bound up the wounds before I helped him into the boat. Sherry had prepared one of the mattresses and we covered him with blankets.

'Don't forget Angelo,' he whispered. I found the long heart-breaking canvas bundle where Chubby had dropped it, and I carried Angelo down and laid him in the bows.

I shoved the whaleboat out until I was waist-deep, then I scrambled over the side and started the engines. My one concern now was to get proper medical attention for Chubby, but it was a long cold run down the islands to St Mary's.

Sherry sat beside Chubby on the floorboards, doing what little she could for his comfort—while I stood in the stern between the motors and negotiated the deep-water channel before turning southwards under a sky full of cold white stars, bearing my cargo of wounded, and dying and dead.

We had been going for almost five hours when Sherry stood up from beside the blanketed form in the bottom of the boat and made her way back to me.

'Chubby wants to talk to you,' she said quietly, and then impulsively she leaned forward and touched my cheek with the cold fingers of her uninjured hand. 'I think he is going, Harry.' And I heard the desolation in her voice.

I passed the con to her. 'You see those two bright stars,' I showed her the pointers of the Southern Cross, 'steer straight for them,' and I went forward to where Chubby lay.

For a while he did not seem to know me, and I knelt beside him and listened to the soft liquid sound of his breathing. Then at last he became aware. I saw the starlight catch his eyes and he looked up at me, and I leaned closer so that our faces were only inches apart.

'We took some good fish together, Harry,' he whispered.

'We are going to take a lot more,' I answered. 'With what we've got aboard now we will be able to buy a really good boat. You and I will be going for billfish again next season—that's for sure.'

Then we were silent for a long time, until at last I felt his hand grope for mine and I took it and held it hard. I could feel the calluses and the ancient line burns from handling heavy fish.

'Harry,' his voice was so faint I could just hear it over the sound of the motors when I laid my ear to his lips, 'Harry, I'm going to tell you something I never told you before. I love you, man,' he whispered. 'I love you better than my own brother.'

'I love you too, Chubby,' I said, and for a little longer his grip was strong again, and then it relaxed. I sat on beside him while slowly that big horny paw turned cold in my hands, and dawn began to pale the sky above the dark and brooding sea.

During the next three weeks, Sherry and I seldom left the sanctuary of Turtle Bay. We went together to stand awkwardly in the graveyard while they buried our friends, and once I drove alone to the fort and spent two hours with President Godfrey Biddle and Inspector Wally Andrews—but the rest of that time we were alone while the wounds healed.

Our bodies healed more quickly than did our minds. One morning as I dressed Sherry's hand, I noticed the pearly white seeds in the healing flesh of her fingertips and I realized that they were the nail roots regrowing. She would have fingernails once more to grace those long narrow hands—I was thankful for that.

They were not happy days, the memories were too fresh and the days were dark with mourning for Chubby and Angelo and both of us knew that the crisis of our relationship was at hand. I guessed what agonies of decision she must be facing, and I forgave her the quick flares of temper, the long sullen silences—and her sudden disappearances from the shack when for hours at a time she walked the long deserted beaches or made a remote and lonely figure sitting out on the headland of the bay.

At last I knew that she was strong enough to face what lay ahead for both of us. One evening I raised the subject of the treasure for the first time since our return to St Mary's.

It lay now buried beneath the raised foundations of the shack. Sherry listened quietly as we sat together upon the veranda, drinking whisky and listening to the sound of the night surf upon the beach.

'I want you to go ahead to make the arrangements for the arrival of the coffin. Hire a car in Zürich and drive down to Basle. I have arranged a room for you at the Red Ox Hotel there. I have picked that hotel because they have an underground parking garage and I know the head porter there. His name is Max.' I explained my plans to her. 'He will arrange a hearse to meet the plane. You will play the part of the bereaved widow and bring the coffin down to Basle. We will make the exchange in the garage, and you will arrange for my banker to have an armoured car to take the tiger's head to his own premises from there.'

'You've got it all worked out, haven't you?'

'I hope so.' I poured another whisky. 'My bank is Falle et Fils and the man to ask for is M. Challon. When you meet him you will give him my name and the number of my account—ten sixty-six, the same as the battle of Hastings. You must arrange with M. Challon for a private room to which we can invite dealers to view the head—' I went on explaining in detail the arrangements I had made, and she listened intently. Now and then she asked a question but mostly she was silent, and at last I produced the air ticket and a thin sheaf of traveller's cheques to carry her through.

'You have made the reservations already?' she looked startled, and when I nodded she thumbed open the booklet of the air ticket. 'When do I leave?'

'On the noon plane tomorrow.'

'And when will you follow?'

'On the same plane as the coffin, three days later—on Friday. I will come in on the BOAC flight at 1.30 p.m. That will give you time to make the arrangements and be there to meet me.'

That night was as tender and loving as it had ever been, but even so I sensed a deeper mood of melancholia in Sherry—as at the time of leave-taking and farewell.

In the dawn, the dolphins met us at the entrance of the bay, and we romped with them for half the morning and then swam in slowly to the beach.

I drove her out to the airport in the old pick-up. For most of the ride she was silent and then she tried to tell me something, but she was confused and she did not make sense. She ended lamely, '—if anything ever happens to us, well, I mean nothing lasts for ever, does it—'

'Go on,' I said.

'No, it's nothing. Just that we should try to forgive each other—if anything does happen.' That was all she would say, and at the airport barrier she kissed me briefly and clung for a second with both arms about my neck, then she turned and walked quickly to the waiting aircraft. She did not look back or wave as she climbed the boarding ladder.

I watched the aircraft climb swiftly and head out across the inshore channel for the mainland, then I drove slowly back to Turtle Bay.

It was a lonely place without her, and that night as I lay alone under the mosquito net on the wide bed, I knew that the risk I was about to take was necessary. Highly dangerous, but necessary. I knew I must have her back here. Without her, it would all be taste-less. I must gamble on the pull I would be able to exert over her out-weighing the other forces that governed her. I must let her make the choice herself, but I must try to influence it with every play in my power.

In the morning I drove into St Mary's and after Fred Coker and I had argued and consulted and passed money and promises back and forth, he opened the double doors to his warehouse and I drove the pick-up in beside the hearse. We loaded one of his best coffins, teak with silver-gilt handles, and red velvet-lined interior, into the back of the truck. I covered it with a sheet of canvas and drove back to Turtle Bay. When I had packed the coffin and screwed down the lid it weighed almost five hundred pounds.

When it was dark, I drove back into town and it was almost clos-ing time at the Lord Nelson before I had completed my arrange-ments. I had just time for a quick drink and then I drove back to Turtle Bay to pack my battered old canvas campaign bag.

At the noon of the next day, twenty-four hours earlier than I had arranged with Sherry North, I boarded the aircraft for the mainland and that evening caught the BOAC connection onwards from Nairobi.

There was no one to meet me at Zürich airport, for I was a full day early, and I passed quickly through customs and immigration and went out into the vast arrivals hall.

I checked my luggage before I went about tidying up the final loose threads of my plan. I found a flight outwards leaving at 1.20 the following day which suited my timing admirably. I made a sin-gle reservation, then I drifted over to the inquiries desk and waited until the pretty little blonde girl in the Swissair uniform was not busy, before engaging her in a long explanation. At first she was adamant, but I gave her the old crinkled eyes and smiled that way, until at last she became intrigued with it all—and giggled in antici-pation.

'You sure you'll be on duty tomorrow?' I asked anxiously.

'Yes, Monsieur, don't worry, I will be here.'

We parted as friends and I retrieved my bag and caught a cab to the Zürich Holiday Inn just down the road. The same hotel where I had sweated out the survival of the Dutch policeman so long ago. I ordered a drink, took a bath and then settled down in front of the television set. It brought back memories.

A little before noon the following day I sat at the airport café pretending to read a copy of the *Frankfurter Allgemeine Zeitung* and watching the arrivals hall over the top of the page. I had already checked my baggage and my ticket. All I had to do was to go through into the final departure lounge.

I was wearing a new suit purchased that morning of such a bizarre cut and mousy shade of grey, that no one who knew him could believe that Harry Fletcher would be seen in public wearing it. It was two sizes too large for me, and I had padded myself with hotel towels to alter my shape entirely. I had also self-barbered my hair into a short and ragged style and dusted it with talcum powder to put fifteen years on my age. When I peered at my image through gold-rimmed spectacles in the mirror of the men's room, I did not even recognize myself.

At seven minutes past one, Sherry North walked in through the main doors of the terminal. She wore a suit of grey checked wool, a full length black leather coat and a small matching leather hat with a narrow businesslike brim. Her eyes were screened by a pair of dark glasses, but her expression was set and determined as she strode through the crowd of tourists.

I felt the sick slide and churn of my guts as I saw all my suspicions and fears confirmed and the newspaper shook in my hands. Following a pace behind and to her side, was the small neatly dressed figure of the man she had introduced to me as Uncle Dan. He wore a tweed cap and carried an overcoat across his arm. More than ever he exuded an air of awareness, the hunter's alert and confident tread as he followed the girl.

He had four of his men with him. They moved quietly after him, quiet, soberly dressed men with closed watchful faces.

'Oh, you little bitch,' I whispered, but I wondered why I should feel so bitter. I had known for long enough now.

The group of girl and five men stopped in the centre of the hall and I watched dear Uncle Dan issuing his orders. He was a professional, you could see that in the way he staked out the hall for me. He placed his men to cover the arrivals gate and every exit.

Sherry North stood listening quietly, her face neutral and her eyes hidden by the glasses. Once Uncle Dan spoke to her and she nodded abruptly, then when the four strong-arm men had been placed, the two of them stood together facing the arrivals gate.

'Get out now, Harry,' the little warning voice urged me. 'Don't play fancy games. This is the wolf pack all over again. Run, Harry, run.'

Just then the public address system called the outward flight on which I had made a reservation the previous day. I stood up from the table in my cheap baggy suit and shuffled across.to the inquiries desk. The little blonde Swissair hostess did not recognize me at first, then her mouth dropped open and her eyes flew wide. She covered her mouth with her hand and her eyes sparkled with conspiratory glee.

'The end booth,' she whispered, 'the end nearest the departures gate.' I winked at her and shuffled away. In the telephone booth I lifted the receiver and pretended to be speaking, but I broke the connection with a finger on the bar and I watched the hall through the glass door.

I heard my accomplice paging.

'Miss Sherry North, will Miss North please report to the inquiries desk.'

Through the glass I saw Sherry approach the desk and speak with the hostess. The blonde girl pointed to the booth beside mine and Sherry turned and walked directly towards me. She was screened from Uncle Dan and his merry men by the row of booths.

The leather coat swung gracefully about her long legs, and her hair was glossy black and bouncing on her shoulders at each stride. I saw she wore black leather gloves to hide her injured hand, and I thought she had never looked so beautiful as in this moment of my betrayal.

She entered the booth beside me and lifted the receiver. Swiftly I replaced my own telephone and stepped out of the booth. As I opened her door she looked around with impatient annoyance.

'Okay, you dumb cop—give me a good reason why I shouldn't break your head,' I said.

'You!' Her expression crumpled, and her hand flew to her mouth. We stared at each other.

'What happened to the real Sherry North?' I demanded, and the question seemed to steady her.

'She was killed. We found her body—almost unrecognizable—in a quarry outside Ascot.'

'Manny Resnick told me he had killed her—' I said. 'I didn't believe him. He also laughed at me when I went on board to do a deal with him and Suleiman Dada for your life. I called you Sherry

North and he laughed at me and called me a fool.' I grinned at her lopsidedly. 'He was right—wasn't he? I was a fool.'

She was silent then, unable to meet my eyes. I went on talking, confirming what I had guessed.

'So after Sherry North was killed, they decided not to announce her identity—but to stake out the North cottage. Hoping that the killers would return to investigate the new arrival—or that some other patsy would be sucked in and lead them home. They chose you for the stake-out, because you were a trained police diver. That's right, isn't it?'

She nodded, still not looking at me.

'They should have made sure you knew something about conchology as well. Then you wouldn't have grabbed that piece of fire coral—and saved me a lot of trouble.'

She was over the first shock of my appearance. Now was the time to whistle for Uncle Dan and his men, if she was going to. She remained silent, her face half-turned away, her cheek flushed with bright blood beneath the dark golden tan.

'That first night, you telephoned when you thought I was asleep. You were reporting to your superior officer that a sucker had walked in. They told you to play me along. And—oh baby—how you played me.'

She looked at me at last, dark blue eyes snapping with defiance, words seemed to boil behind her closed lips, but she held them back and I went on.

'That's why you used the back entrance to Jimmy's shop, to avoid the neighbours who knew Sherry. That's why those two goons of Manny's arrived to roast your fingers on the gas-ring. They wanted to find out who you were—because you sure as hell weren't Sherry North. They had killed her.'

I wanted her to speak now. Her silence was wearing my nerves.

'What rank is Uncle Dan—Inspector?'

'Chief Inspector,' she said.

'I had him tabbed the moment I laid eyes on him.'

'If you knew all this, then why did you go through with it?' she demanded.

'I was suspicious at first—but by the time I knew for certain I was crazy stupid in love with you.'

She braced herself, as though I had struck her, and I went on remorselessly.

'I thought by some of the things we did together that you felt pretty good about me. In my book when you love someone, you don't sell them down the river.'

'I'm a policewoman,' she flashed at me, 'and you're a killer.'

'I never killed a man who wasn't trying to kill me first,' I flashed back, 'just the way you hit Suleiman Dada.'

That caught her off-balance. She stammered and looked about her as if she were in a trap.

'You're a thief,' she attacked again.

'Yes,' I agreed. 'I was once—but that was a long time ago, and since then I worked hard on it. With a bit of help, I'd have made it.'

'The throne—' she went on, 'you are stealing the throne.'

'No, ma'am,' I grinned at her.

'What is in the coffin then?'

'Three hundred pounds of beach sand from Turtle Bay. When you see it, think of the times we had there.'

'The throne—where is it?'

'With its rightful owner, the representative of the people of St Mary's, President Godfrey Biddle.'

'You gave it up?' she stared at me with disbelief that faded slowly as something else began to dawn in her eyes. 'Why, Harry, why?'

'Like I said, I'm working hard on it.' Again we were staring hard at each other, and suddenly I saw the clear liquid flooding her dark blue eyes.

'And you came here—knowing what I had to do?' she asked, her voice choking.

'I wanted you to make a choice,' I said, and she let the tears cling like dewdrops in the thick dark eyelashes. I went on deliberately, 'I'm going to walk out of this booth and go out through that gate. If nobody blows the whistle I will be on the next flight out of here and the day after tomorrow, I will swim out through the reef to look for the dolphins.'

'They'll come after you, Harry,' she said, and I shook my head.

'President Biddle has just altered his extradition agreements. Nobody will be able to touch me on St Mary's. I have his word for it.'

I turned and opened the door of the booth. 'I'm going to be lonely as all hell out there at Turtle Bay.'

I turned my back on her then and walked slowly and deliberately to the departures gate, just as they called my flight for the second time. It was the longest and scariest walk of my entire life, and my heart thumped in time to my footsteps. Nobody challenged me and I dared not look back.

As I settled into the seat of the Swissair Caravelle and fastened my seat-belt, I wondered how long it would take her to screw up her nerve enough to follow me out to St Mary's, and I reflected that there was much I still had to tell her.

I had to tell her that I had contracted to raise the rest of the golden throne from Gunfire Break for the benefit of the people of St Mary's. In return President Godfrey Biddle had undertaken to buy me a new deep-sea boat from the proceeds—just like *Wave Dancer*—a token of the people's gratitude.

I would be able to keep my lady in the style to which I was accustomed, and of course there was always the case of Georgian silver gilt plate buried behind the shack at Turtle Bay for the lean and hungry off season. I hadn't reformed *that* much. There would be no more night runs, however.

As the Caravelle took off and climbed steeply up over the blue lakes and forested mountains, I realized that I did not even know her real name.

That would be the first thing I would ask her when I met her at the airport of St Mary's Island—Pearl of the Indian Ocean.

Wilbur Smith was born in 1933 in the mining town of Broken Hill in Northern Rhodesia—now Zambia—and after attending a university in South Africa he became a businessman. The world of commerce, however, seemed dull and dreary to him, so he turned to writing. His first novel was rejected by seventeen publishers, but that did not discourage him, and his next effort, *When the Lion Feeds*, was both published and filmed. So was *Dark of the Sun*, which became *The Mercenaries*. For eleven years now he has been a full-time writer with each book more successful than the last in both hardcover and paperback. *The Eye of the Tiger* is his ninth novel. Recently published in England, it quickly became number one on the London *Times* best-seller list. A previous novel, *Gold Mine*, was made into the internationally successful film *Gold* and another book, *Shout at the Devil*, is currently in production.

Wilbur Smith lives in Capetown in a beautiful house overlooking the ocean with his wife, Dee, and their three children. He writes for six months and spends the other half of the year on camera safari and fishing. He is also a keen amateur naturalist and anthropologist and an "enthusiastic if unskilled golfer."